A STATE OF EVIL

By

Alan Power

Probity Press Ltd

Typeset by 2QT Ltd (Publishing)
Cover Design by Nicholas Spender

Printed and bound in the UK by
TJ International Ltd, Padstow, Cornwall, UK

"A State of Evil" is derived from the author's non-fiction book, "The Princess Diana Conspiracy", by making constant reference to the facts. It reflects the damming evidence revealed by the author of what happened on the 31st August 1997 in Paris. Where certain names or places cannot be stated, for whatever reason, the author uses creative reasoning. It must, therefore, be considered a work of fiction.
The author uses his rights in British "democracy" to freely air his "honest opinions" and truly held beliefs. He also claims rights of "qualified privilege" under rules of English Law.

ISBN 978-0-957573-8-95
British Library Cataloguing in Publication Data
A catalogue record for this book is available from the British Library.

A NOTE OF GRATITUDE

I wish to thank my Editor, Demi Price, for her enthusiasm and encouragement during the re-emergence of this manuscript that was largely due to her; it had been hidden away for years gathering dust. Demi's cajoling finally made me realise that perhaps the people would appreciate an insight into how this evil act unfolded; whilst the Nation slept.

Contents

ELEGY FOR A MURDERED PRINCESS

Cold Hecate's wanderings in the night
Have put the wings of light to flight
Darkness reigns throughout the globe
Pervading lives; despairing souls

We sought the truth, till now in vain
Embraced the anguish and disdain
Lamenting angels hid their face
Lost in sadness, bereft of grace

Pale, grey men hide dispensing lies
All love, truth and light despise
Yet truth is not contained by sword
It lights the path to our dear Lord

The slain now seek our justice, dare!
To invoke the beast within his lair
We need to fight and standing tall
Pursue the truth; hope not to fall

And trust God will one day decree
That all who love the light must flee
From evil gathered in the hall
Of those who hear hell's darkest call

Let angels gather, trumpets sound
The day is ours; vile truth is found
Reviled grey men no more shall win,
The world now knows; let hope begin

Alan Power

PREFACE

I thought all you good souls might like to know the provenance of "A State of Evil'. It is a story narrated through the eyes and perspective of MI6 (the British Security Services). They were responsible for the planning of Diana's murder but also felt they had a justifiable stance.

The book was first written almost in tandem with my other work on this subject that is non-fiction; "The Princess Diana Conspiracy". There was interest for both works from publishers in New York; some letters I still have on file, all from 2006. But there was no interest from UK Publishers.

The heavily researched non-fiction part, "The Princess Diana Conspiracy", had an exciting beginning but quickly became unavailable due to MI6 criminal intervention. The whole combined book was conceived of, and begun, in November 2003; "A State of Evil" was created by reverse engineering facts taken from "The Princess Diana Conspiracy". I constantly referenced back to ensure the facts stayed on track with the truth whilst writing. But you must consider "A State of Evil" a work of fiction, because some facts, people and places, are abstractly conceived to remain legal and complete the story.

MI6 showed great interest in "The Princess Diana Conspiracy" (Perhaps they will like "A State of Evil" too). Amidst much MI6 activity, I found Patrick Condon, an officer from MI6/GCHQ/Computer section, sitting next to me on a plane from England to the Isle of Man, just before "The Princess Diana Conspiracy's" first release. He was very pleasant but told me, "We will have a problem with your book". It didn't occur then, but I later realized he had just confirmed he had broken the law. It is illegal for intelligence agencies/police to interrogate private communications; it is an abuse of one's civil liberties (my book at that point had not been published). An attempt was made to legalize this practice in late 2014 but it was justifiably rejected by Parliament. Why bother with a law; they do it anyway? Patrick actually wished me luck.

I believe Patrick was trying to establish whether I knew about the errors he had placed in my book to reduce my credibility because clearly, if I did, I would have halted my books release, corrected all errors and delayed publication. It would have then been pointless for MI6 to publish other lies about me (via a conman) because their interposed errors would have been removed; unfortunately, I didn't know. When a book is passed to the typesetters, the author doesn't see it again until it's on the market.

All MI6 errors placed in "The Princess Diana Conspiracy" were corrected in the eBook by mid-November and hardcopy by February 2014 but you still couldn't buy the corrected hardcover on Amazon US or UK during all of 2014. Problems were placed in my way until I was forced to contact the CEO of Amazon, Jeff Bezos. Matters improved but there are still problems. This followed on behind unmarked khaki helicopters hovering near to my house and a gentleman walking down my drive who had already followed me on the ferry from the Isle of Man to England; two more were in in his car. Intimidation was normal before, and after, my book's release.

Do not believe that freedom of speech is permitted in the British Isles nor that censorship doesn't exist. I have endured nothing but censorship for eighteen months; they don't want you to read "THE PRINCESS DIANA CONSPIRACY". My answer to them is "A STATE OF EVIL".

Although we must demand justice and an end to MI6 being the personal police force of the monarchy, also remember that transparency is now much harder to suppress. The people's justice will no longer be silenced. The monarchy must either come clean or face the consequences. The nation needs to see Prince William standing in front of TV cameras, telling the nation the truth; I believe that this is the monarchy's last chance of salvation.

I doubt, in our "democracy", that I shall sell "A State of Evil" unhindered either but to courageous souls who understand my purpose, I say this. Continue to face down the beast and be of stout heart. The truth will out; they can't kill, or bankrupt, us all just to preserve one family. I demand the heads of those that perverted

10

the course of the people's justice and committed, or endorsed, this vile and treasonous act.

I commend "A State of Evil" to all decent MI6 officers; I am sure they will find it most unsettling. They purport to serve the people so I say to them; help to establish the people's democracy and end this evil.

WHITEHALL

John Brooke climbed his office steps and passed through the main door of this large London riverside building. He walked along the brightly lit ground floor corridor, took the lift to the first floor and peered around his office door, bidding his secretary good morning.

'I shall go straight up to number three, Sally, please bring my visitor up when he arrives; just let me know when you are on the way up.'

His unease was expected by Sally Chalmers, Brooke's devoted and long-standing secretary. She was prepared for this morning's meeting and anticipated her boss's probable demeanor. 'I have already had coffee sent up, Sir. Is there anything else you require?'

'No thank you, Sally,' said Brooke, forcing a smile and nodding his approval of her usual efficiency. He walked briskly to the foot of the stairwell that led to the dreariest meeting room in the building, typically selected because of the nature of his forthcoming meeting. He bounced up the stairs, trying to shake of his deepening trepidation, thinking how lucky he was to have such an efficient, likeable, loyal and attractive secretary as Sally. It helped smooth his path with some decisions, enabling him to focus on the issue at hand. Sally would handle all routine matters extremely well.

He entered the room. Many decisions have been taken between these walls, he pondered, as he cast his eyes over a soulless and bare décor that always made him shudder even before any deliberations began. 'The idea is to keep us focused and in the mood,' he thought. 'It certainly achieves that!' Today Brooke was embarking on a journey from which his soul would never return. He felt a deep sense of foreboding, for today he was to receive a man who might make a call for something he had long resisted. If the call came he must answer it! It was his job! It was his duty!

Brooke had been deep in thought for some weeks and his humor was wearing thin. His current Service attachment was to the royalty watch section and his job was to maintain a smooth relationship between the public and the royal household. Royal indiscretions were his domain and needed to be contained to preserve the royal image. 'I feel a bit like Goebbels, the Second World War Nazi propaganda minister,' he self-deprecated, being in an unsettled mood.

A crisis that seemed to have been with him for an eternity had been worsening ever since the Prince and Princess of Wales had first decided to separate. Parker, his main contact at the palace, had been in touch informing him of the latest series of concerns they had over Diana; Brooke was uneasy. He was now waiting for another series of monotonous concerns to be aired during today's meeting; or was there more? Dick Parker had requested an urgent meeting which was most unusual and, when he arrived, Brooke knew he must listen, offer advice and show sympathy; advice he could manage but sympathy – well! He also knew that if the palace asked for action then there were powers in the Service that would require this to be expedited along required lines and he dreaded being involved in something he would have difficulty in countenancing.

It had been a year since Diana's divorce and great consternation remained both at Whitehall and the palace at the direction Princess Diana was taking. All palace hopes that divorce would settle the Diana problem had evaporated and, if anything, matters were now a great deal worse. She wasn't listening to anyone and, with people-power at her command, had become even more dangerous. Her removal from the royal family and her new status hadn't dented her popularity and, if anything, the problem was now more untenable.

It was clear that a very attractive and still young woman was going to seek comforts elsewhere now that her husband's inveterate adultery had been shown to the world and she had been forced to say goodbye to a sham marriage, endured for years from its very beginning to its sad but inevitable end. This experience had ensured a very uncompromising Diana. She was a free spirit who did as she pleased and was causing consternation amongst those who spent their lives protecting the monarchy. She was not disposed towards accepting diktats from the Security Services and by heavens, how they had tried. Diana was now causing more of a stir because she had threatened to reveal dangerous truths, fight the system to the end and not go quietly; she had said this on television. Brooke believed her!

Her attitude wasn't so much of a concern while she had no serious options, because Diana feared losing her children; but what if she had a spouse who could give her the freedom she craved and offer her children protection? She was now becoming a state liability but if one combined her justifiable stance concerning her treatment by the royals with her newfound freedom, then here was a problem; a lethal cocktail that Brooke was not looking forward to resolving. She was ridiculing the system, ignoring the wishes of the palace and didn't care what she said or did. There was nothing to stop her delivering a deathblow to the Windsor family and the Service was feeling powerless to intervene or produce any effective defense. She wouldn't accept advice from those tasked with controlling the political scene and she would never meekly accept a lesser role than goddess, thought Brooke, as he wrestled with a balance between compassion and duty, still retaining his options. It was his job; he must.

Diana had achieved iconic status and now wielded such power throughout the world she could not be controlled by the palace or by his office. He pondered his dilemma, sipping coffee and looking through the window at the bustling London traffic. Having been conned all her married life, she was in inclement mood and most probably intent on seeking revenge. Previous myriad and clandestine indiscretions from the Windsor family had all been managed without too much information entering the public domain; now the genie was wriggling out of the bottle and soon he would be trumpeting his glorious battle cries all over the world. There were a lot of matters that needed to be kept under wraps and Diana knew most, if not all, of the Windsor skeletons. The future was uncertain because the royal mystique had gone and there was going to be a major problem squeezing the genie back into the bottle again; impossible with a hostile Diana.

John Brooke, like so many of the senior MI6 personnel, had earned his seniority from displaying absolute loyalty to the crown but had never made the very top because the Service considered that he possessed an excessive sense of morality and justice. The Service liked to think they stood for these also but sometimes the need arose to perform tasks requiring a cold, steel-like resolve that Brooke lacked. Brooke was likeable, efficient and very loyal but would he be tested on whether to support an action with dubious motive. A tall, bespectacled and erect man with a slim build, Brooke exuded the appearance of a stereotypical British gentleman who one would always expect to open the door for a lady. He was early fifties, with thinning hair greying at the temples, and walked as though he expected to meet the monarch around every corner.

While Brooke waited for Parker, he slowly flicked through the pages on behavioral science, notes he had acquired from a recent Service seminar. Perhaps I should get Diana on one of these, he mused, as he read about the psychology of people controlling power, the triggers that caused them to react and how they resisted provocation. On the other hand she could probably teach me a thing or two, he thought as he read further. He skimmed through as his mood darkened and his mind drifted to the coming meeting. He could be on the golf course rather than dealing with a tedious and spoilt group of people who live in a different world and whom he was supposed to respect and even admire.

The phone rang, jolting Brooke back into the present. Sally informed him that 'his guest had arrived and they were on the way up to number three'. Brooke concentrated his thoughts and decided he was going to let Parker do all the talking. He didn't want to lead him down any avenues and impart new ideas. Let him tell me what he wants.

Moments later Sally knocked on the door and announced, 'Mr. Parker, sir'. Dick Parker swiftly entered the room, not wearing a smile.

Oh great, what a morning I've got, passed through Brooke's mind, and now without humor. 'Good morning Dick, how is life at the palace?' he asked.

'Well might you ask,' said Parker, his face puce from hours spent trying to make sense of the latest palace fiasco and rushing down the Mall from the palace to Vauxhall Road for a meeting he accepted as necessary but one that also unnerved him. Parker used to work in this building and Brooke was one of his underlings. He had joined the palace for an easier life but wasn't getting one. 'I have a problem in controlling the palace and diffusing the excesses of its inhabitants who are doing precisely as they wish and giving scant regard to any reservations from those who do my job,' gushed

Parker. 'I wonder why I don't retire early or move on to something exciting such as janitoring. Perhaps I should come back here, John?'

Brooke was slightly amused and relieved that today might not be as bad as he had at first thought. 'I know your concerns,' said Brooke, 'but what made you rush over here today?'

'You know of course, that Diana and her children are in the south of France with Mohamed al Fayed,' said Parker, obviously with something specific in mind. 'And there could be more to it than that?'

'What do you mean?' said Brooke, his voice now losing its lighter tone.

'You know of Dr. Hasnat Khan' said Parker. 'He has been pursued by Diana for some months, causing us concern. Just as we were beginning to breathe again after that one has almost certainly failed, Diana goes on a holiday to the south of France with yet another Muslim family!'

'Well, is a holiday so much of a problem?' said Brooke, keeping his deliberations silent and knowing what was coming before Parker spoke. He had already received a report on Diana's recent antics from his team in St Tropez, but decided to play devil's advocate, unsure of how Parker viewed this latest episode.

'With Diana one can never be certain, but in Mohamed al Fayed we have a man who is capable of defying us and giving Diana a great deal of power; the very thing we can't control and just as the Prince of Wales is trying to be reinvented as a lovable human being,' said Parker, making a further attempt at humor. 'We need to try and contain this holiday otherwise what if the unthinkable happens and they become an item?'

'Bit of an age difference,' said Brooke thinking Parker was being rather boorish and irrational.

'His son is quite young,' said Parker, 'and he has just joined them at Fayed's house in St Tropez. He is attractive and unmarried so we have a big potential problem'

'We'll look into it,' said Brooke, testing the water. 'What do you think we can do?'

'Well,' said Parker, 'that's your job if this were ever to become a serious relationship. We couldn't tolerate that union under any circumstances and this comes from the top.' He held Brooke with a steady, cold stare.

Parker stood to take his leave, emphasizing that this is what

17

he had come to say. 'Give it some thought, John! We need to prevent this relationship developing because we cannot accept the consequences of a union between Diana and that family.' He repeated his previous statement in case Brooke had misunderstood. He hadn't!

Brooke needed to pinch himself that he had just heard a senior member of the palace tell him they must manage Diana's future union and it was his job, whatever its cost! The Princess seemed to have a predilection for Muslim men and that alone was a problem for the Establishment. The monarchy was in trouble! It was his duty to resolve the matter, catch the genie and imprison him. 'How can we achieve this?' thought Brooke. 'We are really in for a tough ride. Why can't that damn Windsor family keep it in their trousers? One day soon, there will be nothing we can do and the people will awaken. I hope I have retired by then.'

Brooke returned to his office where Sally had just made another pot of coffee, having seen Parker rush past. Brooke knew Parker had just made a comment that he took as code. There was only one way in which this situation could be resolved and hopefully restored to its previous status. What if the Princess of Wales should no longer exist? This is clearly what Parker meant. She should be around for another half century yet and if she had her way either the monarchy would not survive or, even if it did, Charles Windsor would be certain to lose his succession to the throne. He had far too many skeletons to hide and wouldn't survive much longer with certain revelations becoming public – and that was guaranteed with Diana gunning for him. It was not as though he is popular. What in God's name could they do?

'Diana's intelligence history tells us,' Brooke mused, as he began reading through Diana's files, 'that Diana's most recent beau is a heart surgeon. She has been to see his parents in Pakistan and has spent an inordinate amount of time with him both in the Brompton Hospital and at Kensington Palace. Taking the "what if" scenario, suppose Diana married him and went to live in Pakistan then became a Muslim just as one of her friends, Jemima Khan, has done? What about the children? Now we have a further complication, together with a palace that has lost its patience. What about the succession? What about protection for the Princes living over in Pakistan, or when they are visiting their mother if they don't live there permanently? The one point in our favour, at present, is that Doctor Khan's family doesn't appear keen to allow an extended relationship between their son and Diana to continue and we believe it's faltering. OK, but we do now have an indication of Diana's intentions and appetites; this latest information from St Tropez fuels that view.'

Reading more of Diana's files that were placed in his desk drawer before Parker arrived, Brooke was reminded of the pathway that led to the current thinking. He noted that intelligence had confirmed the likelihood of Diana and Dr. Khan being finished, but Brooke thought this new development could be another matter.

'We knew of the invitation of 3rd June to the South of France with Mohamed al Fayed and of Diana's acceptance letter of the 11th June, but we were not concerned because we were focused on her other relationship,' the notes said.

He noted his previous comments in the margins of the agent's notes and saw that following her relationship with Khan, Diana had already spent time with a Pakistani multimillionaire at Annabel's nightclub in London.

'We must now watch any developments carefully because it's clear something will happen soon and a pattern of her preferences is developing. We must be ready for when she decides to "go for it" on a permanent basis with one of her escorts, which won't be long in coming. This has been developing for some time and isn't some passing fad,' the notes continued; 'The al Fayed connection worries me in particular because he is extremely wealthy and if anything goes down there, the palace won't be unable to control her and she will be able to turn on the heat, big time!' Brooke thought as he placed the file on the table. 'Why can't she choose some non-controversial Anglo Saxon country gentleman, enjoy her life and allow us to leave her alone? At the moment she is only on holiday in the South of France, as far as we know, so nothing is certain; we mustn't jump the gun. But neither can we wait for disaster to happen. The problems are endless and I see no solution in sight, since her feelings will most likely be reciprocated by whosoever she settles on; it looks like we shall have a problem. I am going to see Morison and discuss this frankly. There is only one logical solution; God help us. I can't take this decision on my own, I need to discuss it with my superiors and take their view. It's our job to be ready!'

Brooke went through into Sally's office. 'Will you please make an appointment for me to see Morison ASAP, Sally?'

'Mr. Morison is back from holiday tomorrow, sir. Shall I make your appointment for when he returns?'

'Yes please, Sally,' said Brooke. 'On Friday; the sooner this is done the better'

***

Tom Morison returned from holiday feeling relaxed and in good spirits until he heard that Brooke was coming over the following day for an urgent meeting. After spending the day clearing a backlog of accumulated work, he resisted the temptation to phone Brooke, knowing him to be the epitome of the professional Service man who wouldn't discuss anything sensitive over the phone. He wouldn't be descending on him like this if it were not urgent. Morison let his imagination run wild and waited with baited breath for the next day's meeting that he felt sure would soon make his pleasant holiday memories evaporate.

Tom Morison was a distinguished, well-built and good-looking man with piercing but gentle blue eyes. In his late forties with a well-modulated accent, well-dressed in conventional suits and sported well-made shirts, his was a commanding presence. Unswerving loyalty to the Crown had eased his passage to his current status and he was not without an impish sense of humor when the occasion allowed. He had a relaxed manner but undisputed integrity; nothing compromised his loyalty. He was one of the old-school who commanded respect and admiration from his fellow officers and possessed a cold and incisive ability to do whatever was required.

Morison felt he was wasting far too many days on meetings about the royal family with his senior staff. He knew it was important to maintain the status quo but the palace was becoming a nuisance. The Service was compelled to use considerable manpower in watching Diana's every move and then to report back to the palace. He had more important issues on hand, such as protecting the realm from terrorists and supporting requests for assistance from the country's allies. His resources were stretched! He could do without spending days cleaning up after a feckless and self-centered Prince!

Morison had allocated Brooke the task of looking after the royal family's traumas because he had the right temperament for dealing with royalty. He could also handle some of the more delicate fringe operations that the Service frequently needed to embark upon. Morison wondered what had arisen that seemed so important. He had seen all the latest intelligence reports so it must be something else.

The following morning Brooke arrived, spot on time as usual, and was gestured straight into session.

'Good morning John,' said Morison, as he walked Brooke to the comfortable chairs in the corner of his plush office. 'What can I do for you this wet and miserable day? I don't suppose you've brought me some cheer? That's one of the problems with our job. Whenever we see someone we haven't met for a while it's never for a pleasant reason.'

Brooke replied with minimal niceties. 'Dick Parker has visited me and I needed to see you as a matter of urgency. I have been thinking about the ongoing problem we have with the Princess of Wales and Charles Windsor, sir, and I feel the situation could be about to become untenable.'

'I thought they were divorced?' said Morison, holiday mood prevailing and trying to find some light relief from a stern-looking Brooke; to no avail.

Brooke continued, not responding to any attempted humor; he was not in the mood. 'We are spending long hours chasing around after her, guessing what her next move might be and how it's going to affect one or other of our policies, or how she is going to embarrass the monarchy and make them look irrelevant or us foolish. Is it worth having another word with her and trying to persuade her to moderate her behavior in the interest of her country, and to stop embarrassing the Establishment? There must be someone she will listen to?'

Morison didn't need to think long. 'You know as well as I that there is no chance that Diana will change her mind about anything she wants to do. Her obduracy is famous. Her power and influence grow continually and she has good reason not to be too accommodating. That is our main problem,' he said, without pulling any punches. 'We have already tried to persuade her to take a more detached approach but have never received a positive response. Understandably, she sees us as the enemy and if those close to her can't change her mind, we have no chance. The best placed person is probably Parker but I presume he has given up on that one too.'

Brooke replied, 'He has, sir. So you think this will be a problem for ever more and there is nothing we can do about it, even if it destroys the monarchy? It seems we must assess just how dangerous her behavior is, or will become and at some point, if we cannot stop her, we shall need to consider the unthinkable or become a republic.'

Morison was taken aback by this frankness and looked at Brooke intently as he tried to read his thoughts. If one pursued this logic to its conclusion then Brooke was going down an avenue with no turnings, although the same idea had passed through his own mind.

'John,' said Morison, 'first of all I must ask you what has brought this level of response from you? Something must have happened to induce it. I know you will have pondered extensively before coming here today and I can't say what you suggest is illogical, but the consequences of failure would be cataclysmic.'

Brooke described his conversation with Parker and his own perceptions, which left Morison with a resigned expression and a quick response. 'So Dick Parker is on side with what you are saying? You are absolutely sure you did not hear the possible need for something to happen as distinct from a suggestion that there is already no alternative?'

'It was he who intimated the degree of the problem' retorted Brooke. 'What are the consequences of not doing anything? If the Establishment is destroyed then is that acceptable? I naturally don't want to take any unnecessary action but I am saying that if the situation worsens significantly should I approach you again with a plan?'

'Consider this option over the next week or so please, John, and let me know the possibilities,' said a more resolute Morison. 'This has always been at the back of my mind and is regrettable, but you have put me on notice of the prevailing mood; thank you. Maintain a reliable and current intelligence, since this is vital in determining any possible action. Perhaps you have a few operatives in mind but if you choose to test the water don't reveal any detail. Don't say who this target might be. Don't even whisper it. Keep this well and truly between us. Only a select few will ever know about this and we must keep numbers tight. We would probably need to consider using our Increment team and even they must be selected very carefully. I shall asses the mood in other quarters and see what the thinking is with all parties who need to be on side. As distasteful as it is, I shall consider it and come back to you. In fact,' said Morison, 'considering the position, my secretary will arrange a further meeting between us. Shall we say next Friday at Bleak House? That will give me time to make enquiries next week. I shall ensure I have all necessary feedback by then.'

Brooke left Morison's office feeling great remorse for initiating this course of action. 'It's not really my fault,' he mused as he searched for excuses. 'This would have arisen from any member of the team just doing their job. The logic is too clear for this not to be considered.'

During the return journey to his office, he considered the implications of his meeting; the more he deliberated, the more the logic faded and the horror of the moment came upon him. He did what he was paid to do but couldn't stop being a human being. He realized this was something that would carry high risks but either there was a problem or there wasn't. If there was a problem then what was the alternative answer, other than to accept that Diana would probably destroy the monarchy and enjoy doing so? It was his job to protect the Establishment and if there was no other way, then that was that. He had given orders for the ultimate sanction to be applied before, so why should it be different because it involved the Princess of Wales; and yet...!

The conditions existed for the ultimate sanction and he regretted that, but knew he must do his duty. He considered the senior operative most suited to this task that he would need to see. But he couldn't even discuss it!

Brooke revised his thinking. 'All I can do is call my best operative in and test the water. What if he freaks out? I can see a serious judgment call coming with potentially fatal consequences if we get this wrong. I am going to call Jim Winfield into the office within the next few days and see if I am a satisfied with his response before revealing my hand. We shall use the Increment for the hit but I prefer a commander of impeccable background.'

Brooke returned to his office and immediately asked Sally Chalmers to contact Jim Winfield for an urgent meeting.

'He's on holiday, sir,' said Sally. 'He won't be back for a week I believe.'

'Damn these wretched holidays,' interrupted Brooke. 'Where is he?'

'Devon or Cornwall I believe,' said Sally, taken aback by Brooke's uncontrolled and uncharacteristic comment.

'Well, he will have to come up to London by train for the day. I am meeting with Morison again next Friday and I need to see Winfield before then. Tell him to come to my office on Monday; he can return to his holiday afterwards. We're all going to need a holiday if this goes down.' Brooke continued in a more subdued tone, 'Do that now, please Sally. I have an urgent matter on hand that won't wait on staff holidays.'

CRITICAL CHOICE

Jim Winfield made good use of the Mall for his usual early morning jog, striding out sturdily in the mid-summer London sunshine. Two evenings earlier he had received a rather cryptic message, relayed from his boss's secretary via his answering machine that required his presence in London for an urgent meeting this morning. This necessitated a late-night journey on a slow and refreshment-free train with bleary-eyed and drunken types that had left him in not too good a humor. He felt it had better be good, or else; or else what? Jim pondered. That's the way it goes. I could always get a job doing something more mundane but then I would complain of boredom so I can't win.

Jim had been in the country with his wife Jane, and young daughter Sarah, enjoying long invigorating walks in the rolling Devonshire countryside together with their Labrador dog, Mandy. Mandy always enjoyed romping close to her master, cajoling him into throwing sticks and excitedly chasing the occasional squirrel.

'I've been in a few too many situations like that,' thought Jim. 'I wonder what the hell Brooke wants that is so urgent? Why couldn't he wait another week when I'm back in the office?' Jim had not intended to return for a good few days but had no choice now that Brooke had summoned him.

Brooke's call had ended his idyll and Jim had packed at a moment's notice to return on Sunday evening and attend this specially convened meeting. 'All rather sudden and unusual,' he mused. 'Unless we are declaring war or the Americans have sent another request over for "expediting" something or other and Brooke has been caught short.' He wondered what could be happening but he would find out soon enough after breakfast. 'This is what comes of accepting a role on the special operations team. I suppose I have to accept that "special" could be synonymous with downright uncivilized and does not just happen between 9-5 or when I'm not on holiday.'

Winfield had been selected as a leader in the special operations team, which consisted of personnel considered tough, resourceful, highly trained in combat skills and, naturally, extremely loyal. Highly intelligent, experienced people one could call on in a difficult situation and not have to worry about their capabilities or discretion.

Jim hurried back to his apartment for breakfast and to make some telephone calls. He wanted to make sure he wasn't going to be late. The meeting shouldn't last more than an hour or two, at the most, and then he could return to the country and finish off his break. He also needed to phone Jane to make sure she had booked them in at the local hostelry for the following night.

***

Monday morning, 9.30am. John Brooke was preparing for the meeting with Winfield at 10:00am, knowing it was going to be one of his most difficult ever. He had tried to prepare but wasn't quite sure how to play it. His real objective was to determine Winfield's willingness to perform this task, should the need arise. This order was unique because he must appoint his commander before the order was given. If Jim refused, Brooke would be endangering Winfield's life or career for something that might not happen. Nobody would survive if they refused this order once they'd been briefed.

The reason for having him in the office today was to assess, as best he could, whether Winfield would take command; the only way to do that was to look into the man's eyes while telling him as much as possible, which wasn't very much at this stage.

As a senior officer who would act as the man in charge of any special operations team, Brooke was being extremely cautious in putting this team together. Winfield was tried and tested and Brooke had no reservations about his abilities or loyalty, but this was something else. How would he approach this necessary but extremely unpleasant task that could be considered beyond the call of duty and only dubiously in defense of the realm?

What options would Brooke give them, if any? What sanction

could he recommend if they freaked out at this order? Could an operative continue in the Service if they refused? Could he trust them to keep silent?

'I virtually know Winfield's response, so is this meeting really worthless?' Brooke thought. 'I shall at least get some comfort though. I could determine his preparedness to act if I gave more detail but that's been strictly forbidden. No, there is nothing for it other than to take what I can from this meeting and let matters take their course.'

Demons of uncertainty confronted him, until he finally accepted he was just doing his job. 'Anyway,' he thought, steadying the ship, 'I've been told to prepare in case it's necessary; no decision has been made yet. I will go through the usual motions. Either the system works or it doesn't. Either we follow orders or the nation doesn't have a workable system.'

He began thinking about Morison's maxim to seek comfort. Whilst perusing the reasons he shouldn't be feeling this anguish, he thought about the Nuremberg trials. When he was at military college, several years before entering the Secret Service, he had numerous heated discussions with colleagues about whether German officers, during their trial after the Second World War at Nuremberg, had an acceptable defense to the slaughter of innocent civilians by claiming they were only following orders. Brooke held the view that humanity took precedence over orders from any political or military masters and they were therefore guilty as charged. He wondered now if he had held this comfortable view because he had never felt any reservation about orders he had been given; until now.

Brooke felt ill at ease and irritated that he didn't veto the idea when it arose. Maybe he would have to make the same decision that those German officers should have made. What chance of his men feeling differently? Could he face his own personal trial of acceptable behavior? Would he proceed, knowing he could be brought to account? That didn't answer his moral dilemma! Perhaps his conscience would survive and enable him to function normally afterwards.

But then he faced the truth. 'I still fail the test if I proceed, despite believing that all my previously held values were correct. If I comply with this order, should it be given, the main tenet of my Service life has been a lie from to moment it began. How can I order

27

my men to execute a task I know will sicken them to their stomachs? It's already sickening me and I must order it! What if they refuse the order on the grounds that humanity takes precedence? What will be my response? What if some refuse this order, as we believe those German officers should have done in the Second World War; would I then be prepared to deal with my own men in the same manner that those officers feared they would be dealt with by their own evil regime if they refused? What does that make me?'

Brooke's pulse raced and he needed a moment to pause and collect his thoughts. 'I must complete this preparation and take stock, but until the order is given I won't be sure how I will respond, which is one of the main concerns I hold for my men. If I feel this way now then how will I feel if the order is given, and how will my men feel? I must ensure they are suitable for the task before giving orders that might jeopardize their careers or safety.

He had already considered who he could use from amongst his own men and, apart from Winfield there were none he wished to involve. All operatives, other than Winfield, would be chosen from the Incremental reserve. This was made up of SAS and SBS troops who would need to be ruthlessly controlled and carefully chosen.

Brooke had penciled in the most trustworthy and capable squad available from his list of those who has been involved in lethal operations before. Those who met the required criteria were in short supply because they must have shown no remorse when having to dish out lethal expediency, such as was required here. No conscience, no, reservations, no self-doubt and no aftershocks, which are impossible to relieve after the event and very difficult to control without using the ultimate sanction. 'We must avoid that at all costs,' thought Brooke. He would, therefore, need his less sociable men. Those who would not baulk at orders that would turn most men to jelly and, heaven help us, probably be turned on by it. Brooke didn't like these men, but it was not about liking. It was about getting the job done without comeback. Nobody would survive any comeback on this one!

The ground commander, however, must be the very best available. There was no way around that bearing in mind the consequences of failure; that was unthinkable. 'It does mean though,' thought Brooke, 'that I shall have to mix our more unsavory bunch with an officer who won't take well to this union; one of the good guys. I am not comfortable about this mix.'

The man Brooke preferred for the task, and whom he was about to see, was not only the most competent of his officers but also had the right military background. He was a man Brooke both admired and liked, and someone in whom he could have complete confidence. Still Brooke had reservations about whether Winfield would execute this order.

Jim Winfield was with the SAS regiment 22nd airborne for some years before moving to MI6 and deciding to test his talents in a different way. The only drawback was that Jim was used to taking on other soldiers or being in more up-front situations. He might find it difficult to accept the nature of this order but then his MI6 training had made him more devious over the last few years. 'Protecting the realm, in whatever guise; that's what we pay him for,' Brooke thought.

Brooke knew he must assess Winfield and test the water before declaring the nature of the operation. He couldn't do that until standby was confirmed and all operatives had been vetted. He would have a second meeting with Jim if matters were firmed up. His biggest fear was having to order Jim to do this before the order was given and then, subsequently, it could be stood down. He wasn't looking forward to the moment he had to tell Jim the target's name. 'Anyway he will be here soon, so I shall know his initial response and if he looks uncomfortable I will have to look for another operative. In any case the order may not be given,' Brooke kept repeating, feeling the need for comfort. 'If I am not happy he will be OK with this assignment then I have other options, but I would prefer to have a commander with whom I am confident. I think I am really choosing Jim Winfield because I need his support but I mustn't compromise his safety because of my own self-doubt.'

***

The time was approaching 9.45am as Jim Winfield walked from the taxi, dodging the traffic as he crossed the road to the large grey building that was his business home. The office building near Vauxhall Road is an imposing looking structure right next to the River Thames, with views of London from the office windows. It was in one of these offices that John Brooke had his abode.

Jim strode up the steps to the office bidding various staff good morning as he made his way down the long corridor that led to

29

Brooke's office on the first floor, showing his security clearance pass as he proceeded. He knocked on the door and went straight in, saying good morning to Brooke's secretary, Sally. There was a good-natured game the two of them always played when he was summoned to Brooke's office. Jim always aimed his hat at the stand behind Sally's desk, mimicking a famous fictitious spy, and always missed by a mile. He tried to imitate a Scottish accent and a typical James Bond style movement, sweeping past the desk and feigning some flirtatious comments that always made them both laugh.

John Brooke came to his office door and at once Jim saw from him expression that this was not going to be a relaxed and enjoyable session. There was not the usual half-pained comment about Jim throwing hats around the room and disapproval of him sexually assaulting his secretary. This was the most serious John Brooke that Jim had ever seen.

A chill went through Jim as though someone had walked over his grave. He thought, 'Well I did have a prickly feeling about this one. And it had better be good for disrupting my holiday; here we go!'

'Come inside,' said Brooke. 'Sit there; I need to ask you some questions.'

Jim sat near Brooke's desk on the large, green-leather chesterfield sofa, and waited apprehensively for this meeting to begin.

Brooke stood near the window, looking out over the London bustle, apparently deep in thought. He appeared to be oblivious to Jim's presence, lost for a moment as though this didn't have to happen. No! It was definitely happening and the quicker Brooke started, the sooner he would be able to have lunch and wash away the taste in his mouth.

'Jim,' said Brooke, 'when you started with the Service you knew there may be times you would be asked to do something you might not find agreeable, did you not?'

'Yes,' replied Jim. 'We can't expect to choose our tasks when in defense of the realm.'

Heartened by this response Brooke continued. 'So if I asked you to lead an operation that I have been assured, at the highest level, may be critical to the Establishment's survival, you would have no difficulty in complying?'

'That sounds very serious. Many of our tasks are unpleasant; that is the nature of what we sometimes need to do but this seems to be concerning you big time. Just tell me what I must do and I can start the planning and selection of the operatives.'

'The operatives have already been selected, in principle, but I will welcome your input when we get to the next stage,' replied Brooke. Then, diving straight in, Brooke asked the question. 'Just now I need to know that if you were asked to render someone neutral, would you have any qualms about who that person was?'

Jim knew that 'render someone neutral' meant assassinate and he thought, 'Why the hell can't he just speak English, for heaven's sake? There are only two of us in the room.' He responded, 'Well, I might have a problem if it was the Pope, but as long as I am allowed to pray first and receive absolution afterwards...' The look on Brooke's face made Jim wish he'd kept his mouth shut.

'Jim, I wish I could joke with you but I have been entrusted with a task that I am struggling with and I have to gauge the reaction of all chosen operatives, especially the commander, before finally making my selection. If you accept this task, there is no going back, no way out. I need to make a decision by describing the type of operation without actually telling you what it is at this stage. I am doing this to give you as much option as possible to withdraw but that option only exists before you are briefed. This way there is a small chance of my being able to eliminate any mistakes in personnel selection before irrevocably committing them. As I have said, the order has not yet been given but we must be ready. Do you understand?'

Jim was in no doubt what Brooke meant. He now knew this was a very high-profile target and one that most of the guys were not going to enjoy eliminating. 'Oh no, I am going to be working with the low life brigade,' he thought. 'Please God no!' He realized he would be required to lead men from the Service Incremental team, a group of people that would do absolutely anything for the Service; they were totally devoid of humanity or principals. The Pope came back to mind and quickly flashed out again. Who could this possibly be? Why all the great secrecy and intrigue? He knew that Brooke wasn't given to being melodramatic.

'If the realm is being threatened then one person cannot be allowed to jeopardize the good of all. I presume all other options have been considered?' Jim said this, thinking there couldn't be anyone he would refuse as a target. Nobody he could think of whom the Service would contemplate eliminating, surely? He trusted them; he had to trust them; if he didn't, what was he doing in this room?

'That is the one big question I need to clarify when I have my next meeting above, but I assure you that all avenues will be pursued first,' said Brooke. 'If there is the slightest chance we can find an alternative option, then nobody will be happier than me. But are you saying that whoever this person is, you will lead the others and follow orders without reservation? You will know that we have tried everything else and there is no other option available.'

Although Jim was now feeling very uneasy, he had come to the conclusion that if he couldn't trust the powers that be to make decisions on behalf of the nation, then why had he been taking orders for several years; he would need to resign now. He was satisfied he could rest behind the fact he was 'following orders' and could trust the Service not to order an unnecessary or unacceptable action. They were not the Gestapo after all; were they? He communicated these sentiments to Brooke.

'Thank you Jim', said Brooke. 'I shall let you know when I need to see you again; that's all.'

Brooke stood and turned on his heel as if something else far more pressing needed to be done; he didn't give Jim a chance to ask any more questions. Jim bade Brooke 'good day' and left the room, not wishing to waste any more time than necessary. He quickly made his way to Sally's desk, thinking only of returning to his country break and wondering what all the fuss had been about. Surely Brooke could have done that over the phone?

He persuaded Sally to order him a taxi to the railway station and, bidding her farewell, made his way to the exit. 'Why did he need eye contact? He's only asked me to do what I am paid for.'

Back in the office, a thoughtful Brooke was considering that he had asked the question, looked Jim in the eye whilst doing so and could do no more. He had established Jim would rise to the task. He would check through the details on his operatives ready for the meeting next week when he needed to suggest a team in case the operation should proceed.

It was mid-July and he thought he would have to wait a while before taking any holiday. This must be dealt with first. The one thought, however, that left him troubled was Jim's comment about only following orders. Brooke thought, 'If ever it comes to your needing a defense, old boy, that isn't going to save you! Nor, for that matter, will it save any of us.'

RAISON D'ETRE

Bleak House is a large stone, gargoyle-adorned house set in an enormous park in the south of England. Brooke turned towards the gatehouse situated at the beginning of the drive. This building, looking more like a small Victorian mansion, housed Service staff whose job was to ensure no uninvited visitors breached the tight security. CCTV, monitored from the gatehouse, scanned the perimeter fence and there were armed personnel on standby, supported by a number of Land Rovers parked at various points.

Oak trees lined the drive from the gatehouse to the main building, which was surrounded by a large gravel parking area where more armed guards patrolled. To the locals, Bleak House was considered a Department of the Environment administrative overspill. They would not have been amused to know it was used for training MI6 operatives in the ancient arts of espionage and assassination. 'Aptly named place,' thought Brooke.

Brooke had been here several times and was always excited when he was involved in large or important operations. He had felt privileged to be chosen for several previous tasks, at which he always excelled. Embarking on jobs that required serious judgement calls in the interests of the State was one thing; however, where the call was shrouded by doubt because of its dubious morality in defense of the realm, the integrity and morality of Service personnel would be seriously tested.

This was a major juncture for Brooke and dangerous for morale within the Service. He was hoping that the operation wouldn't proceed then he could breathe a huge sigh of relief, having done his duty. His initial reaction when faced with Parker's concern was to go on to automatic pilot and calculate the logical choice for his masters but now he'd had time to think and Brooke the man, not the automaton, had emerged. He was entering this meeting in ambivalent mood, despite the calls of Service logic.

He arrived at the gatehouse and his security was checked even though the staff knew him well. 'I actually engaged you about six months ago and endorsed your security clearance, remember me?' thought Brooke. He didn't say a word, knowing the man was perfectly correct in checking each time he visited; in fact, Brooke wouldn't have appointed him if he cut corners.

He proceeded up the long drive, parked near the main entrance and went straight to the reception desk. He asked the receptionist, whom he always regarded as too prim and proper, whether Morison was ready for him and got the rather curt, if polite reply that if he would take a seat he would be sent for in due course. Brooke thought he would love to have this one put into his department and sorted out, but then decided he would give her the sack and not bother to attempt any improvement in her manners.

He felt agitated! It was most unusual to be kept waiting like this. He checked his watch. He'd only been here three minutes. Everything about this operation, so far, seemed to be out of the ordinary. This didn't bode well.

Time went by slowly from three minutes to twenty before he saw a figure walking down the corridor towards him. The man tried to gain Brooke's attention to lessen the walk all the way to the reception. 'Manners have all gone,' thought Brooke, 'but I mustn't say "like in my day"; a definite signal I am getting old.'

The man beckoned him to follow up three flights of stairs and down a dimly lit corridor to a fully soundproofed room on the third floor, near the center of the building and with high windows one couldn't see out of. These rooms afforded better security than others in the building; all top security, class one meetings were held in these rather stuffy rooms.

Brooke entered and saw three people assembled around a large table. He knew Tom Morison and recognized one of the others whom he had seen at a senior briefing, but never properly met, and whose name he couldn't remember. Realizing the level of security this operation was attracting made him nervous, and confirmed his earlier fears. The look of these people made him feel as though this was a full planning meeting and he wasn't prepared or confident to discuss such a delicate operation with people he didn't know. It wasn't his call, however; he was involved at the inception of the idea so must follow orders and do his job; personal feelings were inappropriate.

Why were these people here? Brooke thought he was coming to discuss options on how to deal with a problem with the Princess of Wales, should it become necessary, and didn't expect to have very senior people present. Had a decision been taken? He immediately made a movement towards Morison who held out his hand in greeting.

'Good morning, John,' said Morison. 'Did you have a pleasant trip down?' Without waiting for a reply he continued; 'so sorry to keep you waiting but we had a few matters to go over. Let me introduce our two colleagues since I don't think you have met. This is Peter Caruthers and this is Nick Stephens.' Morison did not reveal that they had just been appointed to the British Embassy in Paris.

A thought came to Brooke as he viewed this senior array of personnel. 'I wonder which one is missing: hear, see, or speak no evil. I know, do no evil; goes without saying. That job's ours!'

'Both are from our senior directorate,' Morison continued without being more specific as to their precise roles. 'We have been considering all options on this issue and have decided we need a complete planning preparation schedule ASAP.'

Brooke's heart sank! All the thoughts he had been pondering rose to the fore and he was unsure of how to respond. Morison, seeing he had caught Brooke unawares, continued; 'The overview plan you sent me has been reviewed and it's considered appropriate to have the details available in case it's required. We need a plan in place now but the decision is far from being taken yet, John; just a few precautionary appointments have been made. We must have all the options available to us in the event that a decision to go is taken. If this operation is deemed necessary, speed will be important for several reasons. Since this is an operation we would prefer not to be countenancing, we will only decide at the last possible moment. That means all planning and preparation has to be done because there may not be time later if we receive the green light.'

Brooke's reaction was 'whose idea?' The idea came from Parker but here cometh the proverbial buck passing! He knew these people would distance themselves and the palace from this operation and never allow the Service hierarchy to be compromised, so it must

35

appear as though it came from a routine Service decision. The Service then, in turn, would need to find a way to ensure the buck was passed on from them. The thought crossed Brooke's mind that there was nobody left to take responsibility but he quickly redirected his thinking back to the occasion unfolding before him. 'Scapegoat duties over,' he thought; 'let's see how this unfolds.'

Brooke was extremely elated at the news that the decision was not actually upon him yet. He also knew he mustn't allow his feelings to be known, since any hesitant response at this level would be bad for confidence, if not his health. He hoped his slight reticence at the beginning of the meeting had gone unnoticed; these people rarely missed anything! He also realized he had passed the briefing stage and was at the initial operations commitment stage so there was no backing out.

If he showed signs of weakness, his own life could be at risk from his own people. They couldn't take chances on a matter this sensitive, so he must toughen his resolve and remember, 'This may not happen.' He wasn't about to risk his career, or worse, because of reservations about something that would probably not happen.

He kept reiterating this comforting thought and became more robust in his contribution, describing his preparations, the staff he had chosen and why. He was congratulated on his reasoning and choice of personnel, which had mostly coincided with people Morison had in mind. If anyone had suspected his commitment from the first few minutes of the meeting, Brooke was unable to detect it.

'We need to go through the available options and decide on which scenarios are best for our purposes, then where and how we would strike,' Morison continued. 'We shall then come up with a short list of plans that our operatives can test in the field. If and when this goes down, it must look like an accident. The finest detail in planning will make for a much smoother route to that objective. One issue we must establish from the outset is that we never discuss anything regarding this operation, at any time, except in this room. The logistics we shall employ for administering this operation will be sent to you later but in the meantime, never forget this point. All communication between us will be arranged using secure lines and we will use a code when using select e-mail addresses that will be known only to those involved. Before any personnel are briefed, this committee will approve each of them.

'The code name for the operation will be "Swandance" and it will be a full-time category A operation, listed reserve/secret.' Brooke reflected on this being as high as security gets but wasn't surprised. What he didn't like was the code name; it conveyed the image of a dying swan's last dance, sad and unnecessary.

Morison continued; 'I think that once we have considered our initial plans, we shall discuss each option and, after coffee, consider each one more fully. Then we'll put together a first-stage operation preparation document and consider any other business. Oh, and we shall continue to conduct the meeting today as though the decision has already been taken, simply for ease of passage.' Morison saw no point in freaking Brooke out, as he was already aware that his loyal colleague would probably be a victim of this operation and he didn't expect him to be the last.

Brooke thought how routine it all seemed but all operations had to follow the same procedure. It seemed as though Morison was just planning a departmental shindig.

'We are going to assassinate the Princess of Wales, accepting there may have to be collateral damage but we do need to keep that to a minimum.' Morison spoke as though by saying it quickly, it would become acceptable. 'This will happen only if absolutely necessary and I want to spend a few minutes discussing why this action is even being considered. None of us in this room relish the prospect. Even those in the Service at the highest levels haven't accepted this responsibility without a great deal of soul searching. But our Nation's very stability is being threatened and, unless the measures we are putting in place are successful to undermine our target's current relationship, or a complete change of course is noticed in her behavior very soon, then no option remains. We have it from the latest intelligence that Diana's relationship is reaching crisis point from our perspective so we need a plan of action sooner rather than later. Our discussions today are of the utmost urgency!

'The Princess has for some time now been interfering politically with us and various allies and causing embarrassment by forcing changes in policy due to the almost unnatural power she wields throughout the world. Also, our monarchy no longer has the ability to plan its own actions without constant reference to what the Princess may be doing on any particular day. Diana wields more support, and has a bigger following, than all the other royals put together and the monarchy is being seriously undermined. Now

37

that Diana has effectively left the royal family she can no longer be controlled by the palace and may do as she pleases.

'We retain an influence while she needs to consider her children but if she married a wealthy man, and went to live abroad, as she has indicated she might, then we lose all control and are at her mercy, especially with her knowledge of all the royal skeletons. The situation will arise where members of the royal family will be abroad on official visits and all Diana need do is turn up at the same location, at the same time, and the whole trip would be ruined. It's guaranteed that Diana would have a better reception than the royals, leaving them with egg on their faces. You can imagine what that will do for the monarchy's popularity both here and abroad. Should she now marry an extremely wealthy Muslim playboy, she could continue her vilification of the royals for years to come and be in an unacceptably strong position to achieve her avowed aim of denying the throne to Charles Windsor.

'Marrying a Muslim may be a problem, perhaps not, but it is another potential minefield we would prefer not to face. Her stated preference of living abroad could be a bigger problem, especially with regard to her children and the succession. All in all, we are facing a major series of problems. Diana's avowed intention of destroying Charles Windsor in particular, together with everything else, gives us an extremely volatile mix. We believe this action, extreme as it is, is the only way of allowing the monarchy to restore its position and remove the almost iconic aura of Diana Spencer from the scene once and for all.

'If we don't take dramatic action then the monarchy will probably not survive. We believe that the people will ultimately thank us when the monarchy returns to its previous status, and the threat from Diana is removed, but we know they will rage if ever they discover our part in this action. This is why her death must be seen as an accident. As long as there is insufficient proof available to the contrary, then nobody can do much about it even if we fail to completely convince the world it was an accident. We should always be able to maintain our deniability. If, as time goes by, the truth emerges, the government can claim it merely made a mistake by not pursuing it sooner.

'If the act is carried out on foreign soil, we have much more leeway. We can blame it on foreign procedures, make the appropriate and meaningless diplomatic noises and let time remove the problem. We can even stretch the law on inquests by claiming we are unable to proceed until foreign enquiries are completed. With co-operation from that foreign power we could delay the process for some considerable time, if necessary, and our operatives cannot be prosecuted for an offence committed outside these shores. The grey area is the existence of the death penalty for treason. I am looking into that now!'

Brooke felt his pulse quicken. 'He's already decided!' he thought.

'I have already stressed that it must appear to be an accident and I want you all in no doubt as to why,' continued Morison, now getting into his stride and starting to open up the whole concept of what they were facing. 'The very possibility resting in the public mind that it's not an accident would produce the constitutional crisis we are trying to avoid. If we were, for example, to sink Fayed's yacht the *Jonikal*, or engineer any obvious non-accidental violence, the people will know it was murder. In this event it will be extremely difficult to fudge an investigation. Whatever method is finally chosen, it must look like an accident and leave no residual evidence. If evidence remains, we could be in trouble so we must do everything in our power to ensure this isn't the case. We must control the subsequent investigation and, should matters become difficult, enforce deniability.

'If there is evidence of assassination, the reaction from the people will be extremely hostile and, because of the relationship the Princess currently has with her ex-husband, the finger of suspicion will point at him. Public pressure may become unacceptable. They will be of a mind-set to believe she was murdered by the palace and we shall have lost our prime objective, even without an investigation. This will probably be survivable, since the people by and large are extremely gullible and trust officialdom, but they are not stupid so we must achieve a clean operation. We shall from now on refer to the Princess of Wales as POW, for brevity.' The wartime connotation of this abbreviation, and its closeness to Diana's royal misfortune, escaped him.

Matters were proceeding too quickly for Brooke, who felt as though he was in a different world and at any moment he would awaken. 'Morison wants to make the whole operation as impersonal as possible,' he thought. He felt the need to say something but hesitated. 'We don't yet have a "go"; keep calm!'

Despite his reservations, Brooke found he was getting into

the detail, unsure whether from habit or self-preservation. He continued to make an attempt at the same sort of zeal he always brought to these meetings; his true feelings remained hidden. He needed to impress the men before him. He was trying to act as if he were just doing his job; nothing he could do was going to change anything and, after all, today was not decision day.

Morison added, 'Both Nick and Peter are here primarily as observers. The main activity for John and me is to discuss the planning in as much detail as we can; we must create a framework and then make some initial decisions about personnel. John has already given us an overview of the profiles of the people he would use and I confirm my agreement. Firstly, however, I would like to share with you my own belief as to how this matter is best directed when we can consider any other ideas and agree the best and least risky option.'

Morison decided to continue keeping Stephens' and Caruthers' appointments to Paris from Brooke. He felt there was no need to inform Brooke because it could worsen his anxiety. Brooke would then know, barring a miracle, this was going down soon and Morison needed him on side, especially during the planning phase.

Morison continued; 'I have given serious consideration to this operation and believe a car "accident" is the best approach. We have many locations throughout Europe with assets in place to assist our staff where we shall have up to the minute intelligence of the subject's intentions. We have more influence in some venues than others, which is a major factor in deciding where to strike. My choice is Paris for a number of reasons, and I ask that you play devil's advocate during our deliberations. Firstly, as I have already stated, we must do this on foreign soil where we know the law will permit the level of secrecy we require and where we can expect support from that government. If we act on British soil, we shall be criticized over delays in procedures such as inquests, and be in the firing line over our subsequent non-investigation. If it's not on British soil, the investigation isn't our responsibility and we can claim the foreign police are doing all they can. We shall tell the French government after our attack, if our choice is France, that we fear a crisis if murder is suspected and request their support in "investigating" the crime. The French won't want to cause us a problem; they are sympathetic to carrying out certain acts in state interests if it's for the greater good. We cannot be blamed for not pursuing the crime more vigorously if it doesn't reside within our jurisdiction.

'We have exceptionally good support at the Ritz hotel, which incidentally is owned by Mohamed al Fayed and we have some useful assets working there. It's a venue that will almost certainly be used by the subjects and already has been within the last few weeks. These assets can keep us informed of the events and assist considerably with our planning, helping to perfect our chosen program. It may well be that we have no option other than to strike at a completely different moment if we are under some time or event constraints, such as if the subjects are about to make an announcement of their intentions to marry, or decide not to return to Paris; our intelligence will keep us informed. Once we have chosen the team, we shall introduce them to our staff currently on assignment in Paris and St Tropez, where Fayed has a home, to check out the best areas and options.

'In Paris, for example, they will look at routes from the Ritz Hotel to the other usual destinations, the Windsor Villa and the Rue Arsenne-Houssaye where Dodi Fayed has an apartment and where he will take the POW. We are checking the Paris accident figures to see if there are suitable accident black spots on those routes and we will concentrate on these as the best options for the attack, which will reduce the risk of suspicion and increase the probability of success. We shall have a team in Paris to ascertain a location and have them report their findings to the committee here. Armed with this information, we can assemble a plan that must be foolproof and rehearsed over and over again until we are happy with our response times. How does this seem so far?'

Brooke was amazed that an idea of where and how could be arrived at so quickly. Morison had used his time well in contacting operatives and thinking through an initial plan and, yes, on the face of it the idea was sound. The main issue was whether they had secured the best option and then, having settled on the way forward, they must examine the plan again to minimize possible errors.

Morison continued; 'I think John deserves our congratulations for coming up with an extremely sound outline. May I suggest we put on our thinking caps and ponder over the next few days whether a better option can be envisaged and if not then how best we maximize this one? We shall meet again soon to go through the planning and by then will have settled on our chosen operatives. You and I, John, will look at these and discuss them again at our next meeting before we make our final approaches.

'That man of yours, what's his name? Jim Winfield. We must make absolutely sure we get him right. We must discuss him now. Gentlemen,' Morison turned to Caruthers and Stephens; 'I need to spend time with John until lunch. If you wish, naturally you may remain but I suggest there is nothing further for you here today. We shall look forward to seeing you at our next meeting, unless you have any further business.'

Peter Caruthers spoke up first and said he didn't think he could add anything to next week's meeting either; Nick Stephens added his agreement and so it was left that they would attend at some future date to be agreed with Morison.

They would return to Paris and complete the groundwork preparation, unbeknown to Brooke. Morison was joining them the following day so they could discuss anything further then without having to be cautious about Brooke.

Caruthers and Stephens bade farewell and left the room. Brooke said to Morison, 'They didn't have much to say, did they?'

Morison replied dismissively, 'Perhaps, but consider them to be OK. They were only here to report that they are satisfied we are getting on with the job and are on workable lines.'

Morison and Brooke returned to their deliberations, with Brooke more relaxed than he had been with their guests. They could now complete the meeting without the presence of probing eyes that made Brooke feel uncomfortable. They continued with selection procedures, and finalizing the document to determine the tasks each team member would perform, since Morison wanted the basics in place for their meeting the following week.

'One thing I didn't discuss in front of Peter and Nick,' said Morison, who had detected Brooke's earlier mood, 'was how you feel about this affair. For my part, I understand the need to obey orders without which we wouldn't have an effective Service. But although we have a responsibility, we are human and you need to be content that we are not just acting out some evil or unacceptable fantasy on the part of our political masters.'

This caught Brooke completely off guard because he believed there was no questioning the motives or morality of any action the Service might embark on. Also, they had never discussed philosophy with regard to their jobs before, so Brooke thought perhaps Morison was testing his degree of loyalty, or his inclination to comply with these orders. Was Morison sensing Brooke's reticence from the first few minutes of their morning meeting? Brooke had always done what was asked of him without question but this was an atypical operation. Morison would need to know that taking part wouldn't cause him an impossible dilemma. Brooke felt that Morison had most probably detected his reticence and so felt emboldened to air his reservations. He tried to ensure he retained control so as not to undermine his position irrevocably, but he did need answers.

Brooke responded with a question whilst carefully watching Morison. 'You have said we are hoping for this action not to proceed, and we are trying to obviate it by using other methods. But what I would really like to know is who has ordered this? Who has the authority to determine the need for such action? Either the need outweighs the risks, or this is an emotive response darkly veiled in hidden motives. Who could make such an assessment and sanction it without reference to several senior people? Who would take such a decision without knowing it had been sanctioned from the very highest level? What level of power do these people have? If it's not the head of government, then who is involved and with whom has the decision been squared? If it's not been squared then I do not understand who this person could possibly be. Is this a democratic decision taken by someone with the interests of the State in mind? Are we doing our job of protecting the State by allowing an act we know is against the will of the people? If so, how do we justify this in a democracy? Who makes the assessment that the State is so much at risk, especially if the act is also against the will of the elected government? If it's necessary to perform an act we find repulsive in defense of the realm, and we know there is no other option, we must proceed. But should we not first ensure our motive is justified?

Morison felt uncomfortable with the frankness of Brooke's outburst. Perhaps Brooke should be allowed to run his course. He knew this was leading into dangerous waters but he could pull the plug and find out where Brooke stood. Now was a good time; he hesitated. No, the conversation was getting too much to handle.

Morison knew the points Brooke raised were valid but dangerous and he could not answer them. This was a potential minefield. He replied, 'Can there ever be a straight answer? I don't know who

43

ordered it, since the precise details have been kept even from me, and I believe we will never know. I do know it comes from the top of the Service, so whoever has asked me for this operational assessment will be very close to the seat of power. But,' he added, 'I re-emphasise that it hasn't been ordered yet; only its preparation.'

Brooke continued, now in full flow and thinking he might as well complete his points, naively thinking he wasn't giving too much away and not realising it was much too late to worry on that score. 'There is no guarantee the very head of political power will necessarily know of this at all. Is it conceivable we have been ordered to do this with the boss being totally oblivious?'

'Possibly,' said Morison, 'but there's no way we will ever know. We would need to ask the Prime Minister and I think we could find ourselves extremely unpopular, not to say, unhealthy and/or extremely jobless, if we take matters that far. We have no option other than to rely on the directorate to determine policy. The democratic element arises when, and if, the government of the day reduces or removes that power. That's not our call now or ever.'

'I don't suggest we go that far,' said Brooke. 'It just begs the question of whether this carries the government stamp of approval because the implications are obvious. If there is not government support, this operation doesn't carry even the loosest stamp of law.'

'True,' said Morison. 'But what if the government wanted to establish a positon of deniability? The only way they can possibly stand aside from this, in the disastrous event the world gets to know the truth, is if they didn't know what was happening and perhaps some rogue element of our Service was responsible.'

'Yes,' said Brooke, 'but we are now in very tricky waters! How could it be rogue elements when we will be using agents for our survey and back-up work if we go along with the idea you proffered today? It surely wouldn't be difficult to link these people, whose existence will be known, with events taking place in the same vicinity? How would rogue elements of the Service persuade our agents to support an action like this against their will? Everyone will know our agents are in Paris with a duty to protect the Princess. Without Service co-operation, rogue elements would need to operate in full view of our watching agents, so people will know that we know who is responsible. Our presence around Diana is for the opposite reason; we should be defending her. That is not possible! It will be obvious the Service was involved.'

'Possibly,' said Morison, 'but the people investigating this would first need to prove our agents were involved. We must ensure there is full co-operation from the French police, so it will be impossible for anyone to examine alternative theories because only the police will have the authority to investigate in their own country. They will prevent investigative journalists from being involved, so there will be no scope for challenging the police findings from any other source. Also, there's no way we shall allow ourselves to be interviewed on this or any associated issue.'

Brooke looked at Morison. 'Do you mean we are to rely on French police support for this? How can we be sure of getting it?'

'Rest assured,' said Morison, 'I have no concerns in that regard. Naturally we shall not tell them our intentions prior to the operation or of our involvement afterwards, but we have assisted each other before and work well together when either side has a crisis.'

'One other point,' said Brooke. 'What if the Prime Minister doesn't know and, if he did, would not only veto it but also arrest those who have mooted this as an option?'

'Well now, that was an interesting exercise,' said Morison, ignoring the last point and thinking this was a good time to pull the plug. Had he let this go too far? He should bring the day's business under stricter control and get the planning under way. All that had been shown was that Brooke had thought matters through and if he didn't, he wouldn't be much use anyway.

He felt Brooke needed the certainty that there were no alternatives and he would then be OK. He wasn't sure how OK but, hopefully, as much as he was sure; he couldn't expect to improve on that. 'What a perverse world we live in,' thought Morison.

Then, making light of their conversation, he said, 'Well, if anything else comes to mind, speak up. It's invaluable to throw these thoughts around. We need to continue to play Devil's advocate so we understand the way each other thinks and how others may also think. This way we are better prepared. But in the final analysis, we accept our orders and believe what we do is necessary to protect the realm, or we are in the wrong job. Now, let's get down to business!'

Morison watched Brooke for a reaction. Brooke noticed, nodding his assent.

An unsettled Brooke began with the general assessment he had made of the type of people he would be looking for in this operation.

He made the point that he could not be specific on personnel roles until they had decided where the action would take place and how they would conduct it, citing the example that assets at the Ritz would be irrelevant in St Tropez. Numbers should, in his view, be as few as practicable and Morison readily agreed. They needed to select the operatives from those already identified.

'I suggest we focus on Paris and test it thoroughly now?' Brooke said.

Morison replied, 'Yes, I favour Paris for several reasons but I don't want to exclude other sites, especially since we may need to change venue; we need to be prepared in two or three locations. We cannot tell the subjects where to spend the evening or where to go for a meal or, indeed, whether to go to Paris in the first instance. In Paris, however, we know a great deal about their habits, such as where they will most probably eat, where they will sleep. We can also control, to some extent, how they travel in between their venues.

'We have the advantage here of assets who will obey our instructions without question and these are already well embedded. When we select our attack team, we need people who have been involved in this type of work before who haven't suffered any post-operational trauma. There are some who have actually seemed to become psychological elated, where post-operational assessment has shown a positive trait.'

Brooke thought there was a fine line between a good operative and a psychopath. He said to Morison, 'I have those people listed and there are several available. I know we must be sure of no comeback, and I've done my assessment, but what about these assets you mentioned in Paris. Who are they? Do we know they will be up to it? Do you have any personnel files we can scrutinise over the next few days?'

'I am getting those sent over as we speak,' said Morison. 'I should have photocopies for you before you leave the building today.' He knew that at any moment his secretary would enter the room and deliver the details Caruthers and Stephens had left with her. Morison has already instructed this be delivered to him as though it had just arrived. This way, Brooke would be kept out of the loop of the advanced stage of preparations.

No sooner had Morison made this remark than his secretary entered the room. A small, middle-aged and rather dowdy woman, with greying hair and glasses, placed a bundle on the table in front of him together with one special memo. She put this face down in front of Morison which, he realised, was her way of letting him know this might be sensitive.

'Your specially requested files, sir, just arrived from Paris. Will there be a reply?'

'Thank you, Cynthia' said Morison. 'No reply just yet. Oh, you could drop a line and say we should have an in-principle affirmation on venue preferences within days.'

'Very good, sir' said Cynthia, as she left the room.

Brooke watched this with more concern. 'Just who knows what's going on?'

Reading Brooke's mind, Morison said, 'The staff are completely trustworthy and we haven't given details to anyone else. This operation needs to be administered and we shall handle most of it, but it's acceptable to allow the peripheral administration to be handled by Cynthia. Have no fear; all information regarding this will be kept very secure.'

Matters now seemed to have picked up a pace and Brooke was feeling increasingly soulless. He felt that Morison had subtly coerced him into this role and the decision was already made. He wasn't sure how he felt but knew he shouldn't feel like this; he never had before. This was a mind-numbing first he must somehow survive. Nothing escaped Morison's skilful gaze. He knew that if the order came, he would have no choice and, in any event, he told himself, the country had to come first. They wouldn't be doing this if there were any other option but he was finding it hard to take, nonetheless. He was ready to do his duty, however unpleasant, and he had his pension to consider.

Realising that Brooke was uncomfortable, Morison thought it wouldn't take much for him to falter so was at the point of standing him down but he didn't want to lose a valuable and experienced officer. He decided to take on the field role himself and place the intelligence work on Brooke, but to keep this decision from him until Brooke had been utilised to the full, in a week or so.

Morison said, 'I think we have gone as far as we can today. Take those papers with you tonight and prepare your plan based on the Paris option, which will almost certainly be our first choice! Oh, and are you sure of Jim Winfield? We need that decision to complete the picture.'

'I had him in my office last week as you know,' said Brooke, having already given the details to Morison. 'I am confident he is ready for the job but if he isn't, then I doubt anyone else in the Service is either!'

Morison thought, 'Good! With the way events have unfolded there's a probability that if we are not successful in our propaganda campaign against Dodi Fayed, we shall be moving within weeks, not months.'

DARK RESOLVE

The Service machinery was in full swing and planning under way. The teams in France had completed an initial review of the favorite attack sites and detailed initial planning was resolved on the preferred attack format, together with the support of the appropriate Service assets. Since the choice of sites needed to be kept open, Morison had instructed that the initial overview planning should be put in place for the Paris option and they would conclude the others within a few days.

From intelligence already received, Morison was confident they would be using Paris but knew they must have alternatives. The Alma tunnel was the only place he felt ninety per cent confident his goal could be achieved, so he remained adamant this was the site and rigidly stuck to this view, constantly badgering intelligence for confirmation on whether the subjects would be travelling to Paris.

Stephens and Caruthers had been appointed to Paris, because it was the preferred choice and also because it was necessary to establish a nerve centre for the operation, irrespective of where the attack went down, so that all the pieces of the jigsaw could be pieced together. Stephens and Caruthers were well chosen to head up the Paris operation. Stephens handled the planning and controlled the detail, putting round pegs into, hopefully, round holes, and Caruthers took the field role, reviewing attack sites; both coordinated their findings. Morison needed to perfect Paris, before looking at other possibilities because he took the view that once the Paris detail was secured they could then concentrate all resources on the other sites. The main option would be in the bag except for possible mishaps!

Morison intentionally arrived in Paris a few days before Caruthers returned from St Tropez, knowing he would have

Stephens all to himself. He needed to get up to speed on detail before they sat down to review the Paris plan. He thought it would be very unprofessional to meet with colleagues before being sure of all the facts, especially when all decisions were his to make. He continued to hope that, by the time Caruthers returned, intelligence would have given Paris the all clear. This attack must take place by the end of the month; whatever happened!

Morison became increasingly agitated and impatient. The site location continually played on his mind. He pestered Brooke for information on the subject's movements and intentions almost hourly; he knew that for all Brooke's shortcomings about this operation, he could rely on him to do a good job of gathering the necessary intelligence. His main objective here today was to be satisfied that this attack was viable, leaving no evidence and appearing to be an accident.

Morison reached the MI6 nerve centre that had been established in a plush central Paris office overlooking the Arc de Triumph and the northern section of the Champs Elysée. His nostrils met the glorious aroma wafting through the air from the nearby *boulangerie* as he approached the main office building. This was a very tense time for the Service but it had its compensations, if only he could find time to enjoy them. But he couldn't relax; his senses were on collision course with duty. Pleasure would have to wait; he had no time! There was a certain incongruity in being preoccupied with death whilst in an enriching capital like Paris.

Arriving at the top floor, Morison was met by Stephens.

'Good morning Tom', said Nick Stephens. 'Welcome to our humble abode.' He walked Morison over to the window to take in the view from his office window.

The operation was fronted as a trade mission. Boring, as usual, Morison thought but considered it was better not to change a deception that had worked for almost a generation. Being an apparent trade organisation would explain the numbers of different people coming and going, covering the Service both now and from possible post-attack scrutiny. Now, no time was to be wasted!

'How are matters progressing Nick?' asked Morison, getting straight down to business. 'We have anxious people in London who are keen to know how we are progressing.'

'Well,' said Stephens, 'in a few more days we shall have everything ready for Paris. We only have to pursue the other locations in case Paris ceases to be an option; we await intelligence. If they are coming to Paris, we are virtually there.'

'Right,' said Morison. 'I would like to review all you have today and be fully up to speed before Caruthers returns. We shall then be ready for a full planning meeting and I can take that back to London and tell them all is in place. They can't give the order until we are ready.'

Stephens invited Morison into his inner office where they sat down and began taking stock. Morison turned to Stephens, 'Remember, an accident; I value my neck.'

Morison's mind turned to the preparation and evidence of illicit activity that was scattered all around him. His nerves jangled at the thought of a leak that although rare, had been known to happen and the consequences would be more than just a few red faces. He had the macabre thought of protruding blue tongues, one of which would be his, not to mention how discovery of this operation would affect the government or the monarchy. This act, after all, was treason and punishable by death, depending on how one interpreted the position that Diana, the mother of the future king, now held because she was no longer a member of the royal family.

Now she was arguably an acceptable target, provided the Service could justify their reasons for her demise. Her son, however, would be king one day, so one could interpret this act as treasonable. How would future King William view the Service if this act ever became public knowledge? Morison was not a lawyer, and didn't intend having to face once, but the academic points were hard to ignore.

Morison continued to muse that perhaps the death penalty for treason could be removed from the statute book to afford the Service some protection. He would continue to pursue this point with higher authorities on his return to England! All it needed was for the Prince of Wales to die or stand down from the succession, which was not improbable, and they would then be killing the mother of the heir to the throne.

The thought crossed his mind that should Charles Windsor have already stood aside he would not be going through this torment. 'Pull yourself together,' thought Morison, feeling anguish gain ascendancy, unsure whether it was his conscience conflicting with the act he was about to perform. 'We are way past being able to indulge ourselves and just have to get on with it. It still may not happen but we must consider it will and let our professionalism take control.'

Today was the day Morison secretly dreaded. He had been able to rally the troops but couldn't pretend this operation didn't affect him; this was now for real! Today's meeting was for the purpose of enhancing the Paris detail; it could no longer be considered a game of intrigue. This was going to happen!

Stephens reached for his brief case and laptop computer, which stored all his ideas and options, affording a mix of alternatives to produce 'what if' scenarios, so they could decide on the best available. This was kept on his laptop for mobility and was normal Service practice, in case the need arose to vacate the premises in a hurry. He also had to allow for variables because a field operative could never be certain whether some parameters might change at the last moment; one had to be ready for all possibilities so portability was essential.

Stephens had sent an advance copy of his thoughts to Morison, so today should be a feedback session. Stephens sat down at the desk near the wipe board that was centrally positioned. He was now better placed if he and Morison had company today; he needed to be in a better psychological position for control. He had checked through the details of his presentation, reasoning through several different scenarios and then adding variables to see how this impacted on the whole. He ordered a second huge pot of coffee, since he had made significant inroads into the first, having taken full advantage of coming to this wonderful capital, and wanting to be in the most professional frame of mind for the task ahead; he would need to be!

Nick Stephens was a shrewd man. He was more of an academic than a front-line trooper but there needed to be a balance of abilities if one was to achieve the best results for each Service sector. A Cambridge graduate, thirty-five and recruited through family connections, he had an uncertain purpose in life rather than a burning desire to serve Queen and country. He was considered to have natural attributes for the Service that Morison had always thought should exclude most people from entry, simply because those attributes were obvious. This job was not about being obvious! Stephens excelled at planning and reasoning through 'what if' scenario's, which was ideal for the Service and especially suited to this operation.

He checked with Morison whether they could expect any

company today, unsure whether any Embassy staff had been invited. Morison replied, 'No,' with a wry smile. 'There won't be any visitors.'

Stephens breathed a sigh of relief. 'They wouldn't have the balls to piss in the Prime Minister's loo,' he thought. 'They will be in their usual deniability mode of positioning themselves to claim they knew nothing and didn't realise our intentions. We must have been in Paris to review how overseas operations were handled in France. If it's discovered we have used their premises they will claim it was without their understanding our purpose.' 'Good,' Stephens said aloud, 'we shall be able to work much more effectively without others asking irrelevant or obvious questions and wasting time.'

He had set up the PowerPoint presentation and was ready to get started when Morison stopped him. 'Perhaps we had better sit down and take stock of where we think we are first and then spend time running through your planning and testing its substance. We must form an outline of the planning, review the detail and make our assessments within a time frame. During the next few days we are tasked with finalising details on Paris but there is no harm in first recapping on our whole position.'

Stephens asked that Morison start with an overview of how he saw the position so far, especially with regard to intelligence, since they last met. Primarily, Stephens was concerned about the operatives they would be using because all the good guys were unlikely to support this operation and it wasn't a situation where one could expect the operatives just to obey orders. All would be at risk if it became too much for someone to handle and they freaked out so it was in everyone's interests, and certainly that of the operation, to make certain they didn't get the selection wrong. Even for professionals this was going to be a difficult call and very few people, including those hardened to political murder, would escape some feelings of regret. This was their biggest challenge!

Now there was a requirement to prepare an attack plan that would take place subject only to confirmation of expected intelligence and acceptable operational logistics. More importantly, the order specified that it must happen before the Princess made any public announcements of her marital intentions otherwise subsequent deniability, and thence the operation, were in serious doubt. A clear deadline was emerging!

'Firstly,' began Morison, 'I agree entirely that the choice of the team is crucial for numerous reasons. Using our Service personnel is injudicious because of the nature of this operation, since many would not take well to being asked to end the life of the mother of our future king. So it's necessary to use a team from another source where no last minute pangs of conscience could endanger the operation. There is no absolute guarantee this operation will remain secret within the Service, so all risks must be minimised and the ultimate sanction will be threatened to anyone who later reveals what has taken place. We must also ensure the operatives are extremely well paid for this task. By looking at our Increment team profiles, we are identifying the most suitable people who will adhere to a strict set of rules without suffering any post attack conscience. These people must be ruthless, totally remorseless and susceptible to being controlled by threats; otherwise this operation will not work.

'We shall have to be certain they will not falter when the moment comes and also not be indiscreet about their exploits later so we have a tall order to fill! There are a number of operatives whom we are confident will perform this task, although the strict criteria we are using for their selection does limit the choice. John Brooke has this well in hand. The most important role is that of the commander and Brooke has that covered in Jim Winfield. He will knit the troops together and it's up to us to ensure how they function afterwards. It would only take one careless whisper to trigger a complete unravelling and spell total disaster. One or two of the team may well have psychopathic tendencies but the correct frame of mine for this act is the priority, whatever the person is like in their social life. Being a psychopath is probably as good as it gets.'

Stephens listened. He was glad they had these people, since the priority was to conclude this mission without any comeback, and they now had the tools to do it. This saddened him!

'The main discussion today is about Paris,' said Morison. 'But, as you suggest, we shall first go over the overall position as a recap. The only way this action may be stood down is if nothing materialises between Diana and Dodi Fayed. But there are those who think that whether this relationship develops or not, she remains intent on leaving the country with her children so perhaps we had better get it over with now. Some wish we had done it before there was a Dodi Fayed. We are doing all we can to ensure Diana's relationship falters and I believe that if the powers that be order the attack, regardless of her current relationship status, they will get resistance from everyone, including us. I don't believe that that is tenable.

'We maintain constant surveillance on the subject's activities; Diana has had encounters before that have come to nought, so it's imperative that knowledge of her intentions is up to date to ensure this is not just another fling. She has intimated she may choose to live abroad if she remarries. This would mean her children either travelling to visit, probably frequently or, God forbid, going to live with her.'

Morison was in full flow and Stephens knew he must wait. He dare not interrupt. 'If Diana went to live in the USA, as she has declared a possibility,' continued Morison, 'which is now a probability if this affair goes anywhere, then an heir to the British throne may end up going to an American school and effectively become American. OK, but what about security for the Princes; how could they be protected? They wouldn't be able to grow up learning the dark and secret art of their trade and would be imbued instead with a sense of liberty, equality and fraternity. What next?! That is not what the monarchy is about; this would almost certainly finish them off.'

Morison's tirade of what Stephens saw as self-justification suddenly ceased and he calmly asked: 'Would you please give me an overview of where you are with your plan now Nick?'

Stephens began his presentation with a general preamble. He agreed with Morison that a round-table discussion would serve today's purpose better and they could review the full-screen presentations later.

He began; 'We have looked at all the locations and methods for this operation and agree that the best method is a car "accident", with the best area being Paris. The subjects are now holidaying in the South of France on board a superb yacht, purchased by al Fayed for the purpose of wooing the Princess. They sometimes utilize a secluded house in St Tropez that overlooks the sea with its own private beach; this is owned by al Fayed. Intelligence tells us that during this month the subjects will be visiting the following locations in Paris, also owned by al Fayed: the Ritz hotel and Dodi's apartment on the rue Arsenne Houssaye. Al Fayed also rents the

Villa Windsor in the Bois de Boulogne. We have good intelligence, from intercepting their phone calls, that once the Princess and Dodi Fayed are married they are intending to live between the Villa Windsor in Paris and Los Angeles but also retain a home in London. These facts will not become a problem until they return to the UK, which means they won't be a problem, provided we succeed.

'The idea is we shall strike when the subjects are travelling between two of these locations. We shall know beforehand where they're going and make preparations along the route for each strike option. We shall rehearse these beforehand by controlling the direction of their car but we must perfect all sites. We must be ready with the others in case of a police presence or major incident near the Alma; something we cannot foresee. We know they will be taken wherever we wish; the driver will be one of ours! Paris affords a large number of current Service assets who will furnish us with vital intelligence of the subject's intentions and timings, so we shall always be one step ahead; that is crucial to a successful attack. We must decide on the optimum position at which to strike between each of these sites. We have asked our operatives to research the Paris road traffic data to find which spots have the worst accident record, bearing in mind that it's crucial this "accident" is considered as such by the public. We are expecting some serious public reaction and may need to ride out a storm, possibly for months.

'The people are more likely to believe in an accident if the attack takes place where others have lost their lives before but, paradoxically, the fact it's an accident black spot will also increase speculation of murder. People know we would choose such a site; here we can't win but we do increase our chances of success. If there is residual evidence and the police are involved, then questions will be asked to which the people will require answers. We either answer those questions or risk everyone realising the inevitable, that we have something to hide! This is especially true if those questions can be identified by the people and are obviously only ones we could answer if we chose. It's crucial there is no residual evidence so there won't be any questions!

'After a few months we are expecting all will have quietened down but only if there are no major cock-ups. The planning will need to be meticulous and must be rehearsed time and time again, hence the need to identify the target spot, or spots, ASAP. It's only by constant rehearsal that we shall be able to move like clockwork and even then changes may occur for which we must be ready. We need this preparation in place, because we shall only have a moment's notice of the subject's intentions before the order is given.

'The strike will ideally be at night to minimise the number of potential witnesses and hopefully between 1.00am and 2.00am, or later, when there will be fewer people about. The time, however, we cannot control. August in Paris is the best possible time because the city virtually closes down. If we have witnesses then we shall have serious trouble with deniability and, if we have any mishap with the attack personnel that too could be problematic.

'We must allow for all possibilities, such as attack site forensics. In the event of an unforeseen collision, we shall rely on the French police to clear the site. We must be politically deft just after the attack to ensure French political support is quickly available; that's essential if the police are to accept our instructions in clearing the tunnel before people start descending into it.'

Stephens thought he didn't need to discuss the implications of anyone needing hospital treatment post-attack right now; they would be scooped up and taken away to the Embassy compound. He considered that, as long as these people were retrieved, it didn't really matter whether or not they survived but they mustn't be caught or found.

'We shall also need some refinements to the vehicle. The plan will not work if the large Mercedes normally used by Mohamed al Fayed is used because this car is extremely strong, with darkened windows and armour plating. The effect of any "accident" will be significantly lessened. We know that Dodi doesn't like this particular car so it shouldn't be a problem but it mustn't be chosen on the night, or we may have to abort the mission. We shall need to use one of the smaller cars, prepared prior to the attack and delivered to the rear door of the hotel when needed. It's critical this car doesn't have darkened windows, since that would reduce or eliminate the effects of the military strobe that we will use to blind the driver just at the critical moment.

'The subjects are known to wear seat belts, which will decrease our chances of success but we shall ensure they are unserviceable and ineffective. Our assets at the Ritz hotel and staff at the Embassy will provide us with excellent intelligence, so we will know whether we need to change any of the last-minute plans due to a change in the subjects' plans.

'They may, for example, decide to stay at the Ritz for the night and send for their belongings from the apartment. A daytime attack isn't possible, bearing in mind the chief objective of making it look like an accident, because of the number of witnesses we would have, so we may need our draconian mid-air plan which is also in place. This requires a further order, although the plan is ready, and the decision would need to be taken over night. The critical issue here would be to try and ensure the plane crashes into the sea to thwart or delay forensic discovery.

'At this stage, we need to collect details and piece together how to proceed for our most probable method. We have everything available for a successful outcome. This is because the event will take place in France to forestall the inevitable investigation, since this will be down to the French police, not us. This should enable us to ride out any storm more easily.'

A report had arrived from Caruthers the previous evening that both took time to read; the darkness deepened!

'We have it on good intelligence,' continued Stephens, taking it upon himself to paraphrase the report's findings, 'that the subjects are very quickly becoming an item and it's more than a summer fling. It had been suggested they may well be about to announce their engagement and are known to have visited a jewellers shop in Monte Carlo to view engagement rings. There is also a rumour circulating amongst Service hierarchy that the Princess may be pregnant; this is one of the reasons they are bringing their engagement announcement forward. A great deal of credibility is being placed on this relationship because the Princess and Dodi are so well suited and the whole affair so plausible. Where else is the Princess of Wales going to find someone who can offer her the prospect of a relatively normal life that we know she craves?'

Stephens felt an uncommon pang of guilt here so he quickly moved on. 'This union will accomplish all her objectives of defying the palace and removing her need for protection from their continuous attacks, plus establishing her complete security, and with a man who shares the same ideas, likes and dislikes. If the announcement of marriage is made then our options for action evaporate because the people would know this was murder; that knowledge would probably achieve the very thing we are trying to avoid – the fall of the house of Windsor, or at least the Prince of Wales. We must maintain a current and constant flow of intelligence; this is vital in making sure we won't be taking unnecessary risks.'

This exercise had seemed surreal for the past few weeks because they had been playing games with ideas and theoretical preferences. That time was fading! They had now upped the ante and were looking at times, preferred date, which routes offered the best opportunities for striking, and the best positions along the two options were already emerging. The sense of urgency exacerbated latent feelings of remorse in Morison because the moment had arrived. They were not engaged in a paper exercise any longer but were about to end someone's life, someone whom many liked, and for a reason most regarded as dubious.

A dark resolve had settled in Service minds that this was a duty they must perform and from which there was no reprieve. A game, now no longer a game and very much for real! Morison knew he was going to be presiding over an historical act that would leave his nation in grief and run contrary to his life's purpose, but do it he must.

It was August and the Service knew from intelligence the subjects were coming to Paris during this trip but there was no absolute guarantee, so they must retain options to strike in St Tropez, Sardinia or elsewhere. They might need to go for one of the other options if intelligence later indicated Paris was being given a miss; they must be sure.

With nobody in Paris during August, and knowing where they were staying and that they would not have more than a few bodyguards in tow, it was perfect for the job. Morison ran through the reasons in his mind. They must wait for Paris if they possibly could because being forced into taking action elsewhere would increase the risk of failure one hundredfold. With their necks on the line, he didn't like that risk.

One further reason to wait for Paris was that it was the end of the holiday season, giving more time for the Princess to change her mind or for something to go wrong with her relationship. Clutching at straws came to Morison's mind as he resigned himself to an action that was going to change the mood and the psyche of his beloved Service forever.

Morison addressed Stephens. 'I think I would like to see your preferred attack location from the beginning of the intended attack run now. We may pick up ideas if we drive along the route and I would like to see how effective this ramp is at the tunnel entrance because that will be crucial. Let's forego your presentation for now.'

'Yes,' said Stephens, 'let's go after lunch and I'll drive us around the route from the Ritz hotel to the Alma; we can discuss the detail as we drive.'

Both men felt that the usual excitement over these operations was missing. It was more tinged with sorrow and a sense of duty; but personal feelings aside, there was a job to be done and that was that.

Morison continued his reasoning. 'The intelligence must be first rate or no strike is possible if it's to achieve its primary aim of looking like an accident. For this to be successful there must be few credible witnesses, preferably none. If we fail in this, we have to rubbish the witnesses who don't give suitable testimony but if there are too many of these, we lose credibility. A state of total deniability is essential for the Service to stand aside from this.

'Whatever happens, we must never acknowledge anything concerning our presence in Paris. We mustn't ever allow ourselves to be interviewed on any issue even remotely connected to this operation. We must ensure everything is planned to the finest detail and, if there are any credible witnesses, we must ensure they are rubbished while at the same time putting forward the view of those who support our position. Nobody will be able to prove anything if there is no evidence and we have a privileged position that we shall certainly be utilising. Failure in this quest will most certainly cause the fall of the monarchy and most probably the British and French Governments, since I doubt the people will be very forgiving. Failure is not an option!'

While Morison and Stephens were more secure with the feel of the operation and setting its parameters, another brief intelligence report came in from Caruthers in St Tropez. Stephens handed Morison a copy and suggested they both absorb it before further discussion.

Morison quickly read its contents and began. 'Caruthers is saying that electronic surveillance results have confirmed the couple's status. They have definitely decided to get married and have definitely bought an engagement ring.'

He put the report aside and continued. 'It looks as though the Princess has found her man and the chances of her changing her mind are virtually zero.'

Stephens read the report with the same feeling.

'We have been watching them very closely for several days now,' read Morison, 'and their body language and mood definitely confirm our worst fears. The relationship is looking hot. She seems to like Middle Eastern types,' adding cynically, 'especially very rich ones. One of her best friends married a Muslim so there is a precedent, despite comment from some quarters that this will never happen because of her responsibilities. We believe she thinks her duties are bringing up her children in as normal a manner as possible and that alone deviates from the preferred way for the monarchy. Normality is another death wish to the monarchy's survival hopes.' He looked at Stephens. 'The moment is upon us! We must strike in Paris and ensure our agents stay close, informing us of any changing circumstances. We must be updated hourly.

'Paris is a virtual certainty but if they change their minds, as they leave Sardinia, we may still need to consider a less satisfactory plan. We already know a stand-down is not an option unless we have good evidence that they are parting company. The report says that the numbers of bodyguards in St Tropez is prohibitive and action there would be suicidal or, at the least, ineffective since we need for this to look like an accident. Fayed has increased them to around twenty and there will be hardly any light between them and the subjects whilst they are there.

'One of our biggest problems is that any action other than Paris would be off the cuff, virtually spontaneous, and I cannot approve of that. Think of the position! It's imperative we give the impression of an accident, which requires a huge amount of precise and meticulous planning. If we do this elsewhere we cannot achieve this, which means that we cannot strike at all unless we elect for an accident in the jet. This is not ideal but we may not have the time to plan anything else and the job must be done before they return to the UK. Dodi's girlfriend has left the scene and we know they have bought an engagement ring. From their conversations we know this operation is going down within days. Barring a miracle, we can expect the order any time. Be resolved and be prepared!'

REBELLION

Information from Paris arrived on Morison's Bleak House desk first thing on the morning of his return to London. This included a note from the intelligence team, based in St Tropez that described Diana's reaction to the Service's rubbishing campaign of Dodi Fayed. Morison learned that Service actions against Dodi hadn't made an impression on the Princess, thus far.

Morison turned to Brooke in sombre mood. 'I have just received intelligence that our attempts to rubbish Dodi Fayed with his womanising and financial matters have regrettably failed to impress the Princess, so we shall extend our net of possible scandals and affairs to help change Diana's mind! It appears we are unlikely to succeed but we must do all we can. Now it's certain this is more than just a holiday romance; their bond is growing. Our options for a stand down have all but evaporated. This will be more than an embarrassing relationship and is developing into something much more permanent and serious. If anything, the probability of us getting a "go" has greatly increased over the last forty-eight hours. This letter,' added Morison, reading another missive from his desk 'is from the Directorate, saying they need this operation on standby within the week. We shall continue trying to secure a change of heart but I now fear we are unlikely to escape this action.'

Whilst intelligence was being fed through to the team, Morison knew this was going down within days and they couldn't afford to delay full preparations any longer. From 5th August they knew that the subjects were looking at engagement rings in a Monte Carlo jeweller's shop and one didn't look at engagement rings to celebrate a summer romance. This, together with the electronic intelligence coming through, made it clear there was a marriage in the offing and disaster for the British Establishment. It was time to prepare and disengage from the fantasy that all would be well; it would not!

Jim Winfield received the call from Brooke that afternoon and diarised the arranged meeting at Bleak House for the next day. No further information was given, just to contact the office and go through their special procedures to identify the location of Bleak House. He was instructed that a senior officer would be present at the meeting and he should prepare for a few weeks' training. The operation was top secret and he was not to divulge his whereabouts to anyone; including his wife.

'Same tone of instructions,' thought Jim, as he imagined some frustrated clerk sitting at a desk, deriving a great sense of power from delivering a straightforward message under instructions. It always annoyed him. 'It's a sad reflection of human nature,' thought Jim, 'that people derive such pleasure from merely delivering instructions. Perhaps shoot the messenger isn't such a bad idea!'

The day arrived and Brooke had a distinct foreboding about Winfield's imminent arrival. He dreaded briefing Jim before a definite order was given. It was his duty, however, to have Winfield prepared and he had to put him forward, even though the operation could still be stood down. He pondered, 'We wouldn't have time to prepare. We must be ready! How can I ever be satisfied on something like this? I can't do more to reduce the risk of a negative reaction so he must be fully briefed.'

Brooke also considered that if others knew he had reservations about Winfield's possible psychological response it wouldn't do Jim any favours. 'He may respond far better than I think,' Brooke thought, 'and I would then be putting his career at risk on the basis of my irrational and incorrect assessment.'

As Brooke deliberated, Jim Winfield was driving through a wet, early morning mist and arriving for his meeting, as prepared as he could be. He knew this was something special or there wouldn't be all this secrecy and he couldn't forget Brooke's demeanour when discussing this operation in London, which had been the most cautious Winfield had ever seen him. He wasn't happy with the prospect of what was to come. His instinct, following the meeting with Brooke, told him he should feel wary. Well, he had chosen the Service as a career, and he had received instructions before that he wasn't happy with, but everything had turned out OK.

Jim had kissed his wife and daughter goodbye on the steps of their house, saying he would take her on a special holiday when he returned. He knew these special operations meant a bonus and he promised they would have a holiday to remember; there was an important task to perform and he wouldn't be back for at least two weeks. He would try and get word to her if it was much longer, but not to worry if she didn't hear because these operations sometimes took longer than expected and he wouldn't be able to make contact. Jane already knew how the Service worked, so this came as no surprise.

Winfield arrived at the gateway to Bleak House ahead of time and, receiving his pass, went through the regulatory checks and proceeded up the long drive to the main house. It looked appropriately bleak and felt chill on this grey summer morning. He felt an inexplicable uneasiness and thought, 'Why do I feel as though I'm going to a funeral?'

He entered the hallway and announced himself to the receptionist. He was informed that he was fifteen minutes early; would he mind waiting? The others had already arrived and had started an earlier meeting that was to lead into the one he was attending. They may be running late. If he sat in reception, he would have coffee brought to him.

Jim sat thinking how good the coffee was when the call came for him to join the others. Ushered to a room on the third floor in the centre of the building, he entered to find Brooke approaching him with outstretched hand but in solemn mood. 'Good morning Jim, did you have a good holiday?'

'Yes, except for being dragged up to London when a phone call would have sufficed,' Jim thought.

'Good morning Sir, very pleasant thank you. They always end too quickly don't they?' Brooke's terse demeanour indicated to Winfield that he was not in the mood for niceties but out of habit needed to go through this ritual. Winfield thought, 'If these people were uneasy before they began, what the hell was coming?'

'Let me introduce you to Tom Morison,' said Brooke. 'Tom is in charge of this operation and I report to him. We need to fill you in on all the details we have so far and to discuss how we proceed from here with the project we briefly discussed last week. Would you like some coffee?'

'Yes please, sir,' said Jim. 'I have already had some and it is rather good.'

'Yes,' said Brooke, now glad for the opportunity to make light conversation and put himself at ease, let alone Winfield. Brooke went over to the coffee pot, still unsure how to start this whole thing off. 'I just have to say it,' he thought. 'Morison is not prepared to test the water any more. There should be no need! Winfield is paid to do a job and now he must do it!'

'Jim,' Brooke began with his back to Winfield while he poured the coffee. 'We have a duty to perform an action that, as I have already told you, is essential to the health of the realm. A member of the royal family is causing, and will continue to cause, extreme difficulties and embarrassment to the government and to the main core of the royal family.' Then, clearing his throat and trying not to shake, he said, 'We have a solemn duty to perform that I can assure you is being carefully assessed. There appears no other option is available to us.'

As he spoke, a piercing chill was already streaking down Jim's back as he thought, 'God almighty; I am to lead the assassination of the Prince of Wales.'

Brooke continued; 'We have tried everything we could but have no choice other than to face the problem and leading that task has befallen you. We need to eliminate the Princess of Wales.'

Jim thought he must have misheard; 'Prince or Princess?' His pulse quickened, beads of sweat appeared on his brow and his mouth felt dry. He could not help his reaction! He could not have foreseen it! It was sudden, autonomic, and he had no thought as to how this reaction was being perceived by the other two men, nor was he even considering it. His mind was a blur and paroxysms of rage swept through his very being. He had the strongest urge both to punch the two men sitting in front of him and to call the police.

The quick thought raced through his brain: 'How can I call the police? These people are senior to the police. We give orders to the police!'

Brooke and Morison looked at each other in horror! How could Brooke have got this so wrong? This was the worst possible nightmare unfolding before them and all they could do was watch and wait. Jim Winfield was a tried and tested operative. Brooke had tried to test the water; he had reservations but couldn't know for sure. Jim had seemed fine and if they couldn't trust his reaction then...

Jim finally blurted out, 'I am assuming that I have not misheard you. You want me to be responsible for assassinating Diana, Princess of Wales?'

His heart continued to pound but his focus was coming back as the expressions on both Morison's and Brooke's faces confirmed he hadn't misheard. The thought crossed Jim's mind: 'Lord, take this cup from me.' Words couldn't describe his feelings but one thing he knew; he wanted out of here as soon as possible. His thinking wasn't clear and could only rage at the two, by now very dark-looking men on the other side of the table.

'What in God's name are you thinking? Why do you think I joined the Service? Do you think I joined to murder this beautiful woman loved by the entire planet? Why is such a monstrous act even considered necessary? How can you sit there and tell me there are no alternatives to this vile act! Why not declare a Republic if things are that bad and the Windsor's can't cope!'

Jim was not thinking; he'd already said far too much and was in mortal danger. Brooke and Morison moved slowly to the far side of the desk and Morison spoke quietly to Jim. It sounded to Winfield's ears like a hollow, disembodied voice speaking to him, as if in a dream. 'None of us want this Jim, but we must follow orders otherwise we don't have an organisation. We take it that you are refusing command of this operation?'

By now there was no going back and Jim could merely breathe irregularly and look at the two men, enraged but silent.

'Jim,' said Morison, 'I am going to ask you to wait while Brooke and I go into another room and decide how best we can proceed from here. Please take some coffee,' Morison said in a rather banal tone.

Morison and Brooke left the room and went into the security room at the end of the corridor, having instinctively locked the door behind them. Morison called security and both stood, eyes fixed to the floor while they waited for the door to open. Morison said to the security man on duty that he would need him on standby for the next hour or so and would he please get hold of Justin Davidson, the head of security as soon as possible and tell him that Brooke and he would be in the security anteroom where they would await his arrival; it was urgent!

Morison and Brooke looked at one another as though they were both in another time or place and felt the surreal experience of floating and losing touch with reality, both still reeling from this wholly unexpected and very upsetting experience. Jim was a man they both liked very much; what were they going to do?

'There is no point in having any further discussions in that room,' said Morison. 'If anything, it would make matters worse. Now, however, we cannot let him become involved in this mission, obviously, so how do we deal with Jim Winfield?'

Brooke was trembling with the enormity of what had just happened. Not only were they committing the worst and most horrendous act he had ever been asked to perform, but what was Morison going to do with Jim?

Justin Davidson arrived. He was a man who would do absolutely anything for the Service, anything, as to him it was sacrosanct to the survival of the state and any order from the Service was treated as a command from God.

Morison explained the situation they had with Jim Winfield without telling Davidson anything about their operation. Davidson came back in an instant and said, 'You have a rogue runner and there are no options as to the course of action. The reasons for his response are irrelevant, since he has undertaken to obey orders and failed. If you give him a chance to change his mind he will most certainly bottle out when it come to the "hot" section. Can you afford for that to happen? What will be the consequences if he does bottle out, both to the operation and to all personnel involved? This is the worst call any commander has to make but make it you must. Or call off the action and even then, from what you have told me, he may still take it further.'

'Leave us for a moment, please, Justin,' said Morison. 'Brooke and I must have a serious discussion.'

'Where is he now?' asked Davidson.

Morison explained that they had left Jim securely in the middle section conference room. Davidson said he would prepare with his team for whatever they decided. He then left the room.

Morison and Brooke looked at each other, neither able to speak. The enormity of the operation and now this dreadful experience had clearly taken their toll. Both men were old enough and wise enough to know there was no escape from doing their duty on either count. They must get through this day, regroup and proceed. Each knew what must be done, but with greater urgency since they were now compelled to appoint another commander and their deadline for the operation remained.

'We have no choice Brooke,' said Morison. A numbed silence continued between the two men as both were hurting, mainly because both knew this was true. Within the hour Jim Winfield would be no more.

'We cannot risk Jim continuing to be involved in this operation,' said Brooke. 'But what if we could persuade him to keep silent?'

Morison continued to look at the table in a fixed stare but retorted rather angrily, although still hurting. 'He has let us down badly, Brooke. Neither of us wants to do this but we do our duty. We have a major problem with making this deadline that we shall still have to comply with, and now we have no commander, thanks to one of yours bottling out. None of us can be allowed to pick and choose what operation we are prepared to accept at this stage. We gave what chance we could to allow for conscience but when the call comes either they work for us or they don't. When there is a potentially lethal risk to us with the knowledge Jim now possesses, then we have no option. We all signed up to this and it applies to us all; there cannot be exceptions!'

These words pierced Brooked heart. 'We all know what the consequences are of refusing an order at this stage, and of the difficulty we have in appointing someone to a task before they even know what those tasks are. That is how it is and always has been. We cannot afford for one man to cause problems with the press, especially with this operation, even if we do contain it from public view. He has always known the risks and rules of being involved in this kind of work; he is not a child. It's not an option to stand the operation down because of Jim Winfield and, as Davidson rightly said, it makes no difference because we cannot afford to take the chance that he will go elsewhere and report us. You give me an alternative!'

Brooke knew there was no alternative. He had done his best to give a withdrawal option to Jim and he could do no more. He wished that, somehow, he could have told Jim more and given him a better chance, but how could he? He would have been in the same situation then as now, and before they were virtually certain this operation was going to proceed. They were still not certain but it was likely; that still disturbed Brooke. What if the operation is now stood down? All this will have been for nothing!

'We must see him once more,' said Brooke. 'There is a possibility he has had a genuine change of heart. Even you and I freaked a little when we needed to consider this order. We owe him that much at least, even if I share your view that there's little hope.'

Brooke had gone for the only chink of light remaining and Morison knew he needed to allow this because neither would rest if they hadn't done everything possible. Reluctantly he agreed to re-enter the room and hold this discussion, but his greatest fear was the effect that seeing Jim Winfield in his predicament would have on John Brooke, who was already on a knife's edge.

The alternative was to have Brooke believe they hadn't done all they could to prevent this and he was already having serious problems with his trusted aide, even without the Winfield scenario. He felt that denying Brooke this vain attempt to save Winfield would certainly lose him a trusted and loyal senior officer forever so, unhappy with either option, Morison agreed to re-enter the room and join Winfield, after they had seen Davidson.

Justin Davidson returned with the news that everything was arranged and he was waiting for Morison's order.

'Stand by!' said Morison. 'We are going to see Winfield and will be with you shortly.'

Davison's eyes connected with Morison asking for the order. Morison turned fully towards Davidson, his eyes acknowledging assent, but with the implied meaning; 'We are re-entering the room in one last vain hope,' as he turned his glance towards Brooke, his eyes indicating the reason that also asked Davidson to be ready!

'Do not look sad or in any way perturbed,' said Davidson. 'You will do him no favours if he has any inkling of what is about to befall him.'

Brooke quietly responded. 'He will already know.'

'Yes, but you will be amazed how people somehow don't accept what is happening; they seem to blot it out; that will help him, and us,' replied Davidson.

Morison and Brooke returned to the conference room having been gone for about fifteen minutes but for what seemed like hours. They entered the room to find Jim Winfield sitting at his desk and staring at some notes he had prepared for the meeting.

He was now much calmer and greeted them as they returned with an almost normal welcome, saying; 'Would you gentlemen like some coffee?'

'No thank you,' said Brooke. 'Have you had time to consider your position?'

'Yes, sir, it's not very good is it?' said Jim, in the biggest understatement of his life. He calmly continued, knowing he had already done irreparable damage to his position and, realising he couldn't make matters worse, decided to question the reasons for the order and establish his view with these two people who had shattered his illusions of everything he thought the Service stood for. He had nothing to lose and felt that justifying his position somehow gave him a weapon; the only one he had. He felt logic and decency could win the day but secretly he knew this betrayal was more than his being put in this position. It was a betrayal of the British people who trusted him, and those around him, to protect the innocent and the whole realm from harm. How was murdering Diana going to save the nation?

For matters to be that bad there had to be another evil that needed to be expunged but one more entrenched in the social system that could not be so easily dislodged. This evil had now invoked its powers to prevent its own demise. He knew he couldn't withdraw his opinion, so why not tell them and see if Brooke, at least, might waiver.

Winfield began his earnest entreaty. 'We are given orders for the defence of the realm and required to act and to obey but have never been advised that we couldn't question an order or ask for clarification. By giving an opinion, we may be standing against the official view and so always risk incurring the wrath of our masters at any time. If, however, we don't ask questions when we feel it appropriate then we don't do our duty,' he continued. 'Who made this decision? Are we to believe this order has come from the Prime Minister? That's hard to believe and, if not him, then which unelected official within the Service has felt able to make such a decision, presumably under the guise of being in the national interest? If these questions aren't challenged, these people may do as they wish, whenever they wish. Surely we must stand in check on this behaviour.' Jim fell silent, his eyes rapidly searching between the two stark expressions before him.

Morison thought, 'A rational and impressive response under his current stress. I must respond for Brooke's sake. Although nothing, regrettably, will now change what must be done.'

Morison felt he could keep Brooke on side as long as he tried everything but after this tirade he would need to win the point. 'Your reasoning is understood Jim, but in any organisation of this sort a certain amount of decision-making must take place without the constant approval of politicians or there would be no decisions made. With an order of this magnitude we are rarely privy to who is in the decision-making loop. Sometimes the politicians don't want us to know or even acknowledge there is a loop, so they communicate these orders to one of our very senior officers who will then allocate the task down the chain. They always need to establish, and then defend, a position of deniability. The government is fully aware that decisions are often taken without their knowledge but those decisions are always assessed very carefully by us before action is taken. It would be more than the life of a civil servant is worth to take action against the wishes of the elected government.' Morison then thought: 'My God, those were unfortunately chosen words.'

Winfield responded immediately, desperate to retain ascendancy not only because he wanted to save his neck, but also because he wanted to stop this evil from proceeding. 'What safeguards do you have that senior people in the Service made this decision with the consent of senior politicians? Certain people could claim to be representing a higher authority to achieve his or her own ends and, if there is no check, then anyone who has an axe to grind and who has access to significant power could be abusing it.' Jim had unsettled both men before him and knew he would be stopped soon so continued as if driven with Lucifer snapping at his heals.

'Suppose someone has a problem with Diana and wants rid of her and this person knows people who know people in the right places. There cannot be many such people! Influencing the powers that be to achieve this goal wouldn't be difficult because this person would wield enormous undemocratic power and may have undue influence in what would merely require the nod for such an action. Then you must have considered who this person could be? Who do you think would have sufficient power to order an action be undertaken by the British Secret Service of this magnitude? From whom would we accept such a directive? Your list of possibilities will not be long! That is not something the people would approve of, so the whole tenet of democracy fails and what becomes a brutal and selfish murder is committed by the state and against its people. That is not what I believe our nation stands for and it's not what I or, I believe, the Service stands for.'

Amazed the floor was still his, Winfield continued as though this was his swan-song statement and must carry through and be heard, or what had his life been about. 'What will the police do about this when they realise what has happened? Will they play the game when you have the political machinery swinging behind the inevitable disinformation that will ensue from this evil? Will they be coerced and expected to stand down on their integrity, allowing all that is decent to be impugned because you wish to take action to prevent a system from failing that needs this kind of action for its very survival? Who in this nation wants a system that requires this sort of action to maintain power? Doesn't that tell you there is something seriously wrong?'

The points gushed forth in a flurry as though the next one would be his last. Desperate to finish his statement, Winfield glanced at Brooke and could see he was having an effect. He didn't even look at Morison as though to do so would break the spell and he would be forced to return to his pumpkin. 'Has this been really approved by the right people or has a minority manipulated the Service to achieve its own evil ends? Is the head of our Service aware of this?'

Winfield looked rapidly between Morison and Brooke but was met by stark, unsettled expressions. 'If the head of the Service isn't on side, then what is he going to do when he discovers what has been done using his organisation and without his knowledge or approval? Will he make a statement unravelling the truth? No, you will have covered that as well! If you need to coerce him then the person who ordered this must be more important than any senior politician in the realm. This act would need to be an offshore black operation to be possible. It could then be carried out without the knowledge of the head of the Service. This is very dark and sinister.'

Winfield then asked the question, again looking directly at both Brooke and Morison. He knew they wouldn't answer but wanted to observe their faces; 'Who ordered this monstrous act?'

Winfield guessed from their expressions they didn't know any more than he did and that gave him a grain of hope. Did Morison and Brooke now have doubts as to what they were doing; for whom and why? Why were they supporting this? Were they assisting the state in this venture at all? Feeling his time running out, Winfield had one last shot. 'How many people will have to fall because of this act that no decent human being will support?'

Then, challenging the very heart of power, Winfield said, 'This will probably mean the end of the Service, as we know it. If the

Service personnel don't recoil when they hear this news, as you know they will, then they're not the people I know and trust. When the people get to know of this we shall be finished as an organisation and there will be repercussions to make Nuremberg look like a tea party!'

This last point struck a nerve with Brooke, which was clear to see. Winfield had touched on Brooke's own particular fear. He felt the gods were telling him something; something he already knew.

Brooke was unable to hide his emotion any longer and started to breathe erratically, feeling he must leave the room to maintain his composure but managing to stay through fear. Fear that Winfield was right. For the first time he felt threatened by his own team of people. It wasn't only Winfield in danger! Winfield was right and was saying what Brooke also wanted to say but lacked the courage. He was in a dark corridor that had no turning and felt like a murderer, not a loyal servant of the crown, which meant he had reached the end of the line.

He was not, however, going to leave in a box like poor Winfield, so through his daze and grief he decided to wait until today was over. There was no stopping this anyway and no point in joining Winfield but that was it. He had had enough! He would tell Morison very soon that he wished to be stood down from the front line. He couldn't take anymore!

Winfield knew he had made his mark and looked straight at Brooke as if to say, help me. Brooke wasn't listening, whether through cowardice or a lingering need to do his duty regardless of its nature. His eyes were travelling through a watery mist; he couldn't see Winfield for shadows.

Winfield knew when he looked at Brooke that he had failed and his time had come.

Brooke's thoughts went to Davidson's words about helping Jim. 'This will mean you're being cashiered out of the Service, you know that don't you Jim? You have signed the Official Secrets Act and all this must remain totally confidential?'

A huge feeling of relief went through Jim as he heard this; as Davidson had said: 'Nobody accepts that the ultimate sanction is going to be enforced.'

Morison beckoned Brooke to leave and said to Jim, 'I deeply regret that this happened. You will now need to see people outside who will take your pass and security papers, which will begin your removal from the Service.' Morison swallowed. 'Goodbye Jim.'

Winfield retorted 'Goodbye and good luck to my country. God help her!'

With that Morison and Brooke left the room. They now had even more work to do.

Justin Davidson entered the room with one of his colleagues, John Jacob, a sallow faced, thickset man with dead and fish-like eyes.

Davidson spoke to Jim brusquely. 'Would you mind giving me your papers, Mr. Winfield? I understand you have various items that need to be returned. Would you please go with Mr Jacob?'

Jim did as he was bade and walked for what seemed like an eternity down a long corridor that had one door at its end. He saw men discussing matters in whispers. He walked as though he was in a trance, his thoughts never leaving his wife and child as he continued along the corridor, unable to prevent whatever might now befall him. There was no escape, no point. Where would he go? They would find him and then his wife and child could be harmed. There was nowhere to go but retain the faint hope that perhaps he was going to be released; perhaps he was going home.

'Please go in there,' said Jacob in a monotone, 'and fill in this form on the whereabouts of your effects.' He handed Jim a list of Service items that would need to be returned. These people knew how to put a victim at ease. 'I shall be with you shortly.'

Jim entered the room and the door closed behind him. He walked over to a desk and noted there were no decorations in the room and that the heater wasn't on. He started to feel chill and did up the top button of his coat, then began to think about what he'd just done. He had ended his career and had to explain this to Jane. What would he do? Was he right to take the position he did. He sat at the barren desk and thought, 'I don't have a pen. They've taken it from me.'

The door opened and two men walked in. Both approached Jim and one started talking about his belongings. The world started to spin and thoughts crossed Jim's mind of Jane and Sarah. He had the feeling of warm liquid running down his neck and a supreme sense of peace. Jim had not heard the shot from the sound-moderated Sig Sauer subsonic 9mm pistol. He fleetingly knew there was no more pain, then the lights went out. The Lord had taken his cup!

Davidson returned to the meeting room where Morison

and Brooke were sitting down, looking as though they were on a different planet, lost in thought and, although unable to show it, also in grief. Davidson sensed the atmosphere and merely informed Morison it was done and he would take care of matters. "Were there any further instructions?"

Morison gestured no. Davidson left the room and Brooke turned to Morison.

'Do you know Jim's wife?' Brooke asked in almost a whisper.

'No, I never had the pleasure; just as well', replied Morison.

Brooke pressed, 'Are we able to assist her in any way she needs?'

'Well,' said Morison, 'we shall make sure she has her entitlement but we cannot start giving favours or it would look very strange. She will have a good pension and will have to find someone else and start again. Now let's get down to business.'

Brooke suddenly saw red at what he regarded as this cold and indifferent attitude to one of theirs who had served his country well and had just received his reward! His blood boiled. 'You know, sir, I am finding this job increasingly difficult to countenance! Once I have this operation out of the way, I would like to apply for a transfer to non-operational duties. Do you think that's possible?' he asked in a firm and decided manner.

Today was a day that Morison would never forget. One of his best commanders and now one of his best and most trusted senior operatives had fallen and the day was not yet over. He had already been thinking of Brooke as not suitable to lead field operations on this one, so felt able to comply with this request. He knew Brooke was totally trustworthy; Morison didn't believe his objections were on the grounds of complete disgust with the Service, as they had been with Jim Winfield, but that this order was one too far. In truth, he wasn't far behind.

Morison felt as though Brooke was just on side and was not the selfish type. The one way of both testing and securing his absolute commitment would be to make him feel as though he was letting the side down or, more particularly, his colleagues. It was in the interest of the Service, and of Morison, that he had full support from Brooke and he had to find a way of ensuring he didn't falter. He knew Brooke could not continue in the Service afterwards, that he could handle, but he must use him as best as he could for intelligence gathering.

Morison began with a most unusual outburst that Brooke

considered incomprehensible. 'Today we must resolve that we shall be ready to serve Queen and country in committing ourselves to achieving a successful outcome, whatever our feelings or whatever problems we encounter. This operation will probably cause us to lose more personnel from the Service than we can afford but we have no choice. We don't have the luxury of deciding whether it's worthwhile or right or morally acceptable but we do as ordered and we must focus our minds on this objective against all emotions; there will be many,' he uttered, pensively gazing ahead.

Brooke was worried that Morison too was beginning to feel the strain. This was a strange tirade from Morison who was always in control but now indicated he too was having difficulties.

Brooke thought, 'It's all very well for me to feel the way I do and let Morison do all the cajoling,' but he knew Tom Morison, and he wouldn't have been blasé about dealing with this horror story without reaffirming the need and he had no choice. It made Brooke feel more responsible for the task in hand, since he now felt that he must shoulder his burden and assist Morison as best as he could, rather than be a passenger. It occurred to him this was what Morison had intended, and those comments were for the express purpose of making him feel guilty.

'Is he that clever?' thought Brooke, looking across at Morison and then deciding no, that wasn't possible. He didn't see Morison look sideways at him as he turned away, with a wry smile!

'God, what I do for Queen and country,' then, correcting himself, 'well for my peace of mind and ease of passage. It should help to ensure Brooke stays on side for the course.'

'This operation is the toughest I have ever had to undertake!' said Morison, trying very hard to be the commander he was and retain Brooke's support. 'But we do a job that sometimes requires making difficult decisions. We learn to take the rough with the smooth. We shall never have an assignment as tough as this again, of that I can assure you. You are also feeling as I do, perhaps more so, but time will help you overcome that. Let us do the job in hand and discuss this when it's over.'

Morison was deeply regretting that he had allowed the last discussion with Winfield to take place. That was another mistake and he was wondering if maybe he had lost his touch.

Brooke was relieved to have received a sympathetic ear and it emboldened him to say more. 'I accept all you have said, sir, and yes, I will see this operation out, but have you decided what role I am to play in the end game?'

'Yes,' said Morison, deciding to cut his losses and at least ensure he had a good and loyal senior man on this operation, since he would have a major problem in finding anyone whom he could trust, certainly at this late stage. He would tell Brooke now! God knows how anyone else might react to this order!

'I have already decided,' said Morison, ensuring Brooke didn't get the impression his hand was forced, 'that you should deal with intelligence gathering and the feeding of critical information to the troops. As you are aware, intelligence is vital to this operation.'

'Yes,' said a very relieved Brooke. 'I am sorry but enough is enough. I would start to become a liability in the field.'

'I know,' said Morison, 'that's why I am putting you onto intelligence gathering but we must discuss your position with the Service, when this is over. Oh, will you make sure that Davidson sends out the usual letters to Jim's widow in about a week's time. Perhaps you would check in with him before we leave today. We now need to find a new commander; in a hurry!'

22nd August 1997

Dear Mrs Winfield,

It is with great regret I must inform you that your husband Mr Jim Winfield has gone missing whilst performing a special duty. We are doing all we can to trace his whereabouts and will inform you immediately when we have anything further.

Regrets

Faceless official.

27ᵗʰ August 1997

Dear Mrs Winfield,

It is with great regret and deepest sympathies that I must inform you that your husband Mr Jim Winfield's body has been found. Because of the difficulties in repatriating his remains, we have taken all the necessary steps to have his body cremated and his ashes will soon be returned to you. You will be contacted by a member of our department to discuss your pension entitlement. Please allow us to offer our deepest sympathies.

Regrettably yours

Faceless official.

DEEPENING CRISIS

Morison's overriding consideration in this deepening crisis remained whether Diana's intention was to marry Dodi, when she would most probably leave the country and take the children with her, or was she just enjoying a brief summer fling. He needed an ongoing review of events that led to the current position, knowing intelligence was crucial. This was not only to perfect the assassination plan but also to maximize all chances of persuading Diana to change her mind; by whatever means. This could only be achieved by obtaining information concerning the couple's relationships to date and knowing their future plans.

If this attack couldn't be prevented then it was very important it came before any announcement of impending marriage, because this knowledge alone would guarantee people assuming murder, no matter how well it was executed. His plan of rubbishing Dodi Fayed must succeed before the date by which they plan to strike in order to avert it. They could not wait beyond 30th August!

Morison could accommodate Brooke on being stood down from the front line because intelligence was of equal importance and whatever action the Service decided on, and its timing, would depend on this information. Brooke had consequently increased the number of agents for intelligence-gathering purposes and made sure they were his best. Following Brooke's departure from the front line, Morison had become more wary and less certain of his other operatives. If Brooke and Winfield could bottle out; who might be next?

This was not a typical operation where one could predict people's behaviour, as with less emotionally charged tasks, since even the most loyal and hardened men could flounder during this order. Morison felt he could perform the required duties without

Brooke, and was right to shoulder the main responsibility, since this was definitely above and beyond the call. This was going to need a steady hand and nerve! Brooke would continue on his best area of expertise, intelligence and planning; Morison would decide what to do with him after this operation.

In the meantime Brooke's task was to produce a full report on where they were to date with regard to the subject's activities and maintain it daily over the coming weeks. He was asked to produce a complete file on this relationship from its inception, so the Service could scrutinise each detail and understand every move.

His agents would listen to their conversations and glean their intentions. They must use the latest surveillance equipment, usable at considerable range when a collection of small nuances of speech made, or behaviour observed surreptitiously, was more illuminating than major public statements.

Following Morison's instructions, Brooke had ordered his men to report daily, so he could maintain impressive reports to Morison. First they were to produce an overview of Service reports submitted since the beginning of the summer and on Dodi from the beginning of the year. Brooke wanted a complete picture and to establish probable events to come, to include areas of weakness that ought to assist his rubbishing campaign on Dodi and ensure they hadn't missed anything. This way he would be best prepared! They would need detailed evidence of the subject's intent if they were to be successful in their forthcoming operation or, as Brooke also thought, if a chink of light existed to help in preventing this union, surveillance might afford them the opportunity they required. This was Brooke's primary driver!

Brooke didn't have to wait long before receiving the compiled report that was taken from Service information gleaned over the last few months. He sat down to a hearty breakfast in his country-house conservatory with muted resignation, reading through the lead in to Diana's nemesis. The report was prefixed with the following caveat: 'You will be pleased to note that the detail in the first part of this report does not reflect the code level of urgency this operation currently holds. It's an initial overview report compiled with information available from routine but continuous scrutiny of the Princess during the early part of the summer, so only the later part will give the level of information required. As the report progresses, and in subsequent reports, you will note the level of detail is more constant and reflects the higher code level.'

'Covering their backsides,' thought Brooke; well, 'fair enough.'

He then proceeded to read. 'During our normal routine surveillance procedures we observed Diana watching her favourite ballet, *Swan Lake*, at the English National Ballet's performance on 3rd June in the Royal Albert Hall, where she sat near to Mohamed al Fayed. Al Fayed, who was there in a sponsorship role later, sat next to Diana at the Churchill Intercontinental Hotel during dinner and offered her a July holiday at his St Tropez Villa in the South of France. We don't believe Diana accepted this invitation but she had been invited before to several of al Fayed's homes, including those in Scotland and Gstaad, Switzerland.

'Considering Diana's needs for privacy and security with her children, and requiring support from someone known to her, we thought she would accept the offer because of her limited alternatives, which she later did. Diana received offers from other sources but we believed she would accept al Fayed's invitation because he is able to accommodate all her needs.

'Her family have also known the Fayeds for some time and it would be difficult for her to accept an invitation from someone she didn't know and who couldn't protect her children. Diana's stepmother is a non-executive director at Harrods, owned by al Fayed, and her father Earl Spencer has known al Fayed for several years. It was very possible Dodi Fayed would join them on this trip. This is the main reason we reported a possible doomsday scenario unfolding that, in our view, couldn't be controlled by us.

'On the 11th June 1997 Diana wrote a letter to al Fayed accepting the holiday offer and details were sent to her concerning all available amenities at the villa in St. Tropez, so we knew she was going, and with her children. To assess the risk of Diana and Dodi meeting up during this holiday, we checked Dodi's current woman situation. He appears to have a serious relationship with his current girlfriend, Kelly Fisher, and marriage has been rumoured. If this happens, I believe we shall need further instructions on whether this level of surveillance need be maintained.

'We observed Diana and her children being collected by a Harrods' helicopter that was sent to Kensington Palace on the 11th July, which flew them to Stansted Airport, from where they routed to Nice on board the Harrods' executive jet, a Gulfstream IV. On arrival in Nice, they all transferred to the *Jonikal*, al Fayed's new yacht, and sailed down the coast to his mansion in St Tropez, Castel St. Helen, in St Tropez le Parc where the security is very high.

'This is an exclusive park of more than 100 mansions and al Fayed had taken a number of bodyguards, making discrete observation much more difficult. The mansion is set in ten acres on cliffs above the sea and Diana occupied the guest quarters, the Fisherman's Cottage, an eight-bedroomed house set just down from the main mansion. The house has direct access to the beach, so we may be able to use this for observation or access, if required, though we haven't yet made a full assessment. We await your instructions on this point.

'The subjects went into town on several occasions appearing relaxed and off guard. We had to bear the bodyguards in mind so maintained a discreet distance. We blended in with the press photographers and weren't spotted. Diana was happy to have pictures taken and appeared to enjoy diverting public interest from Charles Windsor. This we believe was provoked by the fiftieth birthday party that Prince Charles had thrown for his mistress Camilla Parker-Bowles, at his home at Highgrove, Gloucestershire, the day after Diana arrived in St Tropez. We also believe Diana accepted the Fayed invitation because she wanted to offer the press suitable exotic headlines to spoil the press cover for Charles Windsor and his mistress's acceptance-building program. What better opportunity than swimsuit shots of Diana in sun-drenched St Tropez on board a luxury yacht, with her children and obviously very happy?

'Alarm bells rang when we discovered that on the 15th July, Dodi gave his girlfriend, Kelly Fisher a false story of going to London on business for his father. He left her in Paris and flew down to St Tropez to be with his family and Diana at the villa. Being prepared to lie to his girlfriend, whom he has known for some time and at such an early stage in his relationship with Diana, didn't bode well and we believed our worst-case scenario was unfolding.

Kelly Fisher did, however, join Dodi in St Tropez on the 16th July and spent the next few days on one of Fayed's other boats, the *Cujo*. Dodi spent two nights with her there while the Princess was still at the Fayed's guesthouse.

Dodi went over to the house each day and spent considerable time with Diana, so we became increasingly nervous as a clear choice was emerging from Dodi that must be kept hidden from the public. It was obvious he was deliberately keeping the two women apart during this time, which was a further indication of his intent.

Diana returned to London on the 20th July, two days later than planned, so she wasn't rushing to return home. We guarantee she was enjoying her stay.

'On 24th July, Dodi and his girlfriend returned to Paris from where she continued on to the USA and Dodi to London. We intercepted letters sent by Diana to the Fayeds to thank them for the wonderful holiday, when she spoke of Dodi's family in rather affectionate terms, calling them "hugely special people", adding to our alarm.

'We watched matters unfold and didn't have to wait long, since the day after he returned to London, Dodi took Diana to Paris for the weekend on 25th July. They went to the Ritz hotel, owned by al Fayed, and stayed together in the $10,000 a night Imperial Suite, dining at the Carlton Restaurant near to the Ritz.

'They were very keen to keep this trip quiet and maintain privacy, thus making our work easier. They sneaked out through the rear door of the hotel to avoid being recognised and nobody knew they were there except for the Ritz hotel management, and us.

'We watched this unfold with increasing tension and realised that every bit of information, every word between the couples that was spoken and every move made needed to be recorded and passed on. We had a man who could help in this already at the Ritz hotel, the assistant manager, who is one of our assets, and we arranged for him to prepare the bugging of the Imperial Suite, so there would be no doubt where they were headed with this romance. We told him this was necessary for the Princess's protection, after which we had all details regarding timings and movement. We knew this was a budding love story, much more than just a summer fling, and you will see from our routine reports that we informed the directorate accordingly.'

These words from the report echoed sorrowfully through Brooke as he realised this was unfolding one way; although he would continue to do his best to stall this romance, hopes were fading, especially knowing Diana's obduracy.

Now the report described their man at the Ritz who had helped before in placing various gadgets in rooms so they could listen in to selected guests' conversations. Brooke remembered asking

Morison whether he had decided where the attack would take place and Morison replied it would most likely be Paris. Brooke knew that Morison had been thinking of an idea, not fully explained, that concerned a man called Henri Paul, the assistant head of security at the Ritz. It was mentioned here in the report.

Morison said, 'I think I know how we are going to proceed.'

Brooke felt that whatever this plan, it would now unfold in Paris. The parts were coming together and he knew Morison would inform him in due course. He continued reading.

'The subjects returned from Paris to London on Sunday 27th July. It was discovered they would be going away together again the following Thursday 31st July for a much longer break in the Mediterranean, on board the *Jonikal*. Tension mounted as we observed their relationship deepen; they were unable to be apart for more than a few hours during the whole of that week.'

Brooke set the report aside and pondered the futility of his actions unless he could pull something special out of the bag. The rubbishing of Dodi was one of his main objectives but what of Dodi's current girlfriend? Could they use her in their quest for a change of Diana's heart? A woman in the process of being scorned might prove very useful. He resumed reading the report.

'Diana and Dodi left London again for Nice via Stansted Airport, London, for a private and undetected holiday on board the *Jonikal*, sailing to Corsica and Sardinia. The affair was becoming very intense and we believed the couple were preparing the world for news of their marriage intentions by allowing a Mr Mario Brenna to know where they would be and take photographs of them for press release and thus achieve their objective without suffering the usual paparazzi intrusion. They wanted the world to know they are an item and big changes were on the way with Diana's lifestyle.

'From our surveillance we knew they were deciding on marriage and spending all their time together to reaffirm their feelings. Fortunately for us, they were being very secretive about their relationship, probably until Diana has told her children.

'Their timing is to collect the ring on the 30th and return for the announcement on the 31st or 1st September; this seems perfect.'

Brooke knew the last possible day by which the attack must go down was 30th August, before they returned to England.

The report continued: 'Mario Brenna is a renowned celebrity photographer who has worked as Gianna Versace's personal photographer and is well known on the various fashion catwalks. Versace, the fashion designer, was a personal friend of the Princess of Wales; she was extremely upset by his recent murder and attended his funeral in Milan.

'The public unveiling of this affair was not good news because any indication of this romance blossoming before we take action is going to seriously complicate matters. We need to keep it quiet and disclaim the later public furore that will ensue when we state there was never a romance, merely a summer fling. It will be hard to sell but we have absolutely no choice if we are to proceed with this action.

'It was too late for us to prevent any intrusion on the part of Mario Brenna who located the *Jonikal* on the 2nd August and followed the yacht to several different locations. Then the problem took on a new dimension. On the 4th August at Porto Cervo, Brenna was in position to take photographs including the one called "The Kiss" published on 10th August. That followed the headlines on the 7th August that you will have seen in the British press, the *Sunday Mirror*.

'There will be no misinterpreting this photograph, which has confirmed to the world that Diana is in love. We will never convince the world that Diana and Dodi aren't in love; regretfully, motive has been irrevocably accentuated. No other press coverage was made on this trip because the yacht kept its distance and we did all we could to keep the Jonikal's location from the general media.

'Mr Morison was furious when he learned this had been allowed to happen. He told us to keep him informed of all events from that moment on a daily basis, and immediately should anything significant occur.

'Our team followed Dodi and Diana back to London on the 6th August and the next day they observed the subjects spending the evening together at Dodi's apartment at 60, Park Lane, next to the Dorchester Hotel, leaving at 11.00pm. We had little to do other than keep a vigil and report to Mr Morison daily.

'Diana went to Bosnia on a landmines campaign sortie the next morning, returning on the 10th August. A few hours after returning from Bosnia, the Harrods' helicopter picked Diana up and took her to al Fayed's house in Oxted, Surrey, where Diana and Dodi spent the following day relaxing on the 500 acre estate while al Fayed was visiting his in-laws in Finland. Then they went to meet with Rita Rogers, Diana's clairvoyant, near Chesterfield, Derbyshire and back to Oxted, by helicopter.

'The significance of this is more than at first meets the eye because Diana sets great store by readings from Rita Rogers and Dodi is the first man she has taken to meet her, strongly suggesting she was looking for approval on a decision already taken; marrying him.'

Brooke knew this action was dangerous with so much already in the public domain and everyone knowing Diana and Dodi were an item, but despite that he knew there was no option. They just had to bite the bullet and get on with it. Brooke knew that now even his best endeavours were unlikely to prevent Service action.

More and more despondent, Brooke found his concentration beginning to crumble. While hope existed that this was never going to happen, he could hide behind the idea it was no more than an exercise and he would wake up one morning, go on holiday and think of how dreadfully close he had come to losing all those hard-won values of integrity and self-respect that made him a man, and he thought a good man.

Shivers of pain and anguish ran through his blood; he knew this was going to be a historical event he would rather have read about in history books than be instrumental in initiating. He felt debilitated by his duty, and his respect for the Service had now diminished irrevocably. All the values he held dear began to disintegrate. He couldn't help it. He couldn't reinvent feelings that rarely let him down; he relied on them for his profession. He was paid for his intuition, for God's sake, and it was that this was wrong; very wrong!

A dark mood descended as he found his very soul ranting at the Service for putting him in this position. Who made this decision? What of his pension? What of his further role in this job? What of his self-respect? What of Winfield and his family? Could he hold on any longer and let this moment pass; would it ever pass? These moments of doubt were now becoming more frequent and Brooke knew he was unlikely to last the course.

The one chance was if the Service allowed him to retire early and stand down, or take an even lesser role, but Morison had already been very accommodating; could he expect more? He wasn't sure how to make an approach but considered that, if he delivered the information required, the moment might come for him to depart under acceptable cover. He hadn't been asked to do more than the intelligence, so far, and Morison was very active on all the detail. Maybe, just maybe, Morison might take complete command of this one and then he could withdraw to his previous role and stick out the last few years, albeit without the feelings of justifiable patriotism that had carried him through his career thus far. That was now gone forever! He would try to do his job and bide his time.

The report continued: 'You will, no doubt, have already gleaned some information that we include from the press in this report, because a more open and relaxed Diana has reported certain items freely, but we include them for completeness.

'We have noted comments coming from the Princess that give rise to further concerns that the trend we feared is developing. Diana has been voicing her thoughts on living abroad and, should this relationship with Dodi Fayed develop, a substantial change in her lifestyle is imminent and that is bound to cause us serious concern. Comments to the press don't help our case because as people are given more and more information about Diana, the more it highlights her plight and the more sympathy she attracts. The relaxed mood of the moment had induced Diana to make comments such as: "My sons are always urging me to live abroad to be less in the public eye. Maybe that is what I should do: go and live abroad.'

'We note from press reports that this hasn't gone down very well with Her Majesty, who ordered a new statement be issued disclaiming this possibility. I mention this to highlight that the more speculation we receive from Diana, the more unsettled the people will become.

'A war of words between the Princess and the Royals is the last thing we need right now, since this will fuel speculation later. The people won't take kindly to Diana being forced out of the country with their young princes and living estranged from them all; they will see it as all the fault of Charles Windsor. Having the second and third in line to the throne living abroad and without the level of protection afforded by British security is not an idea relished by the people and most certainly not the monarchy.

'Diana also made a further comment to the press, probably concerning this point, when she remarked to photographers: "You will have a big surprise coming soon with the next thing I do." We must, of course, put a different spin on the meaning but when you take everything else collectively, this will be viewed ominously.'

Brooke poured a cup of coffee, thinking that his operatives had been asked for facts not opinions. Nonetheless, people from all quarters were coming up with these thoughts and that gave some comfort that the Service was justified in this action and had not grossly misjudged the seriousness of the position.

A situation was emerging where Morison, and the senior team, would consider this problem needed dealing with very soon; a stand-down was becoming less probable, even if Diana and Dodi didn't become a permanent item. If Diana was to put out information about her intentions, and continued to feed the press about her activities, a problem was guaranteed. It was never going to stop; Brooke knew this.

He read on. 'The holiday proceeded without us having many operatives on site in the south of France. We felt that we couldn't have too many because the topography didn't allow for agents to remain unnoticed. Since this was more of a reconnaissance operation, large numbers weren't really needed, only our experts in the use of voice recording equipment and all the new toys we had for intelligence gathering.

'There was, of course, security in place surrounding Diana which comprised of both official British police and al Fayed's own security staff that he had beefed up to around twenty shortly before her arrival. This number made it difficult to observe Diana and remain discreet, although we have the police available to give us information if needed. We cannot use them for anything other than routine detail because this could be a dangerous indicator later that we had something going down, and naturally, we can't make the police party to our intentions.

'Fayed's bodyguards took some avoiding, so we had to observe from a distance and just gather information but we were close enough to hear their private conversations. They told us all we needed to know.

'Mr Morison requested we find out what the level of bodyguard protection would be in Paris because he fears a large number of bodyguards would make an operation impossible. We have been unable to gain this information but continue to watch.'

Brooke agreed that if Fayed's guards were good, this could pose a problem. Trained protection people would spot Service men observing Diana and Dodi in Paris and the Service couldn't work with professional interference! Another reason Morison prefers

Paris, he mused, was the subjects wouldn't consider they had need of guards; they would be on home ground with their properties, the Ritz hotel and Dodi's apartment. It was their own turf and they didn't have bodyguards in tow when they were in Paris only weeks before.

He continued reading; 'We have no way of knowing whether the subjects had an existing relationship. We knew they had met on previous occasions, since Dodi and Diana's parents have known each other for many years and there may have been a relationship building that didn't come to our attention earlier. We aren't certain whether Dodi is still engaged to an American model, Kelly Fisher, but we presume this is not so or we expect soon to be stood down from this exercise.'

'Well, we all know the answer to that one now,' thought Brooke.

The relationship between the subjects left Brooke more and more despondent and he relayed as much to Morison! The body chemistry between the couple was beginning to blossom and the Service knew this was going one way only. There was not much time! There were comments from Diana that 'Dodi is so very special' and these weren't given without something serious being under way with their relationship.

The Service's fears were heightened when Dodi finally dropped his girlfriend because they knew Dodi wouldn't make this decision without good reason, indicating he knew Diana would commit to him. Brooke knew they both wanted marriage so, barring a miracle, this appeared to be a definite green light. It would be incredible for it to be anything else and he needed to regard it as such. One of the biggest problems was the amount of time they spent together. People don't stay with each other every minute of the day without good reason.

Brooke knew in his heart that hope was fading when Dodi Fayed's girlfriend, or fiancée, began proceedings against him. Any faint hope of a reprieve from this operation was doomed, unless Brooke could pull off a miracle. This train of news didn't give an encouraging background but Brooke continued to hope this was merely a hot holiday romance.

'The Service cannot yet be sure but neither can they await the outcome,' he thought. 'The order won't be given until absolutely necessary, so there must be a continuous and persistent attack on the relationship by rubbishing Dodi Fayed, since this is the only way they can influence the Princess and avert action.'

Brooke considered going to St Tropez himself but Morison thought it was best for senior personnel to stay away. They would rely on the information coming through from the field because, if senior Service staff were noticed near to the Princess, there could be suspicions after the attack. With British police around, that was likely.

Morison told Brooke to spend his time on the Dodi propaganda campaign to increase any chance of a stand-down; he knew there was nobody more motivated to succeed. Morison thought this would keep Brooke on side, doing something useful and out of harm's way; their way.

'The subjects spent as much time together as possible and on the 13th August, while in London, they went out for a night on the town and then back to Dodi's apartment at 60 Park Lane from where Diana left at 2:00am.

'The following night of the 14th, Diana arrived at 60 Park Lane at 7.43pm and left in the early hours of the following morning. The only reprieve we had from the monotony of observing people enjoying themselves was when Diana kept a long-standing arrangement with her friend, Rosa Monckton, and departed for a holiday in the Greek islands on the following day, 15th August, using al Fayed's Gulfstream IV.

'Once more we flew off into the sun and watched and pursued, but Diana had gone off around the Greek islands with her friend and they gave us the slip. Since they were on a boat, which was out of sight most of the time, we couldn't observe them but we are content there was nothing of any significance that could happen on the water.'

Brooke thought the order was soon to be given anyway and there is nothing she can do to cause much further embarrassment. The Service was waiting.

Brooke instinctively thought Diana was in safe hands. He wondered if Diana knew that her friend's husband and brother worked for the Service. It also occurred to him this should make her feel safer. Both thoughts he quickly put out of his mind, further invoking his sense of guilt.

'Diana arrived back at midday and by 9.00pm that evening was back at 60 Park Lane and in Dodi's arms, leaving at 1.15am the following morning. The very next evening, on the 20th August,

Diana and Dodi took off for Nice at 6.40pm, where they boarded the *Jonikal* for another idyllic cruise around the Mediterranean.' Brooke knew, this was most probably their last.

None of the revelations or rubbishing in the press had the slightest effect on Diana. Brooke knew it was unlikely to work because Diana was too much in love to be persuaded that her beau was not the most wonderful man on earth and she had been used to conspiracies and being lied about for the last fifteen years.

Diana had found Dodi, and nobody else would be able to give her everything she had so far been denied. There was a paradox! Dodi's ability to give Diana what she needed was the reason they were here today because this union would also give her the power she couldn't be allowed to possess. Nobody posed as great a threat as Dodi and it must end! Brooke knew this was not a relationship that would founder easily but it concerned him that, since this was an obvious statement, everyone else would realise this when they found out Diana had been killed in a car 'accident'.

There would be people who might normally support Diana who must change their views when presented with a fait accompli; would this happen? They must be persuaded! It was probable Diana and Dodi would be getting married from when they went into the Alberto Repossi shop in Monaco on the 5th August and looked at engagement rings. When they went in and ordered one on the 23rd August 1997, and arranged to collect it in Paris on the 30th August, it was certain. The Service had electronic surveillance information that left no doubt they would set a date but not before Diana had informed her children; their timing was perfect! The Service timing must be perfect!

Dodi had even spoken to Frank Klein, the manager of the Ritz hotel and overseer of the Windsor Villa, to ask when the villa would be available for occupation. He was told the villa was ready for moving into and Dodi told Klein, 'I've spoken with my father about moving in. My friend doesn't want to stay in England.'

Dodi then decided not to be secretive adding, 'we want to move into the villa because we are getting married in October or November, Frank.'

This was becoming known by the whole world; Diana said she was retiring from public life in November which people would realise would coincide with their marriage plans. This operation was becoming more risky!

It was very clear where this relationship was headed and Morison was glad they did because, from the Service perspective, there was now no guesswork involved, just an effective disinformation package needed, fast; especially with a growing public expectancy of marriage.

Watching the blossoming romance grow around the Mediterranean gave the operatives confirmation of where this was headed but they were going to continue in the streets of London, in and out of Palaces and apartments, at all times of the day and night. Morison knew he must be seen to be doing all he could by his colleagues to avoid this action because even the hardest man amongst them would prefer a stand-down. The fragile air of unification amongst the Service must be maintained, and not just in consideration of those involved, since he didn't want the Service disintegrating when news of this action leaked.

Morison decided that Brooke had done his duty with the information gathering in the south of France. The timing of events in the USA with regard to Dodi's affairs was at its most fruitful for propaganda purposes but time was critical.

A useful result of the 'Kiss' photograph being published was that it triggered Dodi's girlfriend/fiancée into realising that Dodi was having an affair with Diana and commencing proceedings against him.

Morison felt it was time for Brooke to place his enormous talents into this field. He sent for Brooke the following morning and asked that he continue to remain focused on intelligence gathering but to major on the Dodi propaganda. This would help with personnel morale at their next meeting when it could be shown they had done all they could before proceeding. Brooke was to give a presentation of what he had accomplished at the next scheduled meeting and set about rubbishing Dodi Fayed with great gusto, having already begun the preliminaries. It was now time for a full-blown attempt and a last throw of the dice.

Morison knew in his heart that Brooke's activity was futile but it allowed a fair attempt to be made and assisted a friend's, some Service team member's and his own, conscience.

Kelly Fisher had started her proceedings for breach of promise against Dodi in Los Angeles on the 14th of August, so it was clear she was out of the picture, but Brooke must unsettle Diana somehow! The 'Kiss' photograph not only began the fireworks with Kelly

Fisher but also engendered press hyperactivity in pursuing any angle to see who Dodi really was and if he had any skeletons. Thank God for human nature, thought Brooke; it makes our work so much easier.

He continued his preparations for a major push on utilising any negative publicity on Dodi Fayed and tried to ensure no stone went unturned in maximising efforts to win Diana's disapproval. The Service would do its duty in supporting efforts at destroying Dodi Fayed's life but, thought Brooke, as though he was doing Dodi a favour, 'I am probably saving his life too.' He was after all trying to save Diana's life, he pondered in justification of his actions.

Brooke reviewed the position with some of his associates in Los Angeles, where the greatest possibilities for information discovery lay and from where the disinformation process would begin. Dodi's publicist was based in Los Angeles and Dodi travelled there to see his lawyers and try to defend himself against this new onslaught from Kelly Fisher that threatened to take his newfound happiness away.

Brooke needed to be close to the ground and retain a close vigil; he intended being ready! Magazines and national newspapers were all getting on the bandwagon, each trying to outdo the other, with the American magazine *People* using headlines such as; 'A Guy For Di' and 'Is He a Dreamboat or a Deadbeat?'

Mohamed al Fayed was cleaning up Dodi's financial indiscretions by instructing Harrods, the London store, to pursue any outstanding debts and remove them before the press got wind. The Service must work fast because, even if Dodi did have any outstanding accounts, all he had to do was tell his father where they were and there wouldn't be any. They needed to reach these first and time was not on their side. They could hardly tell Dodi's father to leave well alone because they were trying to prevent the need for an attack on his son!

Dodi knew of the furore that was being invoked in the USA and flew out to Los Angeles to visit his lawyer, Burt Field, in an attempt to stem any further potential damage caused by the Kelly Fisher revelations. The Service had done their best to prevent an attack and couldn't do much else other than sit back and wait; they hoped for a change of heart from the subjects.

Dodi was not in the USA for long and caught the plane back to London to make sure he was back in time for Diana's return from her Greek holiday on the 19th August.

Brooke knew he was trying to secure a miracle! He had been looking at all the ways in which he might be able to persuade Diana she was not going in the right direction and Dodi wasn't the guy for her, but knew she had learned to be sceptical of outside intrusion, since she has been the victim of various false propaganda ruses before. He would have to find something that would really upset her such as, perhaps, jealousy or concern for her children.

Despite various, and Brooke thought, effective comments coming from the press regarding Dodi's financial matters, highlighted during the weeks around July and August 1997, none seemed to have the desired effect. In addition to suing Dodi for breach of promise, Kelly Fisher was now selling 'kiss and tell' stories in the British tabloids and problems were highlighted with Dodi's financial affairs by using American Express statements, albeit old ones, but to no avail. These could be considered suitably lurid for Diana's consumption but they were either disbelieved or ignored. None had the desired effect on Diana with regard to her growing affection for Dodi and Brooke began to realise he had failed and couldn't do much else.

It wasn't his failure that grieved him but its consequences. Without success here there was no way of stopping the juggernaut that had now started and would continue to its inevitable end.

The second line of attack was going to be Dodi's women. Brooke felt that here they were on a stronger ground because Dodi's previous sexual encounters might respond to overtures for 'story for reward' and feed the newspapers with lots of relevant titbits of information.

Kelly Fisher saw her lawyer Gloria Allred and sued Dodi for breach of contract using the reason that they wanted the world to know what Dodi was like; the Princess in particular. The story was sold to the British newspapers and serialised in the *News of the World* and its sister paper *The Sun*. This included nude modelling photos of Kelly Fisher and salacious stories of Dodi's preferences. It was personal and should cause the desired damage, thought Brooke.

Stories about other women were added to the list and portrayed across the world's press but all to no avail. Dodi's publicists became alarmed at the amount of invective levelled at their client and thought it might affect his relationship with the Princess.

But Dodi's response was that Diana felt sorry for him and their relationship was getting better and better. Brooke thought it was a fair reflection of the situation that if disclosures over the last few weeks couldn't change Diana's mind, then nothing would succeed. It was not what Brooke wanted to think.

They had run out of ideas and Brooke knew it was time to pack his bags and admit defeat. He telephoned Morison who awaited the call.

'Hello John,' said Morison, knowing what was to come. 'You have done your very best and it's time for me to take control. I wish to thank you for your good work and I am sorry I must take over.'

This attempt at softening the situation for Brooke almost had him in tears. He didn't feel as though he had deserved this support for, in essence, not being up to the job and Morison had taken the responsibility leaving him blameless. He was no longer involved in something that sickened him to his very soul but was still able to remain in the Service. He hesitated on that thought. Yes, he would do his job and retire from the Service as soon as possible after this operation, never forgetting this moment for the rest of his life. He must bid his integrity and the Princess goodbye! Brooke broke down and cried like a baby.

Morison was now without solace. He had many about him but the call was his and his alone. He needed to take stock of the position; having lost Winfield and Brooke was certainly gone after this operation but there was one goal that must be achieved. He must assassinate the Princess of Wales without any comeback. He considered the position…

Diana and Dodi knew their forthcoming marriage was about to cause a furore amongst the Establishment and didn't want to announce their intentions until they were officially engaged. The Service knew Diana wouldn't want to inform her children of her intentions before making the news public which suited them very well and took away any immediate urgency. If Diana was prepared to announce her intentions through the press, whilst still abroad, Service plans would be up the proverbial creek.

The Service knew it was imperative the people didn't know Diana intended to get married because it was a guaranteed motive and so their plans at disinformation would fail. They must complete their propaganda package before the attack.

Morison learned they had ordered an engagement ring from

Alberto Repossi's jewellery shop in Monte Carlo from the 'Tell Me Yes' ('Dis-Moi Oui') range on 23rd August, having previously viewed them on 5th August. Alberto Repossi said he would take the ring to his Paris shop, just yards away from the Ritz hotel, from where Dodi would have it collected on 30th August. The Service knew the subjects would be leaving Paris the following day, 31st August, and return to London with their news.

There were two places they could stay for their last night: either the Ritz Hotel, or Dodi's Paris apartment at the rue Arsenne-Houssaye, near the Arc de Triomphe. The Alma tunnel was chosen, but they must continue to maintain alternatives. Morison knew the Alma was the place to execute this attack, without doubt being extremely lethal and close to both venues they would be using. This would make it much easier and less suspicious for his chosen driver to take the subjects on their final journey to, or from, wherever they had been and it was close to the British Embassy; it was ideal! They had Henri Paul, the Ritz Hotel as a focal point and the rue Arsenne Houssaye as target destinations.

Morison wished to avoid collateral damage but knew he must do whatever was needed to increase the probability of success and couldn't take chances, so this would be Paul's last mission for the Service.

Morison focused his thoughts. 'This is the perfect opportunity. This is what we are going to do! I shall get the order now. There cannot be further delay!'

ORDER GIVEN

The big remaining concern for Morison was to find a new commander and he was assured by Brooke they had a satisfactory candidate. Morison needed to endorse this new commander, and the entire team; there was no time for delay. The order had been given! They would complete the operation within the next week and he prayed that Brooke had chosen well.

Morison knew this was the last major hurdle for the preparation, other than rehearsing the attack sequence and the detail that would be repeated, ad nauseam. He couldn't help but remember that Brooke had chosen Winfield and that was a disaster; he thought he was being unfair. Nobody could have anticipated that one. He wished Winfield was on board but must make the best of what he had. There were several operatives available in the mercenary reserve and it was likely Brooke had chosen the best available.

This evening he hoped to return to France with the entire team and begin an intense training program. He now wanted to meet the people with whom he would be working over the next few days and ensure they gave of their best. He had relied heavily on Brooke for this selection process and, despite Winfield, Morison still had confidence in his colleague. Practice, practice and more practice would be his mantra upon their arrival in France when any of their operatives would be effective, provided they had the right experience and sufficient time to prepare.

Morison arrived at Bleak House, mid-morning, having been collected from Heathrow Airport. Brooke was engrossed with his assembled team and Morison thought it best to speak with him alone before joining them, so he asked a secretary to inform Brooke that he was in his office; he would expect Brooke at eleven o'clock.

Morison entered his office and found Brooke had left him the personnel files for the entire team. He knew there wasn't time to read them all, so he concentrated on the commander and would peruse the remainder. He opened the file for the man Brooke had chosen to lead the attack: Kurt Zimmerman.

Zimmerman served in the British SAS, rising to sergeant before he became available to the MI6 Increment team; he was regarded as a very reliable, if ruthless, soldier. 'What other sort are there; unreliable I suppose?' thought Morison. Zimmerman had been in a few brawls during his army career and, according to his file, had struck an officer but managed not to be cashiered. Morison thought that this showed initiative but also questioned whether it showed a lack of control, as he considered Zimmerman's suitability. But he realised that whatever these files told him about past performance was speculative; nothing really mattered until the moment of truth. That was what unnerved him most.

When faced with such a task as this, nobody could be certain of knowing their operatives' reactions in advance. He knew his own service agents well but not these men, although he hadn't changed his mind on going down the Increment route because there really wasn't an option. The majority of his men were not murderers; men who would follow any order, without question, as were needed here. That thought sent a shiver up his spine.

Continuing to read, Morison saw Zimmerman had also received several medals for courage under fire in various campaigns and clearly had the leadership skills and experience required for this task. The more he read, the more he realised he wasn't going to get much comfort from CVs. Winfield, who was the best, had succumbed when confronted with this so how could he find someone suitable? Perhaps only from those available whom he couldn't find a reason to exclude?

Morison briefly perused the remainder of the files just before Brooke knocked on his office door at exactly 10.55pm.

'Good day John, how is it going in there?' asked Morison.

'Well enough,' replied Brooke, 'considering our needs, I think we've done well. They're not the people we're used to dealing with but we could do worse; they're better than I expected!'

Heartened by this response, Morison thought he would go straight into the fray. There was no point in questioning everything one's trusted officers advised and repeating the process for oneself; time was short! He would enter the room, announce where they were going and ensure he got to know these people as best he could.

'John, I don't wish to waste time in reassessing these people but would rather spend it getting to know them better; after all they are from an established Service unit,' Morison said.

This made Brooke feel better in that Morison trusted his judgment, despite Winfield and his own newfound reticence; that gave him more confidence, as Morison intended.

'Do they have an inkling of who their target is yet?' Morison asked.

'No,' said Brooke, 'they don't know who and they don't know where, just that it's not in this country and they are to be available for eight days then subsequently disappear for a month. They know it's a high-profile target but, considering what we are paying them, they're at our disposal for anybody.'

'At our disposal,' thought Morison. 'I hope that won't be necessary.'

Brooke continued. 'We have been going over techniques, getting them to know each other and assessing their particular skills, so we know who to use for what, and where, depending on the final plan.

'Good man,' said Morison, regretting that Brooke wasn't more up for this operation. It would have made his task so much easier. 'We shall go in there and you introduce me. I shall address them and afterwards ask each to make an introduction to the assembly, or perhaps that should come from Zimmerman. Unless I have very strong reservations during the briefing, then we shall go to active mode and get under way to Paris later today. Is there anything I should know about any of them?'

'They are all murderers,' blurted Brooke unintentionally, but unable to resist Morison's offer to express his thoughts. He immediately wished he hadn't. Brooke knew Morison wasn't enjoying this either but he was doing his job regardless. Brooke felt he was indulging in conscience which was something Morison couldn't afford.

He immediately tried to recover. 'They're from our Increment reserve and just what is needed for this operation. They are all very capable murderers.' Then, regretting this rather banal response, he thought he had better remain quiet and let Morison take the floor.

'I know John,' said Morison, knowing the scope of Brooke's thinking but keen to move on. He had placed Brooke in a locker with regard to the extent of his support, so this comment no longer concerned him. 'Before we join the team, I think it would be beneficial if we met with Zimmerman; alone. Bring him in here, John. It won't hurt to allow some distance between him and his command; let's afford him some kudos.'

Brooke went to fetch Zimmerman while Morison considered how he would play this part of the game. He needed to give Zimmerman the feeling of virtual command to assist his relationship with the team and let him know who the main target was ahead of the others, to build motivation to lead and succeed beyond just a large pay packet.

Brooke re-entered the room accompanied by a large, muscular man who looked like a fit rugby football forward. Morison greeted him with the usual pleasantries and asked him to be seated. He would keep this brief.

'My name is Tom Morison and I am leading this operation for the Service. I thought it best to meet our new commander before we begin the meeting in case you have any questions.'

'I appreciate that,' said Zimmerman, as he viewed Morison in his usual suspicious manner. 'I would like to know who the target is. We shall need to know soon anyway, so we might as well get it over with.'

Zimmerman knew the Service had been cagey about this but they couldn't keep it from their assassins much longer unless they still weren't sure of him or his men.

He expressed this thought to Morison who responded, 'The target is the Princess of Wales!'

Zimmerman's face fell; he quickly recovered. 'I wasn't expecting that,' he retorted; his immediate response had been similar to Winfield's. His automatic thought was, what am I doing here? He then considered that this was what he did: he followed orders and the pay was extremely good.

Zimmerman asked a question, giving him time to regain control. 'Is this a definite hit?'

'Yes,' said Morison immediately, not wanting to give the impression that it might be stood down as that was now improbable. He needed his operatives to prepare for a deadline, especially with such little time remaining. 'How do you feel about that?' Morison questioned, unsure how Zimmerman had taken the news.

'A target is a target,' said Zimmerman, having had time to recover and knowing he must be positive and show he was in control as he could be stood down; or worse. 'I was surprised but no doubt you have your reasons and my job is to carry out orders. I have no particular feelings other than I cannot afford to allow anything to become personal.'

Morison was satisfied; he couldn't expect more. Whoever they appointed was going to find this hit unusual. 'I shall inform your team of the target in a moment and give them an overview of our options for the attack.'

'Good idea,' Zimmerman responded. 'It's best to keep them involved all the way through.'

'Good man,' thought Morison; this mirrored his own thinking so he felt more comfortable that he had someone who could handle this operation.

'I shall have a paper delivered to the room from intelligence after we have informed the troops of the target and discussed our reasoning,' said Morison. 'I shall pass this to you and you read it to the team. I want to build up a gradual but speedy acceptance of what we are doing before we leave here today. They must be motivated before we arrive in Paris and ready to go from their arrival. Do you have any questions?'

'No,' Zimmerman replied.

'Then let's join the others,' said Morison as he picked up his jacket and walked towards the door. 'I shall feel happier when the team is going through their paces in Paris. Let's get started!'

Brooke led the way back to the room where the operatives were finishing an early lunch and called them through to the main meeting room. Morison entered and walked to his chair at the head of table with a grim determination that now replaced the ambivalence of yesterday, followed by a dutiful Zimmerman. A mix of stern-looking and unpolished personnel entered behind them and sat in their respective seats, waiting for Morison to begin. The room held an air of expectancy!

'Gentlemen, we are gathered here today for a solemn duty. You are assembled as our chosen team to know that this is it! We have finished with theorising, soul-searching, procrastinating or hoping for a change of heart on our subject's part. As far as the Service is concerned, all that can be done has been done to avoid this action. The nation's future is at stake and our whole way of life would be threatened by inaction. The order has been given! We strike as soon as the opportunity presents itself and definitely before any announcement can be made of an impending engagement between the subjects.'

The team members looked around at each other with a knowing glint in their eyes. Morison saw this and thought that he would get it over with. They seemed to have already guessed and the decision was taken. 'We are to assassinate the Princess of Wales in Paris; within the next week.' The room grew much quieter and more attentive.

'Our team in France has reviewed three probable attack options in fine detail and you should be able to agree the most appropriate within twenty-four hours of being in Paris. We can then concentrate our energies accordingly. You gentlemen have been chosen because of your professionalism, experience and also because we need to maintain a barrier between this act and the Service. It is a central reason why your team must always remain anonymous. Having worked with you all successfully before was essential in giving us the confidence to appoint you, and we shall be working with you in the planning and supply of ongoing intelligence. Our operatives will be assisting along the death route during the attack but we must distance ourselves from this act and that you will understand. We have examined the attack detail and you will become familiar with this over the next twenty-four hours, after which it will be practice, practice and more practice.'

Morison repeated the words to impress on the team that they wouldn't get away with just turning up on the night. They were going to earn their money on this one – and it was a lot of money.

Morison didn't consider he could motivate these people for his perceived reasons, but he thought it best to try and knit them together, although he knew they would follow orders. But he also needed a team spirit to assist in coordination and to build a common purpose, without which the timing for the attack could be lost. He intended treating them as he would his own Service personnel and expect them to respond in like manner.

He continued. 'I can say we have it from the highest authority that this action is essential if our current Establishment is to survive. You may regard yourselves as blameless in this carnage, although don't expect any official thanks from the state or its people. The people will not understand the need for this action so must, at all costs, be kept ignorant.'

Morison continued to separate out any feelings of guilt that his team may have; he needed them to be focused on success. He knew they were extremely efficient when dealing with other troops in battle situations but murdering a woman, who was loved by the whole world, together with her unborn child, whilst travelling towards a new and happy life, was something else.

'We have prepared the ground to cover any unforeseen eventuality and our sweepers are ready for their instructions. They will study all possibilities and probabilities and will be active from the instant of the strike. Once the attack is over, your role will be finished and you will follow our predetermined exit route both from the attack scene and the country. The rest is down to us. We have done our best to ensure that evidence won't be at a level to make subsequent deniability a problem and it's your task to ensure there are no errors during the attack to cause us problems.

'Post-attack propaganda has been thought through and we need to review the probabilities; each aspect needs to be coordinated. For example, the sweepers will need to know exactly what is planned for the attack, so they can be prepared and move as quickly as possible.'

By involving the team in other aspects of the attack, Morison tried to ensure they would realise the importance of no post-attack debris, no witnesses, etc. and thus increase the probability of success. 'There will inevitably be some people who will later suspect the truth but without any evidence, and with the passage of a month or so, the whole affair should quickly become a distant memory. Even if 10 to 15% of people suspect the truth we shall survive, but if this figure rises to in excess of 30% then we have a problem. We must make absolutely certain no evidence remains post attack otherwise, even having succeeded in the attack, we lose.

'You will familiarise yourselves with the overview and I ask that you raise questions on any issue during this session, then we shall discuss each point in turn and flush out possible flaws. We must certainly assess whether we have sufficient staff for the job and whether we have the right skills present in this room for all attack roles. This must be determined today as best we are able, because the last thing we want is to find that we are short of expertise in some aspect with only a day or so to go.'

Morison needed to present the plan as a simple exercise to remove any tension that he felt was beginning to mount; he couldn't be sure whether this was just the usual pre-attack nerves or something else. He felt a different range of emotions emanating from his team and he must determine quickly whether he had any problems.

'Another reason why we cannot be absolutely certain whether we have enough of the right skills is because, until we know exactly what our plan is, we cannot know what our requirements will be, so the decision of when and how is crucial before we finalise the attack. Later today you will be in Paris, and by tomorrow evening you will have chosen the preferred attack site and from then be enjoined in our mantra of practice, practice and more practice. We have little time left, so let's get straight down to it. Don't forget, your country will owe you a great debt of gratitude irrespective of your personal feelings. I am now presenting you to your commander, Kurt Zimmerman, who takes over from here.'

The new task commander, Kurt Zimmerman, had worked with MI6 on several occasions and had proved his reliability. He had eliminated people before working in the Increment team and had never displayed any sign of regret or post-attack disturbance. Forty-one years old, just under six feet tall and muscular, his was a professional, cold and calculating manner. He was not a man to shirk unpleasant duties and was well-suited to the task ahead, having led soldiers in action and demonstrated clear thinking under fire.

Thoughts came to Morison of how this man compared with Jim Winfield. He was half the man, but with Winfield they had made the mistake of choosing one of the good guys, not considering that such a soulless act also needed a field commander devoid of integrity. Only someone who could carry out such an act with a cold and ruthless efficiency and do it for money, but irrespective of motive, would be suited.

Talk of Increment members having a normal civilised psyche was a joke, and Morison knew it, but he needed to ensure his team remained focused and didn't see this action as unnecessary. Morison knew some didn't think too highly of the monarchy and it was clear this action was being carried out because of them. This was one of the main reasons they had selected carefully, even from within their own Increment team.

They should never have tried to involve one of their best, thought a sad and pensive Morison. He was using the Increment team because of their skills and MI6 knew these operatives from previous assignments. They wouldn't have problems with control and post-operational secrecy; these men were the best option.

He would have liked one of his regular commanders in charge but he wasn't putting another Jim Winfield at risk. These were the reasons Zimmerman had been chosen to lead this operation in the field, since they had discovered they needed a solid, rigid man with few scruples who displayed no emotion. Morison thought he was ideally suited. 'A trained killer and heaven knows what he'll do when he stops working for us.'

The supporting operatives had also been chosen with great care since it was imperative that all those involved had experience in subversive military action and could be entrusted not to falter at the critical moment. It was also imperative that these people never 'grassed' on the operation later. They must be chosen with care and then paid well; very well. They must also be made aware that any indiscretion on their part, post attack, would be dealt with by the Service both swiftly and resolutely. It was with this in mind they had accepted this assignment.

Zimmerman continued to take stock of his colleagues to ensure his confidence matched Morison's. He addressed the assembly in a manner that ensured his presence would be felt from the onset.

'My name is Kurt Zimmerman and I have been with the British SAS, like most of you, for some years finishing as sergeant. I have worked with MI6 for several years and led surveillance teams on anti-personnel assignments; I have also been involved in several previous assassination jobs. I do what the Service requires of me because I believe it's necessary to have a system that works and I have seen some of the problems that can arise in the field when people start to question orders.'

Morison thought, 'Ingrained discipline from his army days; that will help.'

Zimmerman continued. 'We must rely on a democratically elected Government to govern and that means taking some unpleasant decisions, which is where we come in. I can't say the money we are being paid hindered my thinking but I don't moralise, or believe that anyone who does this sort of work can question orders; we would never be offered another job.

'We have a major task ahead of us and little time in which to prepare so I expect professionalism from each of you. I want to make it clear I shall be giving the orders on this operation so each of you will follow them to the letter. This is no more than another assignment; another hit.'

Zimmerman scrutinised the faces before him. It was important there were no dissenters on this point.

'Timing will be of the essence where a second too soon, or too late, could lose us the day, so absolute concentration and coordination will be required at all times. You are being paid plenty for your five minutes work. You will have loads of time to relax in luxury once the job is done. I am now asking each of you to stand and give a brief talk on your backgrounds. Who you are and what relevant experience you have to date. Raise any issues you consider necessary from the briefing materials you have received. Greg,' he said turning to the operative seated closest to him, 'you start!'

Gregory (Speedy) Haussmann stood up. He was in his late twenties, well built with a red-faced complexion and pock-marked face. Nobody had ever seen Greg smile and today was no exception. He began his harangue to the assembly in a matter of fact way, showing calm and control. 'My name is Gregory Haussmann; I am twenty-nine years of age and started in the British military when I was eighteen. For the past five years I have been working for MI6 in the Increment team, performing various tasks including assassinations. My main strength is driving, cars and motorcycles; I can handle either well, so I'm anticipating being asked to perform one of these skills. My motive is money and nothing else,' he said with an air of cold arrogance that was not well received by those assembled. 'I can assure you of my absolute loyalty in this and have no fear about my silence. I wish to enjoy the fruits of my labours and, once this is over, I shall forget it as though it had never occurred.'

Morison thought, 'I really don't like these people. Soulless bloody animals but that's not the issue; for this task he'll do very nicely.'

Without being prompted, Rod Tyler rose and began immediately. 'I'm Rod Tyler, thirty-one and ex-SAS. I left the army two years ago. I find this work very exhilarating! I wouldn't survive very long if not. I was seconded to the MI6 Increment team to assist with a couple of assassinations and I too am doing it for the money, since I need to make one big score before getting married and settling down. The work has no effect on me at all. It's just a job! I follow orders whether on the battlefield or in a civilian role. It makes no difference!'

Tyler asked about the role he would be playing but was informed this would be allocated during their sessions in France, when they had decided on the precise course of the attack.

Morison couldn't help thinking, 'God knows what his children are going to be like, perhaps good gangster material. I can't see this man living a normal existence. He'll be behind bars within a month of being back in civvies; or very wealthy.'

Tyler continued: 'My main expertise, like Greg, is driving motorcycles, so you may find it suitable to place us together if we are going to use motorcycles for the attack.'

Morison had already considered this but said nothing, waiting for Tyler to finish. He would make this decision with Kurt Zimmerman later in France.

'I know Kurt from a previous operation and I am delighted to be working with you again,' said Tyler, looking in Kurt Zimmerman's direction, as he sat.

The remaining operative stayed seated. He was a cold and distant man who looked as though he might erupt into violence at any moment. Sidney (The Hammer) Gould, so called because he had once bludgeoned one of his victims to death when his gun had jammed, sat impassively as though the business of addressing everyone was beneath him.

'Well Gould,' said Zimmerman, becoming irritated at Gould's silence and delay.

Both men stared at each other for a while, neither blinking. Zimmerman knew he must establish control and was about to respond when Gould slowly rose and spoke. 'I am the granddaddy of the team, forty-four years old and been in the military before working with MI6. I have made my living doing this job for so long, I don't think I could adjust to anything else. I am looking forward to many more years of activity before I am forced into hanging up my gun. There is always a job within MI6. I am good with a gun and can take on any task we are likely to need for this job. From what I have heard so far about this operation, guns are unlikely so I shall be interested to hear how we are to proceed and what my role will be.' With that, Gould sat.

Zimmerman was smarting from Gould's deliberate delay. He thought about responding to the challenge but decided he would deal with it later. Gould was probably trying to enforce the view that he was the top guy and could control anything. 'Except his ego,' thought Zimmerman. 'I can't allow that. No operative will work on this job that isn't fully supportive and prepared to take orders without question. What a stupid attitude if he expects to be working with me; how dare he challenge me like that. Has he thought of the possible consequences?'

That moment had moved on, for now, so Zimmerman rose and continued. 'We need to prepare an initial document of the three attack-site options we've been presented with and determine how best to approach each, and then discuss our preferred choice with reasons, allowing for all eventualities.

'A car crash has been decided upon because it's the best method without raising suspicion. We have been told by Mr Morison that it's preferable that assassination is not considered as a possibility by the public but it's essential there is no proof that it was. The establishment must maintain deniability, a word you will hear a lot of from now on. Since we control the investigative activity after the attack, there will be precious little anyone can do about it but we don't want a hostile public. As Mr Morison has said, it could be just as fatal as being caught in the act.'

Morison thought Zimmerman was being too presumptive by assuming this level of authority but then considered he preferred it this way. He could always call it back if necessary and preferred that Zimmerman was motivated to succeed. A successful outcome was much more probable if the commander was motivated and had authority over his men.

Zimmerman placed the three Service plans for Paris on the table. A preference for the Alma tunnel was the clear choice. Morison continued his policy of involving all Zimmerman's men, hoping they would agree with the service choice of their own volition.

Whilst Zimmerman debated the attack plan with his team, Morison pondered what could go wrong. He was still nervous about the subject's intentions. The Service couldn't influence where the attack venue would be; where the subjects decided to go from Sardinia was their choice alone. Intelligence had confirmed Paris was their intention and so they focused on this option but, if the subjects changed their minds, the Service needed to know and quickly.

Time was diminishing rapidly since the action must take place before any announcements of marriage were forthcoming. The subjects might decide to go to St Tropez for a short period, so an option to strike was needed there but this was not for discussion now with Zimmerman and his team; that was a Service call and they had already considered the option of attacking the *Jonikal* or attacking in St Tropez.

This was not desirable because it left too much to chance. They would need to know where the *Jonikal* was headed and then waylay it at one of the ports, or board en route to somewhere and strike as though it was a mugging gone wrong. "No chance of fooling the people that this was a coincidence", Morison thought.

There were also two other insurmountable objections to St Tropez. Mohamed al Fayed had too many bodyguards in St Tropez that would complicate matters. Also, there weren't any agents inside the Fayed household at Castell St Helen to assist, or any surrogates on whom they could rely. It was also going to be difficult because of a British police presence. There weren't many Service operatives working in the St Tropez area, so they would need to fly more in and it would be impossible to discreetly accommodate the number required, especially with the British police and bodyguard presence.

Morison knew he must stop considering possible, unsurmountable changes of plan and focus on Paris with the attack team. Paris must happen or there would be little likelihood of success. There were a large number of operatives always on hand in Paris, so using them wouldn't arouse suspicions and these people knew the area.

Suitable attack options had already been found around the four main locations: the British Embassy, the Ritz Hotel, The Villa Windsor and la rue Arsène Houssay, all of which were close to each other; wherever the subjects went they would certainly be moving between these sites. The British Embassy was very close to both addresses where the targets would be spending most of their time. They would be travelling between the three al Fayed properties and would certainly be using cars, so here was the perfect setting.

The main concern with vehicular homicide was that more people than just the target may become victims but this was felt justified because it increased the probability that it would be consistent with an accident, which was their chief goal.

'We must be certain about where to make the attack and we have operatives already at the Embassy and in the Paris Ritz hotel,' thought Morison.

'We must devise a plan as to how we entice these two people to travel by car at night, without an escort, and accept a particular route that we have pre-determined, leading them to their destiny.' This was a general synopsis that Zimmerman thought from experience fitted the bill but there needed to be a lot more information assimilated before firm decisions could be made. What made Zimmerman more concerned was that Paris, a car crash and all the attendant details just described were too perfect; this would not be lost on everyone else!

'What of it,' he thought. 'The people are gullible and will never be able to prove it. In any case, we will be long gone by then and, after all, the Service possesses a magic word, "deniability". We also have the police and officialdom on side.'

One of Morison's men came into the room and handed him a report. Morison glanced through it and handed it to Zimmerman, as arranged. Zimmerman read the report and spoke to the team.

'Intelligence has come in that our subjects bought an engagement ring in Monte Carlo and they have arranged to collect it in Paris on the 30th August. Not only does this confirm fears about where this relationship is headed but it further justifies this action and further confirms Paris as the site of choice.' Zimmerman, still felt the need to pacify any unsound feelings and to be seen singing from the Service hymn sheet.

'This gives us little time to perfect this operation. We leave this afternoon and will be meeting our Service agents on arrival in Paris, who will run us through the options. By tomorrow, we shall have devised our initial plan. We must be ready to move by the 28th August latest and we shall then have some leeway if we have any unforeseen circumstances. Read the notes on our options and think through what we have discussed; we'll discuss any relevant points then wind up the meeting. I just need a word with Sid. Sid, join me!' barked Zimmerman, as he left the room followed almost enthusiastically by Gould.

'What was all that about in there?' said Zimmerman in an authoritative and aggressive tone, still maintaining control. Gould stared back at Zimmerman, so once more the air was tense and strained. Before Zimmerman could allow his anger to rise, Gould smiled and spoke.

'Kurt I know I was testing you back there and I cannot apologise but I must explain.'

Zimmerman said nothing; he waited, in silence.

'I have been on several of these types of assignments and by and large they have gone well. Twice, however, the leader of the operation was not up to scratch. On the one occasion not knowing what he was doing and the other chickening out at the critical moment, when both situations threatened my life and I nearly got caught or killed. You never know how someone will behave until the chips are down and then it's often too late. I swore after that I would always test the guy in charge to the best degree I could just to satisfy myself. You passed!'

'What were you expecting me to do?' replied Zimmerman, 'other than maybe blow you out or— oh I get it, lose control.'

'Yes,' said Gould. 'The most important thing in these operations is nerve and self-control, without that you're dead in the water.'

'Right,' said Zimmerman, not exactly satisfied but more relieved he didn't feel the need to remove Gould from the team.

'Dangerous game you play Gould,' said Zimmerman.

'That's right,' said Gould. 'What do you call what we are about to do?'

Zimmerman remained unsure about whether this episode had eroded confidence in him with the other team members and thought that, although Gould had a point, he had no right to do that in front of the entire team so he needed to take control.

'I understand your point but the team needs complete solidarity if this is going to be a success and not botched or cancelled at the last moment because someone hasn't done their job. You may have reduced confidence with your colleagues, so you have two choices. Either you go back in that room and apologise for not responding to my request immediately, or you walk.'

Gould was expecting this and prepared to eat humble pie, especially considering the payment he was receiving for this job. He decided he had no choice especially since he didn't know what 'walk' meant. 'No problem,' he said. 'I am content to comply with your orders and will happily apologise to the team, and to you.'

In an ironic way, Zimmerman felt more confident with Gould for the task in hand than before; liking someone was not the issue or a luxury he could afford as he headed towards the door saying to Gould. 'Follow me!'

Gould and Zimmerman were leaving the room as Morison

entered to join them and Zimmerman indicated to Gould that he should continue to leave.

Morison closed the door behind Gould and spoke to Zimmerman. 'What is your view so far?'

'I am satisfied they will do the job, but I thought I had a problem in there.'

'I noticed,' said Morison. 'But as long as you are now content.'

'It's sorted now,' said Zimmerman. 'He will be apologising when we return to the room.'

Morison continued. 'Are you happy with the skills your team possess for the task ahead now you have viewed their CVs and spent some time with them? We have discussed briefly the car accident idea and need motorcycle riders and car drivers of the highest calibre. Do you agree they will match requirements?'

Zimmerman replied, 'Yes, we have studies on these people. They are well tried and tested and have the right skills and experience, so are unlikely to falter at the critical moment. None of us officially work for the Service and I am certain all are reliable both for the job and for silence afterwards. I agree that car and motorcycle skills will be of the essence for this job and they all come highly recommended. All in all, I don't think we could do any better.'

He continued, 'My main concern is whether we are short of a few top-class drivers. There is inevitably going to be the need for some deft interception and after the Gould comments in there, I have a small reservation, since I was relying on him for a major role. We may need another driver. Let's finalise our thinking on the overall plan and bear this point in mind.'

'Good', said Morison, feeling relieved that the man who was leading the operation had picked up on his own concerns. He considered a man who challenged authority in this environment could have an inferiority complex and not be up to the job and, if so, then he was not the man to be given one of the prime attack roles. He thought it was far too risky; there was too much at stake. He would rely on Zimmerman. 'He will make these decisions. He clearly sees the position as I do, so we can now go back in and take it to its final stage before we leave for Paris.'

Morison said, 'I feel we have done all we can here today. I have arranged for us to fly earlier than planned. We shall leave within the hour and be in Paris by 4.00pm. Let's go get your apology.'

Morison and Zimmerman returned to the meeting where the

team had been familiarising themselves with the papers.

As they entered, Gould immediately stood, having been a little nervous that the reason Morison had gone to see Zimmerman was to discuss him and maybe he was history. He thought maybe he had gone too far and saw a huge pay packet going down the drain, not to mention future opportunities. Then again, God, what if…

He quickly addressed the assembly. 'I wish to apologise to Kurt and to you all for being sluggish back there. I am really looking forward to working with you on this. Please accept my apologies and the same to Kurt.' He then sat.

Zimmerman thought Gould was an idiot for putting himself through that but now wanted to move on. He couldn't expect a more elaborate apology; Gould wasn't capable.

Zimmerman, now in his element said, 'Accepted; now let's turn to the business at hand. You now know the extent of the operation but we shan't have a workable platform until we have met up with our Paris people and viewed the sites. We are all going to assess the attack sites, identify them and put you through your paces. It's virtually certain which site we shall use but the Service requires us to maintain a few options.

'The two Service members, who will be available to us for the whole period, have made an initial assessment. They will join us in the apartment this evening and go through these options, so we'll study these and any other details from our intelligence then devise a plan. We shall be repeating this process again and again until we have it absolutely right. Time is short because we can't be sure when the opportunity to strike will arise, so we must have a workable plan within two days, perfected by the following day.

'We know the subjects will be in Paris on the 30th August and this is most probably the night we strike. We must assess the options of where they may go and be prepared for each because, from tomorrow, we have seven days maximum in which to change the course of history.'

PARIS ENSEMBLE

Morison travelled incognito as his aircraft approached a small airfield to the south-west of Paris; he could see the runway appear through a mist from his port window. His team followed separately into Le Bourget airport. All were careful to ensure a discreet arrival; nothing was left to chance as Morison was whisked away by one of his waiting agents to the British Embassy.

The attack team were collected from le Bourget by Service cars and driven to the Paris apartment that was to be their operational base for the next week. They arrived within an hour of Morison, unpacked and assembled in their specially chosen meeting room at the rear of the apartment, knowing all rooms had been checked for listening devices to ensure absolute security. The team was on a high and, although not much sleep would be possible over the coming few days, not much was needed; adrenalin would keep them alert. They could take weeks to recover, after the job was done.

It was considered preferable that the team didn't meet full-time senior Service colleagues unless absolutely necessary. All were instructed to be cautious about their movements throughout this operation; they must not mention each other by name outside the apartment walls.

Zimmerman needed briefing on Service thinking and procedures, so Morison instructed him to attend and digest what the Service envisaged. Having confidence in one's commander was essential but there was no need to risk Service personnel through unnecessary exposure.

At precisely 5.00pm there was a knock on the apartment door, which Tyler opened. Two men were identified as Service operatives and entered, going straight to the main lounge where Zimmerman was waiting. They spoke with Zimmerman briefly, introducing themselves.

Zimmerman spoke to his men. 'I shall be gone for an hour; unpack and settle in! We shall discuss Service thinking on the attack when I return, which will give us a good platform to begin tomorrow.' He suggested the Service men introduce themselves but they declined; that wasn't appropriate. Zimmerman knew who they were! Zimmerman understood their reticence and beckoned that they should now leave.

Driving through the centre of Paris, Zimmerman could feel the ambiance of a city alive with people walking and laughing, going to restaurants and enjoying life as though in a different world. His was certainly a different world because, for the next week, his body and soul would be concentrating on one of the hits of the century and it was his to command.

They reached an obscure building near the Ritz Hotel where they approached an underground car park. Zimmerman realised it was the British Embassy.

The agents led Zimmerman to a room on the second floor where Morison was waiting, together with two serious looking but well-dressed men in dark suits and subdued ties. One beckoned Zimmerman be seated and offered him the usual coffee. Zimmerman thought he would have withdrawal symptoms when this was over. He would need to find where he could get this coffee back in the UK; he allowed thoughts of mundane and unimportant matters to break the tension he was now subconsciously experiencing.

Morison had agreed that Stephens and Caruthers would call themselves X and Y respectively when any essential meetings with the operatives took place. There was no need to put Service personnel at risk, especially to the point of their names becoming known. Service demeanour was to be presented as withdrawn, cold and tenebrous since efficiency was all they were required to deliver.

Stephens and Caruthers introduced themselves accordingly. 'We shall call ourselves X and Y for ease of reference,' said Stephens, who accepted the designation X.

Stephens began. 'This operation, as I'm sure you realise, is very sensitive and the fewer people whose names are known the better, just as the numbers involved in this operation have been kept to a minimum. We have scoured the Paris area for the most suitable attack site and find there are very few when looking at the criteria we are using, namely sites that are close to the venues we know the subjects will frequent. If you wish to view all those we have identified, we understand, but it's our firm view there can be no better opportunity than the Alma Tunnel. We will, therefore, spend our time exploring the reasons why we believe this is the best site and then give you brief details on the others. It's up to you to inspect them and confirm this as the preferred site but this must be done quickly.'

Having spent weeks reviewing the best sites in Paris for this 'accident', Stephens didn't want to waste time with this bunch's opinions but he knew they needed to feel it was right. They must feel involved! Three sites were discussed and the general consensus was that it was right to examine the Pont de l'Alma in detail and then view the others later. It appeared clear that the Alma tunnel was the site of choice and time was of the essence.

'The Pont Alma is situated alongside the river Seine, due west of the Ritz hotel and due south of Dodi Fayed's apartment near the Arc de Triumph,' Stephens continued. 'It's by far the most lethal of road sites in Paris and we can find none better for this task. Its position is close to, but not directly between, the two venues that the subjects will definitely be visiting, so we will need a method to ensure this route is taken. We need to work on that but we believe we have the answer, as I shall explain in a moment.

'We need to be prepared for whatever time they make this journey, so close surveillance is essential and we shall furnish that for the entire period of this mission. The strike would be better made under cover of darkness to minimise the number of potential witnesses. People rarely remember detail when asked about traumatic experiences but darkness gives an even greater level of protection, not only for the attack, but also for our vehicles escaping the scene. This will ensure few people, if anyone, will be able to swear to what they saw, which makes it easier for us to ignore, or deal with, any unwanted witness testimony.

'The idea we have for controlling the car through the tunnel is to use one of our operatives who works at the Ritz hotel and is near-perfect for this role, being impeccably loyal and prepared to take orders without question. His name is Henri Paul and he is the acting security manager of the Ritz. He won't question orders, provided he believes they are in the interests of his employers. He is a key figure without whom our whole plan is untenable, so we must get him right.

'The other asset I mentioned is a paparazzo called James Andanson who has worked for us over several years, in addition to other similar agencies, and has been involved in some high-level French political irregularities. He has been associated with the removal of a previous Prime Minister of France, Pierre Bérégovoy, which made us think carefully about keeping him in reserve. On the other hand, he does have the skills you need and does socialise with several current and key French political figures, which might prove useful later. He also shows himself as very competent. Again we shall discuss him at greater length later, if necessary, after we have given you the core detail. I mention him now because I understand you may have need of another driver.

'The subjects may wish to visit the Villa Windsor, which is in the Bois de Boulogne,' Stephens continued; 'But they will not be staying there because the household effects have been auctioned off, so we may discount this venue as potential accommodation for route-planning purposes. We need to concentrate on the routes between the Ritz Hotel and the apartment at rue Arsenne Houssaye on the Champs Elysée, since we know they will be travelling between these two and will be collecting their engagement ring from Repossi's jewellers shop in Place Vendome, near to the Ritz.

'We have, therefore, three places where we know they will be on the evening of 30th August, and one of two where they will spend the night, so we must have a strike plan prepared to allow for eventualities in shifting between these. We know where they will be on the 30th, and their intentions, because we have people at the Ritz who keep us informed and the room they use, the Imperial Suite, is also bugged, so we have an excellent and continuous electronic surveillance in place. Since, however, we have someone who we know will drive them to the Alma Tunnel then, by acceptance of collateral damage, we shall ensure the car will enter the tunnel and meet the attack.

'It's regrettable that Paul will be put at the same level of risk as the others but it's the only way of ensuring success, especially considering our requirement for an 'accident'. We shall come back to him in much more detail later both for this and other pre-attack roles. This is an overview plan of our considerations apart from looking at the sites.'

Zimmerman was transfixed as Diana's fate unfolded. It was Caruthers's turn to speak; he referred to himself as Y. He moved slowly to the head of the table, not with the same commanding gait as Stephens, tentatively placing his papers on the table as he looked at Zimmerman. He looked uncomfortable and fingered his collar while collecting his thoughts, reaching for a cup of coffee from the nearby tray. This was his first hit and highest level of responsibility yet. He wasn't sure how he was felt about it; this was his moment of truth.

'What a first!' he thought. He was going to murder innocents, including the Princess of Wales and her unborn child, which made it all the more poignant, but coolness was essential in establishing control. He put distasteful thoughts of having to deal with a rabble to the back of his mind and proceeded in a haughty, if defensive, manner.

'In considering the Alma tunnel, we have an opportunity you will not be able to ignore. One of the main problems in the execution of this attack is how to direct the car from either the restaurant or the Ritz, wherever the subjects dine, and then to the attack site you select. This is crucial to our success!

'It's important they eat at the Ritz because that is where we have our intelligence. If they go to a restaurant, we may not know the substance of their discussions or what time they intend leaving. It may be more difficult to find a plausible reason to steer them through the Pont de l'Alma from that restaurant should a large detour be required, without raising their suspicions. It's all about control. It's one thing to have Henri Paul drive the car and dance to our tune but another whether the subjects have their suspicions raised by what is happening. They must not suspect anything or they could order a change of direction and Paul would not ignore that. They could also order the car to pull over and stop, thus preventing the attack. We shall brief Paul to follow our orders precisely and ostensibly in the subject's interests.

'We must try to ensure they leave their bodyguards behind, since a skilled defence team might well realise what is going down and take avoiding action; this is a serious risk! It will then be known to the world as murder, or a murder attempt, and we could never risk trying it again, so we lose. The key is in persuading Dodi to travel without bodyguards and have someone other than his normal chauffeur drive them, which is where the redoubtable Monsieur

118

Paul comes in on both counts. We also need to ensure a car without tinted windows is used, otherwise the military strobe gun we shall use at the tunnel entrance will have little effect, if any, and greatly reduce the probability of a fatal outcome.'

Zimmerman initially felt disgruntled that this operation appeared not to be his. He was supposed to be in charge but it seemed the Service wanted to complete all the preparations and he and his men were just the executioners. He then considered his position. He would have serious problems without the Service; in fact it would be impossible for him or any team of professionals to handle the amount of planning and supply the necessary intelligence the Service were handing them on a plate. He subconsciously chided his foolish thoughts. Any group of assassins would be grateful for the level of support offered by MI6, and think of the money.

Caruthers was continuing. 'We must have cover for our team and ensure the Mercedes is travelling at a high speed at the tunnel entrance, so we shall use the paparazzi. They must remain outside the hotel and not give up for the night, so Paul will assure them the subjects will be leaving and not staying the night at the Ritz. This is one of our biggest risks.

'It will be necessary for the subjects to be pursued by the paparazzi when the attack begins but not too closely, or they will witness the attack. The paparazzi must be informed the subjects are leaving from the rear entrance in sufficient time to begin a pursuit but not so they can catch up with the Mercedes before it reaches the tunnel entrance. Henri Paul must have an incentive to maintain a high speed and he will know the paparazzi are following, so he will go faster to leave them behind.

'We shall have our motorcyclists waiting along the route from where they will pursue the car at high speed, inducing Paul to go faster without causing undue alarm to the victims because they will think they are escaping from paparazzi. So that the paparazzi don't witness the commencement of your attack, our operatives must know how much time they have before the press will arrive. They will be informed by our team at the Invalides Bridge so will know how long they have to strike and vacate the scene. It is important Paul is pressurised and feels as though he's following orders; our orders!

'A major reason for settling on the Alma tunnel is because of a very dangerous curve and destabilising dip at the entrance, and there are no safety barriers. It has been the site of a number of fatal accidents in recent years, so it won't seem unreasonable to the public if this 'accident' proved fatal.

'We assessed the tunnel and have identified the optimum point to make the strike where this 'accident' is most likely to produce a fatal outcome. We must assess the speed the car needs to reach to guarantee this. Once you have rehearsed the correct line for the Mercedes to follow, then you must practise driving through the tunnel, timing the stages of the attack and individual roles. We shall use different vehicles for these practice runs, so as not to raise suspicion, but must make some runs with a Mercedes similar to the one that will be used by the subjects on the night to plan for precise dynamics.

'Once we have viewed the other options, we can make a judgment on the Pont de l'Alma and take our final decision and will know if we have made the right choice. The basics must be finalised by mid-morning tomorrow, latest.'

Zimmerman was keen to proceed to the next stage; killer adrenalin kicking in! He decided he would initiate the review of sites immediately upon leaving this meeting and said, 'We shall go and review the other sites when I return to the apartment then we will all have a clear opinion on each. We shall then reconvene, discuss them and settle on the site.'

'Excellent,' said Caruthers, now in a much more relaxed mood; the ice broken. 'Please let us have your decision as soon as possible and let me know if I can be of any assistance.'

Stephens and Caruthers then left the room without further comment.

Morison walked Zimmerman out of the building, bidding him good hunting and saying he would see him again tomorrow. Zimmerman returned to the apartment and immediately assembled his team. He formed two groups. He would travel with Gould and put Haussmann with Tyler. Both groups were to review all three Paris options, applying the attack criteria presented by the Service, to assess the suitability of each. They must determine the lethal potential, escape route availability and the sites' proximity to the British Embassy. Zimmerman knew the Service was looking for confirmation of the Alma and he just wanted to hasten the process so they could quickly complete their initial assessment.

Both groups returned within two hours. The forthcoming

meeting would be very brief, since there was no issue to debate. The Alma tunnel had no equal from any of the criteria used. The meeting took fifteen minutes and Zimmerman was able to phone Caruthers, confirming the Alma, which they could now focus on and look to detail.

It became clear to Zimmerman that these Service guys knew what they were doing and would give superb support on the planning but especially on the ongoing intelligence. They had also spent considerable time looking at the Alma site, so would help considerably, he thought, as long as they maintained their 'deniability'.

Zimmerman's adrenalin levels were now at an all-time high and he didn't want to waste time, so determined to put the evening to good use. He would ask Y to join him in driving along the death route and then the team could repeat the process once again during darkness, when they could emulate the attack conditions more propitiously. This was to better understand the Service perspective of the route to be taken, the attack scene and also their thinking. It also put him in the best light with the Service for being seen to value their opinions and respond with alacrity. These guys had spent an inordinate amount of time perfecting the Alma and it would be factious to consider an alternative and, most probably, counterproductive time-wise.

He picked up the phone to Caruthers, whom he knew as Y.

'That was quick,' said Caruthers. 'You are all in agreement then?'

'Yes,' said Zimmerman. 'I would like you to accompany me this evening on two runs through the route. We need to establish a basis for the whole attack scenario and would like to assimilate your views.'

Caruthers agreed and said he would join Zimmerman in the apartment in thirty minutes. He arrived in his dark blue Renault, and he and Zimmerman drove to the Ritz Hotel. They spent their time discussing options and personnel requirements from a first reading, both knowing they were feeling each other out. They were going to complete one run before the light faded and another later; when darkness fell.

As they drove towards the tunnel from the Ritz, following the intended death route, they noticed the distance from the hotel to the Alma and how long it would take if driving without too much traffic, how many traffic lights and where they were positioned. They also observed where they knew Service vehicles would be placed en route in advance, and the severity of the dip at the entrance of the Alma tunnel.

Another helpful point was that as the car went over the dip into the tunnel there was a definite sag in the road. Zimmerman thought that if a car was forced to alter the steering line at this point, and at speed, it would be propelled in the direction of the blocked lane. If there was a vehicle in that lane, the driver would instinctively turn the wheel the opposite way and towards the pillars. If travelling fast enough the car would quickly become uncontrollable. If also at this precise moment the driver was unable to see because he had a military strobe gun blazing into his eyes and the steering immobilised, then disaster was certain.

'Nice one,' said Zimmerman.

'Yes,' said Y, realising that Zimmerman had noticed their masterpiece. 'We noticed that! It's one of the main reasons for the Pont de l'Alma being the site of choice. Now add no tinted windows in the car they will use, the paparazzi as cover and with a bit of luck as scapegoats too, and we are building our attack scenario very well, without yet considering the contribution to be made by Henri Paul.'

It was becoming clear to Zimmerman that another driver was going to be needed and, as reluctant as he was to involve anybody else, he said to Y; 'It looks as though the attack is going to need one car in front and two behind, together with three motor cycles. We need two riders on the one cycle, and that we have; but we need another bike rider for post-attack assessment and someone who could block the lane of the Mercedes at the right moment, without being hit.'

'Yes,' said Y.

'Our back-up vehicles will wait by the exit from the expressway, both blocking entry from unwanted vehicles that might enter the attack theatre and hinder our operatives. They must be positioned to join behind the attack vehicles to follow through and pick up injured personnel. Your reserve car driver, and another bike rider, will be needed.'

'Yes,' said Y. 'We have several people available on standby and I know the one for the car-blocking exercise. I shall get back to you with him and the bike rider in the morning for you to consider.'

After a complete initial assessment of the attack theatre, Zimmerman and Caruthers returned to the apartment. Caruthers agreed to assist in the preparation by discussing the route, the overall plan and logic behind Service thinking with the operatives. Caruthers moved better in the dark and was relaxed about entering the apartment at this time of day, since he reasoned nobody would now notice him.

Zimmermann knew the extent of the Service preparation in this operation. They had planned everything exhaustively, even to the point of keeping other attack options open in case of an unexpected change to the subject's plans, but Zimmerman still felt this would be untenable. The amount of work required for the preparation of the Alma tunnel couldn't be replicated with precision for any other site. There wasn't time; it wasn't practicable and Zimmerman couldn't see why it was necessary.

He communicated this to Caruthers who added, 'Yes, but what if for some reason there is an accident at the Alma on the evening we need to strike and the tunnel is closed? Or we drive towards the tunnel for the attack and there are police cars in convoy with us and we need to abort? Having another tunnel means we may be able to redirect the attack and that is why the other two must be planned, at least to a high degree, if not perfected.'

'OK,' said Zimmerman, 'but don't bank on deniability being workable in that situation. It will be hit and miss.' Zimmerman knew the Service were professional in their approach and planning and should succeed in presenting this as an accident; provided it was the Alma. No doubt, at all, that this was near perfect. He also decided he should make use of Caruthers' presence here this evening and run through the Alma with his men tomorrow. He would gather all he could from Caruthers now.

They convened in the meeting room and Caruthers began. 'Right, now to the main questions: how are we going to get the level of support required from Henri Paul? How do we arrange a car without tinted windows? How can we ensure they will eat at the Ritz but leave later? How do we ensure the paparazzi will wait at the hotel for evening pursuit duties? How do we get them to travel without bodyguards? There are also certain post-attack considerations, such as who will be blamed for the "accident"? Either pursuers or the driver are the usual culprits, so we must assist with evidence against the driver. We shall discuss this after we have considered the main points. These are the questions that, once resolved, should allow for a satisfactory conclusion.'

Stephens and Caruthers had agreed they would bond the team in stages and Caruthers thought now was the right time to expand on Service thinking with them. He would describe the Service's role, which should engender confidence and fill in any gaps. He began; 'A principal risk is that the paparazzi might leave the Ritz, thinking the subjects are staying at the hotel for the night, so we need, somehow, to encourage them to remain. If Henri Paul can be persuaded to taunt the waiting paparazzi that the subjects will be leaving, then this should ensure they remain and serve our purpose for pursuit and scapegoat duties.

'If the subject's official cars pull up in front of the Hotel, concomitantly with the subject's departure from the rear exit in the smaller car that should cause sufficient distraction for Henri Paul to get a head start. The car will be delivered to the rear of the hotel and, I can assure you', said a confident Caruthers, 'the subjects will not question it. The paparazzi will serve as cover for you guys, since anyone who witnesses the attack will believe you are the first batch of paparazzi arriving on the scene. We can persuade Henri Paul he is crucial in protecting the subjects and it would be helpful if they exited from the rear of the hotel.

'We must have a car available without tinted windows, otherwise this could negate the whole attack because the military strobe gun wouldn't work and Paul will probably deal with the assault very well if he can see. This is already in hand. Paul is an excellent driver with good reflexes and we need him to accept our reasons for carrying out these instructions. Paul's usual Service handler will persuade Paul, accompanied by a more senior Service member the afternoon before the attack, so he won't have the time to let anything slip. I have given you an overview of our plan but I will now spend a little time expanding on this, so you will understand our reasoning.'

Zimmerman was beginning to wonder why he had needed to visit the Service earlier in the evening if they were going to continue this evening with a presentation to the entire team, but he realised it was to elevate him in front of his team and to observe their relationship with him, thus keeping full control. Clever, thought Zimmerman, who couldn't help but admire how MI6 had constructed this whole plan and handled the psychology, including his. He would just do his job and be thankful for the opportunity of such a high profile and well paid job.

Caruthers continued. 'Should the subjects decide to eat at a restaurant instead of the Ritz, we have devised a way of ensuring they won't want to stay. As soon as we know where this restaurant is, via our surveillance teams, we shall inform the paparazzi who will be there to greet them. There is no way they will eat there in these circumstances, not with the paparazzi sitting in their laps for the entire meal, and the only other place they can eat in total security is the Ritz. Once there, we shall have continuous information of their intentions coming through from our electronic surveillance.

'So, to the four most difficult obstacles! How do we deter the bodyguards, keep the paparazzi outside the hotel for the evening and get a head start to ensure the paparazzi are not in sight of the Mercedes at the time of the attack and, crucially, control Henri Paul? How do we persuade the paparazzi to remain outside the hotel? If Paul remains downstairs, and is vigilant, he can assess whether the paparazzi are thinking of going home; he must go outside telling the paparazzi that the couple will be coming out soon.

'We have examined the car without tinted windows because we need to ensure we have a car that meets our specification; we have secured one of the fleet cars that serve the Ritz to ensure a suitable car is available on the night. As for the bodyguards, only someone totally trusted by Dodi, whose advice he would be prepared to take, will be able to persuade him. Who better than the Security manager of the Ritz hotel who is favoured by Dodi: Henri Paul?

'We must persuade Paul of the need for him to drive, but the bodyguards will require a good reason for allowing it. He could say it isn't far and the car is too small with three people already travelling. If Paul could persuade Dodi to show his father and Diana that he can make his own decisions regarding where he goes and allow Paul to drive, then they could escape the paparazzi and impress the Princess, doing no more than he did a few weeks earlier. The bodyguards will question this decision, so we make certain Paul warns Dodi he will have to say he has cleared it with his father and then they will not dare confirm with London.

'If the bodyguards decide to accompany them, we shall still continue with the attack, albeit with reduced expectancy of success. Our worst case scenario is if both bodyguards accompany them, so we try to ensure they don't but proceed with one, if necessary.

'Paul must stress to Dodi that to impress the Princess he mustn't be seen to be asking his father's permission every time he moves. We shall subtly work on that one! We suggest that Paul persuades Dodi late on, just before they leave, that for the ruse of going out through the back door and using a getaway car to work, and to save the Princess from the paparazzi, his suggestion must be followed. There will be no need for bodyguards because it's only a short drive and it's important Dodi doesn't tell his father, or al Fayed would refuse to allow it. So, by ingratiating himself with Dodi, Paul will see himself improving his chances of promotion. Paul's success in this is crucial, because a veto from Dodi's father would scupper the whole evening. The subjects might stay at the Ritz and then we are into blowing up aeroplanes.

'These ideas will need fine-tuning so we must work together to see whether the plan can be improved on. Will Henri Paul be able to achieve these aims and carry them through? What of his profile?' Zimmerman interceded.

Caruthers spoke in almost laudable terms. 'Paul is an exemplary employee, highly regarded by Dodi Fayed and currently acting head of Ritz security. He is perfect for us in almost every conceivable way, although I am not saying we can take it for granted he will carry this out without some cajoling. He is a good driver and also a pilot with instrument flying skills, so he is not lacking in coordination or reflexes and that may count against us. He is the only person, however, who will be able to carry out the tasks we have identified as essential to this operation. Without Henri Paul this plan is unworkable!

'You will not meet him,' said Caruthers, 'because the need is for us to persuade him that what we are asking of him is not detrimental to his boss but for Dodi's benefit. He will not play ball unless we can persuade him of that so, once we have decided exactly how we are going to play this and what we want him to do, we will see him and be careful not to spook him. We shall send his usual handler, with one of our senior team in attendance, to assess whether this most crucial of assets is going to play ball on the evening. From this meeting the green light will be given, or not, and from this moment we shall be on an effective countdown. We need to agree and decide on each of the issues we have just touched on in much more detail.

'Paul is the key to this whole operation so if any serious flaws arise we would need to rethink the whole attack and that would make matters a lot more difficult. He has assisted us for several years as an informant at the Ritz by placing listening devices in guests' rooms using television sets etc., so he is used to intrigue. This new role will not faze him. He takes orders without question, which probably comes from his military training, and so as long as our story satisfies him of being in his employer's interests, or at the least not against them, then he is likely to comply. He has been passed over now on two occasions for the post of hotel security manager and if we can find a way for him to impress the big boss and increase his chances of being successful next time, that will motivate him. We know we can trust him to take orders but he will need to be very persuasive with Dodi to ensure our plan works.

'We have thought of persuading Paul that on the night of 30th August he ensures he's not on duty. He should remain available to meet us, returning to the Ritz later that evening. We then give him a last-minute briefing and make sure he's certain of what he has to do to remove any concerns. We shall keep him out of the way in case he should discover anything and ensure he's sober and fit for his evening's duties. We are paying him enough! Also, he will not be around to let any detail slip to Dodi and motivated until just before the attack.

'What reason, you might ask, shall we use to persuade Paul? The most probable reason is that to secure the subject's safety we need a driver who is out of the top drawer and we need to ensure the subject's relationship gets off to a good start; a married Diana would take a big problem away from the palace. We know Paul doesn't have much of an opinion on matters royal, so he won't challenge this and why we would be doing this if it weren't for Diana's safety. We can assure him it is important Diana sees Dodi in a more independent light. It won't take much to persuade him on this, since he is clearly not going to guess what's planned.'

Caruthers looked at Zimmerman. 'Is there anything else you need to discuss on the overview?'

'No,' said Zimmerman, 'you seem to have given us an excellent head start, if not done virtually the whole job for us. We need to sit down and plan our route and attack sequence, then go and complete some practice runs. I shall, of course, need both your reserve operatives here by the morning, so we can start keying in their roles. Have you secured some practice cars and motorcycles for us to use?'

'Yes,' said Caruthers. 'We have three cars for you tomorrow and three motorcycles, with each being changed every day for a similar vehicle of the same model, then the day after we have also secured a Mercedes. You will find our reserve operatives very efficient so don't worry about their competence.'

'Thank you for your time,' said Zimmerman. 'Let's get down to business!'

The phone rang in the apartment and Zimmerman answered.

'This is X; is Y there?'

Zimmerman passed the phone over to Caruthers and Stephens told him an extra operative would be at the apartment in about one hour.

'Great,' said Caruthers. 'We had planned for the morning, but let's do it now! I'll tell Zimmerman. I am sure he is ready to put him through his paces.'

Caruthers relayed this to Zimmerman and took his leave for the evening. He felt Zimmerman needed some space and he had done all he could for now.

At just before midnight, a knock at the door brought a well-dressed man into the room that appeared very personable. 'Almost as though he is going to a cocktail,' party thought Zimmerman. 'Let's put him straight!'

'Welcome; in here please,' said Zimmerman, ushering his new team addition into the meeting room. 'My name is Zimmerman and I am running this operation. Would you mind giving me your name and brief background and then telling me how much have you been told so far?'

'Just that you have a high profile hit to execute and we are to report to you,' said Pierre Grossman in his highly accented English. 'I work for the Services from time to time, whether French, British or American, whoever pays me. With the money you are paying on this, everybody I know would jump at the chance. My main strength, as I am sure you already know, is my motorcycle skills but I am also good at driving cars, so I am flexible.'

'OK,' said Zimmerman, looking at the notes on Grossman.

Having briefed the Frenchman, Zimmermann agreed he would take the car with Gould and have Grossman come alongside him at the tunnel entrance as a practice run, although they couldn't continue to use the Alma as their own private 'train an assassin'

128

route, since the chances of being spotted were increasing. They would do most of their practice work elsewhere but first, although it was late, Zimmerman decided to complete a few practice runs and one in the Alma.

The practice runs went well, with Zimmermann feeling satisfied with his new team member. He needed to be; the clock was ticking!

LOGISTICS

The first full day had dawned for the team that received a baptism of fire to this operation in England, followed by a heavy first day session in France. This had served to instruct them that the Service expected perfection, within a specific timescale.

The team arose and, armed with a detailed plan, sped off towards the Alma tunnel, deciding to concentrate on the attack details, incorporating the route, timing and journey planning.

Haussmann and Tyler were riding the powerful BMW motorcycle that had been acquired for the day, after which it would be replaced with another similar machine. They decided to stay with the same motorcycle model for the attack and the Service required them to take a different one each day in case the Paris police should happen to pick out a particular motorcycle driving fast and aggressively in the same spot time after time, when alarm bells might later ring!

It wasn't considered necessary to drive very fast for the first full practice run, just to get a feel for the road's instability at the tunnel entrance and at which precise spot a bike, or a car, would need to turn on the gas to get ahead of the Mercedes; the assassins were determined not to follow it into the tunnel's pillars. The cameras that were positioned near to the tunnel entrance could also cause a problem so, if they were caught on camera, at least it would be a different bike and there was no way the police could identify its rider.

Zimmerman and Gould drove their Renault car along the death route, blending in well with the Paris traffic. They took a mental note of the roads that joined the expressway as they approached the tunnel and looked for sheltered areas where operatives' vehicles would lurk and await the arrival of the victim's car. They drove towards the Alma tunnel.

Zimmerman looked for the optimum point where the attack vehicles would begin moving for the strike and, as they entered the tunnel, they felt the fault beneath them as the car rode over the dip with the wheel pulling to the side and made the necessary adjustment. They knew the fault was there! Henri Paul, hopefully, would not! Now they could work on the best point for the attack and knew the team needed to run through this procedure several times to establish precise dynamics.

Zimmerman said, 'We need to know what speed the Mercedes must reach and at what point we intercept; achieve this, and we have our fatality.'

'Yes,' said Gould, 'we need to keep on running this until we know where to block the car's path. We also have to think about pre- and post-attack issues. If we have lots of debris or injured operatives, the Service will not be happy.'

'Right,' said Zimmerman, 'we need only to block the Mercedes' path to ensure a crash. I feel sure of that!' Zimmerman wanted to move this along. 'Let's go to the Ritz and follow the route the subjects will travel, provided Henri Paul does his job. We can then assess time lapses between control points and look at suitable places for our guys to wait. It's imperative our vehicles are not noticed, or certainly not considered suspicious, otherwise this is something that will be remembered after the attack and add to doubts about it being an accident. I know the Service have covered the whole sequence but they also expect us to practice this whole operation again and again; let's make sure we can't improve on it.'

They noted the best positions for observation purposes and Zimmerman added, 'This isn't our concern, it's a Service job but there are plenty of areas for observing the scene. Let's hope the Service lads make sure they aren't on camera, considering the inevitable press interest that will follow.'

Zimmerman was now thinking more along Service lines. 'We need to know how long before the subjects arrive at the Alma, so when we get information from a particular control point, we know how long we have before arrival at the next. We can therefore start a countdown to the attack and each of our guys will be on a high for as little time as possible. Nobody can sustain high levels of adrenalin for long periods or concentration fails. Let's begin with a marker of 12.00pm for our subjects to depart from the Ritz, with control points established along the route. When the subjects leave the hotel we shall be notified and, if it's 12.15pm, then we merely add seven minutes to the timings and we have our ETA.'

They continued towards the Alma and noted the time from the Ritz to each reporting point, recording the travelling time between each. Passing the Invalides Bridge, Zimmerman realised this was the last control point for the Service team to announce the Mercedes' imminent arrival to the waiting operatives and, having timed the run, they would be able to give a very accurate ETA for the Alma.

'If the Mercedes arrives at the Invalides Bridge at 12.00pm, having taken seven seconds to the Alma with the paparazzi twenty seconds behind, we can inform our operatives at the Alma that they have seven seconds to arrival and thirteen to complete the attack and get off the scene. There should be nothing to prevent the car from reaching the necessary speed before entering the tunnel with the assistance of the pursuing operatives, so our guys will know the time of arrival to within seconds. This should work well!'

Zimmerman wanted to check the whole process through and practise each part in turn several times. Continuing his drive towards the Alma, they checked the dip at the tunnel entrance again but at a higher speed and they felt a pull to the right, confirming that if the right-hand lane was blocked, and the speed high enough, it wouldn't be necessary to ram the victim's car. It wasn't even desirable because of the debris this would leave, and they didn't want anyone to even know there was a car blocking the subject's path. They would ensure that whoever was to make this block was able to avoid a collision. It would require nerves of steel and precise timing!

They drove through the tunnel and emerged, passing the rue des Frères and a few metres further, the rue Débrousse, which they drove up and entered the Avenue du Président Wilson. They checked their maps and drove towards the Place de l'Alma, just above the tunnel, and then into the Avenue Montaigne. They realised that if they travelled via the rue Jean Goujon, it would lead to the Avenue Eisenhower and the Avenue des Champs Elysée, from where it was only a few hundred metres to the British Embassy. The whole journey took them a matter of minutes, which should also be the case at the time the attack was planned; at night!

'Now turn right into the rue St. Honoré and past the British Embassy, then head back to the Ritz,' said Zimmerman. This completed the circuit that would be travelled by the assassins on 30th August that needed going over several times but not in the same vehicle. They wouldn't want to be spotted and reported as being suspicious, so would make one more run checking the route, deciding on the control points and checking the timings and where their Service colleagues would be stationed to report on the position of the target vehicle as it approached the Alma.

In the afternoon they would have Haussmann and Tyler drive their motorcycle the same route and practice the timings and route for themselves, especially the movement over the dip in the tunnel and at what precise point it would be best to surge in front of the subject's vehicle to use the military strobe gun. The timing here must also be perfect because the Mercedes' driver might change speed and avert the attack; strike at the right moment and the car would actually enter a state of oscillation. This was needed to ensure it would go out of control and head into the unprotected pillars.

The main apparatus for a successful attack sequence was now in place; all they needed was to observe the movement of the motorcycle at the tunnel entrance. They returned to the apartment and assembled the team.

Zimmerman asked Tyler and Haussmann to follow the route he had just driven with Gould until it was memorised and came as second nature.

Tyler then had a good idea. 'Let's use ourselves as guinea pigs,' he suggested to Zimmerman. 'You drive the car into the tunnel as the target and the lads follow to make an attack. This way we get practice and we see how deft we are at this most critical manoeuvre.'

Zimmerman thought this was highly imaginative and immediately agreed that they would do it that afternoon, but only once. They would first have some lunch and discuss their experiences, then make a practice run with Zimmerman and Gould acting as targets later that afternoon with Tyler and Haussmann on the BMW motorcycle.

Sitting down to lunch, Zimmerman told the team of Tyler's idea for the afternoon. All were in full of agreement as they eagerly discussed their preparation for the practice run.

'Are you happy with the bike,' asked Zimmerman.

'Very,' said Tyler. 'I was very impressed with the acceleration and the power is enormous on the BMW. I shall have no problems with performance.' He continued, 'We travelled through the tunnel this morning. We rode over the dip at a reasonably high speed but not fast enough for the attack. It was still hairy! A small error of judgement at that point and the bike would leave the ground and kill us both. We have discovered we can ride the bike to the side of the fault in the road, which will enable us to maintain a very high speed, perform our task and not be at risk because the right hand side of the entrance is stable. It's essential we time this to perfection, so we are going to decide which of us should ride the bike and who will use the military strobe.'

Zimmerman pressed for all to decide by this afternoon so the roles would be autonomic and they would have the maximum time left for further preparation and practice. Gould said he would drive the car that afternoon. Zimmerman was now happy that Gould was a very good and aggressive driver who seemed totally in control, so he thought that maybe Gould should drive the attack vehicle after all. He would drive the back-up car himself in case of any unforeseen mishaps during the attack because they couldn't leave anyone behind, dead or injured, so he would follow just behind the attack vehicles.

Zimmerman and Gould left the apartment and sped towards the Ritz hotel. They would drive the now-familiar route and enter the Alma at a steady, but not excessive, pace. Then Haussmann and Tyler would practice their bike interception at the precise moment their car traversed the dip at the tunnel's entrance. They intended practising the military strobe gun elsewhere. There was too much risk of being spotted if they practised on the attack site.

Zimmerman thought the flash didn't need practising, only the bike's critical movement at the tunnel entrance. The flash would be tested in their apartment and then checked again before they left for the attack.

Tyler and Haussmann decided the best place to lie in wait for the car on the night was under a bridge. From here, posing as paparazzi, they could aggressively pursue the car towards the Alma tunnel, encouraging it to go faster, thus ensuring the speed would be adequate on entering the tunnel and maintaining a suitable time lapse between the attack and the pursuing paparazzi.

Gould drove towards the tunnel and looked in his mirror to see Tyler and Haussmann behind on the big BMW. The victims would be escaping from the paparazzi so would not necessarily be alarmed by two riders armed with what looked like a camera. It would be what they expected to see. He was watching to see whether the bike would raise any unusual concerns, other than frustration and anger, because it was important the real situation wasn't guessed at, otherwise avoiding action by the victims would be relatively simple if taken before the tunnel was reached; they could just stop the car!

Gould drove towards the tunnel at a moderate speed and deliberately headed for the dip in the road. At this precise moment, as if from nowhere, Tyler swerved in front of the car at electrifying speed, with Haussmann facing the car sideways on as he drove past, imitating the position he would need to be in when holding the military strobe gun. The movement was smoothly done and presented no problems because Tyler was now getting used to the dip and beginning to know exactly what line he needed to take when preventing the bike leaping into the air. He would ride to the right of the fault; he wanted to enjoy the enormous sum he was being paid.

Zimmerman and Gould were taken aback by the speed and precision of this movement, even though they were expecting it, so they were very impressed after the initial shock had subsided. Zimmerman sensed, however, that Gould had felt something else during this attack. He recognised fear in Gould's eyes and in his breathing as the bike surged past and that was dangerous; he said nothing at the time.

Back at the apartment the team, all feeling extremely elated, poured the coffee and felt as though they had just carried out the deed.

'Not bad for a first run,' said Zimmerman. 'We felt the pressure of the bike's presence without feeling threatened, and your swerve in front of us was very precise. Now, of course, the trick is to do it both for real and at a higher speed. We shall have to build the speed until we reach the point where we instinctively perform as today; but faster and determined by how fast the Mercedes is going. We must get in front, whatever its speed. This will take all your practice time between now and the attack. How did you feel about today?'

'Not bad,' said Tyler. 'A few more practice runs and I should have it cracked. I thought that if I increase the speed by around 5mph for each run until I am comfortable that I am unable to go any faster.'

Zimmerman was grateful for his frankness and objectivity. 'That's fine. Did you check out the escape route?'

Tyler answered that they hadn't really had the time to properly run through the route and were more preoccupied with the attack run but would run through it tomorrow.

'I think you can go and run through it tonight,' replied Zimmerman. 'You will be travelling in the dark during and after the attack, so it's best if you become familiar with it in the same conditions. The route may look different in the dark.'

'OK,' said Tyler. 'Haussmann and I will get a meal and go and run through the whole route again and perhaps try one more go at the tunnel entrance.'

'Don't push it!' said Zimmerman, who didn't want any of his agents having a real accident before the attack. 'Let's just get up to speed on the basics today and do a rerun in the dark and then we can apply the detail and improve on technique. Gould, join me for a coffee.'

Zimmerman led Gould to the anteroom where the usual lashings of good coffee awaited. Zimmerman walked around the table as they poured and talked of the day's practice run. 'Sid,' he said, trying to soften the coming conversation.' How did you feel about today?'

Gould realised that Zimmerman had sensed something and didn't bother to try and hide his true feelings. He was, after all, a professional and if he had a problem he must say so.

'Today,' he said, 'for the first time in my professional career, I felt a moment's hesitation when Tyler came past us at the tunnel entrance. I temporarily froze and I don't know why.'

Zimmerman found himself feeling unusually sympathetic because Gould had been so forthright and he had already experienced similar reservations. He replied, 'This is not a normal hit, even though we all try to pretend it is to get through the day. I understand how you feel, believe me! It's probably a deep-rooted reservation you are feeling and that's nothing to be ashamed of.' But he was ashamed; he had failed in his job. A new experience was emerging for Zimmerman also who was feeling a similar sense of trepidation and he couldn't understand why. Zimmerman didn't let on concerning the depths of his own feelings because that could undermine the operation.

Gould added, 'I will be alright on the night but I realise you can't take a chance. I am truly sorry to let you down on this.'

'You are right,' said Zimmerman. 'I wouldn't be doing my job if I ignored what I saw today and I would be putting too much at risk and that I don't need to explain! We certainly can't let you take one of the prime vehicle movements and I have doubts of my own capabilities in this slot,' said Zimmerman, deciding to risk being forthright. 'We shall use this Frenchman, Andanson, who the Service have available for this attack role. You will ride with me in the back-up car and watch for other traffic and witnesses who may be around unexpectedly and to retrieve any dead or wounded operatives.'

'You aren't cashiering me then?' said Gould, with a note of surprise and utter relief.

'No,' said Zimmerman. 'At this stage we need the entire moral and ground support we can get and I know you need the money, like the rest of us.'

Gould felt almost tearful. Nobody had ever treated him this well before and he found himself unable to speak. Zimmerman realised and said, 'Let's get onto the Service and have this guy Andanson come on over as soon as possible. Will you oversee him please and make sure he's aware of his role?'

'I certainly will,' said a grateful Gould who, feeling guilty over challenging Zimmerman, thought, 'Zimmerman has more steel than I do. I now know why the Service gave him this job.'

Gould knew he would never be available for such a role again. He wondered if others felt the same way because it could jeopardise the attack.

Zimmerman telephoned Caruthers on his Service mobile and apprised him of the situation. Caruthers said he would have his other reserve, Andanson, in Zimmerman's apartment within the hour. Because Zimmerman had already been briefed on Andanson by the Service, Zimmerman didn't feel the need to ask for an overview of his background.

James Andanson arrived within fifty minutes. He was a man in his early forties who Zimmerman quickly felt to be competent; he exuded an air of control. They went straight into session with their new man and, within one hour of Zimmerman and Gould going through the attack scenario with Andanson at the Alma, he was fully familiar with the requirements of the attack sequence.

It was agreed Andanson should go through the tunnel and practise his run, with Zimmerman and Gould driving behind to observe the speed, timing, angle and control that he could demonstrate. Having spent the hour practising, Zimmerman and Gould returned, followed by Andanson, and all three went into session.

'The tunnel is a good choice,' said Andanson. 'I can't think of a better spot. I have worked out the position the car needs to be in to guarantee the driver of the target's car will lose control when trying to avoid me. The speed of the targets car needs to be 100km/h, preferably more, so I shall be relying on Tyler and Haussmann to aggressively pursue the car right up to where they enter the tunnel. Using the paparazzi is a nice touch and I feel confident this will work. I shall block the path of the car at the right position, so forcing the Mercedes into swinging the wheel to the left, just at the part of the tunnel entrance where the road dips, so there will be no traction on the main wheels and the car will take off.

'I still prefer to use my own car for this,' Andanson continued. 'I know it very well and that will increase my chances of getting the timing right. I shall be disposing of it after this anyway.'

'Fine,' said Gould, looking at Zimmerman for acceptance. 'What about the speed and acceleration of your car for manoeuvring yourself into the right spot for the attack?'

'Not a problem,' said Andanson. 'My car is a turbo-charged Fiat Uno that will out-accelerate most other cars and is certainly faster than the Mercedes the targets will be using on the evening. I shall position myself so that, as the Mercedes approaches the tunnel, I shall be just in front and can then accelerate at the right moment to block its path just as it reaches the dip in the road following behind Haussmann and Tyler's flash attack.'

Zimmerman still had reservations about Andanson but time was running short and the options were limited for the precise attack roles. But he had certainly been most impressed with Andanson's timing during the practice run. It appeared, and he hoped, that the Service had got this right too.

Zimmerman was now content with the team he'd got, but had one more thought as he turned to Andanson. 'Are you sure you can execute this attack without colliding with the Mercedes? It's absolutely critical there is no debris left in the tunnel so the Service may maintain deniability. It's imperative you do not collide with the Mercedes!'

'Not a problem,' said Andanson. 'All I need is two more practice runs to make certain I have the right speed and angle and then I shall be able to block the Mercedes without touching it.'

'Good,' said Zimmerman. 'Go and do you're other run now, check the escape route to the Embassy and then report back as soon as you can. We will then be all set for a full practice run this evening.'

This change of personnel still worried Zimmerman, who thought Andanson could use a few more days' practice for timing but he had no choice; it was a Service decision and a 'go' within their specified time scale, whatever his reservations. But the possibility that Andanson could collide with the Mercedes through having had less practice than desirable was Zimmerman's bête noir.

Zimmerman decided that this evening they would practise in the dark, using the same routine they had successfully completed during the day so the team could become accustomed to similar light conditions they would face when making the attack. Morison was in touch with Zimmerman asking for an update on progress, and agreed to Zimmerman's request for the Service operatives to be available for a trial run that evening by manning control points all along the death route. This was agreed, with the exception of the point nearest to the Ritz. They would steer clear of this area to be safe; there may be post-attack CCTV identification issues.

Morison contacted Stephens and asked that he make the control points live for a practice run. Stephens made the arrangements. This would entail Service operatives manning the control points and testing communications with attack operatives, but the ban on contact between Service personnel and attack operatives remained. Unnecessary knowledge of each other would only constitute an unnecessary risk!

Morison stayed in touch with Stephens and Caruthers, who in turn managed the Service agents in their control point activities. Mobile phones had been issued to each operative, with each phone having a simple number already encoded. Zimmerman had number 1, and each operative's number was committed to memory! These phones were non-traceable and would be handed in after the operation and then destroyed.

Service operatives positioned themselves at each of the chosen control points, the Ritz hotel, Place de la Concorde, the Alexandre

III Bridge and the Invalides Bridge, but also above the Alma tunnel. Each would tell the next control point when the victim's car had passed by, giving the next operative an ETA at their reporting point. In this way all parties would know the attack was on track and when to expect arrival.

Zimmerman and Gould would keep tabs on events and Tyler and Haussmann, waiting on their motorcycle at the Invalides, would first receive a signal that the victim's car had left the Ritz and then on arrival at the Alexandre III Bridge. From this point, the victims would be there within seconds and the final attack sequence would begin.

After the run through, Zimmerman felt as though the whole operation was coming together very well, despite a few hiccups, and was feeling a lot more confident. He and Morison met on the morning after the run through in the apartment and, after discussing the previous day's progress, turned the conversation to the other critical point they were to rely on: the unwitting co-operation of Henri Paul, deputy security manager of the Ritz.

Morison kept Zimmerman in the loop by informing him that his men had spoken with Paul and told him there was extra activity for which he would be required on Saturday evening. Paul had agreed to stay on standby. They were fine-tuning the story before being more direct and wouldn't give Paul precise instructions until Saturday afternoon because to do so sooner would give him time to question Service orders and it could raise Paul's, or Dodi Fayed's, suspicions if these two men were in discussion.

Morison left Zimmerman to continue with his practice and went to the Embassy to meet with Stephens and Caruthers. He was happy with the attack planning but needed to perfect the behind-the-scenes finesse of the operation.

Morison decided to meet with Paul because it was considered necessary to establish all would be well on the evening with their most crucial asset, and this decision was down to him. He would accompany Paul's handler, Chandler, to the meeting since Paul knew Chandler well and trusted him. What if Paul survived the attack and mentioned his name or described him afterwards, he pondered. He decided he wouldn't give his name, or perhaps a false one, just in case.

Other than sorting out Henri Paul, all issues had been covered. The Service guys got their heads together to decide how to approach Paul on the issue of his cooperation. Persuading Paul to cooperate on obtaining Dodi Fayed's agreement not to use bodyguards, and also to accept Paul as the chauffeur, were the key issues that needed resolving or the plan would not be viable. Paul, they reasoned, was a man who had great unrealised ambition and had expensive hobbies for which he needed extra cash. It was well known he was game for clandestine activities, having worked with the Service for some time, so Caruthers pondered for a while and began paraphrasing events as he saw them.

'I think we tell Paul that Dodi will greatly appreciate having the opportunity to impress the Princess and show he is able to take decisions on his own. Dodi will want to show Diana that he has flair and daring, so we get Paul to tell him they should leave by the rear entrance, fooling the paparazzi and leaving them well behind.

'This needs speed and the minimum of fuss, so Paul tells Dodi he will drive them the short distance to the apartment because using a chauffeur is unnecessary and would be noticed. They will slip out the rear door and be in their apartment in no time. Dodi surely wouldn't want an angry Princess to propose to, which will be the case if the paparazzi are there in numbers. A smaller car will be used, so won't draw as much attention to the rear entrance exit but, because it's smaller, it won't carry two bodyguards and Paul must use this as an excuse to Dodi for leaving these behind. It's not far to go and what can possibly happen between the Ritz and the apartment? We know Paul is an excellent driver, so we have chosen him for this task knowing he will drive them to their apartment safely.

'The reason Paul must travel via the Alma tunnel is that driving directly to Dodi Fayed's apartment would enable the paparazzi to guess their next move and they will lie in wait for them. If they make a slight detour, it will only take minutes more but they will be able to approach the apartment from the Avenue George V or even Avenue Marceau and that would take him to the Place Charles de Gaulle, which approaches the apartment from the opposite direction. The paparazzi would not expect this and so it affords a better chance of making it to the apartment without being harassed, especially if they drive very fast from the Invalides Bridge. The paparazzi won't know which way they have gone. Also there will be less traffic along this route; they will have escaped. It gives Paul a reason to reach the Alma before the paparazzi catch up. He won't loiter!

'Do you spot any flaws?' said Caruthers, as Stephens pondered their discussion.

'No,' said Stephens, 'as long as our request to Paul is reasonable, and he has no suspicions, he will take orders from us as always. We shall direct him, as you suggest, and make sure the finer details are catered for. We must ensure that when they arrive at the Ritz, having abandoned the restaurant, the paparazzi are at the hotel to greet them with an overenthusiastic display. This will upset the Princess, making Dodi angry, and put him in the necessary mood to accept the idea from Paul that a fast escape is necessary. One point that concerns me is the bodyguards; they are not ours, are they?'

'Regrettably no,' said Caruthers. 'We must ensure that Paul does his best to leave them behind. The car won't take more than one bodyguard anyway because it's too small, but we shall continue with the attack whether one rides or not. My main concern is that if the bodyguards decide to contact London and phone the big boss Mohamed al Fayed, he may well sniff a rat. It is imperative the bodyguards are discouraged from that, so we tell Paul he must prevent this from happening, otherwise al Fayed would stop the rear exit plan. He will suggest that Dodi tells the bodyguards his father has already approved the plan. They won't dare check on this because that would mean calling Dodi a liar and that they would not survive. One of my better ideas, I think?'

'I like it; you're a devious bastard,' said Stephens.

'I know,' said Caruthers. 'I'm learning from you. And, didn't you know? It's what they pay us for.'

SATAN PREPARES

The morning of the 30th August arrived and operatives were on a mix of highs and subliminal feelings of trepidation. None had engaged in an action like this before; here was the test. The moment had come! Even Gould had a problem keeping his breakfast down and everybody held each other with a cold, hushed gaze.

For some, the bravado had gone and reality dawned. They must get through this day but some were questioning what this mood meant. This wasn't a normal feeling before a hit. Why did an air of despondency haunt the room?

Gould was amazed at his reaction and wondered why he hadn't felt this way previously. He had been putting his feelings aside but somehow couldn't help feeling a deep sense of sadness and remorse. 'I haven't done anything yet,' he thought. 'I've been in countless situations where I've needed to assassinate people, but they were enemies of the State and I have never before felt a twinge of hesitation. I must put this behind me, otherwise I will falter when the moment comes; even with just driving the backup car.'

The previous moment of hesitation in the tunnel was clearly more than a blip; this was subconsciously affecting him. Gould thought of his attitude towards Zimmerman during their first meeting. 'My God, I am probably feeling exactly the same as the guy I described to Zimmerman. If I don't get a grip, I will be a liability.' With that Gould put his doubts in a locker and blocked them out. 'Just focus,' he thought. 'This will be over soon and tomorrow is another day. Mine is not to reason why; it's just another job.'

Gould thought he was the hardest man here, not without good reason, but now wondered if he was feeling like this, how were the others coping? That thought made him nervous.

At seven-thirty am and, having demolished their energising

English breakfast, the team gathered around the table, coffee galore, and Zimmerman started his run through of the day's coming events as he saw them unfolding. All was very quiet as he began.

'Very soon, you will have just seconds to change the course of history. All your energies, concentration and steel must be focused on this brief moment. We have rehearsed this operation over and over and you are all looking good. By this time tomorrow, you will have given your debrief and assisted the sweepers with their ongoing clean-up campaign before we disband and return to England. Try to make sure there is nothing to sweep!

'A full report will need to be given by the sweepers to the propaganda team, so that the spin on this operation will not be ridiculed by facts that could prove the reasoning false; that's a Service job. Ours is to complete a clean hit, without leaving evidence; so now to today's business. The Service has their support team in place and will be feeding us with information from midday. This will start from the Ritz hotel, checking whether everything is OK with our agents in the hotel and, each hour during the day thereafter, there will be a health check to confirm that everything is on stream for this evening.

'We must prepare everything this morning and ensure nothing has been overlooked but I don't want anyone to get tense waiting, so we shall keep ourselves busy checking and re-checking details. When the subjects arrive in Paris, the Service will tail them and continue reporting on what they are saying and where they are going. We feel very confident we know their plans but if anything changes, we shall know and can then modify ours accordingly. You will be told immediately the reports come in so you will know whether any change is needed. The Service has ensured the presence of the paparazzi, from the subject's arrival at the airport by tipping them off on the subject's intended activities. The source will remain unknown.'

The nerve-wracking wait continued and various perfunctory activities were carried out by the waiting team to keep them occupied. It was nearing midday and the latest intelligence report gave indications of movement.

Zimmerman addressed the team. 'The subjects are intending to fly into Paris le Bourget airport and are expected to arrive at around 3.30pm.' All personnel knew the day's countdown had begun. 'Tyler and Haussmann will mix with the paparazzi and observe the subjects when they land. As you know, paparazzi presence is crucial as cover for the whole day, since by this evening we need the subjects to be so pissed off they are going to be keen to avoid them, whatever it takes. That's a major part of our plan!'

Zimmerman was happy with the way everything was going except for the one unexpected lapse by Gould. But they did have a very capable alternative in James Andanson for one of the two main attack roles.

**

The Service audio-surveillance team in Sardinia had heard the subjects discuss their intention of flying into le Bourget at around 3.30pm and Zimmerman ensured, via one of their safe sources, that the paparazzi were informed to begin part of the day's most crucial chain of events.

Tyler and Haussmann went over to the airport to watch for the flight and parked their BMW motorcycle in the least conspicuous place they could find: amongst the parked paparazzi motorcycles. 'Very convenient,' thought Tyler, as they went inside for a snack whilst awaiting the aircraft's arrival.

They were beginning to feel excited, if not euphoric, about their forthcoming role. They could only think of this evening's action and the role they were each playing. Tyler said, 'What a lovely lot of cash. What are you going to do with your payment Greg?'

'Haven't really decided yet,' said Haussmann. 'The first thing I thought is to take my girlfriend on holiday to the USA for a couple of weeks and I'll decide on the future while I am away.'

'Yes,' said Tyler, 'I am going on holiday too, probably Greece. I don't think I'll stay in England. I presume the Service have expressed a preference for you to live elsewhere, afterwards?' 'Right, said Haussmann, 'but with one million pounds each, we can go where the hell we want.'

Seated next to a large observation window in the le Bourget lounge, they observed aircraft movements on the tarmac. Each time an executive jet taxied past the window, they watched to see if this was the one.

A commotion on the tarmac and the press group started moving in an excitable manner! Tyler looked down through the window and saw a very attractive Gulf Stream IV plane, coloured dark green and gold, taxiing to the Transair terminal for passenger disembarkation. He knew the Transair terminal handled VIP passengers on behalf of the Ritz. This was the plane! The time was 3.25pm. God this is actually happening!

Tyler and Haussmann knew this was real and could feel the excitement building. Until the moment of actually seeing the subjects in the flesh, it was only words, talk, an exercise, but now! They looked on and waited for the plane to stop and for the disembarkation.

The aircraft doors opened, the Transair staff boarded and Dodi asked if they could assist him in avoiding the paparazzi that he could see from the aeroplane window. First to emerge from the aircraft was one of the two bodyguards, Trevor Rees-Jones, followed by the Princess wearing casual, tan-coloured clothes and designer sunglasses. Next was the other bodyguard, Kes Wingfield, followed by Dodi, also wearing sunglasses and casual clothes, a black shirt, waistcoat and dark jeans.

Tyler couldn't help thinking. 'He looks really relaxed and completely at ease. This seems so surreal.'

As the plane came to a halt, a large black Mercedes 600 that had driven over to the aircraft parked near to it. A balding man in his forties with spectacles also walked to the aircraft steps and waited. The man in the black shirt and brown sports jacket came down the aircraft steps and went over to the bespectacled, balding man, striking up what appeared to be a very friendly and relaxed conversation.

The Princess now joined this discussion group and all seemed very jovial and animated.

'Well, there they are,' said Tyler to Haussmann in a very quiet tone. 'I think I know who that man with the balding head is. It's Henri Paul, one of ours, and a very important man in today's event.'

As he spoke the whole group moved towards the Mercedes and sped off the airfield with Dodi's personal chauffeur, Philippe Dourneau, at the wheel, catching Tyler and Haussmann off guard. Henri Paul, driving Dodi's personal black Range Rover, followed them.

'Come on,' said Tyler. 'We are supposed to tail them.'

'I really don't know why,' said Haussmann. 'What difference does it make whether we know where they are, since the Service lads are doing all the cloak and dagger stuff?'

'Come on,' said Tyler. 'You are being paid well enough, just do as you have been asked, for today. From tomorrow you can do what you damn well like.'

The cavalcade moved from the tarmac and sped off in the direction of Paris followed by the paparazzi, like flies around a carcass.

'Couldn't do that job,' thought Tyler. 'I couldn't be so fucking rude. Just a moment,' his silent self-rebuke reminded him. 'I couldn't be so rude but I am prepared to kill them.' He let that one-drop and turned the bike out of the airport, speeding off in the direction of the fleeting Mercedes. They caught up quickly and, now that the police escort had left them at the Porte de la Chappelle, they entered the boulevard périphérique and couldn't resist the temptation to ride alongside the Mercedes.

As they did, the face of the Princess appeared in the car's window and caught Tyler off guard. He was confronting the face of a human being whom he knew was to be murdered by his hand, and he signalled Haussmann to pull the bike back as a huge surge of guilt hit him. Haussmann fell behind the car but continued to follow. Tyler would do his job and was dismayed at this strange sensation but just shrugged it off.

His instructions had been to phone Zimmerman and confirm where they were and so he gestured to Haussmann. As he did, the Mercedes quickly turned off the boulevard périphérique at the Porte Maillot exit and headed towards the Bois de Boulogne, as Zimmerman had said it might. This move out manoeuvred the paparazzi but not Haussmann who was ready and continued to follow the Mercedes at a discreet distance.

The black Range Rover, driven by Henri Paul, continued on to Dodi's apartment at the rue Arsenne Houssaye and, as they later discovered, placed the subjects' luggage in their apartment ahead of them. It was now confirmed where they would be spending the night, although intelligence had already suggested it would be at the apartment.

The Villa Windsor was soon reached. It was unlikely that the subjects would want to revisit here on this trip, which removed this venue from the attack equation. This was their second visit to the villa during the last few weeks and reaffirmed Service thinking about the seriousness of this relationship, although this was past being relevant.

Tyler had indicated that Haussmann should wait before phoning Zimmerman as the Mercedes made the quick exit from the périphérique but now, as the car approached and entered the drive of the Villa, Haussmann parked around the corner and Tyler made his call.

'They have reached the Villa and we are parked outside,' said Haussmann.

'Right', said Zimmerman. 'Leave now and return to base. Don't wait outside you might draw unwelcome attention, which is the last thing we want.'

'Right,' said Haussmann, 'we are returning to base.'

Tyler now realised why Zimmerman had asked them to go to the airport. He had been kept busy all morning and not sitting around getting nervous, had some practice with the bike and had confronted the people who he had to deal with later that day. Any feelings of trepidation that may have arisen were out of his system and he could focus on the job.

'Good thinking,' thought Tyler. 'Zimmerman is blooding us. If I freaked out, I would have done it before it became dangerous to the mission. Zimmerman seems to know what he is up to.'

Zimmerman thought there wasn't much else they could do to improve on the routine. What they didn't know, they weren't going to learn before this evening. His main task was to ensure the team were kept busy and stayed fresh for the evening's activities so, although content with the preparation, he was still anxious to keep everyone's minds active and didn't want people indulging in maudlin thoughts. He knew that even the most hardened of his men were not going to feel 100% about this job; he didn't! Couldn't allow them to think and have spare time on their hands dreaming up reasons for not proceeding or moralising. Zimmerman thought this very unlikely but didn't want to take the chance, especially considering Gould's, and his own, reservation.

He was especially nervous of the role that Tyler, Haussmann and Andanson were about to play because their roles were the most critical and dangerous, where split-second timing was everything. If these people were not totally committed, or had the slightest hesitation, then the operation would fail and that was why he sent them out to induce a self-test and occupy them. It was just past 4.00pm and within the next ten hours or so, the job would be done so he had between eight and twelve hours to occupy his men and was stuck for what to do with them.

'This is the worst part,' thought Zimmerman, 'no man's land; the time of nervous build up and the anxious wait! I should have prepared for this better. Could go sightseeing; what about the Louvre or the Eiffel tower. Stop thinking nonsense,' he self-reproached. 'Just keep them together and talk through the preparation again and again; at least everybody's mind will stay active and focused.'

Once Tyler and Haussmann returned, Zimmerman addressed everybody together in their usual meeting room. 'We need to keep focused on events, so we are going to have another run through.'

After about an hour, they finished their session and the phone rang. 'Zimmerman please,' said the voice.

Tyler passed the phone to Zimmerman and went back into the room to join the rest of the team.

'Hello,' said the voice. 'This is X; I am giving you your 5.00pm brief for the current state of affairs. The subjects arrived at the Ritz hotel at around 4.30pm and our audio surveillance team has gleaned they intend to go to the Chez Benoît restaurant this evening, one of Dodi's favourites. We have arranged for the paparazzi to be informed once their booking is confirmed, so a paparazzi welcoming committee will await them. They are having the engagement ring collected from the jewellers at around 6.30pm and I believe they will then go to their apartment shortly afterwards. The shop is Alberto Repossi's and is just about one hundred yards from the Ritz. We will keep you informed as the evening progresses, but everything is still a go.'

In the Ritz, hotel activity was normal except for the eager anticipation of one man who believed he was about to improve his chances of promotion and at the same time do his boss a favour. The ambitious Henri Paul had now missed out on two promotions to the security manager's job, despite being well thought of by the management, and with them knowing he wanted this post. He had been offered a chance by the Service to impress the boss and he wasn't missing out. In any event he worked for the Service and found it quite exciting. Orders were orders, especially since it in no way affected his boss. Receiving a healthy cash bung for every job they gave him didn't hurt and was useful with the expensive hobbies he pursued.

Henri loved flying light aircraft and not only held a flying licence but also a full Instrument Rating which enabled him to fly by sole reference to instruments in situations where visibility was down to zero, except for actually landing the aeroplane. This took great skill and concentration and also rigorous and regular medical checks that had recently shown him to be in good shape.

Today he would go about his duties and ensure any wishes expressed by the subjects would be made known to his Service handler, who would then pass them on to the team, purportedly for the subject's protection. The Service needed to keep tabs during the day and, should anything unforeseen take place, they needed to be in a position to respond by varying their plans. The Service would decide whether they had to stand down, if anything radically altered, but this was the last-chance saloon. After this it would be very difficult to commit an act of murder without it being obvious when even with 'deniability', an attack could prove fatal to their cause.

Paul didn't quite understand why the rear escape Mercedes must be small and without tinted windows. These measures, he was told, made it less conspicuous and easier to slip past the paparazzi, which was the purpose of the rear exit escape from the hotel planned for later. He didn't question this explanation. He had no reason to believe his paymasters would want to harm his boss, or the Princess. He had no reason to believe anything untoward was about to happen.

The afternoon went by with the team all on tenterhooks, awaiting the moment. Zimmerman was feeling an unusual tension due to the time lag between preparation and action. They all wanted it to be 7.00pm when the next key movement would begin and they could begin watching the subjects; he must do something!

Morison phoned Zimmerman to see how he was coping and how the team were bearing up, suggesting they go through the plans again, but Zimmerman thought they had exhausted this option and everyone would start losing interest. There was only an hour to go, so Zimmerman told Morison that they were OK and were ready to do the job.

The latest intelligence was not unexpected and so any thoughts of a stand down, that even this group of hardened professionals were almost hoping for, had now greatly receded. Zimmerman started to sweat and feel unsteady. He thought he had better sit! 'God,' he thought, as though he was really expecting God to be listening. 'What's happening to me? I've seen others look the way I feel right now. I can't let the troops see me like this. I feel some are leaning on me for support and, if I fail, so does this mission.'

He went into an empty meeting room and poured himself a large cup of coffee, sat down and began to shake. He wanted to escape this feeling but there was nowhere to go. He couldn't sleep, he wasn't tired, but his body felt listless. 'Thank heavens I am only driving the back-up car. If I was taking one of the main roles in this attack, I don't think I would make it.' His emotions were now taking a grip but he was more concerned with how he might appear to the troops.

Zimmerman considered that all would be OK; he just had to concentrate on playing his relatively low-key part in the evening's action. Tyler and Haussmann entered the room and moved towards Zimmerman who was still seated.

'It's less than one hour to our 7.00pm report from the Service,' said Tyler. 'Should we go through the plans once more as a final refresher? It's nearly time to begin our final attack sequence run through, so have you decided when we are going.'

'Why don't you go now,' said Zimmerman, in a detached voice, almost as though he didn't care who did what and then, steadying the ship, 'go and drive the route between the subject's apartment and the Ritz and through the Alma tunnel just to get a fresh feel but don't take any risks. Just content yourself that you are feeling ready and then return. I don't want anyone overdoing it.

'Only Haussmann and Andanson need to be totally comfortable with timing; the rest of us know what we need to do and its better if we don't spend time rehearsing something we are sufficiently familiar with and risk causing suspicion. We have already practiced the attack sequence over and over, with all vehicles together, and each operative feels confident of where the other parties will be during the attack. I am confident that everyone is ready! How are the others?'

'Fine,' said Tyler. 'They are as anxious to get it over with as we all are, so they are playing cards to take their minds off it.'

'Fine,' said Zimmerman. 'You go until you are satisfied, then come back not later than 8.00pm for a meal. We'll have one more brief during the meal and then be ready to leave the apartment and take up positions.'

Tyler nodded his agreement and went out, followed by

Haussmann who was totally relaxed and couldn't wait to get started.

Zimmerman thought that this is how he used to be. 'Thought I still was but it looks as though this operation has brought me to the end of a dubious career. I think I have lost it! Tonight will end a lot of careers, hopefully not our lives. It's certainly the most difficult operation from the point of maintaining moral that I've ever encountered but that doesn't surprise me. Only money is driving this operation, not the desire to rid the world of some evil person or someone who is holding the state, or any state, to ransom. There is little support for it even amongst the team and that's why the Service resorted to us. Their regular agents couldn't stomach it. God help me!'

Zimmerman really didn't expect God to help and, as that thought crossed his mind, he felt a total emptiness. He found himself reverting to strange and lonely thoughts of his childhood and of having once believed in God many years ago when his mother was alive, but the world had obscured his reasoning and left him a shell of his former self. This job was destroying him and he knew that if he didn't toughen up for the next five or six hours, he may not survive this life much longer. If the attack didn't kill him, the Service would if he failed.

He wasn't sure if he would survive or that he cared. He had spent too long in the business of ending life in order to live and had reached emotional saturation, where life had begun to mean very little.

'Get a grip. I am going to survive this,' he thought. 'And I am going to achieve financial security. What happens after that is another matter; that's for another day.'

The Service meanwhile had been busy with their preparations. The Embassy was bustling with activity and thought it didn't matter that numbers of personnel and the level of activity was much higher than usual because who was going to know the detail of who was there and what they were up to?

'Arrogance!' thought Morison, as he walked through the Embassy entrance, 'is the one thing that could bring us down. Arrogance, complacency and post-attack debris, or any evidence that we cannot stand aside from or reason away.' As he considered the risks run by the Service he thought, 'We should always take care, however confident we may feel. The Embassy hasn't been so busy for a long time; that will be noticed. We can get away with using 'deniability' but that is a last recourse and not our primary reliance. If any suspicious factors arise, post attack, we shall have problems.'

He saw it as a prime duty to identify, and then reduce, the number of factors that could fuel the thought of murder; essential if they were to get away with claiming this as a mere accident. At the same time he had the contradictory thought that they needed to have sufficient staff present to ensure success and he was nervous how many people knew about this operation. The numbers had mushroomed and that was going to make it more difficult to manage afterwards.

The Service team was gathered to collate intelligence and assess the 'go' status. All information at present confirmed a 'go' and there were no current untoward reports; in fact, all seemed OK.

Nick Stephens was in a comfortable anteroom at the Embassy, waiting for Morison as he entered. 'Everything seems in order Tom,' said Stephens; 'we seem to have a go.'

'Yes,' said Morison, 'the team has completed their preparation and Zimmerman seems very happy.'

'Right,' said Stephens. 'What about the situation with this man of ours at the Ritz, Henry Paul? He gives me some concern, since all the others are on side, knowing the truth. He is working for us but not realising what he is about to do. I realise we can't tell him but if he suspected anything he could scupper the whole event.'

'Henri Paul,' corrected Morison, 'he is French and yes, he is as you describe but also under quite a tight control. He takes orders without question but I agree there could be a problem if he suspected anything so we are making sure he doesn't.'

'I presume he will be collateral damage,' said Stephens.

'Yes,' said Morison. 'In fact he is a secondary target because if he survived he would quickly realise what had happened and almost certainly be a dangerous witness, probably going straight to the press. The police we needn't worry about, English or French; they will do as they are told. But we need scapegoats after the attack because people won't believe it's an accident, on that you can rely, so we are ready to fix Henri up with a belated drinking spree; post-mortem.'

Morison suddenly didn't like his own sense of humour and felt a twinge of regret for having said that which Stephens picked up on.

'It's all down to numbers,' said Stephens, trying to take Morison's mind off his previous comment. 'A small number believe it's an accident and no problem, but a large number and we may achieve the very thing we are executing this operation to prevent: the fall of the monarchy and disruption in the status quo, leading to God knows where.'

'I know,' said Morison. 'I'm finding this experience dehumanising. I'll be glad when it's over.'

Morison and Stephens continued to concentrate on the details, still poring over reports they had received in the last few hours to see if there were any glitches.

'Looks fine,' said Stephens. 'Hope there is no major deviation.'

'Right,' said Morison. 'We don't want too much exposure in the Ritz because it could set people wondering what's going on. We have kept our activity there to a minimum. As long as Henri Paul does his job then there is little that should go wrong before the attack.'

'That's another thing,' said Stephens. 'Suppose the subjects survive the attack. Do you think we have adequate measures in place to correct for this?'

'We have a backup team, as you know,' said Morison. 'They will be at the attack scene. They will be on foot, very close to the tunnel entrance and carrying a phial of fentanyl that can be administered very quickly, leaving no trace and ensuring there will be no survival. I am confident we have this covered.'

Stephens asked. 'What about autopsy, post-mortem and inquest.'

'There will not be any,' said Morison. 'Without these all people can do is speculate.'

'Which also worries me!' said Stephens. 'It's all very well saying we control the detail and the people won't know. After the death of Diana, how will we sell the idea why these things aren't carried out? I am not convinced we will get away with it.'

'You will be amazed,' said Morison, 'what people will believe if you tell them even a remotely plausible story and stick to it. We may, however, need a post-mortem in the UK but we'll make sure there's nothing to find.'

'But she is pregnant and the poison will be identified from the blood, if we have to administer it. What a wonderful motive for conspiracy theorists! Poison doesn't allow for a theory; it will be fact. What about the government? I am still not too clear what their response will be.'

'Don't worry,' said Morison. 'We have considered this and the only way of ensuring there is no evidence is to have the body of the Princess embalmed before she leaves France. In this way there will not be any evidence of either pregnancy or poison, should we need to administer it. Also, there is no way a new government of a few months will risk losing power, having been out of office for nearly twenty years. They need to control the truth otherwise they risk a major constitutional crisis and could be blown away, as well as the monarchy. They will be persuaded the best route is to feign an accident in the interests of the British people. As long as they can tell themselves they are doing it for the people, and not to just hang onto power, then they will comply; have no fear. They will, after all, be presented with a fait accompli. Don't worry; leave the politics to me. The people, I assure you, want to believe their Government otherwise who can they believe?'

'Absolutely,' said Stephens, coughing nervously as he agreed with Morison; 'who else indeed?'

The Service team watched the Ritz and wondered why they needed to be here so early in the day. It was now past 7.00pm and there was activity but still a long time before any action. Dodi Fayed had had his engagement ring collected from the jewellers and returned to his apartment, as expected. The Service surveillance teams were nervously seeking more intelligence from the subject's apartment for confirmation of where they were going to eat. If they changed their minds and decided to remain in the apartment, the plan was in serious trouble. There was no safe provision for an early morning attack, which would be far too risky, so, if not tonight, then the subjects returning aircraft would need to be sabotaged and that team was also prepared.

'Not a good option but needs must,' thought Morison. 'If we are compelled to do this then everybody will know it was murder, which is an extremely dangerous option. But if we do nothing we will definitely have a crisis, so we would need to risk creating one we may or may not survive; some choice!'

It was because there was no real viable alternative that this strike was so important. It was the only way of achieving their goal without causing a major backlash from the British people.

'Any information from the guys at the Ritz?' said Morison. 'Has anything unusual happened?'

'No,' said Stephens, 'everything is extremely quiet. The team are rotating about now and have just been briefed. We're not expecting anything to happen before 9.00–9.30pm.'

'From what time did you place our operatives at the control points on the route,' asked Morison.

'They were on site from 7.00pm,' said Stephens, 'and will stay until the job is done.'

'Has Henri Paul left the hotel yet?'

'Yes,' said Stephens, 'he went off duty at around 7.00pm and you're meeting with him at 8.30pm, are you not? That's only an hour or so. Where are you meeting him?'

'At a café some miles from the hotel,' said Morison. 'Not one of his regular haunts but one his handler often uses. We need to stay with him until his return to the Ritz, which we expect at between 9.00 and 10.30pm. In fact we would prefer he doesn't return before his boss, so he won't have the opportunity to discuss this evening's activities with anyone. It's almost time for me to join my colleague for that meeting; I must leave soon.'

'I think I will join you,' said Stephens.

'Would you mind if I asked that you didn't?' said Morison. 'Paul knows Chandler and we don't want to risk him wondering why so many people are suddenly gathering and showing an interest in him; a risk if more than two turn up. As you rightly say, the biggest risk is that he smells a rat and, if he does, we lose.'

'OK,' said Stephens, 'fair point,' realising he mustn't allow over zealousness to hamper efficiency. Morison was very capable, not to mention senior. 'Let me know how you get on when you return. This will soon be over now.'

Morison and Stephens were focused and checking through the final details to ensure nothing had been missed. Morison turned to Stephens and said, 'It's past 8.00pm and our report to Zimmerman is overdue,' as he looked at the clock and saw the hand just past the hour.

'Right,' said Stephens, 'what is the latest?'

'The subjects are at their apartment, at the rue Arsenne Houssay, and intelligence tells us they are still intending to eat at the Chez Benoît. Our first objective is to force them to the Ritz. If they eat at the restaurant, they may well go straight back to the apartment which makes it more difficult to justify the detour through the Alma tunnel. When I meet with Paul this evening I shall stress that he must be on tap to collect them from wherever they eat.'

Morison needed to continually reconsider the logic in case he missed anything. 'If they don't go through the Alma, the attack fails! We have arranged for a reception at the restaurant, so they should change their minds even before entering, and we have instructed Paul to require his night security manager, Françoise Tendil, to recall him when the subjects return to the Ritz. I shall also reaffirm this later tonight. Should our plan to divert them to the Ritz fail, Paul will collect them from the restaurant and still drive through the Alma tunnel. More difficult, but we've thought it through and it's plausible.

'The subjects should be back at the Ritz for around 9.30 to 10.00pm and Paul will be with them minutes afterwards. We are meeting with Paul at 8.30pm to finalise his instructions and settle any concerns he may have developed and shall further enhance his loyalty by paying him a first instalment for his services,' said Morison. 'This will give us an hour or two with him, which should be ample.'

'Won't this be dangerous?' said Stephens. 'He may still have the money on him when we strike. What will the police make of it?'

'He will almost certainly have the money on him but there won't be any proof where it came from,' said Morison. 'How will anybody know? We dare not suggest he takes the money to his apartment because our suggesting it may cause suspicion. We need him to feel in a very positive mood this evening so we have no real option. By being with him for the early evening, and releasing him just before the strike, we can ensure his correct frame of mind and reduce the possibility of contamination with other hotel personnel. We can report to Zimmerman that everything is on track, the ring has been collected from the jewellers and Dodi has gone to the apartment.

'If audio surveillance gives us anything new, we shall let Zimmerman know. Would you just convey that to him?' said Morison, handing the secure phone to Stephens. 'I must go to an important meeting – the last point this evening's operation could be stood down.'

SATAN RIDES

Henri Paul left the Ritz on quite a high around 7.00pm, telling his night security manager, Tendil, to recall him if the boss returned, as instructed by the Service. Henri always found working for the Service exciting; he looked forward to this evening's activity.

He drove from the Ritz hotel in his black mini and went straight home to change before his clandestine evening meeting with the British Secret Service that always spoilt him with excellent food and drink. Henri enjoyed the thrill of these meetings and the feeling of importance they gave him.

He abstained from drink, as required by the Service, and went to the café where he had arranged to meet his handler. An advance instalment had been promised and he was already planning to hire an aircraft and fly to see his parents the following weekend, thinking he would treat himself while making very good money for doing, as he saw it, just a little more than his usual job.

Paul arrived at the café. The room was dark! There were randomly placed tables, some taking advantage of the scant amount of light emanating from the few available light sources. A large mirror behind the counter reflected light from the street to a table in the far corner, still barely affording sufficient illumination for reading.

Paul went over to this table, sat and ordered a large black coffee from an efficient and attentive waiter. He began reading his newspaper while awaiting his handler's arrival. Paul liked his handler, Brad Chandler, and was looking forward to the meeting but wondering why it was needed when the restaurant door opened and in walked Chandler, accompanied by a man Paul hadn't seen before: Morison.

Chandler began. 'Hi, Henri, *ça va*? This is a colleague from

London.' He introduced Morison, but not by name. 'He is with me today to see how we work and to make sure our security is in place for this evening, until the Princess departs for England tomorrow.'

'Hello, Monsieur Paul, it's very good to meet you,' said Morison. 'I understand you will play an important part in protecting our Princess this evening.'

'Yes,' said a delighted Paul, 'I look forward to being of service.'

'Good,' said Morison. 'Let's get down to business but first we'll have some more of your wonderful coffee.' He called over the waiter for another pot and was thinking it smelt better than the stuff served at MI6 country HQ, permitting mundane thoughts to take his mind off what was now going down.

Paul started the conversation, addressing his comment to Chandler. He had no idea of seniority, since he hadn't been properly introduced, and in any case, he knew and trusted Chandler; Morison was just there to make up the numbers.

'Brad,' said Paul, 'what else do you have in store for me today?'

'Well,' said Chandler, 'you know we have a duty to protect the Princess as mother of our future king and must ensure her safety whilst she is abroad.'

'Of course,' said Paul, feeling proud he was to play an important part in protecting the Princess.

'Well,' continued Chandler, 'we have become nervous regarding the behaviour of the paparazzi during the last month. They seem to be more aggressive than ever and have caused the Princess a lot of grief. We think this weekend could be very special for the couple and we don't want the press to know their whereabouts or they will be swarming all over and threatening the Princess, possibly doing her an injury. We have devised a plan to protect them from the paparazzi and let them enjoy a normal night out.

'The difficulty is in persuading Dodi Fayed that he needs to follow our suggestions for their own safety, as you will see when we have explained to you our difficulty in trying to protect them. We persuade Dodi of the best course of action but we cannot achieve this objective alone because we can't approach him directly. How he chooses to protect himself is his business but when the Princess is in tow, we must look after her interests. You understand?' said Chandler.

'Of course,' said Paul. 'I think I can persuade Dodi to follow a set course; he listens to me. What do you have in mind?'

'Our plan will require great skill, but we know you can handle it,' said Chandler, cajoling and hoping to play to Paul's ego and fascination with intrigue. 'We understand the Princess and your boss are intending to go out for a meal this evening, possibly to the Ritz and then back to their apartment. We must ensure this journey is a safe one.'

In making this statement Chandler was presuming the Service would be successful in persuading the subjects not to enter the restaurant. He couldn't explain his real objective to Paul, or how they were going about controlling the evening's activities in directing the couple towards the Ritz, so had to lead with an overall plan and dangle Paul like a puppet, cajoling with flattery and the promise of a reward. He was aware money usually did the trick, even with extremely loyal people, provided they were not aware of the game being played.

If the subjects didn't go to the Ritz, their plan was in trouble, so he had to proceed on the basis they would. 'If they go to the Ritz, or wherever they are,' continued Chandler, 'we must avoid encounters with the paparazzi, so have devised an escape plan by the back door of the Ritz, having first set up a diversion at the front of the Hotel.'

'Yes, I know of the smaller car without tinted windows,' said Paul.

'Right,' said Chandler, 'we need to ensure all avenues are considered in case they choose to return to their apartment from the hotel while the paparazzi are still baying at their door. The car we have chosen will look like any other on the road and the press will be expecting a large car with tinted windows, so let's spoil their fun, yes?'

'Yes,' said Paul, 'good idea, but how do I persuade Dodi to agree?'

'Right,' said Chandler, 'this is what we shall do! Wherever the couple eat this evening, it's imperative you drive them back to the apartment. You must be at the hotel and will be called to collect them if they remain at the restaurant, but we don't want them there; they will be much safer at the Ritz. If they return to the hotel the paparazzi will be gathering outside and this will put them both in a bad mood. There is nothing we can do about that but it's likely they will also be in the right frame of mind to accept your idea of a rear exit plan.

'If you don't get a call from Tendil, we ask that you return anyway at around 10.15pm, so you are on hand. We shall instruct you which route is most favourable for the return to their apartment, avoiding the paparazzi, either way. Our agents will give us information on where the paparazzi are; this we shall pass onto you. You tell Dodi you have devised a plan to help him avoid the Princess being embarrassed, or threatened, by the paparazzi and at the same time give him the opportunity to impress her by leaving the paparazzi for dead. He doesn't want the Princess in a bad mood. It's a very important evening for Dodi.

'Have the chosen car on standby and delivered to the back door of the hotel when you are ready and make sure you have persuaded Dodi you should chauffeur them to the apartment, without the bodyguards. The bodyguards won't like the idea they are superfluous, so you must also persuade Dodi to tell them he has already cleared the plan with his father. They won't dare make a call to London and check. Also tell him you will drive the car, because it's only a short distance to the apartment and, if chauffeurs or bodyguards are spotted by the paparazzi, the plan will fail.

'Another reason you don't want the bodyguards with you in the car, apart from its size, is that Dodi would probably argue about the route you will be taking to the apartment and they mustn't know we are involved, otherwise the Princess will certainly refuse your idea. You mustn't reveal you are working with us. That would annoy the bodyguards and the Princess is famous for her obduracy. Persuade Dodi that this will keep the Princess in the right frame of mind for his proposed question later that evening. You will be seen in a very positive light. Have no fear, we shall be there to protect you, but we cannot let the couple, or the bodyguards, know!

'We appreciate this is more than we normally ask of you but we felt you could deal with it, since you have handled operations for us before and you have the necessary driving skills,' said Chandler, thinking he had better be careful not to overdo the flattery.

'Yes, I can do that,' said Paul, 'not a problem. Only a few weeks ago, when Dodi and Diana came to Paris for the weekend, they went to the Lucas Carlton restaurant and left the Ritz by the back door, for the same reason. It worked then, so it's not a new idea.'

'Good,' said Chandler, breathing an inner sigh of relief that the main part of his remit was complete.

'Let's have dinner,' said Morison, 'and talk of ways to achieve our goal and consider any problems you may foresee. We will just go over the plans for this evening. We don't want anything to spoil the Princess's evening. You have reserved the evening for us haven't you, Henri?'

'Well, yes,' said Paul hesitating. 'I had intended going elsewhere after this meeting but if you think it necessary I am yours for the evening. I would like to ensure that your Princess and my boss are safe.'

'Excellent,' said Morison, 'and I believe Brad has something for you.'

Chandler brought a brown envelope out of his briefcase and handed it to Paul who, glancing inside, smiled and placed it in his inner pocket. He was always paid well by the British Security Services and now had thoughts of a pleasant weekend with more of these proceeds to come. He felt very contented indeed.

Back at Dodi's rue Arsenne Houssaye apartment, there was much activity when the subjects arrived at Dodi's apartment. The paparazzi were aggressive and had frightened the Princess; hot tempers flew! The paparazzi promised to be very nasty in their press comments if not allowed to do their job, so the bodyguards came back out from the apartment to cool tempers. The Service had ensured the mood was set for the evening's purpose and that the paparazzi would continue this unwitting support throughout the evening.

Dodi had decided to eat at the Chez Benoît restaurant, near the Pompidou centre, so the subjects set off at around 9.30pm. Back at the café, Morison's phone rang. It was Stephens, to say the subjects were leaving their apartment. Morison asked that he be informed when they reached the Ritz and immediately if they entered the restaurant.

Morison announced they should break off the dinner and return since everyone, including Henri Paul, had work to do and he wanted to be on hand, especially if the subjects decided to enter the café despite Service efforts.

On arrival outside the Chez Benoît restaurant, the numbers of paparazzi waiting made Dodi decide to go straight to the Ritz to have their meal. 9.51pm, the subjects' car pulled up outside the Ritz, unannounced, and was met by a large crowd of aggressive paparazzi as the Service had intended.

Dodi was angry and took it out on his bodyguards but they

were having none of it. They spat back at Dodi that they should have been informed of his intention to return to the Ritz when they could have ensured a safer reception. Dodi hadn't intended to return, and not even the hotel management knew he would, until the Mercedes arrived at the hotel door, since the decision not to enter the Chez Benoît was taken outside the restaurant and it was only a few minutes' drive from there to the Ritz.

Dodi and the Princess made a beeline for the hotel door and entered quickly for safety where they would remain for the next few hours. Due to paparazzi hustle the scene was irrevocably set for Paul to persuade Dodi to agree to the Service's plan. The Service reported back that everything was proceeding as planned and Morison felt satisfied that everything was now on course. Dodi should be more receptive after experiencing the paparazzi at le Bourget airport, outside his apartment, at the restaurant and now at the hotel. The Service knew the Princess would support the move for an unconventional rear door exit to avoid a fifth, and more hostile, encounter on leaving the hotel for their apartment.

The evening with Henri had passed in the most agreeable way and Morison almost forgot that, within a few hours, the man for whom they had just bought dinner would be dead. They were content, however, that Henri Paul was okay with their plans and was on side.

The phone rang again. Stephens told Morison the subjects had arrived back at the Ritz; all was going to plan!

Morison ended the call and spoke to Paul. 'It was a pleasure meeting with you Henri. We must leave now and I am sure you will soon receive your telephone call about your boss's return. Are you going to your apartment first?'

'No,' said Paul. 'I have already been home this evening before coming here. I probably won't have time before returning to the hotel, but shall be home around 1.00pm. My boss won't want me around tonight except for chauffeur duties, I can assure you of that,' he added with a mischievous glint.

Morison and Chandler took their leave, offering Paul a lift near to where he had parked his car; Paul accepted. Morison and Chandler dropped Paul off and made their way to the Embassy, where the very last assessment was to be made prior to the attack.

Paul approached a gay bar, le Champmeslé, where he had parked his black mini and briefly put his head around the door to say hello. At that moment Françoise Tendil telephoned him from the Ritz, as Paul had requested, to say the boss and the Princess had arrived at the hotel.

Paul promptly bade goodnight to his friends in the bar, returned to his duties at the Ritz at 10.08pm and continued with his normal activities around the hotel for the next one and a half hours. He was obviously excited at his role in this clandestine affair of international intrigue, in which he was to play a major part. Not the part he had anticipated, but one that suited the Service very well.

He spent time talking to various members of staff and had just two Ricards that would certainly not cause him any problem. He had these drinks with the bodyguards but would not have more because he would be busy with his boss and, if he drank too much, it would guarantee his dismissal. His was a major role, as he saw it, and he needed to keep his wits about him; he was intending to improve his chances of promotion, not get fired.

Morison knew that everything was in place for the evening and there hadn't been any deviations from plan. The subjects were suitably pissed off with the paparazzi, so should be responsive to Paul's suggestion and the smaller car was ready. It was now all dependent on Paul's persuasive powers on Dodi and, if this proved successful, all was set. If not then they would have to look to one of their less favoured hit options and that didn't excite them. The Service relied on this option working and, although secondary provisional plans had been made, these were not as attractive bearing in mind the overall objective that this must look like an accident. Their instructions were clear, however; they must succeed one way or another, whatever option was used.

Regular checks were kept on how events were unfolding, in order to ensure no changes were required by the assassins. The subject's room, the Imperial Suite, had been bugged by Paul, so the Service could keep a check on how the subjects were thinking and see how they intended to spend their evening. At first they went to eat in the hotel restaurant, where the Service found it more difficult to check on their conversation but, after a short time and because of a lack of privacy, they returned to their room so now the Service was once more in full control.

All the conversation was listened to and if any doubt had remained, now there was none. They now knew for certain an announcement of marriage was imminent! The subjects intended going to their apartment later that evening but they were still angry with the paparazzi and keen to avoid another battering.

Paul had managed to persuade Dodi to allow him to drive the car, without bodyguards, and that they should leave with a speedy and unobtrusive exit from the back door of the hotel. The Service was content all was set so would monitor the next hour and execute the attack, without leaving evidence.

As the evening progressed, the Service became nervous as to whether the subjects would change their minds and remain in the hotel. They sought, through their listening devices, whether it could be determined that the subjects would be leaving and, if so, when. They asked Paul to confirm that it would be by the rear exit and at roughly what time so they could prepare for their protection. There was a risk the subjects sent for the engagement ring, and their clothes, but Dodi felt it was not far to drive and he would be in his apartment proposing to his Princess within ten minutes; he wasn't yet sure.

Having spent time ensuring the paparazzi remained outside the hotel, by going outside and goading them with promises the couple would leave that evening, Paul had already maintained the essential paparazzi cover for the attack. The throng of paparazzi outside the hotel also ensured that Dodi would accept the idea of leaving by the back door. The Service needed to know whether the subjects had accepted the idea of the car and the bodyguards.

At around 11.00pm Paul contacted Dodi and discussed the exit from the rear of the hotel, the car, the bodyguards and the timing. Dodi accepted that it was a sound plan and Paul gave confirmation to the Service.

At 11.15pm Dodi went outside his room, at Paul's request, and told the bodyguards what he wished to do and that he had cleared it with his father. The scene was set! The bodyguards wouldn't question the order from Dodi because it would require them to call him a liar, a job-losing exercise, so the path was clear for the evening's plan to proceed.

A slight problem then occurred! The bodyguards had accepted the subjects would be leaving from the rear of the hotel but refused to allow it without them. As planned, it was stressed the car was too small and essential to maintain obscurity, so a compromise was reached that one of the bodyguards would travel in the car.

At 12.00pm the Service had a slight palpitation when they

listened to Dodi's conversation with his father. Hearts were pounding as they waited for Mohamed al Fayed to tell his son to stay in the hotel for the evening, which he duly did. Breathe again; Dodi had persuaded his father he would be OK and that he was going back to the apartment. He told his father he was proposing to the Princess and the ring, his present and all their clothes were there.

At 12.15pm it was considered time to leave, so the subjects went down to the foyer and waited by the rear exit for their car to arrive.

Service operatives were in position at each of the control points along the route and a number waited outside the Ritz to inform the first control point that the car had left the hotel. The attack had begun! They reported to Morison that all was set; Zimmerman was informed and the entire attack team was firing on adrenalin. This was another job, that was all, and they were professionals who would do a first class job.

All except me, thought Zimmerman. The irony of the leader of the team having problems was not good but he was keeping it under wraps and it was only minutes before it would all be over; he would be, as leader, two million pounds richer.

The entire attack team and Service operatives were in position along the predetermined route. Andanson was positioned for the interception and could time the start of his run better if he could see the Mercedes approaching. He would wait and time it to the second before the car was upon him and then accelerate as it arrived at the tunnel entrance and execute his strike. He would be notified when the Mercedes reached the first control point and then, crucially the Invalides Bridge, giving him precious and precise seconds to prepare.

The attack bike with Tyler and Haussmann was positioned near the Invalides Bridge; from here they could join behind the Mercedes, posing as paparazzi, and begin their aggressive pursuit. Tyler had his flashgun ready but hidden in case anyone should realize it was not a camera. Grossman was to ride behind Tyler and Haussmann and check the occupants after the strike to see whether the attack had been successful. If in doubt, the two operatives waiting near to the Alma would be called in to administer the coup de grâce. This would take place ahead of the pursuing paparazzi, which mustn't see the attack vehicles; the assassins must be gone by the time they arrived. The operatives would be informed how much time they had to complete the attack before paparazzi arrival, from when the Mercedes passed under the Invalides Bridge; they would have a precise number of seconds to execute the attack. Zimmerman waited with Gould, in the white Mercedes back-up car.

Staying in the shadows, Zimmerman and Gould would follow behind the attack vehicles, prepared to scoop up injured operatives. Gould sensed a very pensive and anxious Zimmerman sitting next to him. He said nothing thinking it best if they concentrate on the job in hand. He thought that each person has their own way of handling such moments.

Zimmerman's mind wandered from the scene for just one moment. Seconds to go! He saw a young mother about to be torn from her children and denied the only true happiness she was ever to have in her life. She had been about to become happy and the beast had come to claim her; he was the beast. His mind seemed to drift into a semi-conscious state where he could see his own life panning out before him and he felt a cold sweat break on his forehead.

This was not him, he thought. 'I'm finished! Will I ever recover from this moment? God, will I get through this? This was pure evil! This moment will pass! This moment must pass!' A cold darkness reached into the night! He was about to become rich but had no feelings for wealth at all.

Gould nudged him. 'Are you all right?' he said nervously. 'They'll soon be here.' Seeing the boss in a distant state was not comforting.

'No,' said Zimmerman, 'but I shall do the job; have no fear.' He was thinking what the Service lads would do if they knew this was happening to him.

'Should I drive?' asked Gould. 'We are only back up so it might be best if I took the wheel; it's nearly time.'

Zimmerman was reluctant to relinquish control but this was almost over and it was more important to complete the job, so acceded to Gould's suggestion, knowing he was finished.

Gould said. 'Don't worry, one good turn deserves another,' realizing that Zimmerman was suffering.

Both men, who had changed irrevocably through this operation, now changed seats. Zimmerman found himself thanking God once again, this time for allowing him a back-up driver.

The secure mobile rang and Zimmerman answered the call.

'This is the Ritz control point,' said the voice, 'how are things your end?'

'Fine,' said Zimmerman; still trembling.

'Good. They are standing by the rear entrance and the Mercedes is just pulling up. The attack has begun!'

Zimmerman had abandoned hope of feeling better, so just accepted he must survive for a moment longer. He didn't even have to drive the car but it didn't stop the whirring sensation in his head and the pounding of his heart.

'Get ready!' Zimmerman murmured, as Gould started the engine and warmed the car for the imminent move to be behind the attack bikes that were now revving their engines. Service operatives would continue to block the exit from the expressway and then come behind the attack vehicles; following the same escape route.

Tyler checked his flashgun was in position and asked Haussmann if he was ready.

Haussmann replied, 'Never better!'

Zimmerman called Grossman to find he too was in fine form and had no reservations. He called Andanson and got a very terse response. He was fine and waiting! Zimmerman realized that people on a high didn't want to discuss the time of day or make irrelevant conversation. They were in total concentration! The Service would handle the aftermath, so all the team must do was execute the attack and disappear.

The second control point came on the line. 'They are approaching, you have seconds left. Be ready!'

All extraneous thoughts went into the ether as everyone concentrated. The subjects' car was reported at the Invalides Bridge, and Tyler and Haussmann put the bike into gear, revved the engine and waited.

They pulled alongside the Mercedes to let Paul know he needed to go faster. Zimmerman and Gould waited for the attack vehicles to come through and follow.

The Mercedes was moving at speed, followed closely by Tyler and Haussmann, who aggressively and dangerously closed in, encouraging Paul to drive faster still. The acceleration of the BMW bike was stunning; no car could live with it!

Andanson saw the vehicles approaching and started towards the middle of the road, so as to be in a position to block the Mercedes' path when it entered the tunnel, and then began accelerating rapidly as it approached the tunnel entrance.

Zimmerman and Gould moved behind the whole group mindful of where the pursuing paparazzi were because, as the last of the attack vehicles, they were the ones the paparazzi would see, if anyone, and that must be avoided.

The Mercedes started to go faster now they had seen the bikes behind them, thinking, as they were supposed to think, that these were aggressive paparazzi and not that their lives were in mortal danger.

Inside the Mercedes, Paul was trying to keep the car ahead of the pursuing bikes and wondering how they were able to keep up with him so easily. He must negotiate this tunnel, take the next turn off and get his boss to the apartment. The bikes continued to press the car, forcing Paul to enter the tunnel at far too high a speed to permit it to stay on the road.

As the Mercedes reached the fault in the road at the tunnel entrance, Haussmann accelerated his bike to get in front of the Mercedes, carefully avoiding the road fault and Tyler delivered his deadly stun directly into Paul's eyes. Paul was now blinded and unable to further control the car as it leapt into the air when it travelled over the fault at the tunnel entrance.

At the same instance, the explosive device fitted to the Mercedes was triggered, but didn't seem to have the desired effect. Paul was still in control of the Mercedes and was fighting to steer the car away from the pillars. Andanson's Fiat was well positioned to the right of the Mercedes blocking its path and, when Paul tried to avoid colliding with the Fiat that he knew was there before he was blinded, he was forced to swerve in the opposite direction thus striking the Fiat.

Paul's reflexes were outstanding, considering his sight had been impaired. He maintained control of the Mercedes and avoided smashing into the Fiat, although he clipped its rear and bounced off the kerb at the tunnel's entrance. The Mercedes continued into the tunnel because Paul had maintained control and straightened up. A further connection from the Fiat, after massive acceleration from Andanson to get in front once more and Paul, unable to see, had instinctively turned the wheel back away from where he knew there was a car and braked hard. It was too late for braking and the car was already skidding into the thirteenth pillar.

'Moron!' thought Zimmerman, who saw the action as he

approached the tunnel entrance. 'Andanson swore he wouldn't collide with the damn car! We now have a major problem. There will be evidence all over the place. The Service will have to act fast.'

Pierre Grossman came alongside the wrecked Mercedes and slowed his bike down to see the damage. Had they been successful? He saw severe damage to the Mercedes and, believing the Princess was still alive, accelerated his bike out of the tunnel, following the others to the Embassy and telephoning Morison to give his account of the scene. The signal was that the Princess was still alive but it was believed all the others had perished. The job was not complete.

Tyler, Haussmann and Andanson were long gone! Having delivered their deadly stun, they drove straight through the tunnel and turned right up the rue Debrousse towards the Avenue du President Wilson and then into the Rue Jean Goujon and straight back to the safety of the Embassy enclosure. Pierre Grossman followed after he had made his assessment of the wreck. Andanson drove his damaged car along the same route and Zimmerman and Gould followed in their White Mercedes and were the last to leave the scene. Their work was done except for the debriefing that would come later to assist the sweepers in cleaning up and prepare the spin for public consumption.

If any vehicle had been incapacitated then it would have been very difficult to explain away but, apart from the Fiat, they were home free. At least the Fiat could be driven away from the scene but they would need to find an explanation for this collision with the Princess's car. The Service had already prepared the ground in case there should be any errors such as this. They had come this far and they were not about to lose now because of one man's incompetence.

At the Embassy, the vehicles all returned within five minutes of each other and drove in through the large gates. Zimmerman and Gould returned last and the gates were closed; all operatives then gathered together in a pre-prepared room. All were relieved and, although still on adrenalin highs, the tension had gone. It was over and appeared to have gone very well.

'Fine,' thought an angry Morison, 'your work is done and now ours begins.'

No more need for private discussions was felt necessary, as he approached Zimmerman and said, 'What the fuck happened with Andanson? Does he know what he's done? He promised he wouldn't collide with the Mercedes and has jeopardized the whole operation and God knows what!'

Zimmerman was expecting this response and was feeling fine, since the pressure had gone and the act was fait accompli. 'I know, it's a risk you run when you are murdering someone,' said a sarcastic Zimmerman, thinking that a criticism at this stage was an irrelevance.

Andanson walked over to Morison and said, 'It was impossible to prevent the collision. The reason we collided is Paul was blinded and if he had been able to see he would have instinctively avoided me. But he only knew roughly where I was and I couldn't get out of the way without letting him off the hook. I think you would have liked that even less!'

Morison didn't reply, but moved to his team and whispered something to them. Then another person entered the room who addressed everyone without introducing himself.

'I shall prepare you for the return trip to England but first you will go into session with some of our officers for a full debrief on any unexpected events or witnesses you may have noticed,' he said, looking in the direction of Andanson. 'Your time with us will be brief. We shall start very soon so enjoy your coffee. You will soon leave in the darkness. Nobody must see you depart this Embassy.'

DAMAGE LIMITATION

As the Service team expected and hoped, the whole tunnel was alive with people within minutes of the attack. The police would take a while to arrive but even then couldn't achieve much until sufficient backup arrived.

There had been ample time for Fred Atkinson and his men to ensure their target wouldn't survive and then disappear amongst the gathering throng. Atkinson and his team, who had been lying in wait in case there was a major blunder, moved across from the edge of the Alma Bridge and approached the Mercedes. Their worst-case aftermath scenario was where all their intended victims survived the attack but they were ready for whatever was encountered.

Zimmerman had been driving the white back-up Mercedes for the purpose of removing dead or injured agents but this hadn't been required, so he and Gould drove straight back to base. They were relieved no disabled or dead agents needed lifting to the Embassy but now had the problem of the main target having survived the attack. A report was received from Pierre Grossman, who had slowed down and checked the Mercedes just after the impact, it appeared that the Princess was alive. Atkinson knew there were seconds remaining, pre-mayhem.

Tenebrous killers swept from the darkness and opened the Mercedes' door. They thought all the occupants were dead except for their principal target, so they administered a lethal dose of slow-acting poison to the Princess, ensuring death within hours, and slunk back into the shadows.

Atkinson telephoned Morison and Stephens to apprise them of the position. Now, with their predetermined task of administering the coup de grâce complete, the Service needed to assess the damage caused by a semi-bungled assassination. Bungled, because the people would now be aware of the probable truth through the unexpected collision with the Fiat but they must never know the actual truth. 'Deniability' was needed; in fact, they would rely on 'deniability' from this moment on. The one blessing: no operatives had been killed or injured in the attack but now this new danger threatened! Because the Fiat and Mercedes had collided, more evidence had been placed into the public domain. This was going to accentuate and accelerate the dangers MI6 must prevent because it increased the probability in people's minds that this was murder, focusing attention on the party with the greatest motive; the monarchy. The last thing MI6 wanted!

In the minute of Atkinson's departure, a number of passers-by and paparazzi began taking photographs and some entered the Mercedes to see whether the occupants were still alive. Two passing policemen arrived and tried to control the pandemonium that engulfed the scene but all Service personnel had long gone.

Stephens and Caruthers couldn't resist driving by the crash posing as ordinary motorists to observe the site. They concluded that all appeared satisfactory and, in any event, they had just received a report from Fred Atkinson and knew the job was done. Next on the agenda, and where speed was crucial, was the clean-up plus the careful handling of information that must, at all costs, be controlled.

While Stephens and Caruthers were watching the scene from their car they could see paparazzi arrive: on one bike there were two riders. One of these dismounted and walked over to the Mercedes, putting his head into the rear of the car while the other remained by the bike.

'The cover gets better,' thought Stephens, as he smugly reclined in the seat of his Renault.

Caruthers asked Stephens when an answer on the level of French police support could be expected, but both agents knew Morison had begun his charm offensive with the French authorities within minutes of the attack. He couldn't approach the French before the attack or it would be known the British Secret Service had planned and carried out the murder, so the request was made immediately afterwards. Then, looking suitably distraught but efficient, a request made to political contacts for help in preventing a British national crisis; they knew the French authorities would respond favourably.

The discussions took place at the highest levels with the French Interior Ministry, and the decisions taken were difficult for those in authority who were not party to this crime but knew it was a crime. They were forced to set aside all within them that was decent because of their State's perception of 'the greater good.'

From the perspective of the French Government, who knew this was murder, there was the choice of telling the truth and letting the British take the consequences or acceding to their request to cover up the murder and propound a convincing argument that this was an accident.

'Thank God it's a new British government,' said Stephens. 'They've hardly had time to get their feet under the table, so should be very malleable. The previous government under Prime Minister Major would have taken the consequences, not to mention our heads.'

Full French political and police support was needed to keep all evidence hidden. After 12.21pm on Sunday 31st August 1997, the most complex and dangerous pack of lies ever thrust upon the world concerning a sudden death was about to be launched.

The sweepers were on site and had begun their work; like carrion flitting through the darkness, cleansing the result of pure evil. While Morison was ensconced with his French connections, considering all priorities for the cover up, an assessment was being conducted of the murder site. It was clear there was a pressing need for the evidence to be removed from the tunnel and destroyed, so the cooperation of the French police was of the utmost urgency. This must be immediate, to contain the truth about Diana's murder; if not, then momentum would gather and people would quickly realise the truth.

The Service would deny the existence of any car colliding with the Mercedes and have the police remove all the debris from inside the tunnel before anyone noticed. They must also cover the Mercedes, so that nobody could see the white marks from the collision with the Fiat clearly visible on its side and move it to a safe police compound away from prying eyes. It was very important that nobody should conclude there was another car and, heaven forbid, even determine what model and type. It was important the French police were able to deny the existence of another car and, if they could, then the biggest and most dangerous error of the attack could be eradicated. It was also crucial the Princess's body was treated in such a manner that any remaining evidence of pregnancy and poison would be expunged and any witnesses who saw the attack, silenced.

It was going to be difficult to persuade the French police that they should take statements from witnesses, accepting those that supported an 'accident theory', whilst rubbishing all those whose testimony suggested even the possibility of murder. Nobody must be allowed to interview witnesses or else the subterfuge would be revealed.

Morison thought, 'People will believe this is murder unless we're successful; we must be prepared. There is certainly going to be a conspiracy theory around this attack but we must try to eliminate all evidence because, without it, any theory is just hot air that's going nowhere. They can theorise all they want! If any evidence leaks out, we can still refuse the people an investigation by just not saying anything but would still have a problem that could cause serious damage.'

They were asking a great deal of the French police and many favours were going to be called in this day. Morison knew the importance of dealing with this as number one priority, but also needed feedback from the attack team to ensure everything had been covered. It was, therefore, crucial that Zimmerman and his team were de-briefed quickly to identify areas where this was needed.

Morison thought, 'By the end of the day I must have a full report from the team censored and leaked to the police. I am not expecting anything from our guys, since they were busy doing their job and then escaping the scene, but we must make sure.'

An immediate debrief was essential or valuable time could be lost. If they had nothing much to tell, as expected, then it wouldn't take long to recount anyway. Morison needed to identify all action points by the evening so precise instructions could be given; it was crucial nothing leaked out or the game was up.

The MI6 Service team of Stephens and Caruthers et al that had been flown in especially for the hit were returning to England from an airport south-west of Paris while Morison continued his cajoling of the French authorities for their support on the crisis that now enveloped the British nation. This was going to require assistance from the highest level because of the evidence. The only reasoning they could use with the French authorities was that Diana might have been murdered by some unknown group of people and, if known as murder, it would cause a major crisis in the UK, whoever was responsible. People would blame the monarchy and that could be fatal.

Morison's task at this stage was to persuade the French to assist by investigating, but to keep the facts from the press and reveal them only to the British authorities, to avert a major crisis. The French were almost certainly going to help, as the British would in similar circumstances, but they mustn't know Diana was murdered by her own people because that could freak out the French President and his cooperation was essential. Morison knew people at the highest level in the French Interior Ministry who were ultimately responsible for the investigation of this crime, so was well placed to seek favours.

At a now much quieter Embassy, Zimmerman was numbed! To outside eyes he had recovered, and gave nothing away, but this operation had destroyed him. He just wanted to get away. He thought, 'A few more hours and I will be in a sunny clime away from all this deception and starting a whole new life.' He felt much better than before the strike but knew he had reached the end of the line with this sort of work and wasn't sorry.

Fred Atkinson, the sweeper in chief, looked around as he walked into the room, where Zimmerman and his team waited in muted anticipation, eager to leave. Atkinson was a short, small and bespectacled man with thin, wiry grey hair, in his early fifties, with a narrow face and dark brown, lifeless eyes. He did away with the niceties of an introduction; everyone knew who he was so he began not expecting the meeting to last more than five minutes.

'We need to move this meeting quickly because the team on the ground are waiting for a report they must have immediately. During the attack you will have been focusing on the job in hand but did any of you see anything by way of witnesses, either before, during or after the attack?'

Tyler said, 'Before we took up position to wait for the Mercedes to arrive, we did have several cars go past us but were fortunate during the attack. As you say, we were concentrating on other matters. It's certain that there will be witnesses. At the speed we were travelling, and with cars and bikes surrounding the car, someone must have seen us.'

'Anybody else have comments?' asked Atkinson.

James Andanson spoke up and described how there were more people than he had expected and some must have seen what happened. He said he noticed a few details while waiting for the Mercedes and recounted the moment before it arrived.

'While I was waiting, I saw several cars going past and was very conscious of who might be looking my way. A few people noticed my car near the tunnel entrance but I really don't think anybody took any serious interest. It's impossible to say who those people were. After the attack some cars spotted me leaving the tunnel because my exhaust was making a noise from my collision and drawing attention. Someone must have seen me but I couldn't say who. I was in a hurry not to be there!'

He felt foolish to have botched the attack but didn't feel totally responsible. It was the blinding of Paul that caused the cars to collide and he hadn't calculated for that. It wasn't his fault! Paul would instinctively have steered the car away from the Fiat if he had been able to see, but was travelling at a high speed and quickly became disorientated. Andanson said he needed to stay close to pursue the Mercedes further into the tunnel or it might not have crashed into the pillars and the attack would have been a complete failure. He had never been involved in a hit where military strobe guns had been used and he had no way of calculating the consequences. The Service, however, had used them before so should have realised and briefed him.

Zimmerman thought this was a perfect example of preparing the ground well before any action and not bringing in people at a late stage. Andanson was brought in at the last moment and, if it had been sooner, this possibility might have been considered. Zimmerman thought Andanson had a good point, and he sympathised. Andanson's awareness of witnesses was similar so it was apparent nobody really saw anything that could help to identify possible hostile witnesses.

'Right,' thought Atkinson. 'Not much information but it completes the picture. There were a significant number of people present! We do have a witness problem!'

The adrenalin rush of the operatives was damping down but would take hours to completely subside. 'Have we succeeded?' Zimmerman asked Morison, anxious to know whether he had earned his blood money.

'Yes,' said Morison, 'but we had to help the principal target on the way. We think she was the only one who survived.'

It was now Zimmerman's turn to feel disgust at the manner in which Morison spoke of someone for whom he had considerable respect and he thought Morison didn't have to be so callous. Perhaps, thought Zimmerman, its Morison's way of dealing with his own feelings; anyway, it's over for us.

Without further comment Zimmerman left the room, feeling unwell, and went outside into the night air. He reached the steps to the building and steadied himself against the pillar of the outer wall. Holding the side of the edifice he sat, pressing his head in his hands and raised his head, looking blankly into a hazy distance on this warm summer evening. He knew this feeling of nausea was not transient. This was his soul crying in despair; his very being fleeing into the shadows of his mind. His life's purpose scurried into the darkness. A rage and anger overcame him when he realised that his life had, on this day, irrevocably changed forever. Money wouldn't change this! The feeling would not be gone in the morning. This anguish was his new place in the world; his new self and a living hell that would endure until the day he died.

The team were driven straight to the airport at Le Toussous, west of Orly, and took a prearranged private flight back home, very keen to leave French soil. The Service had not given details of the return flight to the operatives before the hit, just in case one of them had been incapacitated in the assault and was rescued by the emergency services; in error! Who knows what someone might say when under the influence of morphine? 'It wouldn't have gone that far,' thought Morison, but it was best to be safe. Now it was down to the sweepers, the political wizardry and lies of the spin-doctors to fool the people that this was a dreadful accident and get back to normal.

Morison had an urgent need to control the availability of evidence that would ensue from an examination of the tunnel and deny the existence of another car being involved in the murder. The police were confident this could be achieved by closing down the crime scene as quickly as possible and collecting evidence to hide it from prying eyes. They had now received instructions from the Ministry.

The Mercedes needed to be removed from the tunnel and impounded, together with all the evidence to ensure nobody gained access. But Morison thought this mustn't be done with indecent haste because it would raise suspicions why the car was being removed so quickly and they couldn't afford to be obvious. The car should remain in the tunnel, in his view, and the scene guarded to give the impression of a thorough job being done. But due to French police indifference, it might be difficult to persuade why road users should be inconvenienced any longer and the French weren't as motivated as the British to maintain an image.

Morison might have problems getting the police to do as he wished but couldn't afford to press too strongly or he might not like the answer and have further support refused. The car would be taken to a police barracks and remain unavailable to anyone. They didn't have to give a reason.

'Like us,' thought Morison. 'Thank God we are also unaccountable or we would never survive.' His main tasks were hiding the car debris from the press and dealing with Diana's body, to ensure the evidence of pregnancy and poison were removed.

The paparazzi arrests were convenient but wouldn't stick because there were too many witnesses and forensics from the tunnel, so he needed to invoke plan two immediately. 'We must prepare the ground for Mr Paul to have his drinking spree and ensure the samples taken from his body are switched with another subject. We should find one in one of the morgues so that Paul's body will yield an excessive amount of alcohol so he can take the blame. This will necessitate tampering with test results, so we must keep both options open for a while and hope for a suitable cadaver. It's critical the paparazzi assist us in focusing media attention away from the truth, at least until we have prepared the ground.'

Meanwhile MI6 were busy back in London and away from the murder scene. Morison continued to reason the Paris position. The photographs taken in the tunnel showing white marks on the Mercedes' side from where it collided with the Fiat must be seized. The world would otherwise know there was more to this saga than there seemed. This must be prevented at all costs!

'We need to establish who took photographs in the tunnel and all must be retrieved by the police, confiscated and destroyed as fast as possible,' Morison thought.

He ensured the police moved very quickly and by Sunday afternoon, the afternoon of the murder, photographers had either been interviewed or their homes raided and photographs seized, using the cover that it would be indecent to publish them. MI6 got wind that the Sipa and the Sola agencies had photographs that were going to be sold for high sums and they moved very quickly to seize them.

Back in Paris, the tunnel had been cleared within a few hours of the murder and the police hadn't taken any notice of Morison's pleas to delay. One of the reasons France was chosen for the attack in the first place was because the police had effective carte blanche in doing as they pleased and nobody dared question their behaviour. This, together with the French medical profession's secrecy rules, and MI6 had a wonderful platform from which to exercise control over the ensuing 'investigation'. It was inconceivable to the police that people should be allowed to question their autonomy and, since the French people accepted all their police explanations, they expected the world to concur.

Morison was grateful for French cooperation but frustrated that he couldn't run the show and must liaise with the French police. The next stage of dealing with the propaganda must be ready before news was released to the media. It was crucial he sold the worlds public that this was, despite all the evidence now available, a very tragic accident; it was undoubtedly the biggest sell of his Service career.

Morison didn't waste time following the attack. Senior people at the French Ministry of the Interior were approached and their help requested. Morison had raised the Ministry at 12.55am and, portraying his best ham performance of the grieving British national, persuaded his opposite French number to play ball and order police to follow strict guidelines.

He needed to meet his counterparts and look them in the eye to see whether they would cooperate. It wasn't known if, or when, permission would be forthcoming so he asked the police to ensure nothing was done that would jeopardise their request, should it be granted.

It was approaching 2.00am on Sunday morning but everyone was wide-awake. This was a once in a lifetime event and Morison needed to be at his best. The French police were already on site with a variety of senior ranks, and the head of the criminal brigade was on the way, together with the Chief Paris prosecutor and Chief of the Paris police. This alarmed Morison who thought that having police personnel of this rank on site, specifically trained to deal with criminal matters, meant the press would quickly pick up on the police regarding this as a crime, making it more difficult to persuade the public on Service reasoning for the crash. It would be obvious to anyone this was being treated as a crime, so they needed a good and persuasive response ready for the inevitable questions.

In the event, the police made a statement confirming murder that caused heightened nervousness in the Service; this would need to be turned around quickly. Having received high-level French political support, but not before the first police statement had been issued, the Service ensured the French police followed up with a second statement, only hours after the first, saying they attended the crash site with high-ranking officers from their criminal brigade in case there had been any criminal activity, but they were now content it was an accident. There was no evidence to suggest otherwise.

'OK, we can handle that,' thought Morison, 'but not if proof exists of a Fiat in collision with the Mercedes. We either admit to that now, in case it emerges later, or we try not to reveal it and then say later that we didn't want to warn the driver of the Fiat we were on to him. Yes, that fits nicely with our reasoning. This way we also get the chance never to reveal the existence of the Fiat, unless absolutely necessary and we have the perfect reason why we didn't tell the truth straight away if caught.'

Morison met with his Ministry of the Interior contact, Jean-Pierre Blanc, at a police station near to the Alma tunnel, where they were able to discuss the evening's activities in some detail and privacy. They were joined by a high-ranking officer in the Paris police department, Jean-Claude Chantais, who had rushed over to this meeting with his political boss, Monsieur Blanc and this MI6 agent who was ostensibly attempting to defend his country from serious political damage.

Chantais welcomed Morison and Blanc with a stern and weary bearing and asked they join him in one of the rear rooms. He ordered a pot of coffee be brought in, thinking they were going to need sustenance for this session. The police chief was sympathetic towards Morison, believing that his feelings of sorrow were genuine and placed a hand gently on Morison's shoulder beckoning him to be seated.

Morison shrank from the gesture, as deftly as he could; his disingenuous comments were not marrying up with his emotions. He let it be known he had a duty to perform and excused his response behind the front of doing his duty. Morison began to speak, knowing he couldn't afford to rush this meeting and give the indication of being indifferent or arrogant; he had a job to do.

He began; 'Thank you for meeting with me at this tragic time, gentlemen. In the morning the British nation, and indeed the world, will be shattered with this dreadful news. The Princess is still alive, so we must hope she survives, but we need to prepare the world, God forbid, if she dies.' Further disingenuous comments slipped from his tongue with a natural ease. 'We have our concerns about this accident or, indeed, whatever else you may determine it to be when you have concluded your investigations, but we have a serious problem whatever the outcome, and whether it's an accident or not.

'We cannot win either way because if it's an accident nobody will believe us, and if you find that someone has carried out a strike against the Princess then, as you may never find the culprits, the world will believe the British monarchy ordered it and we have a full blown crisis. This will also have serious implications for our political status in the world and especially within the European Union. Before you find those responsible, even if you find the culprits sometime in the future, it will be too late because the public reaction to this will be immediate and we would have a constitutional crisis in the UK that would destabilise the monarchy and, possibly, the government.'

Morison knew he mustn't tell these people what to do, so he needed to suggest ideas and ask opinions rather than dictate. He also knew he mustn't appear to be asking them to withhold from seeking the murderers of the Princess, since that would give the game away. He needed to give the impression of a clear desire for justice but for precedence to be given to the survival of the Establishment; that the French would understand.

He continued, 'This incident must be portrayed as an accident to the world. All evidence must be covered up and details presented to support that idea and then we have a chance. If, of course, you find sufficient evidence for murder and who is responsible at an early stage in your investigations, that is another matter; we would be most grateful but, being realistic, do you think it likely these people will be found? We can always explain ourselves away should this occur.'

Jean-Pierre Blanc thought for a few moments and replied, 'It will be difficult for us to authorise the covering up of any facts that we find during an investigation. It couldn't happen without authorisation from the very top because no one else would accept the responsibility, especially with one of the victims being Diana. If our people found we had withheld justice from them, they would never forgive us. It would be political suicide!

'I do understand your concerns, however, and am prepared to see what the view is from our side. You will need to prepare your top opposite number to speak with him and put this request personally, before he would even consider such a plan. In the meantime I shall instruct our police to go about their duty but ensure all evidence is kept under wraps. If this is going to happen it will need to be within the next few hours, so we can prepare our presentation.'

Blanc turned to Chantais; 'Will you be able to contain the evidence from this scene and divert attention from the thought of murder for the next twenty-four hours, at least, so as to retain our options of resuming the pursuit of a murder enquiry, or of maintaining the covering up of evidence, if this request is agreed?'

'Yes', said Chantais; 'We shall pursue this in our normal manner, carefully controlling the witness evidence that we gather and information from the crash site.

'The one thing that may seem out of the ordinary is our early opening of the tunnel. We have made our checks, bagged the information and removed the vehicle to one of our compounds, refusing access to anyone.'

'Yes,' said Blanc, 'keeping sensitive information secret in no way prejudices our final decision. Also I understand from our commander at the crash site there is an initial feeling the paparazzi have been heavily involved in this and taken into custody, so we shall pursue them. We may find our guilty party lies here. If not, we should continue to prosecute this line of reasoning until we decide on our course of action which is useful in diverting attention away from our true course. Does that seem reasonable to you?'

'Yes,' said Chantais. 'We can show good cause why the paparazzi were arrested and this will calm the public. We shall also be seen to be taking action which will buy us time.'

Morison breathed a sigh of relief! He knew these people were about to receive political instructions they wouldn't wish to comply with and all that was needed was for him to deliver a slight faux pas to give them an excuse to thwart him. Turning his thoughts back to current requirements, he knew he must focus on the other critical areas needing immediate attention; he turned to Chantais.

'Do you think there is anything else requiring our immediate attention that would make it impossible to satisfy our request if it's approved by your side?' Morison was concerned that the police must be on side now or it would be too late.

'Yes,' said Chantais. 'There are a few more matters we must control if your request is to remain viable. We need to interview the witnesses of the crash and list all their observations. It depends on the witnesses but we need to emphasise the evidence from those who support an accident and suppress what we don't want to hear. We must ensure that none of them speak with the press within the next twenty-four hours. If your request is denied then we will still have the witness evidence to use in the normal pursuit of our investigations. We must order this now!

'Another thing that needs to be controlled is the footage from the CCTV cameras along the route from the Ritz hotel to the Alma. This will show us what cars were in the vicinity and whether any cars interfered with the Mercedes; this must be seized and kept top secret. It may assist in identifying the attackers since it is probable this is murder but, if we wish to assist the British, this footage could be fatal.

'If it shows us who murdered these people, we can move quickly and not need to pretend to the world. We can secure justice instead. However, working on the lines this won't be possible I shall continue with our immediate needs.'

Chantais' police instincts of bringing people to justice were always going to cut across any order to refrain from a genuine pursuit. He continued, 'The one other crucial requirement for a successful subterfuge is that we need a judge who will support our requirements if we are to present the information as you have requested. He must be of impeccable character and, not only respected by all, but also someone who will follow a political line, if required. There are judges on whom our top people have previously relied to follow these requirements and that person will need to know why we are doing this, otherwise he would feel his integrity impugned.

'If we don't have a judge who is supportive then we shall fail, because any judge may find evidence and follow that, not necessarily taking the course we wish. He must be in the confidence of our senior political hierarchy! There is one that comes to mind who doesn't hesitate to take on powerful or dangerous people when asked by those in power. He has dealt with sensitive political matters before and would suit extremely well I believe, but that is not my call. All routine matters will be conducted as normal and, so long as we know which way to play this soon, we should be OK. We need this decision urgently, and shall inform our side accordingly.'

'Right,' said Morison. 'We shall seek to obtain the necessary clearances from London and prevent a catastrophic blow to our Establishment.'

The evening wore on and the Princess had finally been collected by ambulance from the crash site and was on the way to the hospital. Officials from the French judiciary, the Interior Ministry and the upper echelons of the Paris police had arrived in the Alma tunnel by 1.30am and were making decisions concerning the running of this enquiry.

Caruthers met with senior colleagues in London; all went into immediate session, knowing they were under great pressure of time. The British Prime Minister had been woken and briefed by the Service who knew what the outcome of the Princess's visit to the hospital would be but the French authorities did not. They all anxiously awaited news.

The witnesses were the most important immediate threat, should the British request be approved, because they were the least controllable. They must be identified as a matter of urgency and their testimony checked.

The police interrogations had already begun but more witnesses would come forward most probably during the next few weeks; this was virtually certain. The police couldn't be sure whether the testimony could be controlled, but they could give credibility to the favoured ones, discredit the others and reinstate them later if the British request was denied. Witnesses who gave very damning testimony must be ignored or ridiculed, and depositions refused. If there were a large number of hostile and determined witnesses giving accounts to the press, then all was lost. They must be interrogated at once and the most potentially damning ones controlled or 'advised' not to come forward.

The Minister of the Interior, Jean Paul Chevènement, told the chief of police, Philippe Massoni, to retain all information for his eyes only.

Some witnesses started to give their accounts of what they saw, first to the two police patrolmen who arrived on the scene and subsequently the senior officers who quickly followed. The first indications were that this was a crime and so the Criminal Brigade Commissioner, Martine Monteil, was put in charge of operations. She felt there was sufficient information to decide that this was an attack on the Mercedes and wrote a report confirming this view, completed by 2.00am, only ninety minutes or so after the crash. She had now told the world this was a murder inquiry.

The paparazzi's evidence was ignored because they needed to be treated as suspects but the evidence started to build from witness accounts and some was extremely damning. The Brigade Chief's report went against the British, because, at this stage, the French had still taken no decision with regard to cooperation on the cover up. Once approval had been obtained, the police and the Interior Ministry knew they must reverse this statement. The report had gone to the foreign press as follows:

"According to the first witnesses, the Mercedes, proceeding down this portion of the road at high speed, appears to have swerved because the chauffeur was being pursued and interfered with by the vehicles of the journalists who had given chase. The driver must have lost control of his vehicle and failed to recover. Again, according to the first witness, the paparazzi who were pursuing the Mercedes, hastened to take photos after the incident neglecting their elementary gestures of assistance to people in danger. Based on these observations, the first policeman on the scene proceeded to take the photographers in for questioning."

This was unfortunate if they were assisting the British, since it clearly showed the chief person in charge of the Paris criminal brigade, in whom the French have a justifiable pride, was of the opinion that vehicles interfered with the Mercedes just prior to the crash and this was supported by several witness statements. Now the police needed to reverse this view if the British request was approved and explain why they had changed their initial view. To say there were no vehicles interfering with the Mercedes, that they had been somehow spirited away, was the difficult part and impossible if existence of the Fiat became known. How were they going to justify their continued detention of the paparazzi when evidence from the witnesses indicated they were right first time?

Morison was informed on the status of current events by his Paris agents and was getting nervous. Matters were not going well! The French police and authorities were being cooperative, but were taking too long to decide on their course of action; everything else was moving fast. Caruthers also needed to move fast to prevent a total catastrophe. The logical consistency of information that Morison had wished to present to the world was not going to happen and cracks were already beginning to appear. If they weren't careful, the press would realize there was something amiss; fatal! Matters had to move faster still and decisions made now or it would all be too late. The French police must retract this statement and make an attempt at steering public thinking away from murder but before this could happen it was necessary to obtain the French authorities support for the cover up; this was urgent!

Caruthers had been met at City Airport on his return to London and taken to Vauxhall Cross, MI6 London HQ. The top brass hastily convened a meeting, having risen from their beds at an ungodly hour on Sunday morning, to take crucial decisions that could affect the future of the monarchy forever. Their first consideration was how to approach the French and they were swift in their decision.

'We need,' said Caruthers, 'for the French to accept our request in full, as already briefed to you. They must involve us with the investigation so we can keep tabs on events. If they get close to suspecting our involvement, we have a problem but, with the support of the Prime Minister, I am confident they will back our line provided they don't have evidence of our complicity.'

Peter Caruthers was keen to resolve this and return to France. He knew Morison had been right and they must involve the Prime Minister, who had been informed of the crash within the hour. Diana was still alive, so they would need to act before the world knew what they already knew; that she would not survive much longer.

Caruthers spoke again; 'We shall brief the PM on the position and tell him we need to ask this of the French authorities, otherwise we face a major crisis. He will need to get his head around our reasoning, since he was not party to it so we must allow him time. I shall tell him time is of the essence and we must act within hours to preserve the status quo. I don't anticipate any resistance. It's plausible, and if he doesn't comply, he risks losing his new found power and the monarchy will be at serious risk! We must act decisively!'

Within the hour, a phone call was made to the French and all was now set for the Security Services to be singing from the same hymn sheet on both sides of the Channel. Caruthers ordered his plane be made ready forthwith and sped to the airport, contacting his French colleagues and Morison. A meeting between the French police and MI6 was arranged to determine the level of disinformation needed to achieve this British objective. A whole raft of ideas must be agreed, at once, because people would soon be clamouring for news and God knows how they were going to react.

Each item for consideration was now taken separately and a course of action agreed. The meeting began with a list from the police describing what evidence existed that needed to be neutralised. There hadn't been much to implicate MI6 and Morison was at least thankful for that small mercy. If the French police had realised the people they were about to help had executed this deliberate attack, there would have been a serious reaction. The police would now remain on side and jointly lie to the public about the whole affair, telling them whatever MI6 wished, even though they had a different perception of what they were supporting. The French believed they were helping the British people prevent a crisis; the British knew the French were helping them escape with the most brutal murder of the century.

Morison was impressed by the list the Ministry of the Interior presented. He knew this level of detail was needed and read the entire document, making copious notes, waiting for the French to begin.

Jean-Claude Chantais was very thorough in his presentation and felt this was his big moment to impress his political boss sitting next to him. He waited half an hour for all present to review his document and then began.

'Gentlemen,' said Chantais, in his very good and almost unaccented English. 'I have produced a report on where we are with the investigation and listed the main items we need to address in order to control the information. Our current position is that we know a Fiat did indeed collide with the Mercedes both just before entering the tunnel and then seconds later about 100 metres further on. There were motorcycles and cars following and surrounding the Mercedes in a very suspicious way, and witnesses saw one of the motorcycles swerve in front of the Mercedes just before it entered the tunnel. There are also reports of a very powerful flash of light as the motorcycle swerved in front of the Mercedes, just before it entered the tunnel. White marks can be clearly seen on the Mercedes and these alone are complete giveaways. We believe the press may well have photographs of them and once the public see them; that's it!

'This is a deliberate attack on the Mercedes; there is too much evidence to suggest otherwise. We have informed the police of our requirements for this whole business to remain secret but there is evidence we have been unable to contain. I fear we shall need to acknowledge the existence of other vehicles soon.'

This one Morison noted! He was going to flatly refuse to allow anyone to admit to the Fiat because this was fatal to their chances of keeping the lid on.

'No,' said Morison, 'we need to keep that under wraps. Nobody must know of another car! I would like for the police to continue to deny its existence for the foreseeable future. We shall relent only if absolutely necessary.'

'Then, God help us!' he thought.

In the meantime, at around 4.00am, the police issued a further statement, countering the one they had made at 2.00am about this being murder. It reads as follows:

'None of the testimony heard thus far permits us to establish whether a vehicle could have approached the Mercedes to the point of touching it or making it leave its trajectory.'

Chantais knew how sensitive the British were about the Fiat because it was nigh on impossible to explain away and was as near to absolute proof of murder as the British public needed. He didn't realise the potentially lethal consequences to MI6 personnel who could not, under British law, be prosecuted for any off-shore crime but could still be hanged for treason.

189

He agreed, to Morison's great relief, that it would be best kept under wraps, so and agreed they would continue to deny the Fiat's existence for a while longer. A few more weeks might give them something else to use as an excuse for the Fiat's presence and thus minimise the damage. In the meantime they must continue to pretend that either the Fiat didn't exist, or was irrelevant to the investigation; this position must be maintained. Morison needed to go through all these areas of the 'investigation' and make specific decisions on each.

By 4.00pm the evidence on the extent of the witness problem was apparent and the initial reaction from the British and world public could be calculated. A major problem was clearly about to engulf them. Chantais was expecting the British contingent to be nervous and he was not wrong. His view was conceived from the perspective of an honourable French police officer who was collecting evidence and containing it, under political instructions. It didn't sit well.

Whilst these deliberations were continuing, news came in that caused a deathly silence to descend. The Princess had died! It was 4.10am and they had been notified of Diana's death although she had died a few hours earlier. The bodyguard was holding on to life and the doctors were hopeful.

Chantais felt anger! His work was about justice and defending life, not this! He wasn't enjoying the prospect of investigating the death of a person he personally admired and then sidelining the evidence to suit the agenda of people whom he didn't know and for whom he didn't much care. He had a duty to perform, however, and was following orders from on high, so had no option. Now he had the task of informing those assembled on measures he was taking that were way beyond his normal remit.

He had needed to do things before that were unsavoury, in the interests of his own country, since it went with the territory but this was for someone else and he didn't trust their reasoning. Why were they assisting in covering this up? He wasn't sure of British motives and was particularly concerned how a very well planned and executed attack involving several people, totally reliant on good intelligence, could possibly be carried out by anyone other than a large and well connected organisation.

He had received reports that there were a large number of people at the British Embassy that night. He couldn't help wondering why and where the British Security Services were when the attack went down. Why didn't they stop it? Why should he help them now? Morison knew the task ahead would be performed with less enthusiasm than normal unless he took great care. Chantais also knew he couldn't afford to fail! Why should he suffer in his career prospects through feeling natural concerns over what these people were doing when it wouldn't help anyone? He would be ignored or worse. If he didn't comply with these orders then the judgment would be that he was not doing his job, as it had been required of him from very high sources, so knew he must put these feelings behind him. It was more important to impress his political boss and concentrate on the job in hand. And now he had another item to add to his list: a possible survivor.

'This is an extremely sad moment for all of us but especially Tom Morison,' said Chantais looking in Morison's direction, testing his British counterpart's reaction. 'My deepest sympathies go to you and your nation.'

Morison was unsure of how to respond, so just sat impassively. It was better to let all think that he was in a state of shock.

Chantais didn't believe it but couldn't allow his thoughts to wander from his duty; only he would suffer if he did! He continued and described his view of the position. 'Let us all concentrate on the matter in hand and list the areas that need investigation. Bearing in mind the British request, all information must be restricted to me and a few of my officers. We have seven areas to consider, all of which could cause us to fail in this venture, so here they are:

Witnesses
Fiat collision (containing the crash site)
Henri Paul (Drunk, or not)
Appointment of a suitable judge
CCTV footage of murder route
The Princess's body
Paparazzi and their photographs
The Survivor

Taking each in turn, Chantais began: 'Witnesses. We know more witnesses will come forward so we shall review the implications of each testimony and decide how to deal with it. We have four so far, other than the paparazzi that you know we are treating differently.

191

Some will go to the press, expounding their own views and I can tell you that, from these testimonies alone, the world is going to know there were vehicles surrounding the Princess's car and that there was a collision; I don't see how we can avoid it.'

Chantais spoke, looking at an impassive Morison, who just sat searching his note pad. 'I have my doubts we shall succeed but we shall do our best.

'As you will see from your list these witnesses are: Gaëlle L'Hostis together with her boyfriend Benoit Boura, and two off duty chauffeurs Clifford Gooroovadoo and Olivier Partouche. These are the first four who came forward very soon after the crash. In précis they have all told us there were cars and motorcycles surrounding the Princess's car, just prior to the crash, and describe a scene that lends itself to a definite assassination. The criminal brigade was clearly right in their first instincts. I must tell you, with much regret Mr Morison, that your Princess of Wales was murdered.'

Morison sat, still looking at his notes, preferring to give an impression of despondency rather than ham it up with an act that could falter. 'I never was much of an actor,' he thought, 'so in these situations it's best to pretend I am upset or I risk giving the game away. They will sympathise with that and move on.'

Sure enough, Chantais continued with his report, having paused briefly. 'There are going to be several more witnesses from the number of people who were around last night; more than usual for a Sunday evening, despite its being the end of August. Had it been last weekend, there probably wouldn't have been any. We shall revisit the witnesses again in a few days and see where we are then.'

'Damn again,' thought Morison, 'but we couldn't determine when they would be in Paris. We just had to do the job when they arrived and that's that.'

'The Fiat collision,' Chantais continued. 'There was definitely a white car that collided with the Mercedes and it almost certainly influenced the crash. We shall need to find the owner of this car as quickly as possible.'

Morison had to think quickly and chipped in. 'We naturally want desperately to find whoever was responsible but, if we are trying to dumb this whole event down and deny the existence of a white car and then the press get wind that you are looking for it, there will be no room left for doubt on whether there was another car. The police have already regretfully made a statement that there were vehicles interfering with the car at the moment of impact and that, together with pursuit of another car, would be too much. It would in fact render the support you have kindly agreed to give us superfluous. Regretfully I must ask that you do not look for the car but concentrate on finding out what you can from evidence available in the tunnel, CCTV and from witnesses. We shall find the other car later if we have proof this was indeed an attack on the Princess of Wales.'

Morison was clearly thinking that he must keep the police concentrating on the investigation and keep a tight control on their activities. That way MI6 would get to find out what evidence had been inadvertently left behind and have the time to neutralise it; it was now all about suppression of evidence. The CCTV footage he needed to handle with great care! The French police would support this because they were following orders from their high command to assist, so MI6 should win both ways.

Chantais said, 'It's imperative we retain the evidence from the tunnel, keeping it and the Mercedes away from prying eyes, but we have a problem with the paparazzi photographs. We have tried to seize these over the last few hours and found nothing but have reason to believe much has been sent electronically abroad and here we have a major issue. The press agencies have been told to prevent photographs from entering general circulation and, since it will be considered indecent to show photographs of the wrecked Mercedes with dying people, we are reasonably optimistic of reclaiming most.

'One, however, will cause a problem! We believe images have been transmitted to a Mr Cherruault, who is the London agent of the Sipa agency, and must prevent these reaching the front pages of the press. We shall continue with our denials of the white car's existence, which we will have to do if we're not looking for it, otherwise people will wonder what's going on. No car; nothing to look for!'

Morison responded immediately; 'Let me have the details on the London agent of the Sipa agency and I shall convey them to the appropriate authority with a request to expedite a recovery.' Nobody needed to ask anything further on this point.

Henri Paul. Who and what they were going to blame for this crash was paramount in all their minds. The paparazzi would soon be cleared from any wrongdoing and then what? They needed a reason for this crash and the most logical, if not the only one available, was that Paul was intoxicated when he got into the car. If they fabricated the results of his samples then nobody would ever be able to prove otherwise and that should cause a dead end to any possible future investigation. They could ensure no independent tests were carried out and that nobody got close to Paul's remains but needed to begin these rumours quickly, in tandem with sustained aggression against the paparazzi, and then launch into the news it was Paul being drunk that caused the accident'.

This should also help with their inactivity on the white car because, if people believed they had their man, then the Fiat would quickly become irrelevant; or so they hoped. It was quickly discovered from tests that Paul had been drinking but the amount didn't satisfy their purpose. He must be seen as the reason for the crash and was the obvious scapegoat. He couldn't object; he was dead! This should satisfy an information hungry public that they had found the cause of this tragedy; so now to task. How were they going to raise the levels of alcohol in Paul's blood, and other samples, to achieve these results?

They couldn't contaminate the fluids in a corpse where the blood had ceased to flow, or in other tissues that would normally be investigated such as eye fluid. They must find a cadaver in the morgue and make a switch where samples had already been taken. It must be from one of the morgues; all were controlled by the police, and preferably the one Henri Paul had been taken to, where switching samples would be less risky.

Morison had already thought this through and was keen to ensure few people knew what was happening, but time was again critical. They needed to have support from some medical personnel and morgue staff who were needed to make the switch.

Chantais was clear this would require cash and quite a lot of it. He made it clear this would not be forthcoming from the French budget.

Morison nodded his acceptance of this position; this was going to be very expensive. He knew the French had taken the bait on the reasons for Henri Paul being used as a scapegoat and they must never know MI6 had planned it from the beginning. They had set Henri Paul up knowing he liked a drink but was also extremely conscientious and would never drink excessively whilst driving his boss. Having arranged for him to be off duty and brought back, they had allowed him to relax, have a few drinks, albeit insufficient for their purpose, and create a non-provable myth. Their half-truth, half lie was well embedded.

Appointment of suitable judge. There was no point in having a judge upset the apple cart by stating this was murder, since in France the judge has the dual responsibility of both investigating the crime and judging it. They needed a judge who would respond to the wishes of those in high political office otherwise they were wasting their time. This was something they agreed must be taken to a higher authority, and with some haste, but there wasn't much they could do today. This was an important issue to add to their growing list. Having found the chosen candidate, they would need to replace the duty judge and find a suitable reason for doing so without raising suspicions.

'CCTV footage of murder route,' Chantais continued. 'Witnesses have described vehicles surrounding the Mercedes as it approached and descended the ramp into the tunnel and there will be CCTV footage of these vehicles all along the route from where they joined the expressway, probably from the Ritz hotel. We are seizing this footage and it should help in determining what really happened.'

Morison interrupted; 'We must indeed seize this evidence but what will these tapes show? Presumably vehicles close to the Mercedes, but will they show us definite intent to do harm or just aggressive pursuit of a fast buck? We need to seize them and keep them for our attention. We can then decide later what to do about the detail if indeed there is anything to be done.'

'Yes,' said Chantais, 'we have taken the tapes to the local police station. They will be delivered this afternoon when we can review them; shall we reconvene at say, 2.00pm.'

'Could we not review them straight away?' asked Morison, very keen to know if they had a hot potato and something that needed urgent handling.

'Very well,' said Chantais, as he picked up the telephone and called the local station, tasking an officer to deliver them forthwith.

'Which part of the route will be shown by these photographs?' said Morison, hoping he wasn't showing his nervousness. It could show the bikes and the two cars they had used with registration numbers which, although false and untraceable, allowed witnesses the opportunity of saying they placed them here or there and gave more credibility to the stories that would be abounding that Diana had been brutally murdered. Anyhow, no need to speculate, we shall soon see for ourselves.

Before they could begin with the next item, the CCTV tapes from the tunnel arrived and all immediately departed for the dark room that had been prepared. Morison's blood ran cold as he saw the Fiat waiting near the tunnel entrance and the team pursuing the Mercedes. All was visible and left no doubt that this was a planned execution!

Chantais looked across at Morison, who felt the need to attempt a ham performance of horror and disgust. Chantais looked disturbed! He felt numbed! They would look for murderers but there was an instruction from on high not to let the public know. 'These are dangerous times,' thought Chantais.

Morison urged the French to find the killers but to continue to keep everything hidden.

'The Princesses' body.' Chantais was suppressing a natural suspicion of Morison. This didn't feel right! It was not his problem, however; but, having expressed his concern, he was instructed to keep an eye on his British protagonist.

He began, 'One of the most difficult items to overcome when perverting the truth is controlling the information emerging from post-mortem scrutiny. In France we control such results but what about the Princess's body when it's returned to the UK? Do you have the same level of control that will enable us to continue with the deception? There is no point in handling a situation here to find that she goes to the UK and the doctors make us all look like incompetent fools. What about other doctors doing further tests and what about an inquest that will be required under your law? In this situation you will have lost your objective.'

This was all directed at Morison, who knew that Chantais was asking for an immediate response. 'We have considered this point and you are quite right. We need to control the situation back home, or we are wasting our time.'

Morison acceded to this, knowing Chantais wasn't happy with his role, or with him, and wanted to try and reach out as a genuine grieving British national might. 'The British doctors involved will be difficult to manage, although we are optimistic about receiving support because those we shall ask to assist will be told we are protecting our country. Taking these people into our confidence will be essential, to a point, but only certain aspects of what we are trying to achieve.

'The Princess's body must be embalmed before it leaves France, so there won't be any evidence available to scrutinise. Can you handle that for us?' asked Morison.

'That will require permission from a relative,' said Chantais, 'and who would give it? It's illegal in France without such permission and what reason can you show? What reason can you possibly give?'

'We shall find an authority to grant it and so long as we have a loose reason, it will be fait accompli and voilà, the risk has gone,' Morison replied. 'I can assure you nobody will question us. You are able to control matters at your end because you have these very useful laws governing what medical information can be given out on any patient. One thing you must ensure, however, is that any blood samples the surgeons may have taken during last evening's treatment are seized immediately, together with the records.'

'Why is that so important?' asked Chantais, suspecting, but not knowing, that Morison's motive had a much darker aspect in not wanting evidence from blood testing to show.

'Because it completes the picture,' said Morison, 'and a pregnancy shown at this stage, should there be one, isn't terminal but could fuel more conspiracy theorists to embark on far-fetched ideas. It's best not to allow that opportunity, yes?' Morison continued with his attempts at cajoling, knowing Chantais wasn't on side but he must retain a semblance of unity.

Chantais nodded his head in acquiescence but now felt even less easy about embarking on this venture with this dubious coterie of British agents.

Was Morison losing his touch?

'The paparazzi and their photographs,' said Chantais. 'We are all aware the paparazzi took no part in interfering with the Mercedes, but we must continue to hold them in custody until we have decided upon a course of action. We need to understand what we are up against before we can safely release them because, as soon as we do, then people will say OK if it's not them, then who was driving those aggressive vehicles? We must have an answer.

'The greatest problem with the paparazzi is far more dangerous. We have a situation where there were several dozen photographs taken of the crash scene and of some people who were in the tunnel last night seconds after the crash, who have yet to be identified. Who are these people? Where are those photographs? If we can find these, together with the CCTV, then we have a chance of finding your murderers and without causing a problem to your monarchy. We have no way of being certain we have seized all of these but one indiscreet photograph could kill this project stone dead and some of us with it, career wise. We must continue on our present course and see if we can solve this and then deal with it more openly.'

Morison stayed silent!

'The survivor. The last major problem we have is the man who got away. If he survives then we have an issue that will be hard to resolve. How shall we keep him quiet when he recovers and tells all? His testimony will be impossible for us to defend against. He was there! He saw it all happen! Everyone will believe his testimony and all the cover up in the world is not going to change that fact. Whatever story we settle on, his testimony could still sink this whole subterfuge.'

Morison had been considering this problem for some hours now. It wasn't expected that the bodyguard would survive but he was in very good hands and holding his own, so there was that possibility. Morison knew this was a sound point but equally well there was no other action that could be taken, other than the ultimate sanction, and that was considered excessive and very risky with the level of support the bodyguard was receiving at the hospital.

Another cock up! Why couldn't Atkinson have been more alert? This was a situation that must be kept close and watched over the coming weeks, but there were more pressing matters on hand and Morison decided they had a good start but couldn't do any more here today.

He rose and spoke to the group. 'Thank you, gentlemen, for your tremendous support at this terrible time. We much appreciate what you have done and are prepared to do for us. We owe you a deep debt of gratitude for all your understanding and the risks you are prepared to take on our behalf. You have the thanks of Her Majesty's Government. I ask that we pursue the points of our agreement reached, so far, and then revisit them tomorrow when they've matured. We need answers to all questions raised today and need to meet every day for the coming week to review witness statements, then discuss the changing situation; agreed?'

'Yes,' said Chantais, 'we have the main items of activity agreed and have been given consent to support your request, so let's get to work and meet again tomorrow. We shall see what we can do to preserve your monarchy.'

On Monday morning, 1st September, Morison's orders to act quickly and seize the possible damning photographic evidence of the attack on the Mercedes that they believed were sent to M. Cherruault, had been carried out. The task was passed to the domestic arm of the Service, MI5, who visited M. Cherruault's home, uninvited, at around 3.30am.

The raid was twenty-four hours after the Alma when MI5 raided his home in Kilburn, north-west London while he and his wife Christine slept upstairs. Computer hard disks believed to contain photographs of the Mercedes and damning evidence of the existence of the Fiat were stolen.

Morison was disappointed when these contained nothing; still, he thought, 'If we are to suppress evidence, we must pull out all the stops.'

Monsieur Cherrauault added to Morison's embarrassment by calling the police, after the break in, and asking whether they were 'grey men' who had broken in, meaning the Security Services, to which the police replied, 'Call them what you like, but you were not burgled.'

This wasn't helpful to Morison, who complained to the police that they should do as they were damn well told! If they wanted to run the Security Services, then lobby Parliament for a change or else keep secret matters secret.

It had always been a major concern to Morison, emphasised by the Winfield situation, that the majority of his own people, including the Secret Services and police, were going to baulk at this operation. This is why the information and numbers involved must be kept to a corruptible few. Although he had chastised the police, he knew he was sailing close to the wind.

Morison stressed throughout his meetings with the French that this operation must be pursued with the utmost urgency. The general consensus amongst the more gullible might accept the paparazzi diversion whereas the rest of humanity would certainly know that Diana had been murdered.

'This is a disaster,' thought Morison. 'We have failed and it's imperative that any leakage is prevented or we're done for. Damn that bloody Fiat! Damn Andanson.'

He realised it wouldn't now take much to cause revolution. What in God's name had they done? They had probably killed the monarchy off, not preserved it!

POLITICAL FALLOUT

The people were devastated! Grief gave way to rage within days of Diana's murder, which terrified the Service more than anything they had encountered before or probably ever would again.

This had been a mistake; non-rectifiable! Survival mode replaced the killer adrenalin previously displayed by some of its officers, and many in the Service, who had joined for the laudable reason of defending the realm, wished they had chosen a different career.

Morison knew morale was low and hoped there wouldn't be too many resignations. Only those within the Service chosen for this operation knew the detail but it was guaranteed that many colleagues would learn the truth. Morison believed that by continuing as usual, it could all blow over, given time. Nothing else could be done but press on.

Concerns about his colleagues' reactions were something that he couldn't dwell on because he had a more contentious deployment of lies to place. He must now persuade a sceptical nation, and world, that this was an accident and nothing more. That was a possibility before the Fiat collided with the Mercedes but there was now a different hue to the Service's perspective on the probable outcome. Not only must Morison persuade the nation this was a mere accident but do so having failed to prevent substantial evidence becoming available to the media and, also, despite having been forced into a cover up that was much too transparent.

The Fiat had heightened public suspicions and people would now be looking for evidence, rather than blindly following the Service's propaganda. Morison had to overcome the suspicion, soon to be prevalent, concerning the swapping of Henri Paul's forensic samples and having the Princess illegally embalmed, not having a post-mortem, not allowing an autopsy and the continued silence of

MI6, when everyone was going to know they were there that night, and in numbers. People knew that several vehicles surrounded the Mercedes before it impacted with the pillars since this had been confirmed, but initially ignored, by the police; and that bloody Fiat Uno. The list was endless and people were not fools. They would realise that MI6 had no choice other than to stay silent; rather like a guilty defendant trying to prevent self-incrimination, clearly indicating there was something to hide. This was going to speak volumes to the thinking public and, although MI6 knew they didn't have to answer to anyone and could do precisely as they pleased, their remit had been to keep the public on side and in that Morison knew they had failed. Now he must limit the damage, irrevocably done, and hope and pray they pulled through. Any dangerous revelations would guarantee a violent public response, so they were not only defending the monarchy but also their own necks and those of the British and French governments.

Morison realised he had his work cut out to ensure the French police stayed on side, so needed to recap and move quickly. He first considered the issues that were down to endure their continued cooperation plus also the French Ministry of Justice, who were central to this mission; he listed the areas where the process could best be influenced. The main areas were the debris from the tunnel and to ensure that the wrecked Mercedes remained off bounds to everyone. He must continue to divert public attention by maintaining pressure on the paparazzi, seize all the photographs that were taken that night to keep information under wraps about the Fiat Uno, and ensure the French police handled witnesses by rubbishing those who gave evidence suggesting murder but highlighting those whose evidence could be interpreted as an accident.

To lay the blame for this 'accident' at the feet of Henri Paul, he had found a corpse of some poor soul in a morgue who had committed suicide by drinking a bottle of vodka and then gassing himself in his car using its exhaust fumes. Samples taken from this cadaver were very high in alcohol and they needed to switch these with Paul's. A downside was the samples also contained high levels of carbon monoxide from the exhaust fumes but, Morison thought, 'we can't avoid that. If we wait for Mr Perfect Corpse, we might be waiting for months, unless I go out on the tiles with the boss and top a more suitable specimen.'

Morison felt his world had become full of impossible tasks as a sense of futility began creeping in! 'Not a lot to do,' his mind wandered. 'In fact, I think I'll go on leave and let them all get on with it.' Morison often had bizarre thoughts when he was feeling the pressure.

He knew that success or the ultimate failure of this venture relied heavily on the French police and he was only playing a support role; that irked him. He believed the police needed constant cajoling and were already becoming uncertain over continuing with this deception. The French police didn't possess the same determination as the British Secret Service for succeeding in this venture, so Morison would need to stay close and maintain his cajoling. The photographs were snuffed out, he believed, so there shouldn't be any to show the Mercedes with the white marks from the Fiat on its side and reveal their subterfuge to the world.

The police continued to deny the existence of any car collision, as the Service had requested, let alone a white Fiat; while they maintained this position there wasn't much the people could do without further evidence. The debris from the tunnel was a well-handled affair except, in his view, for the speed of removal and the propaganda side of matters that the French police didn't take seriously enough. They were focused on complying with orders and collecting evidence. Morison couldn't get them to see they could win the battle and still lose the war by allowing too much evidence to leak and he desperately needed to keep the public on side by controlling the evidence in a plausible way. A weak, or even laughable, "reason" was better than none.

The French took the view that as long as the evidence was kept hidden then the public didn't need an explanation and they would all eventually go away. Morison needed to keep the public thinking that they could be wrong about the obvious, which was never going to be easy, but the differences in the French police and MI6 tactics were causing Morison problems. He must maintain the pressure on the police, who were not only growing tired of this charade but also its cost.

Commander Mules, who gave the order for the removal of the car from the tunnel and had been put in charge of the operation, wasn't very convincing about his reasons for closing it. This only served to fuel more speculation about why they had rushed to close it. Neutral investigators and reporters wanted to see the wrecked

Mercedes and were denied access for obvious reasons but that was the problem; there were obvious reasons!

A major fly in the ointment was about to envelop and sting Morison. Dodi Fayed's father was intent on unravelling the whole affair. Mohamed al Fayed was about to prevent the Service from achieving its goal and nerves started to flutter at Vauxhall Cross. Instead of being able to steer this event into the thought process of it being an accident and then waiting for people to eventually accept the will of the Establishment through boredom or growing indifference, they would have to face a world where the truth was going to be dangled in their faces for a considerable period. This increased the chances of the people realising the truth and, perhaps, one of the murderers being tempted to spill the beans for the right sum of money.

Mohamed al Fayed was not contained by normal confines due to his considerable wealth and extreme determination. He could afford private investigators with considerable experience that could be deployed in the pursuit of justice. By murdering his son alongside the Princess, the Service had incurred the wrath of a very wealthy and determined man who would never relent.

Al Fayed's view was, as of instinct, that this had been a brutal murder even before evidence began emerging that enjoined the vast majority of the world in agreement. Pursuing the truth and incurring the wrath of those who wished to contain this crime subsequently caused him to be vilified by the Establishment, in the hope that people wouldn't listen to the truth he was expounding.

These were dangerous times for MI6. Its possible proscription was not far from Morison's mind, not to mention charges of high treason that could be brought. He pondered the logic of this for a moment. Theoretically he could be executed for high treason, if caught, for being involved in the murder of the Princess, which he considered highly unreasonable, but much too risky to ignore. He didn't intend getting caught but mistakes happen, they already had, and he shouldn't have to bear this unnecessary risk. He would again see what could be done through appropriate channels to expedite the removal of the death penalty for this offence from the statute book. It would be in common with current European thinking, in any event, so why not complete the picture and possibly save his skin and those of his colleagues? He must press for this as soon as possible, just in case.

Morison knew that in order to win this war, one he must win, he must fight with whatever he had in his armoury using all except the ultimate sanction. Any more violence and the people might well respond with violence. Already the British police had to advise the monarchy that they should be careful when stepping out amongst their own people due to the people's awareness that all was not as it seemed; an unprecedented experience that indicated tolerance was very near to snapping. That bloody Fiat Uno once more came to Morison's mind.

Success in containing evidence of murder, so that people couldn't rise above a level of disbelief to one of knowledge, was now all that stood between an unstable or revolutionary populace. The response was astounding and if MI6 had thought, pre-attack, that this reaction was even possible then the operation would never have been sanctioned. Morison knew he must tighten the reins on French activity and ensure that his policy of denial continued because there wasn't room for error; none.

How could they reduce the effect of Mohamed al Fayed's truth onslaught? They would need to work behind the scenes and drop pieces of disinformation into the public domain, recreating old wounds and persecutions of yesteryear rather like a political party when losing its way needs to refer back to events concerning their adversaries' past, in order to achieve their objectives, because they have nothing detrimental to say that is current or relevant.

'The people might not fall for that,' thought Morison. 'We thought they were very gullible but we now have 90% of the population realising the truth, so allowing ourselves to consider the people gullible has induced us to enter into an adventure that could achieve the very thing we were trying to prevent. Lose the people; lose the war! Whose fault is that? We couldn't know how much the Princess was loved. Right, we need to continue with our course of action in France, maintain a close watch, and rubbish Mohamed al Fayed and try to make people lose sympathy with him. Let us see what we have to help us make the people believe he is lying for some self-serving purpose.

'We shall instruct the team to seek detrimental information and release it in dribs and drabs. We must, of course, refer to the money-for-questions scandal that helped bring down Prime Minister John Major's Tory government just months ago before we executed the Princess.'

A thought occurred to Morison that if there hadn't been the money for questions scandal then perhaps the Tory Government would have survived the last election and it would have been impossible to execute this attack. A Tory Government would in no way have tolerated this operation and would have dealt very swiftly with its perpetrators. Knowing this, MI6 would almost certainly never have allowed it.

'We also have the issue of the Tiny Rowland affair and the purchase of Harrods. Sour grapes really,' thought Morison, 'but it might help our purpose. Then we have the son, Dodi. We can major on strengthening the information discovered during our recent rubbishing campaign against him when we tried to change the Princess's mind before the order to execute was given. We must build on that and divert attention for the next month or so.' Morison hesitated. 'No, that could induce sympathy with the public. We had better stay with the father! Other than this, we need to monitor whatever the al Fayed team do and say, then ensure we have a counter to everything. We must reduce the impact of what is being claimed and make people believe there is another reason for what is being stated other than the truth, perhaps that al Fayed is trying to glorify his position. We should be able to handle that. It's what we are paid for and rather good at.'

Al Fayed was increasingly giving a lot of stick to the Service campaign by illustrating points the Service were desperately trying to divert from people's minds. Were the Princess and Dodi going to get married? Were they going to live at the Villa Windsor in the Bois de Boulogne near Paris? Was the Princess pregnant? Did the Dites-moi (Tell Me Yes) ring that Dodi ordered from Alberto Repossi's shop in Monte Carlo on the 23rd August, together with the Princess, represent their intention to marry? Was it an engagement ring? If not, then what question was Dodi going to ask Diana to which he expected the answer to be yes? This was obviously a very special evening for them. Was the Princess alive when she reached hospital and could she speak? The Fayed campaign stressed the fact that this was more than a summer fling and there was motive for murder. The Service needed to stress the opposite, that this was merely a fling; therefore, there wasn't any logical motive. The battleground was for the minds and hearts of the people and the prize either success for murder, or justice possibly standing some chance when the current British Government was replaced.

Morison needed to win all these battles so went overboard. Every time the al Fayed team made a claim regarding the Princess and Dodi, he set out to neutralise it.

Several witnesses who had indicated support for the Fayed position changed their minds when confronted by the bully tactics of the Service. Alberto Repossi, who had said the ring was an engagement ring, now said that he couldn't say whether it was an engagement ring or not. Richard Kay, a *Daily Mail* journalist who was friendly with Diana and had spoken with her on the night of her murder, had said it was likely that Dodi and Diana were going to get married. Now he couldn't be sure what their intentions were, but didn't think they would have got married. Rosa Monkton stated that Diana couldn't have been pregnant because she was experiencing her menstrual period during their recent holiday around the Greek islands together a few weeks earlier.

This, of course, was helpful to Morison but knowledge had once more seeped into the public domain and people had found out that Rosa Monkton's husband worked for MI6, which rather reduced the usefulness of her statement and Morison thought, might even have made matters more suspicious. He arranged for surveillance to monitor all activities in the al Fayed camp so he would be prepared for whatever was thrown at him.

The inevitable war of attrition between the parties continued and the Service hadn't expected quite such a competent or ferocious onslaught. They had no choice other than to ride out the storm and hope time would take away the pressure now building from the public. The Princess had died in the Pitié Salpetrière Hospital and arrangements were being made for an autopsy in England. Morison had to think quickly if he wanted to prevent a disaster from engulfing them following an examination by British doctors, where pregnancy and poisoning would come to light.

The only way to prevent the Princess's body giving away secrets that would add to the existing motives for murder would be to remove the proof. All they could do was remove further damning evidence that would irrevocably tip the scales against their 'accident theory', so the Princess must be embalmed in France, despite knowing he couldn't give a reason for doing so, if asked; but then, who was going to ask to whom he would be required to give an answer?

Morison knew the risks of increasing the inexorably growing

suspicion of murder but he balanced this against people finding out that she was pregnant and had been poisoned; knowledge that guaranteed murder! This was an end-game scenario! They were playing for keeps! If knowledge of the Princess's pregnancy were known then this would put enormous pressure on the authorities and that was already very significant. If poison were discovered, there would be no more hope of pretending this was an accident and the focus would inevitably be upon the royal family as the ones with the greatest, if not the only, real motive with MI6 as the executioners. Poison identified; murder certain! The consequence, total mission failure and a Service that wouldn't be able to withstand the ensuing public rage!

'How are we to complete this?' Morison asked himself. 'It's illegal in France to even obtain medical information on a hospitalised or deceased person, let alone take action on their remains when you aren't related to them. On the one hand we shall rely on the French medical system to unwittingly protect us because they are unable to give information on the Princess to anyone, including their own police. On the other hand, we are expecting them to embalm someone without permission. Would people notice this conundrum?'

The press would notice inconsistencies and this wouldn't assist his cause but some decisions needed to be taken this day, come hell or high water. Time was not on his side and the ineffable consequences of possible failure would not leave him.

A number of problems faced Morison. The Service had to deal with more witnesses who saw what happened, other than those who came forward on the night, who would not help their cause. There were some in the Ritz hotel who commented on whether Henri Paul was drunk and the Service needed to prepare a series of stories for background support that would fit their picture of drunkenness. The Service would need to spend more of their budget, ensuring suitable support stories existed.

The survivor from the crash would be able to say that Henri Paul was perfectly normal before leaving the Ritz but the Service could discount that by adopting the line: 'He would say that, wouldn't he, since it was his job to look after the Princess.' They would ignore the point that he also got into the car, so could not have had any thoughts of incapacity on Paul's part or his own life was at risk. Morison didn't believe people would think matters through that far.

But what of the British post-mortem? They could delay the inquest by fabricating the reasons why it was not possible to hold one just yet. 'For a year or so,' thought Morison, 'after which people will have gone away and be pursuing some other glamorous celebrity. The post-mortem, however, is a more immediate problem and is why Diana's body must be embalmed but, even so, what if the British coroner discovers something suspicious; could we trust him to support the State's position?

'We have already impugned the integrity of the British police and this will be catastrophic for public order and confidence if people ever get to know. We must control the medical profession in like manner.'

He considered this was unlikely unless they could be persuaded it was necessary for public stability. He would ask them to make it known, publicly, that Diana wasn't pregnant for the purported reason that the Service were concerned with conspiracy theorist drivel that could cause catastrophic problems; they should accept that in the interests of the country. 'They don't need to know the truth. It's for the sake of Diana's children and to prevent embarrassment to the Crown! There shouldn't be a problem with supporting that; they will know nothing of our involvement.'

Another concern to Morison was that the British people would want to know why their own police were not involved in the investigation, which routinely happens in sudden deaths of a British subject abroad. Why would they not do the same for the Princess of Wales? How would the police find a reason to stay at home?

'Pressure will be coming from the people but we don't want to be drawn into finding excuses as to why the police aren't involved because that wouldn't stand up to scrutiny. We need to avoid criticism at all costs otherwise, if the investigation is seen as tainted, there will be more ammunition for all conspiracy theorists that will run counter to our objectives. There is a serious danger that if the British police were involved, we would be far too close to the investigation and questions would be asked and need answering. We would be seen to have control and that would engender an even greater degree of criticism of not doing more than we are.

'Not a chance,' thought Morison. 'We stop that dead in its tracks. Finally, we have one of the biggest problems to overcome. People will know we were in Paris in larger numbers than usual and that will cause suspicion. These items in isolation are not particularly significant but collectively...? Much too much information has seeped out and the French police, although cooperating in part, have not really got into the spirit of our operation and don't have the same motivation to succeed. I think we are in for a very hard ride!'

The people's reaction was one of disbelief and the thought of this being a murder committed by the Establishment was now prevalent. No further cajoling, or propaganda, by the Service could dislodge this from people's minds. Morison's thoughts were travelling through the pitfalls and options open to him and the scenario of his beloved Secret Service and what damage this operation had done.

He began rationalising the probability of forthcoming events that could change his world forever. This was a murder too far and one where subsequent emotions were not going to fade. The British police and Government realised they were not far from a political catastrophe that could blow away the monarchy and the newly formed Government of a few months.

The new British Prime Minister had hardly got his feet under the table at No 10 Downing Street when he had to deal with a monstrous act from a Service that, theoretically at least, reported to him. Whatever they chose to report, however, was another matter and then the ability to question and disprove anything from them would need another Service to oversee them and to ensure both Services weren't in cahoots. The one difficulty in having Secret Services is that they tend to be very secret and there is nobody who can interrogate the façade that they are there for the benefit of the people. If the Prime Minister is in control; how was MI6 able to murder the Princess of Wales without his knowledge?

'The suspicion will remain that the Services are there to support those whom they wish and not necessarily uphold the law. They make the ideological decisions without reference to anyone, so there is a separate kingdom within the Establishment that answers only to itself. There is no process whereby they can be controlled and policed and one needs to rely on those who run the Service being decent upright citizens who will always follow the needs of the State, supporting the maintenance of the status quo. What happens if one doesn't think the status quo is worthy of support?'

Morison pondered, extending his reasoning to a logical end point; a common process when seeking the enemy's reasoning.

'This, naturally, depends on that person's own political standpoint and if the people who support the status quo believe it is threatened then they will act as they see fit without reference to any other opinion. They will take the view that the needs of the many outweigh the civil liberties of the few. A view also held by the French political system, which had been most helpful post the execution of the Princess. The question then posed is whether this is what the people want and, if not, where is democracy? The Service will survive discrepancies of small relevance, because they would be quickly forgotten, but in murdering the Princess of Wales they were way out of step with people's emotions. This the people will never tolerate; it is probably the end of the Secret Service as I know it,' Morison mused, as he considered his next step in this unsavoury saga of evil.

There was nothing for it but to soldier on with the propaganda, even when all looked bleak. The only other option was to emerge, tell the truth and have done with it and there were many decent people in the Service who would have loved to do just that. The usual considerations of jobs and pensions, not to mention being imprisoned for breaching the Official Secrets Act or summary execution had the salutary effect of curtailing any desires for decency and justice from within their ranks.

Morison was thinking ahead to when the inevitable and various television companies and press reporting had finished describing their own view of what happened in Paris. The event that most disturbed the Service was the forthcoming post-mortem with the royal coroner, and that was the first problem on Morison's mind. They were going to need the coroner to announce his findings that Diana wasn't pregnant, otherwise the conspiracies would mount up and, without the people having something to hang their hats on, they would go on believing that Diana had been murdered. Each potential problem must be countered as soon as it emerged. If the belief of murder became embedded in people's minds then the monarchy might as well pack their bags and the Service would have great difficulty in surviving.

The announcement must appear spontaneous, so a formal announcement was of no value. The best way of doing this was to have the coroner make an announcement, during the post-mortem, that Diana wasn't pregnant so the staff would hear and attest to this later. It was always important for the Service to maintain a distance, partly in case events took a wrong turn, but also because they have a greater impact if the Service was not involved. Putting it another way, it would kill the value of the announcement stone dead if anyone knew they were involved!

The preparation of scrubbing down at the Fulham mortuary for Diana's arrival had been completed with an assistant present for the post-mortem. Despite being embalmed, no surprise was noted or announced, although this was most unusual if not downright suspicious. The coroner duly stated aloud, 'Well, she wasn't pregnant,' as though that's what people had gathered to hear.

The Queen's attitude had remained steadfast by refusing to allow Charles Windsor permission to go to France and collect his ex-wife's body, which seemed the least decent act that could be performed by the royals after all the trauma they had put Diana through. The charade continued regarding the use of the Queen's own flight to collect and return Diana's coffin to British soil because she was not considered royal any longer, so her body was not entitled to this privilege.

When the coffin arrived in the UK it was sent to Fulham mortuary, for the post-mortem and the Queen refused to allow it to enter any of the royal palaces; later she relented and it was sent to the palace chapel of St James.

This, together with the Queen's refusal to return to London from her Scottish retreat out of respect for Diana (A move expected by the people) was considered extremely insensitive. The situation was exacerbated because Diana's grieving children had asked why they were not in London when, 'Mummy was there.'

Not being prepared to acknowledge Diana not only fuelled unsavoury thoughts of the monarchy but was also considered an insult to the British people who valued Diana above all the other royals put together, perhaps with the sole exception of her children. Morison knew this was playing into the hands of the conspiracy theorists in fuelling ideas that the monarchy not only wanted to get rid of Diana but had also played a part in her demise.

This was an inevitable thought process that couldn't be easily averted. Whether the royals had played some part, or not, Morison knew that the people already knew Diana had been treated as an incubator and non-person and then subsequently discarded. This was sufficient to cause a major public storm. Now to find the royals continuing to treat Diana as a non-person, even in death, was too much for the public whatever their views on the monarchy might be.

Morison had already briefed politicians in his plans to avoid a disaster at home ahead of Diana's body arriving and all were aware of the situation's sensitivity. The political machine swung into action very quickly, sensing a major crisis that was looming on top of Diana's murder that was, quite frankly, considered inexcusable by the Service. They had performed to their best ability and gone beyond that which many of their number believed were reasonable bounds to protect the monarchy and they were being given two fingers by the royals who didn't even bother to play the game for a few weeks and look as though they might care; if only a little.

Political handling and control of this growing public mood couldn't be left to the machinations of palace sensibilities any longer. The Prime Minister was doing his best to prevent a major crisis from enveloping both the royal family and his government and believed the least the royals could do was give the impression of grieving for a couple of weeks, if only out of concern for Diana's children.

Regret or remorse by the Royals was out of the question. Although the British public are known for their tolerance, that week there was much in the air that would lead any observer to believe the monarchy was in its death throes and a republic in the offing. They couldn't sit back and rely on time to heal, so something must be done or a crisis was about to unfold. To add to their woes, the Queen refused to allow the flag over Buckingham Palace to fly at half-mast out of respect for Diana, since convention decreed this never happened, except on strict protocol. It was of no concern to the Queen that people were asking for this gesture and she refused, clearly showing not only her contempt for Diana but also her subjects in their time of grief.

The Queen clearly believed convention and formality were more important than the feelings of her subjects and it was becoming obvious that a gulf was opening between the monarchy and the people that wouldn't revert. The magic had gone; the genie was out of the bottle. He was kicking and screaming and refusing to be shoved back in again.

To repair this damage, it was decided the Queen must deliver a speech to the nation with the government first ensuring it was satisfactory. Times had changed where a message from the monarch could be delivered from the heart. They now needed to be contrived and regulated in order to keep the people in their place, offering proof that the monarchy had lost its ability to understand the people. No more speeches from the heart would be heard because it was too risky to allow the Windsor family the freedom to be let loose on the public. The government knew what needed saying to placate the people, even if her Majesty did not, and promptly corrected the speech the Queen wished to deliver.

This was handled by the Prime Minister's spin-doctor in chief. These were people used by the government when their actions required the truth be distorted, otherwise either their own, or the establishment's, popularity could be endangered – and possibly their survival. Why this was considered necessary, the people could only surmise; Morison knew!

The funeral arrangements were quickly upgraded from a small private affair to full state regalia, not without resistance on the part of Queen Elizabeth, who once more was compelled to bow to the populist view. Emotions were not abating but becoming more charged as time went by during those first few days.

Morison prayed that nothing more explosive would tip the fragile balance of control they had somehow managed to retain. Those in power had managed to coax the Queen down from her high horse to consider the wishes of the people and that at least gave some breathing space for the monarchy. Morison knew that support for the royals wouldn't rise to another high but as long as emotions were kept in check this would suffice; for now.

It had been necessary to involve Service personnel from the highest level to advise the government of the action that must be taken, and they didn't require any instruction. It was clear that some of the senior royals must show concern for Diana otherwise the obvious reaction would be that not only did the royals abuse her during life, but they didn't even have the magnanimity to respect her in death.

Morison felt a desperate need to rationalise his perception of the royals and understand how people would feel towards them after this murder now that too much had leaked out. He must stem all undue public feeling and thoughts before they became an issue.

A few members of the royal family recognised that playing

along with the people's wishes would help ensure their survival.

Royal attempts at sorrow were not convincing and there would inevitably be some acting by the royals during the funeral because they could not pretend that Diana's death wasn't, at least, extremely convenient for their survival plans. Showing compassion during the funeral would not erupt spontaneously but needed to be induced. Diana was a thorn in the royal side for years. She revealed various truths and ignored conventions that permitted the royals to continue with their archaic behaviour. She was trying to survive and had the effrontery to be her own person and defy the will of the monarchy. She lived her own life without complying with a seventeenth-century attitude of treating women, especially non-royals within the royal family, as though they were chattels one could abuse and cast aside at will.

'One sometimes wonders what planet the royals live on,' thought Morison, 'but it's becoming apparent; not one inhabited by the rest of us.'

Morison knew there were going to be many people still not satisfied with the newly found respect suddenly on display from the royals. It smelt of self-preservation rather than anything genuine, so their efforts must continue to the end of the week and possibly the week after that. It was a small price to pay; what would the royals do if they lost their jobs? There would not be many people who would want to employ them.

The final act of contrition came when the Queen was required to bow her head to her ex-daughter-in-law's coffin as it went by the gates of Buckingham Palace; on orders received.

All the stops were now pulled out to try and subdue the populace and induce a catharsis that would bring them back into the fold, at least to the point of abating their anger. The monarchy would never be the same again but they would survive to whatever fate held in store for them on another day; a day most probably not too far distant.

'The inquest must be delayed,' thought Morison, 'because if it went ahead now, we would risk details emerging, and questions being asked, not yet fully understood by us. We don't yet know whether one of our assassins is going to be tracked down. Other witnesses will come forward or existing witnesses will decide to take a chance on stating the truth, despite police intimidation.

'We have tried to curtail those witnesses that have given

unhelpful testimony but if people have a mechanism whereby they can channel their complaints, comments, thoughts or whatever to a source such as an inquest, this would act as a focal point and provoke dangerous information coming to light that could be impossible to quell. It will raise questions that will need answering. We shall continue to seek out those who have made unhelpful comments to date but we cannot guarantee all will toe our line. Until we have control over all these matters, and know their extent, we cannot allow an inquest to proceed.

'It will be for cosmetic reasons only anyway but, as far as the public is concerned, we shall say we cannot have an inquest until the French have finished their investigation and then we shall also make sure that they don't finish for a long time yet.'

Morison wasn't sure how long they could continue to fool the public but did know that without a focal point there was very little people could do. It was a question of delaying and reading the situation as the months unfolded. How could people challenge the State over not holding an inquest when another power was involved and how could they be sure of what the legalities might be that would perhaps enable an inquest to proceed sooner? The government would intervene should anyone try to challenge this position, so their success was guaranteed.

Charles Windsor, who had been involved in this whole process of repatriating his ex-wife's body, was keeping his appearances to a minimum and staying with his adulterous lover, Camilla Parker Bowles, the first person he telephoned on being informed of Diana's crash, just after 2.00am on the Sunday morning. This role-play was crucial in ensuring that the woman, whom he had detested, abused, ignored and treated as a chattel for years, would somehow be seen as a past lover tragically torn from his embrace by a dastardly act of fate that had left him forlorn and his soul lost.

'If anyone believes this,' Morison thought, 'they need psychiatric treatment for an untreatable condition. What better way of endearing himself to those who regarded him as an adulterous monster and were already on the brink of cashiering the whole royal bunch at one fell swoop? What is more worrying, perhaps, is that Charles Windsor spent some time only months before, from about March onwards, being much friendlier to his ex-wife than ever before. One could argue this was fortunate before her rather nasty demise but some think he was trying to give an impression of being on better terms for a good reason. His demeanour during the time of Diana's death certainly helped to save his position.'

Morison couldn't help feeling that the people will soon rebel and he was entering an end game for the monarchy.

RISING STORM

Grief continued long after the funeral and would remain with people all over the world for some considerable time. Morison's problems did not abate! He had come near to losing the battle to save the status quo, with too many curves being thrown into the equation, but he believed he had come through his ordeal in reasonable shape in that the monarchy was still intact, the government was still in power and the initial problem had gone. But he now knew the aftermath was something he must contend with and realized there couldn't be any relenting on his propaganda campaign to neutralize negative comments emerging.

The world was still a dangerous place for MI6, with the main and continuous thorn in Morison's side being Mohamed al Fayed who was never going to give up the pursuit of justice for the murder of his son. The Service's murder of Diana had left the sword of Damocles hanging above them and they must assuage the people's rage or they would have done it all for nothing. This would be the end!

Al Fayed had detectives pursuing witnesses for any thread of evidence in France and elsewhere. The French had followed MI6 dictates that other interested parties be kept at bay and total secrecy maintained; not a problem for the French police, since this was how they normally worked.

The main thrust of the investigation by al Fayed's team had centred on the Fiat Uno that so mysteriously disappeared after 'interfering', and then colliding, with the Mercedes. This was the car the French police refused to acknowledge for two whole weeks after the attack, at the behest of MI6. The police decided enough disinformation had been disseminated to claim this as an accident and that a drunken chauffeur was responsible. It was imperative no further information leaked out about the Fiat, which must never be found.

All leads received by the French police were notified to the Service because Morison wanted to know, immediately, if anyone came close to the Fiat. Being ignorant of the real reasons lying behind MI6 requests, the police obliged. When the police inspected James Andanson's car, after identifying it from CCTV footage, it was confirmed this was the one. They already knew James Andanson but believed he had been working with MI6 and sent to protect the Princess.

Al Fayed's team also found the car, by different means, and pursued the vehicle's owner to his farmhouse near Lignières in south-west France. The Fiat had been sold in October 1997, one month after the attack, and had received a new rear brake light; the same as the one smashed in the Alma tunnel.

The French police intervened and warned al Fayed's team to lay off, threatening them with a criminal charge if they were caught trying to interfere with the French judicial process again. Morison felt they should have said thank you very much and then suppressed the evidence, having warned al Fayed more gently to leave the investigating to them; instead they had exacerbated the situation. Everyone now knew they had something to hide.

The Fiat had been found. If al Fayed had had any doubts about French complicity, notwithstanding their possible lack of culpability, then these were now dispelled. There was no way an investigative team could approach the French authorities because they were obviously facing both state-sponsored and suppressed murder; everything would be thrown against them. It was obvious to all who considered the facts that the police knew about the Fiat and weren't prepared to do anything about it; there was clearly a hidden agenda.

Those living in so-called democracies came to realise they were able to speak the truth only until the interests of state came between them and an unpalatable truth; then the individual and the truth emerged second best. The French police wouldn't have supported this crime of their own volition; further indicating that MI6 had conduct of this crime and would go to any lengths to prevent the truth emerging.

Morison was not concerned because he knew al Fayed was aware of the truth and would never back off, so his certain knowledge of murder only guaranteed that his pursuit would continue forever. He had hoped that after, say, three years al Fayed's pursuit would fall away but now he knew this was a forlorn hope.

If al Fayed didn't have any concrete evidence after a year or two, then Morison's reasoning was that he was never going to cause a problem to the Service by way of proof but merely remain a thorn in its side. It did mean, however, that having found Andanson, the man who was instrumental in killing his son, al Fayed would be looking at ways of pursuing this man to obtain the truth from one who could give definitive evidence.

There was always a risk, as Morison knew, that if temptation was placed in the way of some people, they could find it difficult to resist. This was one of the biggest concerns he had about using people outside the Service, because one couldn't rely on the discretion of people employed to kill for money who will easily go against you, as history shows.

Andanson did the job for money and that was his greatest motivator. Al Fayed was in a position to offer huge sums to someone who could offer proof of murder, so Morison knew another major threat could erupt at any time. MI6 would continue to keep an eye on Monsieur Andanson, and observe his behaviour, but if al Fayed got too close, then something would need to be done. They couldn't risk losing now because of one man's incompetence and subsequent indiscretion or greed. Morison put his men on to the task of checking where Andanson frequented to make sure the Service had people at hand. If problems arose, the Service would be close.

The death of the Princess of Wales had raised such a furore amongst the people that there was no way of knowing where it would lead. In the UK, the popularity of the royals continued to plummet with people openly saying they were not sure they wanted a monarchy and some that they wanted a monarchy but not Charles Windsor as heir. This meant the palace would have to work overtime to try and reverse the image of their supposed future monarch, now embedded in people's minds. Special photo calls were made of Charles with his children, and points made about all the good causes to which he lends his name. The propaganda machinery was in full swing but it was apparent to most people that, if the Establishment needed to remind them of what some people do in their spare time in order to make them popular, then that person was already a lost cause.

Documentaries about the life of Diana showing negative behavioural traits, expounded by sycophants, became the order of the day. Attempts were made by the Service to put everything back on course by continuing the lies about the Princess in the hope that time would allow people to rekindle thoughts of the royals, pre-Diana, and not be so critical of the monarchy. Nothing changed! Acceptance by the public of Charles Windsor's mistress, Camilla Parker Bowles, would never happen and Charles's statements of having no desire to remarry then later, in contradictory terms, that even if he did his new wife would never become Queen, were meaningless gestures when it would have been suicidal to say otherwise.

Once more it was the idea to tell the people what they wanted to hear and then do precisely as one pleases when a convenient time arrives. Charles apparently married Diana, someone he didn't love, in the interests of the state but found it very hard to leave someone he did love, in the interests of the state. The Service knew he would do precisely as he pleased and to hell with everyone else; after all, 'He would be King'.

How long could they leave it before holding an inquest into a suspicious death for anyone, let alone the Princess of Wales? What excuse could they use to explain why it had taken so long? Morison was going to have another problem in convincing people there was nothing suspicious and that this was normal procedure. It was anything but normal procedure; it was a grotesque miscarriage of justice and abuse of police powers. This the people would know! How was he going to square this one?

Morison was beginning to despair of ever getting on top of this debacle, believing more and more that this was a lost cause and he would have to withdraw from any positive action. All he could do was assist in the ongoing palace propaganda that would continue unabated, probably for years. What other evidence could emerge to add further embarrassment to the police, government and the Service that would put their necks on the block? How many more of Diana's secrets were hidden somewhere that could later emerge and cause a monumental crisis? They had to find out quickly.

They could probe forever but it was unlikely there would be anyone other than Paul Burrell tasked with keeping Diana's secrets. It was probable she would allocate trust to her personal butler and ask that this damning information be placed into the public arena, as and when it was felt that justice might be served, should it ever prove necessary.

Burrell would never reveal such innermost confidences until it was safe because he knew the police would confiscate everything before it could be circulated; or hand it over to us, thought Morison. Pity he isn't a fool! Burrell will await a change of Government and take it to the new Prime Minister; untainted by our Paris attack. So, what else was there? He must find out soon and the police may need to intervene by investigating after all! Risky but he needed a plan where the Service could continue to stand aside from this debacle and that might necessitate British police involvement. Perhaps a retired officer or..? Well, he would consider this one further. There was no immediate need!

Paul Burrell was a loyal servant to Diana and always there for her, both doing his duty and offering his personal support when she was feeling isolated. Here was the danger of a man who knew Diana, so if she had any secret boxes or other items that needed stashing, then here was a likely candidate. What did Burrell have up his sleeve, or in boxes hidden away under floorboards, that could incriminate anyone else within the royal family? What other evidence existed that could shatter the illusion of monarchy further than Diana had already done, and take it closer to the abyss?

In order to expunge the memory of Diana, and the potentially lethal mix of hidden secrets concerning the royals, the Service must ensure all evidence was seized, especially following advice from a reliable source that it did. The Service must find a way of finding and seizing this evidence without raising public suspicion so would use the police to make the search less obvious. A spurious summons was needed to give justification for this search, together with interrogation of all parties associated with Diana, in order to maximise the opportunity of finding these royal secrets of which the Establishment were so terrified, and then eliminate them. To unravel the royals further at this time would be their end; the public couldn't tolerate much more.

'What could a loyal servant to the Princess, who was totally trusted by her and besotted with her, possibly be guilty of where the police would be required to intervene?' thought Morison. 'Ah! What about those items he has been keeping on behalf of the Princess? Is there proof he had permission to retain them? Were any disposed of whilst they were under his care; for any reason? If we can find there is no evidence of innocence then we may presume guilt, with police assistance, and pursue him down that path; then we have him.' Morison locked away these thoughts; for now!

Murmurings were heard about the presence of the Service on that fateful night in Paris. Although Morison knew they didn't need to make any comment, it was difficult to placate public opinion whilst concomitantly taking advantage of the Service's ability to remain silent and defy both the law of the land and common justice.

'What else can we do?' thought Morison. 'If we make a statement then people will say we know you were there that night so, either you weren't doing your job by protecting the Princess, or else why were you there? Are you saying you know absolutely nothing about that evening? What will we be able to answer and also pacify people with; nothing whatsoever? We have no choice other than to maintain our silence and not open the floodgate of questions that would certainly ensue.'

Leaks now occurred from disillusioned operatives within the Service who took the view that this was not a Service they wished to be associated with any more and wanted the truth to become known. This was the most explosive mix that Morison had yet to counter. These were trained and trusted people who had lost faith and, more importantly, respect for a Service that could take such action.

Meddling investigative journalists from *Time* magazine spent significant energy in gathering evidence from within minutes of the attack by interviewing people and collecting evidence and then producing a book: the most damaging item to emerge from the whole operation other than the Fiat. The evidence from this book, "*Death of a Princess, An Investigation* by Scott MacLeod and Thomas Sancton", indicated quite clearly that nobody could possibly regard this as anything other than a murderous attack on the Princess and it left the way wide open for conspiracy theorists to put together the obvious scenario.

The proverbial cat was out of the bag and all the Service could do was carry on, in the most negative of circumstances, and hold their nerve. This book needed to be silenced without raising yet further suspicions as to why. Other rumours now abounded about members of the Service advising some of their colleagues not to follow Diana and Dodi to Paris that night and the whole affair was beginning to crumble. Even the French judiciary were known to have made the comment that, 'There is a terrible secret that hangs over this dossier,' and there was not much being left to the public imagination.

Morison thought, 'What else can we expect? What else are people going to think? What would I think, if I didn't already know?'

The French police had agreed not to make public statements without consulting the Service but this promise was waning. They were weary of being criticised on how long the investigation was taking, how much it was costing the French taxpayer and also of dancing to the British Secret Service's tune. Why should they? They had complied with British requests and wanted this affair to disappear and be left in peace. It just wouldn't die!

They knew their investigation of the whole affair was considered a display of French incompetence and this annoyed them. They knew that if they hadn't been required to comply with the British in this game of intrigue then they would have brought the perpetrators of this vile crime to justice long ago. Now they must endure being considered useless and that hurt their pride, not unreasonably.

Some officers within the French police would have loved to allow evidence to emerge and be dealt with in the proper manner but orders were orders and must be obeyed. It became clear that it would be seen as suspicious if the police didn't give at least one substantial interview to try and assuage fears of a cover-up or that, somehow, the investigation was not properly conducted and there should be a re-run.

The biggest danger was about to descend on Morison, to the point of producing sleepless nights and having him think that the truth was about to emerge whatever the Service did. Because Mohamed al Fayed's investigators had found the Fiat Uno, existing doubters now needed to face the truth about this car. The police had done their best to destroy knowledge of the Fiat but they must never permit its driver to be questioned over Diana's murder by anyone other than the authorities.

The Service had already informed the French police that Andanson was one of their people, just after the attack, because they had no choice. The French knew Andanson had been in the tunnel, and that the Service were also there, so what explanation could the Service give other than Andanson had been there in the tunnel, on their orders, assisting in their operation to protect the

Princess and had inadvertently collided with the Mercedes when he tried to slow down before entering the tunnel.

Now the French police were faced with these investigators, one ex-Scotland Yard, who had found Andanson and his car so their colleagues in MI6 would face the embarrassment of having to rely on a man like Andanson to stay silent. The French had little confidence that Andanson would remain silent because they knew he was motivated by money and now their necks were on the line, as well as their British counterparts. Mohamed al Fayed had lots of money and, if Andanson was offered enough, he would talk.

Monsieur Puteaux of the French Interior Ministry contacted Morison who, after a very brief conversation, knew he must go to France and discuss this latest potential crisis with his French colleagues. Andanson was the biggest remaining risk to the whole affair unravelling. Morison realised that Puteaux wouldn't telephone without good reason but, now that Andanson was being looked at closely by the French, his greatest fear was that Andanson might inform the French police he had been working for the British Service and not in the manner so described to the French police by MI6. Should this occur the game was potentially up!

Morison arrived in Paris amid much speculation within MI6 that the Andanson affair was about to blow up in their faces. He went straight to the Ministry of the Interior to meet with Puteaux; a very agreeable man with only the usual French vices of wine and women. As for his professional role, Morison thought him too gentle and couldn't see him taking some necessary decisions.

'Like a fish out of water,' thought Morison, 'but we can't always go on appearances.'

He entered Puteaux's office and was greeted with the usual courteous handshake and the offer of a cup of glorious coffee. Puteaux had crossed paths with Andanson whilst working for the French DGSE and was well positioned to give Morison a briefing on Andanson's past behaviour and proclivities. Morison needed to first assess the immediate danger and then take a wider view of just how big a risk was posed by Andanson and, although he had studied the operative's files at the earlier planning stages, he knew Puteaux's files would yield more.

Seated, they began to discuss Andanson. Puteaux thought it best if he gave a full and detailed account of all he knew from his own experiences, as well as detailing Andanson's files, since he didn't know precisely what Morison needed.

Puteaux began, 'Andanson is a very talented paparazzo and occasionally works for us as an agent. He is well known to our equivalent of your Special Branch, which has been investigating him for offences not associated with the incident in the Alma. In the past he was associated with the murder of one of our ex-Prime Ministers, Pierre Bérégovoy, so he is something of a renegade when it comes to the fast life and daring escapades and is not a man I would trust too far.'

Morison was already feeling nervous about Puteaux's stance and knew that if Andanson was arrested by Puteaux and got into a tight corner, or if Mohamed al Fayed persuaded him to come clean for several millions of pounds, then the Service was in trouble.

'Andanson took a photograph of your Prince Charles kissing his children's nanny, I believe her name is Tiggy Legge-Bourke, and for that one photograph alone he was paid £100,000. He has been friendly with several of our top politicians, including two of our Prime Ministers, Lionel Jospin and Bérégovoy. I don't mean just to say hello but people who would visit him at his home and with whom he would actively socialise. I know that Jospin has been to his home on a few occasions and has a shared interest in motorbikes.

'A while ago Bérégovoy was killed in a town called Nevers and we put out the story that he shot himself with a revolver; unfortunately, Bérégovoy was causing problems to our Government but it's known, generally that Andanson was in Nevers on the day Bérégovoy was shot.' Puteaux was playing down the pulse-racing encounters he was describing, because he wanted to be seen as a cool man of the world.

'We managed to get away with calling that suicide although whoever shot him,' said Puteaux with a knowing look, 'messed up in not only shooting him from too great a range for suicide but also with a .357 Magnum revolver that nearly blew his head off and which Bérégovoy didn't own. We will not go into details that are not relevant but some of our assets are not as thorough as we would like. Some tend to be arrogant when it comes to eliminating people and think that if they obey their orders, they can leave us to clean up the mess. We cannot seem to persuade them to ensure they leave no unanswered questions, so our public don't become alarmed; a possibility if the press get to hear something. They tend to rely on the fact that we rarely have a problem with persuading our public, who are very trusting of our politicians, and us. They have a very positive attitude!

'I thought it best to give you a full description of the man from our files and then discuss our way forward,' said Puteaux and, without waiting for an answer; he continued to recount the facts. 'As you are aware, we found the Fiat Uno some time ago and agreed to keep the details hidden from the press after you informed us that you had used Andanson in your protection operation of the Princess. Because Mohamed al Fayed's investigators found the car also, we were made to look rather foolish; it gave the impression we were unable to find a vehicle that others did with relative ease.

'We warned those investigators off, but couldn't prevent them from revealing their findings so people will know of Monsieur Andanson and ask questions, making him feel more important and putting him in temptation's way. He is arrogant at the best of times and thinks he is invincible! He has suddenly started to spend even more on cars and is raising eyebrows, with everyone wondering where all his newfound wealth is coming from. Now we have rumours that he's bragging about knowing who killed the Princess of Wales, even telling some friends he was there in the Alma tunnel.'

'Right,' thought Morison, suddenly feeling a cold chill rise through his spine. 'We now have a situation where our hosts and colleagues don't know what we have done and we must maintain that. We also have to deal with this problem, with the help of the French police, but with them having a different perspective of why they are doing it. Andanson knows both scenarios! He knows he worked for us, and the French don't currently know that we ordered the hit in the Alma tunnel. If he decides to play us off against the French for more money, using his contacts here in France to protect him, this becomes a nightmare scenario. We cannot take him out because the French would be up in arms and if we don't then we risk losing everything. This man screwed up the hit on the Mercedes and now is threatening to end our existence. Some choice! What choice?'

Puteaux had described a man he had come to think of as a possible liability largely because of his lifestyle and connections. One never knew what Andanson was saying and to whom, since he had contacts on a very cordial basis with many top people. He would only need to say something indiscreet to powerful political ears and the whole world of the British and French Secret Service could be plunged into turmoil.

Puteaux continued. 'It's come to our attention that Monsieur Andanson has been talking to his friends and jeopardising our positions. We need to watch him very carefully, staying close and, if he talks too much then we shall need to act.'

Morison was now impressed with Puteaux's more menacing stance and surprised to see this man prepared to do whatever he felt necessary. He was more content than a few moments ago and grateful for the speed with which Puteaux had brought him over to discuss what was, at this stage, only a potential problem. Having the French need the same protection from Andanson as MI6 was most gratifying.

Morison now knew that Puteaux believed Andanson posed a possible threat and Morison would have to put surveillance in place immediately because of the potential damage Andanson could do to both parties. Puteaux's concerns were of being found out by the French press for cooperating with British intelligence in covering up the murder. Morison feared French intelligence would realise the British had been lying all along.

'Some of our people have been watching Andanson at his home and followed him on some of his recent photographic assignments,' said Puteaux. 'We have an agent inside his circle that will pick up on any indiscretions and report on his behaviour. We thought you might like to be involved in setting up a joint observation team until we are satisfied what we've heard isn't exaggerated. I have called you over because I felt a serious disquiet, so thought it better to play safe.'

'Thank you very much for your concern,' said Morison. 'We always prefer to be prepared. Yes, I think we shall join you and take the opportunity of seeking more information.'

Morison was thinking, 'Not only did Andanson screw up the hit by making contact with the Mercedes, but now seems unable to keep his mouth shut. Normally we would have used our own men for a hit but this was very atypical. It illustrates the problems of using people who kill for money. If only Jim Winfield hadn't rebelled! I hope to God I never need to use the Incremental reserve, ever again!

'I cannot take action here, without my French counterpart's

approval or risk diplomatic problems but as long as we watch Andanson, we shall be ready when, and if, necessary and the French remain on side. We must ensure Andanson doesn't speak with the French police because under pressure he may tell them of his real role at the Alma. A window of opportunity may come our way, but as long as we keep the French on side and I stay close to Puteaux, we shall be in a position to strike as and when necessary. We must maintain our Entente Cordial, if possible, but strike soon; whatever the cost!'

CATHARSIS

The interminable torment of controlling this operation had now continued for much longer than Morison had predicted and seemed as though it would never cease. Another week, month or year; how long before this resource wastage and nightmare of having to constantly deliver spurious propaganda would end?

'Wouldn't it have been cheaper and more effective to get rid of Charles Windsor?' Morison thought, as he prepared for his next meeting on an analysis of the current status of the people's mood in relation to the monarchy. 'Like banging your head against a brick wall,' he mused, as he considered the role he must play. He read through the recently prepared files on Charles Windsor's current standing in the public's psyche and his chances of being able to marry his mistress while still remaining heir to the throne.

'Charles has made it clear his coming marriage isn't negotiable, so there is no issue of whether he will get married, or not, but rather of when he does and what then do we expect from the public. I can see why some of my ex-colleagues have joined the palace, since we seem to be spending an inordinate amount of time acting as nursemaids; might as well get paid extra for it!'

It was now a matter of MI6 continuing and doing whatever was needed so palace routines could continue as near normal. Any requirement for action would come from the changing mood of the people, so the Service would report untoward behaviour, or mood swings, to the palace and then assist in supplying the appropriate disinformation.

Morison couldn't escape being involved in any new threat to the monarchy, because the people's furore over the Paris attack hadn't abated. He hadn't found the peace of a full night's sleep since and still there was no end in sight. Service personnel were now looking elsewhere to rebuild their lives, although still under the effect of the Official Secrets Act.

Not only had the shock of the Princess's murder affected many of the public, much more than anyone within the Service had anticipated, but also many in the Service were greatly disillusioned. There were those who felt they joined the Service to protect the state and its people and had now been responsible for hurting those whom they were sworn to protect, more than they had ever been hurt. They were witnessing the biggest outpouring of public grief ever known; all because of them. This was not conducive to good public relations. Many in the Service thought they couldn't continue to serve.

Morison knew of possible problems that could still come from Paris and was disappointed, albeit not surprised, when Monsieur Puteaux of the French Interior Ministry telephoned him to say that he urgently needed to speak with him and would be travelling to London later that week. Morison asked his secretary to arrange an appointment for that Friday morning at 10.00am. 'Better get some decent coffee in,' thought Morison!

Puteaux arrived with a present; two jars of coffee that had been preferred by Morison when he was in Puteaux's Paris office.

'Good morning, Françoise, did you have a good trip? Morison said in his usual casual tone and, seeing Puteaux's gift, 'Thank you so much Françoise, what a nice surprise! I was wondering what coffee to serve you today, so that's one problem solved. There, a good start, you see!'

Morison handed the jars to his secretary with instructions that this coffee was to be used today and was, thereafter, for his personal use only.

'What's your latest feedback on Andanson?' asked Puteaux, coming straight to the point and not responding to Morison's attempt to lighten the occasion.

'I asked for the latest report, which arrived a few days ago,' said Morison, 'and it suggests Andanson is behaving well enough. We have no untoward reports on anything we could regard as dangerous.'

'Regrettably,' said Puteaux, 'my feedback is different.'

Morison sat back in his chair, very focused and all ears.

'We are very reliably informed that Andanson has been very indiscreet,' said Puteaux, intensifying eye contact and scrutinising

Morison's every flicker.

'Really,' said Morison, unable to find the words to ask what Puteaux was thinking and subconsciously preparing himself for the worst.

Puteaux continued; 'You already know he has been saying, according to one of my most reliable operatives, that he was in the Alma tunnel at the time of the Princess of Wales crash.' Before Morison could respond Puteaux stated; 'that's not all! He is claiming he was involved in the Princess's murder and that the operation was controlled and organised by British Intelligence; that he was paid by you.'

Puteaux's face was no longer smiling or looking relaxed but fixed and holding a steady gaze at a man who had just been struck by lightning but where much depended on him not showing it. Puteaux watched and waited for Morison's eyes to yield the truth.

Morison went apoplectic! He knew he must give some meaningful response or the game was up but he mustn't allow his expression to betray even a flicker of truth. He must respond and in an animated way because he couldn't contain his growing tension.

He erupted. 'What is this man doing? We pay him to look after the Princess; he fails and now claims he is the hit man of the century. What's coming next, a large cash hand-out, I shouldn't wonder, for him to keep quiet about something that manifestly isn't true? You don't believe this for God's sake, do you Françoise?'

Puteaux was quick to respond. 'We always listen to our operatives and our man is not saying he has evidence of your complicity, only that it's what Andanson is saying, so we put this to you for your comments before we approach him.'

'Good enough,' said Morison, 'and to that you are entitled.' But he was thinking: this is dangerous! This moment could change history! He must continue; Puteaux wasn't convinced!

'We paid Andanson to act as an informant on the paparazzi, who we knew would be present in large numbers on the night of the 30th August. His task was to be close to the Princess's Mercedes and assist in ensuring it travelled to the rue Arsène Houssaye apartment without being harassed. He was appointed to report on the intentions of the paparazzi and if there were any problems that needed our response since, being one of them, he was likely to obtain better feedback. He was not supposed to get close to the car and we came to regret involving him.

'Are you telling us Andanson is saying that he was acting as our agent and paid to murder Diana? Convenient: he fails to protect the Princess and then says he didn't fail but succeeded in killing her and for that, I have no doubt, he will require a great deal more money, from us. Ego enhancing nonsense and blackmail, said Morison, 'and he's using you to achieve it. What a wonderful twist! He screws up and wants our fucking money as well.'

Morison's disingenuous comment and contrived rage was intended to offer Puteaux an alternative concept to his currently held view that the Service had indeed murdered the Princess, and project an alternative. He was on safe ground because Puteaux had already told him there was no evidence of MI6 complicity, so he could throw this into the curve and hope the idea of Andanson being an agent, or creating a situation to exact more money from the British, would unbalance the clear view Puteaux held.

This meeting had come out of the blue and was the most potentially lethal Morison had ever been required to deal with off the cuff. This needed a careful and balanced response that was both plausible and as near the truth as possible, because Morison didn't know whether Puteaux was telling him everything he knew or what he might later discover. As the best lies are those that are closest to the truth, Morison felt that his dialectic must now proffer this position, without deprecating Andanson. Morison must retain his sangfroid! This was his greatest test! Today, he would earn his money!

'Let us look at Andanson's purpose,' said Morison, feeling that Puteaux had now at least allowed his reserve to subside. 'He is driven by money, more than most, and although he was chosen to assist us in protecting the Princess, we had some reservations about his suitability. But time was short and we didn't feel he would have a problem handling the simple task of reporting on paparazzi plans and intentions. You will recall that you expressed serious concerns over his suitability for roles such as these, which you made known to me earlier; well, it would appear you were right. We shall not use him again.

'If he wanted more money, how would he create the opportunity for this? He would need to persuade that he had information it was worth us paying him for. If he doesn't have any information, that leaves him with the need to create a reason for us to pay him,' concluded Morison, looking across at Puteaux to see whether such devious reasoning had carried his counterpart.

'That means he needs to spread stories, not too far afield,' chanced Morison, 'otherwise the game would be up and he would jeopardise any possible pay out.'

Puteaux's eyes reflected deliberation on the points Morison had just delivered and that he might be thinking there was sense to what Morison was saying. He didn't want a problem because the effects of such an upheaval would be catastrophic to Anglo-French relations, not to mention the well-being of the respective heads of state who had endorsed the current position.

'So the Entente Cordial remains intact,' Morison quipped, sensing Puteaux's thinking and preferring a spontaneous response rather than a well-considered one, he immediately continued. 'How do we deal with a man who puts us in this position for money? What is he going to do next? Not only could he incriminate British Intelligence but also you, because if we did as Andanson says then, in the eyes of the people, you must be party to it. They would never believe otherwise!

'What shall we do?' asked Morison, leaving the decision with Puteaux and wanting him to decide on what action to take.

'I shall need to assess the position,' said Puteaux, because we have a new system for this sort of problem, where I need to report with my reasons and personally confirm the need for such action and that there is no alternative.'

Morison's perversion of the truth had worked; Puteaux was softening!

'We have people near to Andanson now,' said Morison, 'who will handle this, if you wish, once you have obtained clearance.'

Morison was keen to get the job done sooner rather than later because as each moment passed there was no way of knowing who Andanson was speaking to or what his next trick might be. He never had qualms about this sort of job because people like Andanson knew the score. If they put the lives of others, or the operation for which they were engaged, at risk knowing the pre-operation agreement for silence, the consequences were inevitable. Neither man had mentioned the action required; both knew!

'I shall get back to you,' said Puteaux. 'Please accept our apologies for questioning you on your motives but you understand our position. We had to ask you the question eye to eye.'

'Don't worry,' said Morison. 'We would be in the same position.

Just let's ensure this situation with Andanson doesn't worsen and permission is swiftly granted.'

Morison couldn't believe he had just managed to escape that test without faltering and felt rather proud of his spontaneous response; this is what he was paid for, but by God didn't he earn his money? But wait a moment: what if Puteaux's team didn't give approval or what if they wanted to try something else first, such as interrogating Andanson, and perhaps offering him some inducement to talk.

Morison was nervous that the French objective to prevent a man talking about covering up the death of a foreign princess wouldn't require them to pull all the stops out. After all, they didn't murder her!

'Their reasons for requiring a hit on Andanson may not be strong enough,' Morison thought. 'And what if Andanson gives the game away and proves to the French police he was involved in the murder of the Princess and that we engaged him? What if he does have photographs of the attack? Why would he reveal those? He then stands convicted from his own evidence, so surely he wouldn't do that. But who knows what motivates the man and what the French may be prepared to offer him to talk.'

Another thought crossed Morison's mind, as he considered what the French may elect to do rather than commit to the ultimate sanction, and one more nightmare possibility occurred.

'What if,' Morison continued his professional self-torture, 'what if the French decide that the risk to them doesn't justify the ultimate sanction and they can afford to be generous? What if they change their minds and decide that, since they have used him themselves, it would be too risky because others whom they have recruited will know one of theirs has been eliminated, and this won't go down well with future recruitment campaigns? Nobody wants to work for an organisation that executes its employees. What if they decide to run a fake on his death and send him into exile, under the threat that if he ever returns he will be executed?

'But then,' sighed Morison, 'I could go on all day with possible scenarios and, let's face it, anything could happen. We make decisions based on our intelligence and that's it. We get some right; some we don't.'

Morison knew that whatever the French did he had a clear duty: he must ensure Puteaux dealt with this situation quickly.

Andanson must go and now!

'I shall speak to our people who are currently over there and perhaps go and talk to them myself. If the French delay, we may need to pre-empt them.'

***

Arriving at Villacoublay airfield south-west of Paris, Morison went straight to the safe house established by the team he had sent over to observe Andanson's behavior. This was purely an observation team and his objective was to assess the position, make a decision and then appoint the appropriate new team within hours. He must have the situation under control before his French counterpart returned with an answer on Andanson because by then it may be too late if the French decided to play for an easier option.

What had Andanson been saying during these last few months and to whom? How many others knew what happened that night in Paris? The Service had gone to great lengths to remove any evidence of the Fiat brushing against the Mercedes and failed.

'Look at the disaster that created,' thought Morison. 'Let's suppose one of the world's top paparazzi was in the tunnel and has photographs that he hasn't yet declared. He is probably keeping them for another bung later. Not only was this man responsible for the Fiat colliding with the Mercedes, blowing the whole operation, he now threatens us with revelations to the press. He is one of our less fortunate choices of assassins. We need information on Andanson's activities before we take action, otherwise there could be several other people popping up demanding money or, even worse, selling their information to one of the newspapers. We shall have to elicit information from Andanson the good old-fashioned way.'

But then Morison hesitated briefly before continuing his deliberations. 'If he's uncooperative, people will certainly know he has been interrogated, so will need to disappear. This becomes more complex! We need him to be found, because a suspicious disappearance would ignite all the conspiracy theorists around the world and tie him in with that night in the Alma. No, he needs to commit suicide, but after we have our information. We need to resolve how we can achieve our required objectives without allowing others to know we have been involved.'

Satisfied with his conclusions, Morison reached his decision. 'Monsieur Andanson will disappear, one way or another, with or without the French, and soon!'

Tom Murphy greeted Morison as he entered the apartment like the old friend that he was. He and Morison had joined the Service together many years before, but they had gone their separate ways when Morison started to climb the dizzy Service heights. Tom Murphy had stayed in the ranks doing the job he felt was the most important in the world, that of protecting his country. He was an honest, forthright man whom one instinctively trusted, not the type to reach the top of the Service! Murphy knew nothing of the Paris hit and that's the way it was going to stay. Morison had religiously kept the knowledge of that night to a select chosen few and would never break that code.

Murphy said, 'Hello Tom, how's my namesake doing?'

'Well, thanks Tom,' said Morison. 'Have you got all the information on this character we asked for?'

'Of course,' said Murphy, 'don't I always come up with the goods?'

'We have been watching Mr Andanson for several weeks and he has certainly got a vivid imagination. He has claimed to some of his friends that he was involved in the death of Diana. Is that what this is all about?'

Morison didn't like dishing out disinformation to his own people but he had no choice. 'Andanson has worked for us,' he admitted, 'but only as an informer or observer. He has a vivid imagination and the French warned us he is intending to sting us for more money. The biggest danger is, as you have just said, that he is claiming all sorts of things which, if they got out, would cause unbelievable damage to the Service. The truth, as you know, is not the issue. Once an accusation has been made, some dirt will stick which we cannot afford and certainly not about this particular matter.'

'Sounds serious,' said Murphy. 'Not much you can do to persuade him otherwise, I suppose.'

Morison didn't answer but instead asked Murphy to join him in the meeting room to go over his report and clarify some details. 'We can catch up on old times tonight, Tom,' he said. 'I am staying for a couple of days, so we have plenty of time to talk.'

Morison thought perhaps Murphy had the better deal within

the Service. He just did as he was ordered and didn't have any of the headaches. 'Should've stayed in the ranks,' he thought, as he sat down to make yet another life-and-death decision. 'At least I'd see more of the wife; then, on the other hand…'

Murphy began with a description of the assignment Andanson went on during the Service surveillance, and his associates, which produced nothing of much concern or value. He said, 'Tell me how you came to know that Andanson was saying he was involved in the Princess of Wales's death. Where did you obtain that information?'

'We heard word of mouth from one of Andanson's friends who is known to one of our informants, said Murphy. 'It's during the intimate or private moments he lets his guard down and we see the real Monsieur Andanson, especially under the influence of alcohol. His tongue is very loose and he doesn't seem to have the control we expect from an operative.'

Morison thought, 'That is precisely what I was thinking. Even if Andanson didn't have any untoward intentions it really didn't matter, because someone who's indiscreet, even if they don't intend disclosing restricted information, is still dangerous. Information could be blurted out at any time without intent or reason.'

'Do you know precisely what he said,' asked Morison?

'We were told he claimed to be in the Alma tunnel and to have taken photographs of the Mercedes before and during the crash,' said Murphy. 'Oh, and he said he has photographs of the others who were around the car just before it struck the pillar.'

Morison's blood ran cold! He knew there was no time to waste! If the police knew this, they would already have Andanson in custody, being interrogated and trying to solve this murder, no doubt thinking they were doing British Intelligence a favour.

Morison pondered his position. 'Would the French give the go-ahead for action on Andanson if they feel he could be of use in solving this crime? We must raise the stakes with the French and ask that we be allowed to take action before they interview him. We must fabricate a reason why this should be done now so I shall telephone Puteaux and stress the urgency. We can interrogate Andanson to find out what he has said, and to whom, but if the French are present they will want to know all Andanson has to say and respond accordingly.

'If Andanson realises the plight he's in he will spill the beans to save his skin. We must decide on how we persuade the French to move now,' thought Morison, 'and give them a plausible reason that they will have difficulty refusing. We must carry French support otherwise we are severely restricted in obtaining information from Andanson since, with a corpse, we shall have minimal interrogation techniques available if we have to worry about his post-mortem condition. Without state assistance, fabricating suicide may not be feasible.

'This is one I shall need to sleep on. I must decide on the approach to Puteaux and will telephone him first thing in the morning. What about a pleasant evening out at a good local restaurant with a bottle or two of wine Tom?' said Morison; 'Let us relax for one night. This problem will still be with us in the morning.'

***

'Good morning Tom,' said Puteaux, as a hung-over Morison answered the telephone.

Morison drank his coffee with one hand as he fumbled the phone with the other, trying to awake to this new dilemma that must be resolved today. How many more of these last-minute problems, any one of which could sink us, he wondered, as he considered how they should deal with a very unstable and unreliable assassin.

'Good morning Francoise; do you have any information or report for me on Andanson yet.'

Puteaux responded with a reply that made Morison sober up immediately and feel like he hadn't touched a drink for weeks. 'Yes,' said Puteaux. 'We have the green light to proceed. It's not only for the reasons we discussed but our special branch of police have been investigating Andanson for months and say he has been causing severe problems. I cannot go into detail but their investigations show some rather embarrassing facts.

'You already know of Andanson's presence in Nevers on the same day Prime Minister Bérégovoy was shot. I am forbidden to go into detail about that, or some others, but our undercover teams tell us Andanson has been talking out of turn and brought some of my colleagues into a dangerous focus. He is becoming known to many people and putting our state security at risk.'

'I understand,' said Morison, not really listening. He could only think what a stroke of unbelievable luck. He could proceed with the blessing and cooperation of the French instead of having to deliver a fabricated story. There was always a chance of being rumbled and now the French wanted the same thing, albeit for a different reason. One more assignment using their best team and they should be home free.

The only issue with Morison was the uncertainty of what precisely the French police knew. Did they know anything about Andanson's comments concerning the death of the Princess of Wales, or were they just dealing with one of their own problems?

Morison was reluctant to start questioning Puteaux on this point, pushing his luck he thought, but also wondered whether they knew more and had told someone at a higher level. Were they testing him again? If the police knew the details, it was fait accompli. If not, all well and good!

'If I push for more information I risk raising suspicions about why, and after my recent meeting with Puteaux I can do without rocking the boat. He resolved to accept the good graces of the police, get this job done quickly, and be prepared for a possible awkward question later, when proof would no longer be available.'

Morison knew whom he wanted for this role and must find out whether he could reach him quickly since, as always, time was of the essence and there must be no delay.

REDEMPTION

Richard Stedman had just returned from the first holiday he had had in the last four years and was feeling fresh and invigorated on returning to the office. Thirty-four years old, with a sporting build and good looking even without a suntan, he now had all the women's heads turning as he entered his London office. He wished he was back in the Caribbean with his beautiful wife and three children but all good things come to an end and it was the first-day-back blues engulfing him when the call came from Morison.

'Good morning Richard. I understand you have just returned from holiday. Have a good time?' Completing the usual meaningless pleasantries that everyone expected but few valued.

'It was only the absence of the usual pleasantries that caused offence,' thought Stedman, 'so everyone complies; strange world!'

'Wonderful, thank you,' said Stedman, playing the social game. 'I know where I would rather be, especially now you have telephoned me. I could do without a heavy job for a week or so.'

'Now, now,' said Morison, never quite sure whether this was Stedman's famous sense of humour or a serious streak. 'All in the course of duty, you know. We have a problem and I need you in Paris right away. So you see you are travelling again within hours of your return.'

'Yes,' said Stedman, 'but there won't be smiling faces, bikinis and laughter where I am going, I'll wager.'

'You can always get a job stacking shelves or perhaps a nice City job complete with bowler,' quipped Morison, trying to compete with Stedman's humour. 'Perhaps you would like me to put out some feelers for you.'

'I'll be there in the morning,' said Stedman.

'No, today,' said Morison. 'I've booked you the flight at 2.00pm from Heathrow. You will be met at Charles de Gaulle and brought straight to me. It's very urgent Richard, otherwise I wouldn't ask you to travel so soon,' he added more seriously; a tone that Stedman quickly picked up on.

'OK, I shall see you later. Anything I need to bring?'

'No,' said Morison. 'I shall brief you before we go into our meeting when all will become clear. We have arranged accommodation for you. This is of major importance to the State!'

'Aren't they all?' said Stedman, as he put down the phone and went home to pack his bag.

***

Puteaux asked members of his security team, who understood the machinations of the British Secret Service, to brief him on what to expect before meeting with Morison at his Embassy. It was necessary to understand how they would proceed with Andanson's removal and what role the French would be asked to play. Puteaux also needed support! The decision to proceed was taken but it still rankled that this operation was his and not the property of the British Secret Service; irrespective of them having requested it. It was still French soil and a French citizen they were about to eliminate. He had been asked, however, to cooperate and give all assistance to the British and allow them to lead the operation because the French preferred to wash their hands of Monsieur Andanson.

Puteaux discussed with his team what had been gleaned from reports on Andanson over the preceding few months; had they missed something?

'Why were the British so anxious to deal with Andanson? Any startling information?' he asked. 'Anything you have heard Andanson say?' Smoking guns is what he was looking for but nothing new was available. He still retained a niggling question mark over British motives.

Puteaux's main man was Jean-Paul Pettit, a balding, short and mid-forties heavy who knew the art of persuasion, using few subtleties. Puteaux wanted him to work alongside the British to retain some influence. He was a man Puteaux believed could deal with any situation; even a strong willed British Security Service.

Puteaux confirmed to Pettit what role he was to play, which Pettit shrugged off with indifference. He didn't much care for the

British and, together with Puteaux, was suspicious of their motives.

Puteaux was determined to stamp his authority on the meeting and not let Morison take over, so decided to say what was required on behalf of the French state, rather than have Morison dictate process.

He needn't have worried, because Morison's smooth approach always disarmed people. He was aware of the sensitivities this operation would engender on French soil, not to mention the ongoing support he needed from the French. He wanted to keep it that way! This operation could have been a problem instead of a relative formality but for the amazing good fortune of Andanson also having caused problems for the French.

Puteaux decided he would tell Morison that he had received authority on how to proceed and had decided to ask him to lead the assignment, with limited French participation, for political reasons. They would have a few of their agents present to observe. Puteaux would decide on any further requests that might arise and Morison was required to keep him informed. With his approach determined, Puteaux felt better than a few moments ago and his mood changed from apprehension to one of routine commitment; both he and the British had a job to do.

***

Richard Stedman arrived at Charles de Gaulle airport and was taken to the Embassy to receive a full briefing. He took a pragmatic approach to life and his orders but, like most people, he wasn't averse to knowing the truth. He would rather have been at home enjoying the dinner party his wife had organized and talking about their holiday experiences but thought, 'Here we are. I can't control where I am when a job needs doing; anyway, I have probably saved our friends from a boring dissertation on my wonderful holiday.'

Morison waited in an Embassy room and brought Stedman up to the speed on the job, not telling him anything about the role the Service had played on the 31st August. Stedman was one of the ethically flexible personnel, but not one on whom Morison had relied for that evening in Paris. Stedman could probably, however, be relied upon to be very unhappy if he knew the details, as with most of the mainstream personnel and Morison wasn't prepared to take a chance. He would only know about the job in hand; the need to remove one person but to first seek information from him on what he had said during the last few months and to whom.

Stedman would hear details from Andanson, damning to the Service, so Morison would forewarn Stedman of this and be present at the interrogation. It was the only way Morison could achieve control, since he couldn't rely on anyone else.

'Good morning Richard,' said Morison.

'What are we about to do?' asked Stedman. 'I presume this involves the ultimate sanction?'

'Yes, said Morison, I'm afraid it does.'

'Don't be afraid,' said Stedman, 'it's what we are paid for.' He not only found niceties irrelevant but also had little time for the old-world charm comments to which Morison was prone, especially when about to embark on an ultimate sanction.

Morison had no time for indulging in irrelevant preferences! He just wanted to get this job done and so invoked a more stern and matter of fact approach, knowing Stedman would respond.

'We have a Frenchman who has worked for us on some occasions and also for our French colleagues, who has begun causing problems. He is now an embarrassment to the French so they are cooperating to remove the problem; that's where you come in. His name is James Andanson and he is a paparazzo freelance journalist who has spent several years pursuing the rich and famous for a living.

'During August as you know we lost the Princess of Wales and Andanson was one of the surrogates we used in her protection by feeding us with information on what the paparazzi were up to and photographing any that were becoming too aggressive, so we would be able to target them for her protection. He has decided his pay wasn't good enough and he's trying to blackmail us into paying for his silence. He is threatening to claim we were involved in the Princess of Wales's death; an idea, no doubt, fuelled by all the conspiracy theorist drivel we have endured from the media.'

'Nothing serious then,' retorted Stedman. 'That should do it nicely. Is he mentally unstable or what?'

'Just greedy and extremely arrogant in thinking we will submit to this threat,' said Morison. 'He believes the French police protect him but doesn't realise he has also outlived his welcome with the French so his protection there has gone. We are doing this in conjunction with the French, so there won't be any come back.'

'Sounds straightforward,' said Stedman, and then as a bolt out of the blue: 'What exactly was Andanson doing in the tunnel in Paris?'

'All these operations are classified, as you are well aware,' snapped Morison, 'and you should know better than to ask but just for you...' Wanting to keep Stedman on side but not wanting to appear to be giving excuses, he kept it brief. 'He was watching her movements and we messed up that night. We really don't want to go over the reasons for the operations failure. It would be extremely embarrassing. There is still an internal review ongoing but I shall let you know when we have our report; provided you keep it secure.'

Stedman considered these to be excuses. He knew the Service well and read between the lines. He sensed all wasn't as Morison had described, but it was not his job. He thought, 'If the truth lies elsewhere then I will never know and am not sure that I want to know. Sounds more to me like Andanson messed up; my employers never were of a forgiving nature!'

Morison completed the detailed breakdown of Andanson's activities and then decided it was time to go to their meeting.

'Anything you desperately need before we join the others?' said an irritated Morison.

'No,' replied Stedman, 'but when do we move?'

'Within the next few days,' said Morison. 'It's best we deal with it as soon as possible.'

'Good,' said Stedman. 'I would like to get this over and done with. I have missed my meal this evening but Mary has another planned for next Saturday and I would like to be home for that.'

Morison could never understand how these people could be so matter of fact when about to initiate the ultimate sanction. 'I suppose, he thought, 'he's always distancing himself from the act despite being its instigator; morality is hardly in the job description.'

It was always lost on Morison, because he never allowed himself to consider it, that without those who initiate and create these operations, like him, there would be no ultimate sanction to invoke.

Morison and Stedman went down the Embassy corridor and directly to the room where they knew the meeting with Puteaux was to be held. Puteaux's team was waiting, looking more unsettled than Morison thought they should but courteous as ever and refreshments had been provided. Morison began what he hoped would be his last field meeting on this operation.

'Here we are again,' he thought, trying to ease the tension both he and Stedman were feeling. Morison couldn't help wondering what Puteaux really knew and had Andanson given him any evidence of their complicity in Paris? That would be lethal? There was, however, nothing he could do. He had to continue with the meeting and resolve this problem; he hoped no more surprises awaited him.

Puteaux was nervous but this was nothing to do with knowledge of Andanson's role in Paris. It was more with his French pride and how he would control today.

Morison could always sense these situations and retorted; 'François, thank you for your kind suggestion for this meeting. Please let me know when you wish me to present our request and how much time you can allow us; we shall then fit in accordingly.'

Morison had immediately passed the reins to Puteaux whose fears of being side lined now evaporated, leaving only an operation to be performed!

Morison asked Puteaux to begin with a description of Andanson's more recent history and give background reasons for being here, because he wanted the French to talk everyone into wanting what he wanted before making his request, so it should be granted automatically. They might even think Morison was doing them a favour, and that placed Morison in his best position to exact the support he was going to need, now and later.

A bemused Stedman had been listening and thought he could never do Morison's job. He thought he too was becoming more devious, but Morison's behaviour needed years of practice. He considered Morison's approach creepy and his own manner more forthright; he wouldn't have Morison's patience. 'Still, horses for courses,' he mused, as Puteaux began a dissertation that was to end yet another life in this never-ending story.

'Andanson has been aggressive in building wealth at whatever cost, capturing photographs of famous people whether from stage, the sporting world or royalty; nothing is beyond his remit and he succeeds where others fail,' said Puteaux. 'If someone considers anything impossible, it's Andanson whom one can expect to prove them wrong. Whether it was a fast motorbike chase through the night to make a deadline, or persuading reluctant celebrities to comply with his request for a photographic pose, Andanson was your man.

'The issue today, however, concerns the darker side of Andanson's proclivities. Known for his inclination to do and dare, his whereabouts during the sudden and, in some cases inexplicable, deaths of various celebrities appeared more than a macabre coincidence. The French Secret Service has used him, as well as the British, and now he has crossed the line between being helpful to the authorities and becoming a liability because of his increasing notoriety and loose tongue; he has been noticed! The Services required anonymity from their agents as a prerequisite for success, not a self-serving egocentric.'

Puteaux recounted an overview of Andanson's presence in the town of Nevers on the day of Bérégovoy's supposed suicide and other known activities. Morison knew the detail but this new Englishman needed his intended victim's background.

'Our police know Andanson has been involved in the deaths of a few people, not under their orders,' said Puteaux. 'That means he is obviously open to bribery, so his attachment to us could become known so, like you, we must now render him no longer a threat. Any questions?' Puteaux asked, directing this to Stedman.

Stedman asked about the people to whom Andanson has been speaking out of turn, remembering Morison's recital. 'Are you intending to interrogate them and assess what damage has been done?'

'We shall first interrogate Andanson and determine to whom he has been speaking,' said Puteaux. 'Then we shall know the scope of the problem.'

'What if you find there are other people who now pose the same threat as Andanson through these indiscretions?' said Stedman.

'One step at a time,' Puteaux responded. 'That is what we expect from the interrogation.'

He clearly hadn't given this point much thought and Morison wished that Stedman hadn't asked the question, because any delay of this operation was going to go against the interests of the British Security Services. It also made Morison nervous that the French police would be handling any interrogation, which meant they could discover the truth about the Alma.

'We don't need to review any future possible requirements, I am sure you will agree,' said Morison, addressing his remarks to Puteaux, and seemingly making the comment to protect and support Puteaux's position. Only Morison knew his real objective was to pass over this remark and ensure it wasn't given much airtime, although an increasingly suspicious Stedman was now giving a lot of thought to the logic of Morison's intervention. Making it look like he was doing someone a favour came as second nature to Morison and he just continued as though nothing further need be said on the matter.

'Would it be appropriate for me to proceed,' said Morison?

'Shall we have some more coffee and what I believe you refer to as a natural break first?' said Puteaux, 'and then we should hear your views and the method you intend using.'

Morison used the break to have a brief chat with Stedman about not prolonging Puteaux's decision by mentioning further ideas on how they should proceed. As Morison put it; 'They can do what they like when we have dealt with Andanson.'

The possibility of second-hand and unproven comments from strangers concerning the night of 31st August didn't worry him so much but Andanson's direct knowledge and probable evidence did.

Stedman didn't understand the problem that seemed to be facing Morison. He just nodded his acceptance. Why was Morison so nervous about the French interviewing Andanson, unless his initial reservations had been correct?

Morison needed to keep this as brief as possible and obtain agreement, so they could proceed to the operational phase and fix a provisional date to arrest Andanson before they closed the meeting. He didn't want to appear too keen but was caught between fearing the police might find something out about Andanson's involvement in Paris on 31st August before the Service took action and also that Andanson might tell even more people if there was a further delay thus causing another crisis!

Morison converted his eagerness to one of determination that neither French nor British objectives should fail, once again to draw Puteaux on side to his reasoning.

Morison began, 'We have a major problem here that needs immediate resolution. If we don't proceed quickly, then I believe that both of our governments risk severe embarrassment, if not worse. I am not familiar with the detail of your particular experiences with Andanson, which I know are not for publication, but action now will contain that risk otherwise you could lose as well.

'Like you, we have used Andanson on a few occasions for surveillance and some photographic work and he was perfectly satisfactory. The big problem for us is that on the 30th August 1997 we unfortunately used him in a surveillance role on the Princess of Wales when he inadvertently brushed against the Princess's car in trying to prevent other vehicles getting near to her as it approached the tunnel.

'We cannot say for sure whether his actions were negligent but they were certainly incompetent and as a result the Princess car smashed into the pillars of the tunnel. Whether this was a direct result of Andanson's contact we cannot be sure, but you can imagine what the press would make of it. We would have been responsible for a deliberate attack and, if that is believed, as it may well be, then we have a major crisis.

'Andanson is now threatening to go public with his fabricated notion that we instructed him to attack the Princess's car and he was paid to assist, unless we pay him a very large sum. That's it gentlemen! We either do this immediately or risk losing more than I care to imagine.'

Morison's French colleagues had already been briefed on what he was going to say so there were no gasps of astonishment. Most of those assembled believed it was necessary to do what they had come here for anyway, but the French were going through the rigmarole of requiring the British to ask, despite the fact that they wanted the same result, for very different reasons. They would have proceeded without the British.

No apparent problems had been thrown up from the meeting and it seemed that Puteaux was going to approve the hit. They would move into the operational phase straight away. Stedman felt the need to add a further point that he thought was relevant to complete a professional job.

He looked straight at Morison as he addressed the assembly, as if entreating his boss to realise that he considered this point necessary. 'When we have completed our task,' said an unusually subtle Stedman, 'we shall have the remains of someone whom we shall have been persuading to reveal information. You have said that for Andanson to disappear is not an option; he must be found. If so, then this limits the persuasive techniques we use to extract the required information and reduces our chances of success. It seems incongruous for us to enter into an operation without maximising our chances; any ideas?'

Morison was furious! Stedman was right but their main objective was to keep this operation on track, not introduce something that might delay the decision. Stedman had now compromised their position and Morison was angry that he had, only minutes before, forbidden any further spontaneous comments.

Morison cast his eyes past Stedman addressing Puteaux directly, to try and ensure he carried him with his answer. 'This is a valid point and we shall resolve it,' said Morison, 'but we mustn't side-line what must be done. May I suggest we proceed with the interrogation now? We won't know the answer to some questions until this task is completed; there is too much risk in delay and we may find Andanson very cooperative.' He was trying to keep Puteaux on side.

'Very well,' said Puteaux, also convinced they couldn't delay and had spent enough time discussing what they knew must be done. 'Let's consider our roles and when we intend moving on our target.'

Morison nodded his agreement.

Puteaux began; 'Intelligence tells us that Andanson will be at home around the 3rd or 4th of May, which gives us ample time. Our agents, who are watching him, will notify us of any changes in his plans but may I suggest we ask Andanson to meet us near to his home to discuss his ongoing role with us following the attack in Paris.'

This was a slip from Puteaux in admitting that he thought of the Paris crash as an attack, not an accident, and this was not lost on Stedman, who just continued to look ahead without showing a glimmer of emotion. Morison also wondered what Puteaux had found out about the 31st August and once more felt compromised but was unable to do anything.

'Stedman didn't miss that either,' thought Morison, as he glanced across at Stedman, feeling he handled his nonchalant response rather well. 'No point in worrying about what one of our own operatives thinks.' He needed to retain his caution because, although Stedman was considered ethically flexible, so was Winfield.

It was lost on him that some will kill for their country, as in war, whereas others will draw the line between that and killing for convenience, without any moral code. Morison never allowed himself time to ponder this point because subconsciously he knew he wouldn't like the conclusion that must be drawn. He didn't differentiate; others did! He was initiating these acts and Winfield drew the line, so what did that make him by comparison?

'We don't employ fools, so there is bound to be some questioning going on, just so long as we don't have to give answers,' pondered Morison, maintaining his momentum. Not dwelling on Puteaux's unintended faux pas, Morison turned an expectant gaze on him as if to request he should continue.

'We believe our agents should work in conjunction with yours so we can facilitate the meeting between you and Andanson,' continued Puteaux. 'We also prefer that you handle the attack because of your history with Andanson. People will believe it was us but you give us some breathing space.'

'Wonderful,' thought Morison, 'but at least that suits our purpose rather well. Now, how do I control the interrogation?'

'My people have just located a remote dwelling near to Andanson's home for our meeting with him. We can then take the necessary action'.

'Good,' said Morison, in his matter of fact way. 'We must decide who plays what role in this and you have kindly given us conduct of the operation.'

'Yes,' said Puteaux; 'We accept that you should lead the operation but my instructions are to remain involved, so our interests are protected. We need to minimise damage Andanson may have done and be prepared for any comeback.

'Right,' said Morison. 'Richard Stedman here is our man in charge of eliciting the facts from Andanson. If I could ask Richard to liaise with your people to agree their respective roles, then I think we can rely on them.'

'Very well,' said Puteaux, gesturing to Pettit and turning to Richard Stedman. 'I have appointed Monsieur Pettit to assist you. He will know what is needed from Andanson but I confirm you are in overall charge of this operation. Do you need anything from us for your interrogation apart from somewhere to take Andanson?'

'Do you have any state of the art thumb screws?' asked Stedman, never being able to resist a joke and now pushing Morison to the limit. 'No thank you, Monsieur Puteaux,' he continued, quickly recovering his position and realising Morison was becoming impatient with his flippancy. 'I am sure we shall manage.'

Puteaux was still wondering what Stedman had said. 'What is a thumb screw?' He was in the process of reaching for his English dictionary when Morison joined in to offset any possible embarrassment.

'We shall both be on site for this rather important interrogation, so I shall also be able to inform you of anything that is said of significance. Rest assured we know this operation is of equal importance to both of us.' Stedman's crass comments couldn't be allowed to cause Morison any upset; he was, after all, the best they had for the task about to be performed.

Stedman and Pettit stayed behind to discuss their respective roles, time scales and methods, so Morison and Puteaux retired to the hotel bar for a relaxing drink, whilst the two whose role was about to be played out remained to establish the basics of who would do what and when.

Pettit was not the intellectual type of agent with whom one could enjoy or risk some irreverent banter but more of a man that even Stedman preferred to stay on the right side of, especially since they were now going to be working together and relying on each other. Two killers together and neither seemed able to relax. Both felt suspicious of the other and knew this mood would remain. Stedman knew his own capabilities but felt that Pettit was not a man who could exhibit self-control and would need watching.

An unspoken understanding seemed to exist that allowed them to discuss the job in hand and nothing more. Pettit had been told by Puteaux that Stedman was in charge and that made for an easier passage when discussing who did what.

'We need to get Andanson to the house for our meeting, by telephoning him just before we are ready to see him, said Stedman. 'I don't believe he will be prepared to attend a prearranged meeting, since he will be nervous of whose there. I understand he has powerful friends, so we can't be sure he won't warn one if the meeting is prearranged. We need to keep the details of this operation to ourselves. No political figures are to know when or where, or any of our intentions. Nothing, until it is fait accompli!'

Stedman was to be surprised at how well Pettit responded to these comments. It seemed as though he was thinking along the same professional lines, thus giving Stedman some leeway with Pettit's initial recalcitrant stance.

'I agree,' Pettit replied. 'We need this done quickly and without interference from our bosses. We know what's required and have all we need, with one exception. How do we interrogate Andanson and meet the boss's objectives of having the body discovered? There is only one answer; he must commit suicide and the body found but in an unrecognisable state.'

'How are we going to do that?' said Stedman, thinking that Pettit had now lost his marbles. 'If we present this as a suicide people will find him in a condition not conducive to suicide.'

'Not so,' said Pettit! 'He will be depressed, go a long way away and set fire to himself. That way there will be no remains left for post-mortem and no evidence remaining of his encounter with us.'

'But we can never destroy all the evidence; some is bound to remain,' said a bemused Stedman. 'And why would a man burn himself in that way? Nobody will believe its suicide!'

'Not if enough petrol is used and whatever the judge says happened is what happened,' said Pettit with a wink.

Stedman pondered this for a while looking for flaws and said, 'Well, I can't think of any other way of doing it but it will be obvious.'

'Obvious doesn't matter,' said Pettit rather arrogantly. 'There is this thing called proof and there won't be any. If one of our judges says it's suicide; it's suicide!'

Stedman knew how close this was to his own Service's thinking but in France this could have an even better chance of success.

Stedman considered the idea more acceptable after thinking about it. 'We are in France after all and pulling this off over here is a lot easier than in Britain. We do, however, need to carry British and world opinion, so this job, although not directly linked with the Princess of Wales' death, will inevitably have some making the connection.' His thoughts continued. 'Whatever a French judge says won't be seriously challenged, so if there is no other way then I suppose this could be the answer.'

Passing on from these thoughts, because there was no better solution, Stedman said, 'What method of interrogation should we use?'

'We shall invite Andanson to meet us near to the venue where we'll be taking him but not mention the actual address, because he may tell whoever is in the house where he is going,' replied Pettit. 'There is a public call box near his house that we shall use because the call must not be traceable to anyone. We shall call and invite him to join us close by and then take him to our chosen location, so he won't have time to contact his powerful friends. If he refuses then we will use more persuasive methods. We shall initiate the interrogation by gentle means because he may decide to be cooperative.'

'Unlikely,' said Stedman, having read through Andanson's notes. 'It's more likely he will demand we do as we are told and threaten us with being reported to one of his highflying friends if we don't. We shall administer the coup de grâce and take him to a remote place for disposal. If his remains cannot be identified, how will the authorities be satisfied that it is Andanson? What if he commits suicide in his own car? If it's his car, at least people will know it's likely to be Andanson, even if there is little remaining of him.'

'Good thinking,' said Pettit, warming a little to his new colleague. Stedman's gruesome and decisive responses seem to have won Pettit over and now they were actually looking forward to their work, as only graduates of the dark arts could.

***

It was 3rd May 2000. Stedman and Pettit departed for their secret location at a rented farmhouse near Lignières, arriving at 8.30 a.m. They began setting up the apparatus for extracting information from Andanson to end this nervousness felt by both French and British Services.

A local telephone box close to Andanson's house would be used for persuading him to meet at a local and secluded location not far from his home. There were no buildings between the roadside meeting place with Andanson and their venue, so there was little chance of anyone witnessing them take him in an enclosed van to their abode, bringing his car behind.

Intelligence had told them Andanson was at home and would be for a day or so, but he was given to taking off on assignments at a moment's notice, so the Services knew they couldn't wait for the perfect moment but must move while they had the chance. They must make it happen!

Pettit suggested he should phone Andanson and arrange a meeting now and Stedman replied; 'Speed is important but we mustn't scare him off or give him time to phone his friends. We must act within moments of phoning, to maintain the pressure. Yes, we prepare now and call him in an hour; say you need to meet in fifteen minutes and note his response. Give him no more than ten minutes to consider his decision. Is his wife at home with him?'

'Yes,' said Pettit, quickly realising what Stedman was implying as he smiled his agreement.

Pettit travelled to the public telephone kiosk and telephoned Andanson, who answered the call and immediately knew who this man was.

'Good morning, James,' said Pettit, in a friendly manner that required a concerted effort. 'We understand you want to discuss a further advance on your British fee and we need to talk to you about how much you expect.'

Andanson thought, what fee? Perhaps I should find out?

'I can't make it today,' said Andanson, 'I am very busy for the next few weeks. Why don't you call back then and we'll arrange to meet up somewhere, perhaps in my lawyer's office?'

'We have instructions to deal with this immediately,' said Pettit, responding closer to his real temperament. 'These matters cannot be held over for long periods, so we must see to you now.' Then, trying to sound more conciliatory: 'It won't take long, I promise you.'

Andanson told Pettit to call back and he would see what he could do, then put down the phone. Pettit used his mobile to call Stedman and recount what had just transpired.

Stedman said, 'Give him ten minutes and call him back but this time be insistent.'

'Right,' said Pettit. 'I'll give him five.'

Five minutes passed and Pettit phoned again. Andanson was still reluctant but now Pettit's voice changed. 'We must meet now otherwise we shall come round to your house and discuss the whole affair in your living room. I am sure you won't mind your wife listening in, will you?' Pettit retorted sarcastically, leaving no doubt of his determination. 'I have other pressing matters to deal with and I can't hang around in the countryside waiting for you.'

'Very well, where are we going to meet?' Andanson asked.

'We aren't far from you now,' said Pettit. 'In fact, we are just at the end of your road, so will meet you there and proceed to where we can discuss this whole matter properly.'

Andanson had been thinking of escaping this meeting but

realised they were much too close and his wife was in danger. She was vulnerable to these people! They could do as they pleased and he knew it. He thought they must have heard of his comments to friends of being in the Alma tunnel. Perhaps they really wanted to talk and resolve this; perhaps he could apologise for any indiscretions and they would let bygones be bygones.

'Not a chance,' he thought. 'These people don't forget or forgive or take chances. I have made my bed, he thought, and perhaps this time I have gone too far. I must go but will arm myself to have some chance if things get out of hand. I will also write a letter to my bosses so, if things go completely wrong, that at least will give my family some protection.'

Andanson left his house at 10.00am and went to the agreed location to meet his nemesis. There wasn't much hope in his heart this was going to end well but his mind was in a whirl and there was always a chance. He tried to remain positive as he drove towards the secluded location chosen by the Services.

He posted his letter on the way; a French agent noted this and ensured the letter would be intercepted later. A car was waiting for Andanson at the meeting place. Andanson got out of his car and stood by the driver's door as if ready to leave quickly but knowing he couldn't do that or he wouldn't be here in the first place. Logic wasn't functioning on a high while under threat for his life, as he believed he was.

Fingering his automatic handgun he made a move towards the end of his car's hood as if to allow one more chance of escape should all hell suddenly break loose, but the Services were ready. Experience had told them to take their prey into the web slowly and gently, then, as calmly as possible, take the necessary action. People will always believe there is hope, until it's too late, so it was down to the Services to ensure that Andanson had few concerns.

He allowed his semi-automatic to slip back into his pocket and moved towards the waiting car, managing a 'good morning, nice day for a conference', bravado greeting to the waiting agents.

Pettit, who had arrived to meet him in person, moved towards Andanson and gestured him to get into the rear seat of the van, next to one of Pettit's colleagues but first he had another agent frisk Andanson and remove his pistol. Sensing a serious unease with Andanson, Pettit started talking in normal terms about how this must be resolved today or else there could be serious consequences for Andanson, the police and them.

Andanson felt relieved and considered that Pettit genuinely wanting to discuss a solution. Perhaps he was being foolish and melodramatic to think of anything else; perhaps he should relax and not show his nerves. That might go against him! His newly assured view of his position allowed him to feel he could make a gambit for a reasonable settlement rather than take whatever they decided to throw at him. He had gone from feeling terrified to exhibiting his usual arrogance, all within a matter of minutes, and was mentally preparing for the meeting. Perhaps he could make money out of this? Perhaps they wanted to pay him off?

Pettit had done his job well!

They drove through the beautiful, green and leafy French lanes, in the spring sunshine, past grazing cows and horses frolicking in the fields, to the house they had taken for one purpose. Shadows from the tree-lined drive were falling across the lawns of the house and the breeze that had now risen was gently wafting the tops of the trees and cooling the warm air as the car drove through the wrought-iron gates and pulled up at the front door.

Harbouring feelings of resignation, tinged with an ethereal hold on hope, Andanson allowed himself to be taken through the front door of the house and into the kitchen where Stedman plus others were waiting. His heart sank! He knew that an Englishman here, together with the French Secret Service, meant one thing. They were working on something together and he knew what that something must be.

Hope now slipped away and despair crept inexorably into his psyche, blocking out any considerations of escape or defence or reason. An aura of state power pervaded the room and he knew this was his most dangerous moment. The Services needed answers but because of Andanson's apparent resignation to his plight, they felt that gentle persuasion might work so felt the machinery of inducing a response the 'good of fashioned way', contrary to all the tenets of democracy and decency, could be put on hold.

They all sat at the kitchen table, as if to enjoy a pleasant meal with wine and banter and, since Andanson's autonomic defence mechanism was collapsing, all questions were answered without resistance.

Stedman began, 'We understand you have been seeking a higher pay out from the Services for the last few assignments; how do you justify that?'

Andanson was still in a state of shock! 'I have no desire for any further payments. I have received all I was promised and am content. I have not sought further payment,' was his honest response.

'That isn't what we heard,' said Stedman. 'You have been saying you believe you are worth more and you have been telling people things about your involvement in the crash in the tunnel in Paris on August 31st 1997. What are you saying your role was in that crash?'

Morison, who had been sitting quietly on the side, now interceded, not waiting for Andanson to reply. 'You were involved in the operation to protect the Princess of Wales and your car accidentally collided with her car, causing us some serious potential problems, but no matter to that. What else have you been telling people you were asked to do that evening?' Morison had quickly shifted the question to require answers from Andanson concerning his loose tongue, knowing this is what the French would be expecting and required.

Andanson now knew why he was here! If he had been compos mentis he would have realised he was having questions asked where truthful answers would cause serious embarrassment to the British Services. He was not, however, in a reasoning mode due to extreme stress, and didn't know that the French Secret Service were not in cahoots with the British in the Alma venture. Morison must keep it that way!

This knowledge would almost certainly have saved Andanson, and caused a major problem for the British, but all he could do was automatically support Morison. He knew it was what he was supposed to do and felt he must say something that might please those present and perhaps end this nightmare. They might release him! Yes, he would give them what they wanted and hope they might be satisfied. He would not brag anymore concerning his role in Paris on 30th August.

Andanson blurted out, 'Yes, I did collide with the Princess's car, but it was not my intention to do so. I was acting in close surveillance for their protection but they swerved into me.'

Morison now wanted to end this line of questioning before it extended to include what Andanson's precise role had been near to the Mercedes on that night. The man was in self-preservation mode but he might slip. Moving on, Morison pushed the boat out slightly by provoking the point in Andanson's mind that, once confirmed, would settle Service fears.

There was no going back, but Pettit was waiting to ask this question anyway so Morison maintained control and continued; 'Why are you telling people that you were involved in the crash and giving the idea it was deliberate and that you were part of a greater plot?'

'That was not my intention,' said Andanson, now seeing through his haze some remote chance of escape. 'It was an accident and I regret I was there at all.'

Andanson had now made the statement and Morison withdrew from further questioning, leaving the remainder to Stedman and Pettit who were both listening from different perspectives.

Pettit was waiting for his turn to discuss why Andanson had been present on some occasions where people had died suddenly when he knew the French Secret Service had not been involved. He had little interest in the current line of questioning concerning the 31st August 1997. He wanted to know to whom Andanson had been speaking about secret French matters and how much embarrassment, or worse, was in store for them.

Morison wanted to know what Andanson had said concerning the Alma incident and to whom. Stedman knew there was something unreal about Morison's questioning and wanted to satisfy his professional streak. He desperately wanted to ask questions burning in his mind, but knew he must resist. He knew there was more to the Service's involvement in Paris than Morison was admitting.

Morison remained agitated. He must bring this to a close! From the French perspective, Andanson either didn't know what they felt sure he did know, or he wasn't going to divulge it. From Morison's perspective, Andanson would always be a major threat, and for Stedman this was a storm in a teacup and he wondered why the ultimate sanction was about to be invoked unless, of course, his initial feelings had been right and something more had indeed gone down in August 1997. Morison's urgency and rush to execute a man for making frivolous claims, if that was all they were, didn't stack up. Stedman was one of the trusted, ethically-flexible types but not a man of great moral pretensions, so could allow this to pass and discuss it later if he got Morison in a relaxed moment. It was just another job after all!

Stedman spent thirty minutes interrogating Andanson and then retired to the anteroom with Morison, while the rest of the team delivered coffee and stood guard. The names of people to whom Andanson had been bragging were listed and seemed to be given without hesitation.

'We have all we are going to get,' said Stedman, directing his comment to Pettit who nodded his agreement.

Both turned towards Morison, who neither smiled nor moved a facial muscle but looked towards the door as if to say, let's get on with it. As all the agents re-entered the room Pettit caught the eyes of one of his henchman who was standing on guard. He gave the nod.

Andanson was invited out of the room and towards the waiting van that could be seen outside in the courtyard. Turning, he looked back at the three men standing in the corner of the room and saw three unsmiling faces turn away. He walked thought the doors and into the waiting agents who were expert in their work and shot him in the head with a sound-moderated pistol.

When it was over his body was taken into the waiting van and driven to a town called Millau in the south of France, with another member of the team driving Andanson's BMW car behind. When they arrived in Millau, the BMW was taken to a remote part of an army range and Andanson's body was placed inside, soaked in petrol and set on fire. The team stayed long enough to ensure cremation was complete to prevent detailed post-mortem examination and poured more and more petrol over the body until it was utterly destroyed.

Their task was now complete and the team reported back to their respective controls that all had been carried out and they were now closing the operation down. This was with the exception of the French needing to arrange for a judge to determine the cause of death, once the body was found. This could be a while, because the BMW had been placed in a very remote spot to give the Services time to leave the area, ensuring there was no way of linking this new murder to them.

But Morison was still concerned with the degree of French support because they didn't worry about their population's opinions. Morison knew Andanson's body had been incinerated in his car to avoid the cause of death being known but the BMW car keys had been taken away from the cremation site and the killers had stayed so long to burn Andanson, that everyone knew this was not suicide. A corpse would need to continue pouring fuel over its remains for some considerable time if this was suicide! But the French authorities are never concerned about their people because they have carte blanche in France and the people believe officialdom, without question. A French judge would say this was suicide. But the rest of the world would now know this was state-sponsored murder and linked to Diana in Paris.

Morison and Stedman, however, had returned to England within hours, feeling they could now look forward to the rewards of a mission successfully concluded and with a real sense of pride. They had secured the safety of the monarchy, messy as it had been, for years to come.

END GAME

Thoughts of dark days, narrow escapes and near miracles passed through Morison's mind as he sat in the Mediterranean sunshine. He was on holiday at one of his favorite locations in the South of France, relaxing and reading the British papers, having now handed his role as royal watchdog over to another colleague.

Pondering previous achievements and moments of exhilaration, he cast his mind back to all that had transpired over the previous few years; it was often in these moments he had his best and most creative ideas. With his years of training, and having lived the life he had, he couldn't just turn off the tap.

'Thank God I'm out of that whirlpool,' he thought, as he sat, reminiscing and watching the world go by. Nothing much had happened over the last few years after his biggest command, the Alma tunnel. 'Looks like we made it through that horrendous period between Charles Windsor's separation from Diana and our current position,' he reflected.

'How the Establishment survived I will never know. We got through, tainted but intact, which surprises me considering the variables we had to deal with and the risks we had to run.'

Morison's thoughts turned to the fate of Jim Winfield and the premature demise of John Brooke's career, but he quickly dismissed maudlin thoughts with his most successful and well-worn escape route: duty. 'We were following orders! Soldiers get wounded and soldiers die!'

How close he had come to disaster with people demanding answers. Why didn't they join the French police earlier, answer questions about blood samples, inquests, embalming and that wretched Fiat? God, that very nearly sank us!

Charles Windsor was still around; not the most popular man on the block but even they couldn't perform miracles.

Scanning through the papers, Morison noticed a piece concerning Diana's ex butler, Paul Burrell. 'What's he been up to?' thought Morison, as he sipped his coffee and read down the page. Then, pushing the cup away and burning his mouth in the process, he read that the police had just arrested Paul Burrell for theft.

'What's happening now? What on earth are the lads up to?' He knew he shouldn't be responding because he'd finally managed to be excused from royalty watch, but still felt a duty to consider the best way forward with anything that involved the Princess of Wales.

'I hope Longford knows what he's doing,' he thought, with the impervious air of superiority that he always maintained concerning one of the biggest hits of the century. It was his hit after all!

'This is the work of our bunch and involving the police can only mean we are trying to find something well hidden. Yes, I'll wager Longford is after something from Burrell,' he continued to muse as he read the remainder of the article, 'and probably for the reasons I suggested a few years ago. It's better to keep it transparent by bringing in the police, provided we can fabricate the evidence, and it's the only way of investigating whether anything else lurks in the archives of those who were close to the Princess. But bullyboy tactics against well-known people associated with the Princess is not conducive to survival in our current climate. What has sparked this off now?'

As a matter of interest Morison decided to telephone his replacement on royalty watch, Longford, to see what had prompted him to take this action and whether he had discovered anything. 'I should learn to leave well alone,' he thought, as he picked up the phone and telephoned the office to see if Longford was around.

'Hello Tom,' said a plummy voice at the end of the line. 'I thought you were enjoying the fruits of your subterfuge.'

'Funny,' said Morison, 'I am just wondering, none of my business I know, but nonetheless wondering, what you are doing with the Burrell situation.'

'Have reliable information he has evidence relating to the Princess's death,' said Longford. 'Some of it may be rather incriminating.'

'Like what,' said Morison, an uneasy tingle once more creeping up his spine.

'Like letters about or to various members of a certain family,' said Longford. 'I am not too happy discussing this on the phone. Pop in and see me and I shall bring you up to date. It's going to take a while to process and we have only just started searching and asking the necessary questions. You might be able to help.'

'OK,' said Morison. 'Look forward to it, after I have endured some more of this torture,' as he slid into his chair and pensively put down the phone. 'Ah well; it's not over yet! Will it ever be?'

Morison returned to London, ten days later, having given no more thought to his conversation with Longford because his wife had become annoyed with business getting in the way of her enjoying this rare and precious interlude with her husband. He was supposed to be entertaining her and relaxing.

The return to his office was met with enthusiasm, in the wrong quarters from his perspective, because another overseas problem had occurred that he must now oversee. He thought of Longford and decided to take a stroll down the corridor and pay him a visit before departing and becoming engrossed in yet another politically balanced intrigue.

'Good morning Nick,' said Morison, as he entered Longford's office and helped himself to a seat in front of his desk. 'How's it going?'

'We haven't found anything,' said Longford. 'It doesn't look good! We're continuing because we can't just fold up and withdraw this early. Hopefully he'll cave in or these incriminating letters will appear if we keep the pressure on. They could be extremely damning to the monarchy and especially to Charles Windsor.'

'Not again,' said a sarcastic Morison, which raised an eyebrow of mock concern from Longford. 'You mean you're not surprised these wretched letters exist, shame on you.'

'Surprised,' said Morison. 'I'll be very surprised if there aren't several! Any idea what the letters contain?'

'Oh, something about Charles Windsor's homosexuality and there's a tape containing a statement by the Princess,' said Longford, 'one that purports to contain shocking details. You will recall we needed to arrest another of Diana's butlers for theft, a few weeks before we arrested Burrell, also looking for this same incriminating evidence.'

'Becoming a bit of a habit, isn't it? Aren't you risking the press becoming suspicious; good job there won't be a number three,'

Morison quipped.

'Hot stuff if it exists though,' said Longford.

'Where else are you looking and what about the effects of the Princess's boyfriend; anything there?' said Morison.

'We've looked,' said Longford, 'but can't expect cooperation from Mohamed al Fayed. This problem came up recently through conversation with someone who knew the Princess and believes those compromising letters do exist. This reliable source told us Burrell is the man to watch. That elusive tape has also been mentioned, so it gets better and better and we couldn't afford to let it go; God knows what those letters might say.'

'Any idea what they're supposed to say?' asked Morison, naturally wondering what could have induced Longford to use the police and raise a high-profile campaign against someone in the public eye on hearsay. He presumed there should be more evidence to justify police action.

'Not certain,' said Longford, 'but as I've said, a small bird told us they could be damning to the Prince of Wales and he's still vulnerable, even though his ex-wife is no longer causing him apoplexy. The monarchy's popularity has plummeted and anything critical at this stage could cause the pack of cards to fold.'

'You think it's that bad,' said Morison, knowing the position of the monarchy wasn't good but thinking it should have improved by now.

'People are not forgetting,' said Longford, 'and they may never forget. Diana will remain very strong in people's minds for a very long time; if not for ever. We both know Paris was a huge mistake; but that's now history. We may well be acting as nursemaid to the monarchy for the next twenty years.'

'Well, at least you'll be fully occupied until retirement,' said Morison, finding humour a shade easier now he was no longer involved in royalty watch; and was he glad!

'What is your new assignment?' Longford asked. 'When are you starting?'

'I believe within the next few days,' said Morison. 'I haven't been briefed yet.'

'Is there a chance you could stay with this for a while?' said Longford. 'You know the players and have more experience on this than anyone. Your input would be invaluable!'

'Well,' said Morison, pleased that his services had been requested but ambivalent about returning to royalty watch, even briefly. 'I'll see what I can do, but only for a short time.'

'Of course,' said Longford, with a twinkle in his eye.

Dealing with sensitive information that must be curtailed was becoming a continuous occupation for the Service and their palace colleagues, who were hardly ever able to relax. The British police, under orders from the security services, were continuing to suppress all possible leaks of information that could still blow the lid off the whole Diana affair.

Some measures were best taken by the police because transparency was required to investigate certain people, especially where the victim was well known, and the public would never accept a more draconian action. The police had to find cause for searching someone's house and hold them for questioning! The trappings of democracy must be seen to be observed, so any move on their part needed careful orchestrating and reasons shown to the public for this behaviour. The only way was for a spurious charge to be made and then pursued through the courts. If they found something fine, and if not, then the victim could be spat out and that was that. No comeback on the Service or the police, because it was all above board in the eyes of the law.

'Wonderful, now let's delve into Paul Burrell's home life and rip it apart to see whether he really was Diana's rock and trusted accordingly,' thought Longford, who was itching to get this whole affair over. They continued to delve but still nothing crawled out of the woodwork.

'How did you get something that will hold up in court? Do you actually have anything on him?' said Morison.

'Nothing genuine,' said Longford. 'He's as clean as a whistle; very boring and inconsiderate! It makes our job so much harder. It was discovered there was a missing dhow given to the Wales's by the Emir of Bahrain and worth £500,000. There's no evidence Burrell was keeping it for the royal family and we have testimony that we believe should stand up in court. We shall say he didn't have permission to hold all those items belonging to the Princess. There's no disputing many of the items don't belong to him.'

'Did we need to arrest him?' said Morison. 'These things can get messy. Has there been any come back?'

'Definitely yes to the arrest,' said Longford. 'There was no way we could ask him because if the answer was no then where did we go from there? Comeback, not at present, but we tried to discover whether he had the two main items of interest to us when they first arrested him. He had no dhow, of course, but neither has he started a book on his memoirs and doesn't seem to have the box, despite our informant being adamant that he does. There were no sensitive papers found.'

'All in all a bit of a disaster really,' said Morison.

'Yes,' said Longford, 'but we can't let up yet because he may be playing a clever game and we won't get another chance, so we must continue in the hope he caves in!'

The main target was now in the dock on trumped-up charges in order to extirpate information on the murder of the Princess. Nothing was too much trouble for the Service because, of all the targets, this was the main one. Changing the mood of the people was a gradual process but dealing with these problems was essential to enable the Service to remove all dangerous remaining issues and create the best foundations for the people's mood to recover. What they were now doing was their best for Queen and country, well Queen anyway, thought Morison, as he took a briefing on where the court case stood as of today.

Time lapsed with nothing forthcoming but that was now considered unlikely; a further problem arose when they realised that Charles Windsor would be called to the stand. With or without the tapes, Paul Burrell could give evidence of their content in court because he had already admitted seeing them and discussing them with the Princess. Charles Windsor would then be called and compelled to give evidence to counter, under oath, and this will mean him having to lie.

'God, we can't allow that,' said Longford. 'The whole thing has backfired. The defence will be calling witnesses to prove the royal family knew of Paul Burrell taking those items home for safe keeping, all along, and in any case they're bound to raise the point about the contents of the box and what's inside it. There's a distinct possibility, if Prince Charles is called to give evidence, Defense counsel will raise the tapes issue, including their content, in open court. Not to mention the possibility that someone could deliver them to court. We cannot allow that to happen! It must be stopped immediately!'

'How can we do this without losing face after two years?' said Morison.

'I know,' said Longford, 'you mean looking like idiots or worse. But there's another facet to a larger web of intrigue that won't be lost on thinking people. They will know this whole affair was a put-up job and is associated with our murder of the Princess of Wales.'

'We need,' said Morison, 'an unexpected discovery of evidence that cannot be questioned because we don't want anyone questioning us over details of the investigation and looking at evidence and our motives; evidence we don't have, motives – well! There is far too much at risk and this must never be linked to Diana's death.'

'What if Prince Charles withdrew the charges?' said Longford.

'No good,' said Morison. 'People will say the only reason he's withdrawing is that he doesn't want to give evidence and is afraid of what might be revealed. People already know he may be called as a witness, and they know of the existence of the tapes, so what a good time to suddenly find a reason to say it was all a mistake. No, the only person who would not be questioned is the Queen. If she were to remember something and make a suitable statement, then continuance of this trial would be untenable; that would work. We don't have time to chance different ideas and we cannot afford failure. What do you think?'

Longford pondered for a brief moment, having followed Morison's logic, and agreed that this would be ideal. 'My main concern is the timing. To suddenly remember something just at the moment that Charles is about to give evidence in a court of law isn't likely to be believed by anyone.'

'Here you go again,' said Morison. 'I know, once more, this isn't ideal but we aren't playing in an ideal world, far from it. Think again of the alternative. If Charles Windsor has to give evidence in court, he must tell the truth. If he lied in court, imagine what the press would do if any flaw were discovered. He would be finished! Everything we have done will have been for nothing. The people might raise an eyebrow if the monarch makes a statement but they will give her the benefit of any doubt.'

Longford agreed he would have to contact his man at the palace to see how the land might lie.

On the 31st October 2001, Morison contacted Longford to see how things stood, since he knew the trial would soon be halted, and was advised it was being brought to a close that morning as the prosecution had decided not to offer further evidence due to the Queen's amazing memory.

'Once even thinking minds have settled,' said Morison, 'this too will be forgotten.'

Longford remained bemused but realised Morison understood the sycophantic British psyche rather well.

The public mood was the barometer by which the Service gauged the level of activity they must engender to retain control. The mood was dark, and ever since the funeral of the Princess there had been a public fury over what had happened and questions raised over why there had been no investigation, no inquest, no respect shown or even a modicum of sympathy from the monarchy for the public's grief. A theatrical production team would be appalled at the way the characters were allowed to act this scene out with no thought being given to the overall desired effect, which was to placate the people and then move on.

This was never going to happen while there was this level of mistrust and disbelief amongst the public. A whole new series of initiatives was needed to bring about a dramatic change in the public psyche and this must begin with the two most influential aspects of the problem. First the memory of Diana must be tarnished, thus reducing her saint-like memory and, secondly, Charles Windsor must be reinvented, yet again, to be someone he was not but more of what people would like him to be!

This process must be established over a period of time because too much too soon and the people would realise the ploy. It was going to require someone who knew the royals well and who had a creative thought process. A very creative thought process! Longford knew that by asking Morison to stay, if the necessary clearance could be obtained, he was making the best move because this was undeniably the man for the job. He would have Morison work with him and between them they could continue the process they had begun by removing Diana and give people what the Service hoped they wanted: a trouble-free monarchy.

A thought flashed through Longford's mind that when he used the word 'they', was he referring to the people or the Service; but no matter, the establishment gave the Service their orders and their wishes would inevitably clash with the people on some occasions when the people would always do as they were told. It was, after all, the Service's job to provide disinformation and control the true wishes of the people by making them think they were getting what they wanted. But they were still working overtime on this fiasco. How were they going to begin this Herculean task?

Longford first decided to see whether Morison was going to be seconded to this mission, and for how long, before embarking on a venture he couldn't afford to get wrong. There may only be one more shot and he must proceed on that assumption.

Morison came bursting into Longford's room grimacing and sighing petulantly as he caught Longford's hopeful gaze. 'Well,' said Morison, 'I have some bad news.'

Longford's face dropped! Here was his and the Service's best chance of success being barred from this campaign. Morison saw his colleague's face and began to laugh. His newfound mischievous mood now became apparent as he said to Longford, 'The bad news is they have agreed to let me work with you for a time. They have passed the other assignment over to Stephens. I am pleased to be at home for a while but still have mixed feelings about the likely outcome of this reinvention. Looks like my destiny is to change duties and be a nursemaid after all.'

***

Public estimation of Diana and the Prince of Wales were the main points at issue which must be reduced in the first instance and elevated in the second. Propaganda had been in full force for almost a decade, and books written both supporting the Princess and the Prince. Morison was sure the public were sick and tired of hearing the same old stories over and over again.

Documentaries had been made trying to appear fair in persuading the public that whatever the Service proffered was true. Some documentaries gave dangerous accounts of Paris, and were uncomfortably close to the truth, but these would be rubbished by having the friendly press write articles refuting views unhelpful to the Service.

'People will weigh this against our explanations and believe it's six of one and half a dozen of the other,' thought Morison. 'That will do nicely when the alternative is to know the truth.'

He thought the trick of giving an impression of balance and then weighting the evidence in favour of Prince Charles hadn't worked and had even become counterproductive by acting as a reminder of what people already knew to be true.

'We have to accept that the feelings of disgust, even loathing, felt by many were going to continue unless they could pull off a major change of heart. Why couldn't the monarchical succession follow from a list of royals, which would then be a democratic choice of the people? If it were a matter of choice, then we wouldn't need to battle against superlative odds to retain something the people don't want. They could sidestep any oddity that might occur; that is democracy, isn't it? This would save the Service a great deal of time and cost and also make certain unsavoury behaviour unnecessary.'

Morison knew this new initiative was an uphill struggle because when dealing with a perversion of the truth, people have a habit of seeing through the lies; the situation could become dangerous.

People don't like being taken for fools, so the Service needed to be very careful. They must decide what was worth pursuing and once more create a planned and carefully monitored approach. They had been working on the age-old adage of tell them, tell them what you've told them and then tell them you've told them, so that as much subliminal information as possible would adhere to the public psyche.

Morison reasoned that since Diana was no longer around, people should feel less protective of her. The Service no longer had to be concerned with being countered at every turn by the Princess; but still it wasn't working. Another attempt at shifting public opinion would be dangerous in the present climate, with most people still believing that Diana was murdered, since this would take away any sympathy the Service might engender on behalf of Prince Charles.

Creating stories about Diana wouldn't work because the whole process of divorce had been far too transparent, so they would play on one of the classical idioms that the most effective lies are the ones that are closest to the truth.

'Everyone knows Diana had lovers during her marriage; we must stress that and create a salacious woman who couldn't resist temptation. Her poor husband must endure this for the sake of the crown. Fine,' thought, Morison, 'but with this being against a background that she wouldn't have done anything if she hadn't been abused and deceived from the very beginning of her marriage, and with the people knowing this, we really have our work cut out for us.

'The public still hold the view that Diana was treated as a non-person, so this process could backfire and make matters worse for the monarchy by reminding people more of Charles Windsor's failings than his battered wife's understandable and imposed misdemeanours. That's the risk we run,' thought Morison, 'but there's nothing else for it. We have tried everything else. The only other course is to lie low for a long while and hope matters go away. If the people aren't reminded about matters royal they should, eventually. We must decide soon what we are to do and if it's a reinvention then we must get started.'

Decision taken on who was in the team, Morison and Longford retired to their club for a long relaxing lunch to discuss the implications of attempting a reinvention versus lying low. All points considered, it was decided that because Charles Windsor was continuing with his lover and making it public, even reneging on his previously stated intention of never getting remarried, there was no choice. The silent response wasn't viable because the monarchy was in the public's face, whether or not the Service risked a new campaign; there was nothing to lose by going for it.

'He's going for broke,' said Longford. 'We might as well have some fun and follow suit. So what do we do first?'

'First,' said Morison, 'I order some of this wonderful claret; look,' he said, pointing to a vintage bottle of claret the club had recently replenished by popular demand.

'Right,' said a lightened Longford, 'important matters first. I'll join you in that, let's start with two bottles. Not going back to the office today are you?'

'No,' said Morison, 'we need to get our heads together now and decide in the morning; decisions through a misty haze aren't such an unreasonable notion in these circumstances.

Morison debated the issues with Longford. 'What's your view on our chances of succeeding with another reinvention program?' Morison asked.'

'Limited,' said Longford. 'We start from a very low esteem. It's only the people's ingrained acceptance of the monarchy that's keeping it afloat. If they think one day and decide to reduce its scope to the immediate royals only, and allow for a vote on who succeeds, they could retain their monarchy and control it concomitantly. These excesses that we have to clean up after wouldn't occur anymore.'

'With current thinking that could be construed as almost seditious,' said Morison, finding it curious that here they were in

272

charge of the monarchy's destiny and becoming as critical as many others. 'We are supposed to protect, serve, nursemaid and put up with it.'

'Yes,' said Longford, 'but we both know it won't be forever. The decision on how we deal with this particular problem is not the only one. We have to deal with a great deal else when we take on this reinvention program. We need cooperation from the royals and not have them behaving in their normal manner, producing more scandals and giving the people less reason to respond favourably; we shall have to see our men in the palace about this.'

'Wasting your time,' said Morison. 'Nothing will change the monarchy's thinking or behaviour; they're incapable. Hundreds of years of privilege have eroded a normal concept of ethics from their repertoire. There are, of course, exceptions but one bad apple is inclined to spoil the barrel and could be fatal for more than just the bad apple. We must put a huge amount of disinformation into the public domain and decide what we use and when to deliver.'

'Yes,' said Longford, 'we must prepare this plan and implement it soon, otherwise the disposal of the Princess of Wales will have been for nothing and Charles Windsor will be gone as well.'

A gentle realignment of the truth continued but achieved very little. The main issue was the reinvention of Charles Windsor and there was little chance of success with the knowledge people had of him and the scandals that had further discredited him coming to light. With the revelations about Charles' behaviour over the preceding years, this endeavour by the Service was going to be impossible, but it was their duty to try.

Not only did they have to deal with the people's knowledge of the abuse Diana suffered but also evidence concerning Charles Windsor's other sexual predilections coming to light by way of this tape that they had gone to so much trouble to find. One of the royal servants, George Smith, claimed he had been raped by a senior member of the royal family, and the police had failed in their attempts at extirpation; the primary driver in arresting Diana's two former butlers.

The Service still believed the tape was hidden in Diana's famous box. 'God,' thought Morison, 'these aren't the sort of people to invite home and meet your parents.' He was already regretting he had agreed to return for this assignment. 'Must be my own sense of loyalty to the crown,' he thought and then, hesitating, 'I don't think it would take much for me to change my mind.' That thought bothered him! If he changed his mind, how would he then view his actions in having murdered Diana, Princess of Wales?

'We shall contain this as far as we are able but it's just part of a larger, bleaker picture. It's known the investigation in Paris was, at least, seriously flawed and the people are never going to accept it was implemented with the intention of seeking the truth. What we need is for the British government to be seen taking this whole issue seriously and send people to Paris, ostensibly with the intention of conducting a proper investigation. They must be seen and photographed in all the right places and meet and talk with the relevant French police authorities to afford credibility.'

'Come on,' said Longford, 'that will never work. The people will fall for all sorts of tricks but that one will cause a huge outcry of disbelief. It will be seen by the people for what it is: a sightseeing trip and a further confidence trick. How are you going to persuade the people it's necessary for us to investigate this act when we didn't go over within hours of knowing about the crash? They already know we were in Paris, in numbers, and did nothing.'

'How do you explain away six or seven years of waiting for the people to demand we do something before we actually do anything?' Morison responded. 'I think we are in some difficulty if we try to pull this one off but if we do nothing then the fury and disquiet over our non-investigation will continue. Not only does this harm the monarchy, it also reduces credibility for the police, and there is a danger the public will feel they can't trust them anymore. They will question why the police didn't take action and must have been prevented by political forces; there is no other explanation. It's clear the police are being controlled by political forces and not by the desire for justice or truth; that's dangerous. We must do something to re-establish police credibility, eroded due to our inaction over Diana's death. A politically acceptable move is needed, or our system may well implode.'

The Service knew they needed to continue dispelling public disquiet over the murder and that people knew what had happened; from this there was no escape. Reaching for a huge dose of 'deniability', Morison drew up the position report the Service must adopt in order to survive. This would involve ridiculous ventures that he doubted would succeed but he knew people were, fortunately, fairly gullible in wanting to believe their government.

If not, what could they turn to?

Relying on this goodwill, he produced a tissue of nonsense behaviour in the hope of placating a dark public that continued to be mistrusting of the authorities. Had he caught it in time and would his ruses work amongst a sceptical and still distraught public? Apart from assisting with the propaganda campaign for Charles Windsor, that Morison expected would continue forever, he must consider placating the public over their non-investigation in France.

He made the suggestion that the most senior policeman in the UK could be asked to visit France in a high-profile visit to give the impression of now having some sort of involvement. He should visit the French capital and walk in the tunnel where the Princess had died, several years ago, and then go back for one or two further visits and talk with some of the authorities. They would then gauge whether it was necessary to escalate this into the appearance of a full and proper investigation or maybe this would be sufficient to placate the people. They would control leaked information and stem continuing public disenchantment and disbelief, then admit to what the people already knew about the murder and appear to be on side. They must be prepared to direct activities towards a satisfactory end game!

The Service needed to consider reviewing the leaked evidence on Diana's murder and construct a more believable package for the people. Memories were never going to be dimmed; if anything, the beacon was glowing ever more brightly!

Morison later came to realise these efforts had been a huge faux pas and, not only hadn't worked, but had alienated people even more than before. Having one's intelligence insulted wasn't the way to persuade the populace all was well; in fact, there was no way of convincing people there was an investigation.

Morison's day continued to consist of checking the public mood and assisting the palace in neutralising negative vibes coming from the press or other sources. He was constantly updated on whether Mohamed al Fayed was making any progress in the discovery of Morison's trained killers or were any being tempted by offers of wealth in exchange for the truth. He continued to supply disinformation to lessen the public view of the Princess, at the same time bolstering Charles Windsor's image and was now giving serious thought to the idea of sending the police to France, full scale. He knew something must be done, fast.

The British police involvement must be stepped up. If the police admitted details already known to be true, they might be perceived to be actually doing something and this should help placate the people. 'We can then close it all down at the most opportune moment, having done our best,' he pondered. 'This should work!' Any idea must be considered to give an impression of police concern; any idea to keep the public at bay.

Morison was now disenchanted! He had set aside personal feelings, knowing these didn't matter. The status quo came first! He was looking forward to moving on and wanted someone to take over. He had helped for a while; that was enough! He knew there was no chance, whatsoever, this would be permitted.

'What about the inquest' said Longford? 'It's causing as much of a problem as our non-investigation. People know there's no logical reason why there hasn't been one, especially if we are going to raise questions of the French police by sending our own people to France several years after the event. Our reasoning has been we had to wait for the French investigation to finish and now we are effectively admitting that there was no investigation.

'People will also know that we assist in foreign investigations where a British subject has been killed, even when that police force is investigating the crime for real, so what reason do we give for not bothering to go to France when Diana was killed? And then we subsequently say that the French investigation is flawed and we should have gone after all. Why didn't we go; why now? I suppose it's true that by starting an investigation of our own we might placate and control the public mood but can we extend the time before we need to hold an inquest? We could claim we can't hold one until we have completed our own investigation and perhaps the PM will have been able to slope off the scene by then.'

'O ye of little faith,' said Morison. 'Don't you remember your basic training? The people will believe what they are told by their government. It's been shown time and time again because they haven't an option. When do you recall people asking questions about anything to do with matters political and actually receiving a viable answer? Never! Who is going to raise questions that we would need to answer? Nobody, and that's the way it will stay! The people will have to believe us unless there is clear evidence what we are saying is untrue otherwise they are the facts.

'I know it's not ideal but look at the alternatives. If we don't make something positive happen then the police risk losing the trust of the people and their excellent position in British society. The people will believe so much and then rebel, which would be extremely unfortunate for my pension plan,' he quipped, unable to stop his new and emergent rebellious streak.

Longford knew what Morison said was correct and there was no alternative, but felt the need to play devil's advocate. 'What about the non-obsequious press,' said Longford?

'Ah, that's another problem,' said Morison. 'We must keep them misinformed, as always, but they have done their worst, so we make sure they don't get any more sensitive information. The remainder of the press we nurture with our propaganda and there is nothing else for them to say on the question of inquests; unless we raise the issue there will be nothing much else they can do.'

Some degree of control continued but there were too many imponderables for complacency. Diana had written a letter stating she believed her husband was planning to kill her in a car crash and given it to her Lawyer, Lord Mishcon, for safe keeping. The police ignored this letter for six years even after Diana's lawyer, Lord Mishcon, had handed it to them after the attack. Police hands were tied by political instructions. They had to announce their intention to interview Charles Windsor in connection with his ex-wife's death, which they would do later, but only when nearer to having an inquest.

In the event, the police didn't interview Charles at all because Lord Stevens, who met with Charles, had left the police some time before so was no longer a police officer. The letter was also kept hidden from the press for years but now all was beginning to unravel.

'God, we have a problem,' said Longford, running into Morison's office and handing a paper across the desk to his colleague.

'What's up now?' said Morison, slowly putting his cup back into its saucer and intently scrutinising the missive.

'Some of our people who were in Paris have been named. This just about caps it all.'

'Where the hell did they get this,' said Morison? 'One of our disillusioned ex-players, who left a while ago, has gleaned something and handed it to the press,' Longford replied.

'Who has been named?' said Morison.

'Two senior people who were in Paris in August 1997, for starters, Nick Langford and Richard Spearman, but I don't yet have the details on the others.

'This is becoming very dangerous indeed,' said Morison, looking more agitated than Longford had ever seen him. 'We must get them off on leave now and make sure they don't return for a few months. Just keep the lid on all communications as usual.'

'I cannot say I am surprised something has leaked,' said Longford. 'Asking our agents to take the Princess's murder in their stride was optimism in the extreme; they were bound to talk to their colleagues so we were guaranteed some rebelliousness. Having kept quiet this long is what surprises me. What else has been said, that is the problem. What else has this person found out and communicated to the press?'

'They can't pass it on to the police,' said Morison, 'because it will just be passed on to us as whoever has it will know. They won't want us knocking on their door.'

'Yes, but it puts pressure on us and on the police who have been trying to keep a low profile citing the responsibility for this remains with the French. Now they will be forced into doing something or else risk people making the inevitable comment about police being in on it and that will be disaster for them and public order. Their credibility is really on the line and they can't say, "Oh well, MI6 asked us to stay away." We need to begin this police flag-waving exercise in Paris and we need to ramp this up immediately.'

'Yes, it needs to be seen as more than a day trip or the police have a public order problem in addition to their integrity being questioned,' Morison replied. 'We can't even refute comments in the press because confirmatory sources may come forward. The police need to point out they are looking into any allegations. When we have a full report we shall give our verdict that the French were right all along. Finally, the matter will be closed; and then we pray!'

Reviewing their position, Morison and Longford's direction was being taken in a way neither wanted nor had any option about if disaster was to be averted. Morison couldn't help thinking about his recent tempting of the fates on holiday by allowing thoughts of having got away with it.

Other matters were now unfolding and getting out of hand, with more bad news arriving, and Morison thought, 'It usually comes in threes and here cometh number three.'

They had just been informed the French had decided to give their TV interview after all. 'Not a good idea,' were the words Morison would have liked to say to the French, but couldn't. It was out of his jurisdiction and he must persuade and cajole and then grin and bear it.

The French told Longford they were under great pressure to go public with their dossier. Longford looked at Morison and expressed his concern. 'They don't have the same degree of commitment to continue with this subterfuge and aren't as skilled at the disinformation methods we use.' The French people needed information.

Morison replied, 'You mean they aren't as good at the bullshit,' seeing no need for pretence. 'They don't need to persuade their people quite as much as we do.'

'OK, whatever the reason, what if they screw up and give more away than is safe.'

'Nothing we can do,' said Morison. 'We have tried to delay them but they'll do as they please in their jurisdiction. We shall have to ask them, very politely, to be careful. Who's giving the interview? Some of them are more skilled at this than others.'

'I don't know,' said Longford. 'I shall find out. You think you can influence the choice?'

'Probably not,' said Morison, 'but at least we'll be prepared.'

'Let me call them,' said Longford, picking up the phone and going straight through to Paris.

'Hello. is Monsieur Chantais there please,' said Longford.

After a brief pause a voice came on the line and Morison whispered to Longford, 'Is that Jean Claude Chantais?'

'Yes,' said Longford. 'Hello, Monsieur Chantais, this is Nick Longford from the British Security Services; I wonder if you can help me?'

Morison was gesturing to Longford to hand the phone over. He knew Chantais from meetings in Paris during September and October 1997 and Longford happily obliged.

'Hello Jean Claude, this is Tom Morison. I trust you are well occupied with various intrigues? We understand you have decided to give a press interview on the dossier.'

'Hello Tom,' said Chantais. 'Yes, we have no choice with the furore still going on over the Paris incident. We have delayed as long as possible but the press are demanding more information and we must hold a conference to refute all that's been said about our not conducting a proper investigation. We have had enough, Tom! Our people are becoming restless! As regards more intrigues, I have had enough of yours to last me a lifetime; and yours probably will.'

Morison knew Chantais had a sense of humour, so thought it best to ignore it. 'Will your man be able to handle the questions?' said Morison, unable to think of a more subtle way of asking.

'I think so,' said Chantais, 'but we have no choice and can hardly ask British Intelligence to take the questions instead can we?'

'Well, no; who is taking the questions?' said Morison.

'Do you know Commander Mules?' said Chantais. 'He's the one responsible for closing the tunnel in Paris that night. We thought he should take it because he will know most of the answers to their questions.'

Morison was thinking, 'That's what worries me. He knows the answers to most of the questions.'

'OK, thank you Jean Claude,' he said out loud. 'We shall meet again soon no doubt.'

'Well if you want to come over for this conference, you are welcome,' said Chantais, unable to resist provoking Morison.

'No thank you,' said Morison, 'but I look forward to seeing you again soon.'

The interview with Commander Mules was an unmitigated disaster from the British Service's point of view. Mules gave straight answers to questions concerning the handling of the investigation all right, destroying any idea all would be well if they left it to the French. The premature tunnel closure of 31st August 1997 was questioned and justified by saying it was inconceivable the tunnel could close and inconvenience road users. It was claimed all evidence had been gathered in around two hours; it clearly had not. It wasn't mentioned that the tunnel was in fact closed again, a few weeks later, ostensibly to seek evidence not collected on the day of the murder and yet again, later on, to further placate a growing public disquiet. This clearly showed that since it needed opening again on two further occasions, it should not have been closed on the day of the crash when there was the best chance of securing further evidence? These points made Morison despair since, despite all the work they had put into this operation, it was now unravelling before their eyes.

Commander Mules made a statement during the filmed interview of how he pursued the investigation and described his normal procedure. He said that when investigating a crime he first establishes a hypothesis and then pursues the investigation. If he encountered something that didn't fit his original hypothesis, he would find a way of discrediting this evidence by more vigorously pursuing leads that helped him prove what he originally thought was right. In other words, he refuted the conspiracy theorists' thinking, despite the evidence suggesting it, because he wasn't prepared to consider any evidence that suggested murder. It just wasn't a part of his original hypothesis!

This totally bizarre attitude converted a lot of doubters to thinking this tantamount to admitting that the police hadn't investigated Diana's death as a possible murder. One or the other must be the case! It led many people to ask what a man with an attitude like this was doing in the police force of any country, in the first instance, let alone involved in investigating the death of the Princess of Wales.

These issues added further to Morison's woes, because now people were asking what was being done about this level of incompetence in searching for the murderers of the Princess. It was also very clear to all but the simple-minded, or those given to extreme obsequiousness, that the Princess had been murdered and nothing was being done about it by the British; for a reason!

Morison waited for the demand to come from the public for an immediate British police presence on French soil to re-investigate. This had been a last resort because it would bring the British authorities under direct responsibility for evidence and reporting to the British people, and would mean the removal of the buffer between truth and the disinformation being engendered by both the British and French Governments.

The Service needed to perfect their tergiversation and maintain a tight balance between evidence leakage and public statements, which should always take account of information recently leaked to the public. This way the Service delivered acceptable reasons to counter the leakage and gave the impression of sincerity. At the same time they gave nothing! The French police would continue to hold the front line and Morison must rely on them not to allow any leakage. This was on their soil and the decisions theirs, so he would watch and wait and dread the moment for when he must

281

further intercede.

The Service knew these slips in logic fuelled the imagination of all who doubted the Princess's death was an accident, and that was the vast majority of the populace. Evidence from all areas of activity, when taken collectively, had given the public proof that Diana was murdered by those whose salaries they pay; the monarchy was going to suffer. That in turn put more pressure on the British police to do something about it, years after the murder, and clearly indicated they should have responded but didn't; the people were wondering why?

Mules' comments concerning his method in approaching the investigation made the Service cringe and wonder how anyone could remain in the profession with this attitude. Mules' statement that the criminal brigade spent their time proving they are right rather than pursuing leads from new evidence with an open mind was a thunderbolt to Morison. It was inconceivable that any police force would seek to prove they were right rather than pursue the truth and also admit this to thinking people.

'Anybody else, whether a police officer or not, would have more sense than to accept this as a reasonable position to take. Everybody else believes one should look for evidence available and then look at the most likely ensuing scenario. If anyone starts off by intending to disprove evidence in favour of one's own unproven theory then one will, naturally, miss vital facts that could have made all the difference. Further evidence for every conspiracy theorist in the world,' thought Morison, 'who will now know this is because the police didn't want to find out who murdered Diana, otherwise no logical alternative reason exists for making such silly statements. French police incompetence was the only alternative.'

Matters got worse!

'How are we going to survive this?' thought Morison. He really believed they were finished and there was little point in continuing with the royal charade; not to mention the possibility of MI6 proscription.

'This is too much to handle,' he griped to an equally fatigued and despondent Longford. 'Have you heard the entire interview?' said Morison. 'I have just heard the juicy bits that are going to destroy any hope of saving us. A main point of interest was Mules' admission that he didn't ask questions about our involvement because secrets are secret and he could never have pierced the secret.'

'So,' said Longford, 'he has admitted, on our behalf, that there is a secret and then admits he couldn't do his job, which is to pierce it. Hasn't he done well! Now everybody knows there is a secret he wasn't permitted to pierce!'

The next item on Mules' endless list of faux pas was to describe how he didn't bother to look for the Fiat Uno any further afield than two departments of Paris. How he didn't bother to investigate why Henri Paul had a large amount of cash on him when removed from the wrecked car and didn't bother finding out where the money in his thirteen separate bank accounts came from, which contained around £300,000 in total. This, for a man earning around £20,000 per annum, was rather suspicious, unless of course Mules' hypothesis hadn't permitted him to consider this might have been our paying him off over several months.

'Well we know why they didn't investigate,' said Longford, 'but he didn't have to tell the whole bloody world in the process. This has totally discredited our sham investigation and means the pressure is now squarely on our shoulders.'

***

'Where are we heading for now?' said Longford, as he got into the Service's car that was taking them both to their official country retreat, Bleak House, for a full review meeting.

'God knows,' said Morison. 'I have lost any hope of ever being able to control this. It's probably best to just let things happen and settle where they will.'

'We can presume today there won't be some miraculous new idea to save us,' said Longford.

'There is no magic left in my bag,' said Morison, 'how about yours?'

'No; whatever action we take at correcting some error, we are always undermined by more revelations. It seems as though the gods are watching and waiting for us to make a move and then preparing something to neutralise it. We need to go to ground on this whole debacle and I shall address the meeting today accordingly. We can discuss their options, if they have any, but I am sure they'll see the sense of what I am suggesting.'

'What else is there?' said Morison, 'Give me your best shot now before we arrive.'

Longford thought hard. 'Perhaps we ought to suggest they have a plan on a reduction of the monarchy available in case things get out of hand. We can try sticking plaster, if we are ordered, but there must be a realisation the world has irrevocably changed since we murdered the Princess. We haven't fooled the public and grossly underestimated their common sense.'

Longford's mood worsened, as he muttered, 'Murdering Diana was the biggest mistake the Service has made. We have alienated the people; everyone knows it was murder and that we were responsible. Whether they can prove it determines whether we are criminally tried or proscribed but our objective was to preserve the status quo and in that we failed. It is fortunate we managed to have the death penalty repealed for high treason, so our families should receive our pensions, come what may. The people have already convicted us and we have probably induced the very thing we were trying to prevent; the end of Charles Windsor.'

These words sent a chill through Morison! He knew what he was hearing was true. They were the words he had used during and prior to the attack. He was responsible and had failed. They hadn't made the decision but they had carried it out; God help them all.

'These events have, regrettably, been terminal for the monarchy, as we know it at least but they will want to fight on,' said Morison, 'and I shall support you but they will ask what else can go wrong.'

'Anything might go wrong with a decaying institution that has become an anachronism,' said Longford, finding his despair very difficult to conceal.

'Well,' said Morison, his mind passing through shadows on a failing enthusiasm. 'Perhaps one day we shall have a system that's just and fair and there won't be need for this intrigue. We can then get on with the job of protecting the country from its enemies and not become embroiled in internal matters involving the innocent and not have to survive as the bad guys. We are after all there to protect and serve not find the people baying at our door for following orders and defending the indefensible. This would require all those who influence decisions, purported to be in the people's interests, but without reference to an elected body, lose their power.'

'Very profound,' said Longford. 'You talk of an ideal it would be nice to achieve but will it ever happen? There must always be someone at the top of the Service who can be trusted to make the right decisions, without any bias, but this will always be down to that person's judgment and they could be out of step with the people. Accountability means that all those in elected office are unable to stand aside from the consequences of decisions we have endorsed so the option for deniability is lost. This means the advantage of being able to strike against the politically acceptable norm, by devious means, is no longer available.

'We need to rediscover democracy to be more of what it should be. The secrecy must go and, where matters are sensitive to national security, there must be a team of responsible people acting under strict guidelines and headed by a Minister of the crown who reports directly to the Prime Minister. The people will then hold sway over their behaviour, through elected officials, and the Service will be accountable.'

Morison replied, 'The current system was born from world war trauma, where it was necessary to be as ruthless as the bad guys. The problem is that we haven't changed an outmoded but still politically useful system, which is why we were able to murder the Princess. Diana was a victim of a system that should have gone out with the Ark. If we don't strive towards an ideal, then we shall always have to tolerate the current system, because there are too many people in power who wish for it to remain. The monarchy is dependent upon it; it couldn't survive, as it stands, without it! We must pursue the options of steering this country away from its current path.'

'OK,' said Longford, 'I agree. But back to today; what shall we tell them?'

'You ask of the risks,' said Morison. 'Who knows what lies around the corner tomorrow or the day after that? What if another of our operatives decided to kiss and tell? Then it would depend on who that person is as to the damage done. What if the government changes and the new Prime Minister demands that we tell the truth and is prepared for the nation, and us, to take the consequences of our previous actions? What if one of the assassins involved in the tunnel that night, or one of our own people, decides that enough is enough and comes clean; then our number is up and heaven knows what might happen!'

Suddenly, in realisation of a truth he was reluctant to hear himself speak, Morison paused. 'God; what if – what if he writes a book!'